PRELUDE TO EXTINCTION

ANDREAS KARPF

D0188410

PART 1: APPROACH

Chapter 1 – May 10, 2124

Jack Harrison walked briskly down the bare, gray hallway. The rhythmic rattle of the metal-grate floor under his shoes echoed lightly off the hard-plastic walls, making him conscious of his pace. Though there was no rush, he didn't see the sense in slowing down and wasting time. The corridor grew dark as he passed beneath a row of burnt out lights; reflexively, he made a quick mental note of its state of disrepair. The shuttle bay door lay a few meters ahead. On reaching the steel bulkhead, a momentary feeling of irritation crossed his mind as he was forced to brush aside a layer of dust from its control panel. There was no reason to be surprised – no one had been down this way in at least a year. Their journey between the stars had offered them little use for shuttles and jump-pods. The heavy door slid aside, releasing a gust of stale air. One by one, the bay's lights flickered to life, revealing a room that was both expansive yet barely large enough to hold its two shuttles and three jump-pods.

Though dormant for years, the shuttle bay felt chaotic, like he'd walked into a scene of frantic preparation frozen in time. Metal tool cases with open drawers lined the wall. Service hoses snaked along the floor to their respective shuttles, and short step-ladders were parked next to each craft. He'd have to have a few words with the crewmen who last used the bay.

Two four-man shuttles stood over him and dominated the chamber, leaving little space to squeeze by. Their thick, white, delta-shaped bodies and stubby wings cast long shadows across the smooth, gray deck. The one-man jump-pods in which he was interested were tucked off to the right, almost as an afterthought. The small, spherical craft were barely as tall as he, and comprised of little more than a seat and support equipment. He peered through the curved, glass window that was the front half of the vehicle, and though that it really wasn't much more than a rigid pressure suit. There was no propulsion system – just a complex set of small wheels and guides on its back and underbelly that allowed it to crawl along the outer skin of the main ship.

"Computer," Jack called out.

"Yes, Captain," the machine answered in a smooth, passive voice.

"Ready jump-pod one for launch. I'm going to try to manually free that probe bay door."

"I will prep seven hundred meters of cable."

"That's about what I was thinking too," Jack said. A compartment door along the base of the wall slid open, and a small, four-wheeled, silver cart carrying a spool of high-tension filament sped to the row of pods. Unfolding its thin, metal arms, the machine adeptly connected the spool to the back of the nearest pod. Then, just as quickly, it retreated to its alcove.

Jack walked to a terminal and brought up a schematic of the ship's exterior. The Magellan's design harkened back to the dawn of space travel. Like the Saturn V that took the first men to the Moon, it was over ninety-five percent fuel tanks and engines; the remaining few percent reserved for the crew and their support systems. The similarity ended there. The Magellan's antimatter ram-drive was a complex array of superconducting magnets, RF field generators and lasers. Half of the equipment was needed to generate a five hundred kilometer-wide magnetic funnel that captured and fed Hydrogen from the interstellar medium into the drive: harvesting atoms adrift in open space removed the need to carry thousands of tons of fuel. The rest of the equipment had the job of accelerating streams of captured matter and stored antimatter into the engine. Moving at nearly the speed of light, the streams were compressed and fed into a small, ultra-dense target zone barely a millimeter across. The extreme energy of the resulting proton-antiproton annihilation generated an intense blaze of gamma rays, and yielded the immense power needed to propel the ship across the void between the stars. All of this was hidden from direct view of the crew by a blast shield and mammoth fuel tanks. Calling them 'tanks', though, was a misnomer as each was a shielded array of specialized magnetic bottles holding the antimatter. At well over a half-kilometer in diameter, each of the six spherical fuel tanks was more than twice the size of the entire habitable portion of the ship. Arranged in two separate rings of three, they flanked the smaller globe-shaped habitat, keeping it nestled safely between them. The blast shield, a broad, squat cone several hundred meters across, dominated the aft, and protected them from the intense radiation streaming from the drive system.

Jack ran his finger along a line depicting the equator of the habitat until he reached a pair of small red circles. He tapped lightly on the image, and the computer obediently enlarged the region until two identical circular ports were centered on the screen. Each had a pair of white, semi-circular doors. The port on the right was highlighted in a computer-generated crimson glow, as was the upper door in the adjacent port.

"Computer," he said, "any change in their status?"

"No, sir. Port-two is still completely fused. The lower door on port-one appears operational; however, I am unable to retract the upper door."

"I assume Kurt tried shaking it again."

"Yes. Lieutenant Commander Hoffman attempted a variety of approaches, as did Dr. Martinez, but none have succeeded."

Jack drew a deep breath. "OK, let's get this done."

The computer answered, "Understood." It then quickly added, "Regulations require that I remind you to spend no more than thirty minutes outside."

Jack grunted in acknowledgement as he climbed into the cramped pod. He knew well that even though they had been decelerating for years, their current speed of ten-percent of the speed of light was still fast enough to make every atom adrift in interstellar space the equivalent of a high-energy cosmic ray. Nature didn't care whether you were in Earth orbit being bombarded by high-energy particles accelerated by some distant cataclysm, or if you were rushing toward atoms that were just drifting in space. In either case, the result was the same: too many high-speed collisions with these tiny particles would be fatal. The only thing that was surprising was how short the safe-exposure time was. The habitat itself had adequate shielding to protect the crew from those particles that did penetrate the blast shield and fuel tanks. The thin skin of the tiny jump-pod, however, didn't. All of this added up to the fact that he would have to work quickly.

Jack strapped himself into the pod's seat, and called out, "Display on." A holographic image of the pod's amber gauges and controls appeared, flanking the main window in front of him. He pointed to the status indicator and it responded by changing from 'Stand-by' to 'Ready.'

"Open the bay door," he said softly. A second later, there was the muted rush of the room's air being pumped into holding tanks to await his return. As soon as there was silence, a pair of three meter, semi-circular doors slid aside, revealing the pitch blackness of space. Even though he'd spent years piloting vessels throughout the solar system long before the current mission, he still felt a little rush of adrenaline as the pod automatically inched toward the opening. It had been nearly three years since he last ventured outside. So long, in fact that he actually felt relieved two days earlier when the computer first informed them of the problem.

The only unnerving aspect of jump-pod excursions was the mode of travel. He would be effectively rappelling in interstellar space down the side of a four-hundred-meter wide globe. The perception of down was provided courtesy of the interstellar drive. The Magellan had accelerated at a little over one-third of a "g" for five years' ship-time, before turning around at the midway point in the trip. It then decelerated by running its engines at the same thrust in the opposite direction. The constant thrust from the antimatter drive meant that down was always in its direction. It was this constant acceleration that provided the crew with an apparent one-third Earth gravity in which to live. Jack's current destination, the probe doors, lay a hundred meters to his left and one hundred and fifty meters straight down.

His path required inching along the skin of the habitat until he was directly over the target, before sliding down on a line to the doors. It was the dangling by a cable part that he didn't like. Even though it didn't make any sense, he wished that he could just drift alongside the Magellan in a space suit and perform the repairs – the normal method when coasting between the planets back home.

A tone sounded when the jump-pod reached the threshold of the door. The metallic click of the safety cable connecting with an outer receptacle prompted him to touch the word 'Proceed' floating in front of him. The pod moved to the left, creeping along its guide track in the habitat's skin. As soon as he was clear of the bay doors, they closed, terminating his only exterior source of light. Jack stared into the darkness, waiting for his eyes to adjust. The black, ghostly forms of the ship's fuel tanks surrounding him were barely perceptible. Ironically, when his eyes became accustomed to his surroundings, there still wouldn't be much to see. Star light itself would be too feeble to illuminate the Magellan. And, even if their target star system Epsilon Eri wasn't hidden by the blast shield, its distance of nearly thirty billion kilometers would render it too dim to add any meaningful light.

Jack mulled the number over in his head: thirty billion kilometers – two hundred A.U. – two hundred times the distance from the Earth to the Sun. Despite knowing it meant they were only three months from the end of their trip, his mind focused on how much further they still had to go. Even lonely Pluto back home was six times closer to the Sun than they were to Epsilon Eri. That, and the surrounding darkness, drove home the ever present reality of their isolation.

Jack's thoughts were brought back to the task at hand as the pod came to an abrupt stop. He activated the grapple and heard the solid sound of it latch onto one of the myriad of support sites that dotted the outside of the ship. "Exterior lights on," he said.

The jump-pod's floodlights illuminated the drab, metallic skin of the habitat. The square plates covering the outer hull showed their wear. Years of exposure to the interstellar medium had left them pitted and marred with thin, black streaks: the result of innumerable collisions with space-borne debris. His eyes followed the grid-like pattern of plates as they stretched away, disappearing in the distance around the curve of the spherical structure. As he gazed downward toward his target, Jack was reminded of being atop a ski slope, looking to the bottom of a steep run. The difference here was that his feeble floodlights were unable to illuminate the bottom. The slope simply curved away toward a black abyss. The only indication that there was any more to the ship was the collection of mammoth, round silhouettes of the fuel tanks climbing out of the darkness below to surround him. The immense disks blotted out all but the stars directly in front of him. Despite his intimate knowledge of the ship's structure, the view was disorienting. Without any light, there was no frame of reference, no perspective to gauge how large or far away these shadowy figures were.

Jack looked over the status indicators and held his finger just above the word "Descend" before touching it. The pod rotated slowly until he was on his back, his feet pointing toward the surface of the sphere. The stars above hovered peacefully over his head for a second; then his stomach dropped as the spool of cable began to unwind, starting his descent. He accelerated quickly and the passing hull plates became a blur. Plunging into the depths below, the jet-black fuel tanks rose around him, engulfing the stars above. His body felt light against the padded back of the seat in the near free-fall plunge. As quickly as it started, the braking mechanism engaged, whining against the spinning cable, and pressing him firmly into the seat's padding. The pressure of deceleration ebbed, and Jack found himself lying motionless again, staring at the curved, paneled wall as it ascended back toward his starting point.

The pod's automated guidance system continued through its program, rotating until he was upright, and then slowly lowering itself on a cable until he was hanging only a meter from the probe launch door. The habitat then curved away toward its base hidden in the darkness a couple hundred meters below. The external lights revealed two brushed metal, semicircular doors that met directly in from of him. Painted across them in bold maroon letters was the label, "Probe Port 1 – Keep Clear." Looking to his right, toward port two, he immediately saw the source of the problem: A ten centimeter hole was punched into the plate separating the two ports – an impact crater from some high-speed piece of debris. Thin, jagged cracks radiated outward from the blackened cavity in all directions. It was closer to port two, deforming its frame, and thus providing the reason why those doors wouldn't budge. Port one, however, didn't look that bad. The fissures from the impact site just barely reached it, and its frame seemed undamaged. Jack moved in closer, carefully inspecting the upper portion of the door; however, it showed no defects. His eyes shifted back to its frame and he uttered a quick "Gotcha!" A razor thin fracture ran the width of the frame.

Without breaking his gaze, he called, "Computer, get me Kurt on the comm."

Looking back to the crater, he noted some of the charring reached the outer edge of each port. He focused more closely on edges themselves, looking for embedded debris...

"Hey Jack, what's going on?" the much too lively voice of Kurt Hoffman announced over the comm-link. Though originally from southern Germany, Kurt's years of working in North America and off-world had left him with a barely detectable accent. Two of those off-world years were spent serving with Jack on the Lunar Polar Outpost.

"I've found the source of our problem," Jack replied seriously.

"I've known what the problem has been for a while," his friend quipped. "You keep hogging the EVA missions to yourself, leaving the rest of us boxed up here like cargo." Kurt paused for barely a second, but continued before Jack could get a word in edgewise, "You know, I wouldn't put it past you to have created this little mishap yourself, just so you could get outside for a while."

Jack allowed himself a smile and a shake of his head as he answered, "I'd probably have broken down within the next week and done exactly that, if this didn't happen first."

"So, what's so complicated that you need the help of your Chief Engineer?"

"There's a pretty nice impact between the two probe launch ports."

"Impact? How...I mean that area's pretty well shielded from direct exposure. What's the angle of incidence?"

Jack studied the site again and answered, "It looks pretty close to head-on."

"I don't see how. Unless..."

As Kurt's voice trailed off, Jack completed the thought, "Unless it happened during turnaround at mid-point." Turnaround was one of the most dangerous parts of the mission. For about ten minutes, the habitat was exposed to open space at high-speed. It was a remarkably short period of time considering it required turning a two-kilometer long ship 180 degrees. But it also represented a window during which any debris floating in interstellar space could impact the habitat at over 90% of the speed of light.

"How large is the site?" Kurt asked.

"Maybe ten centimeters across, and about half that deep."

"It didn't penetrate the hull?"

"No, doesn't look like it. Auto-sealants weren't deployed, and the logs show no record of any pressure loss. It looks like whatever it was completely vaporized on impact," Jack answered.

"Too bad..." Kurt started.

"What the hell are you talking about?" Jack shot back.

"It's not what you think Jack. But just imagine if there were some debris we could recover. What Don wouldn't give to get his hands on that!"

The scientist in Jack quickly saw where Kurt was coming from. Turnaround occurred at 5.2 light years from Earth. The nearest star was 4 light years away, and Epsilon Eri itself was still another 5.2 light years off. Though his original training as a planetary scientist was over twenty years removed, he knew that whatever struck them was true interstellar matter: something humanity had not yet had a chance to sample and directly study. For all they knew, it could easily have predated all of the local star systems, making its scientific value unimaginable. A sample of that material would have been nothing short of a dream-come-true for Don Martinez, their chief science officer. "It would have been nice, but there's nothing left of it," he finally said to Kurt.

"Actually, I'm not that surprised now that I've thought about it," Kurt said. "With that impact speed, there couldn't have been more than a couple milligrams of material in the first place. Anything larger would have done a lot more damage. Basically, we got lucky."

"Captain," the computer cut in, "you have only fifteen minutes of safe exposure time left."

"Thank you," Jack answered. "Kurt, let me get this done quickly. Just stay on-line in case I need your help."

"OK. I'll let you tell Don what he missed," Kurt added.

"Thanks," Jack retorted, emphasizing the sarcasm in his voice. He looked again at the thin fracture. It was a safe bet that a piece of the frame had separated underneath and was wedged into the door mechanism.

"Activate arms," he called out. Two polished, metal appendages unfolded from the sides of the pod. They resembled an artist's stylish interpretation of the bones in the human arm and hand, and precisely followed Jack's every move. He reached into an outer tool case with them and retrieved a large, but simple crow bar. "Sometimes low-tech's the way to go," he muttered to himself. Sliding the flat end into a small gap between the upper door and the cracked frame, he began pushing down. "Increase force slowly up to four thousand Newtons."

Nothing happened.

"Increase to eight thousand Newtons," he said.

Again, nothing happened.

"Computer..."

"Sir," the machine interrupted. "I would not recommend increasing force any further. There would be a significant chance of damaging the door's sliding mechanism."

"Understood." Jack withdrew the bar and said, "Try retracting the door now. Maybe we got lucky and loosened it a bit."

There was a brief pause before he heard the answer he was expecting, "The door is still unable to retract."

"Damn," Jack whispered. He returned the crow bar to the tool case and withdrew a pair of metal cutters that reminded him of large gardening sheers. "Let's see if we can pull away some of the sheet metal around this frame..." He tried forcing the edge of the blade into the crack, but even at its thinnest point the blade was too thick. Rotating it for a better angle, he made another attempt but quickly realized it was futile. The sheers couldn't get enough of a grip to cut into the metal sheathing.

"Captain," the computer said.

"What is it?"

"You have ten minutes of safe exposure time remaining. You will need to begin returning to the bay within three minutes."

Jack didn't answer as he stared at the thin crack. What should have been a quick fix was becoming a real problem.

"Captain, did you hear my..."

"I know...I know." Though the damage didn't directly threaten their lives, or the ship' function, it was essential that they be able to launch navigation and exploratory probes during their approach to Epsilon Eri system. Without these remote eyes, they would be literally flying blind into an unknown system. "Is there an airlock mechanism between the probe loading room below and these doors?"

"No, but the launch tube has its own set of interior doors, and there is an emergency, air-tight bulkhead in case the doors are breeched."

"Are they closed?"

"Yes."

"Good. Keep both sets closed and retract the lower door here."

"I don't understand."

"Just retract the lower door. I need access to the tube so that I can completely remove the upper door. All we need is a clear opening so we can launch the probes tomorrow."

As the door pulled back, Jack retrieved a powered socket wrench. "If I remember right, there are four retaining bolts holding the door onto the retracting mechanism."

"Correct," the computer answered.

He pulled close enough to the door, so that the glass of the pod's window was nearly touching the frame, and reached in as far as he could with both arms. "Activate left arm camera – display center."

A computer-generated image of the interior of the launch tube appeared in front of him. A small lamp on his mechanical arm illuminated the front section of the darkened tube. Easily visible were the four bolts he needed to remove. Twisting his arm, he maneuvered the artificial limb into position and began removing the bolts.

"Sir, your time is approaching critical," the computer warned.

"I know," was all Jack said in response. The last bolt came off quickly and he pulled hard on the door, but it didn't budge. He reached in further with his left arm, and lost most of his view as the arm-mounted camera pushed up against the tube wall. There was no choice though, and he began grasping blindly, trying to get a hold of the door. The arm's pressure sensors served as his sense of touch, and on the fourth try, confirmed that he had a good grip. He pulled back hard. The readings showed the door shifted slightly. Pulling again steadily, he called out, "Computer, increase force to maximum."

"Sir that may damage the retractor mechanism..."

"I don't give a damn at this point, just do what I said!"

The pod lurched to his left as the door finally broke free. Jack used one of the mechanical arms to stabilize himself, before awkwardly sliding the door out. Peering down the long, dark launch tube, he confirmed that it was indeed clear and let out a barely audible, "Yes." The problem now was what to do with the door. At nearly two meters across and over fifty kilos, he could hardly toss it aside. It would likely puncture a fuel tank if he dropped it from this height. There was only one real option: he'd just have to carry it back inside. Without any further hesitation, he commanded the pod to maneuver to ascent position and return to the bay.

Though the machine climbed quickly, it didn't compare to the speed of his descent. It took nearly a minute to reach shuttle bay level. By the time the pod had scurried along its track and was back in the bay, his clock was down to a bare twenty-five seconds. As the doors closed behind him, the computer lightly admonished him for cutting things so close.

"But we made it back in time didn't we," he shot back with a smile.

The machine knew better than to answer.

Chapter 2 – May 11, 2124

Kurt stood alone in the primary conference room, studying a large map of the Epsilon Eri system. A brightly colored, holographic schematic of its twelve planets and their orbits floated gently over the simulated pine table. Large, banded Jovian globes were strung along sweeping outer ellipses that spanned the entire table, while four small rocky-brown worlds and a lone blue and white globe circled the bright central star on a set of tightly bunched inner orbits. His eye jumped from planet to planet, examining the system that he would be seeing with his own eyes in only a few more weeks. He was of course familiar with its population of planets, moons, asteroids and other bodies. His gaze was more of a futile attempt to glean some extra shred of information from a map he'd seen hundreds of times before. Compiled from the rudimentary information first collected by the powerful telescope arrays back on the Moon, and updated with details from the advance probes launched from the Magellan nearly three years earlier, the map accurately laid out the orbits and positions of Epsilon Eri's planets. However, the bottom line was, they really didn't know much more now than they did before they left Earth. The advance probes, released while the Magellan was traveling at over half the speed of light, carried that high velocity with them. It was impossible to fit them with engines powerful enough to slow down, and as a result, they had traversed the entire star system in under two days. To say this severely limited their data-gathering ability was an understatement. In essence the probes did little more than confirm what they already knew. The truth was, they were flying blind into an alien system.

Today's launch of a new set of probes would give them their first detailed charts. Starting out at a tenth of the speed of their predecessors meant that their engines would be capable of doing some meaningful deceleration. These would be more than ephemeral fly-bys. Though not strong enough to stop and go into orbit around any of the bodies near Epsilon Eri, the probes' encounters would last long enough to provide detailed maps of several of the planets, as well as identify any debris down to one kilometer across that may lie in their path. The mere thought of debris drew Kurt's attention back to Epsilon Eri's Kuiper belt. Traveling across this expanse was arguably the most dangerous part of the trip. Lying on the edge of the star system, and spanning nearly ten-billion kilometers, this belt was thick with dust and contained hundreds of thousands of comets and planetoids. The couple dozen that rivaled the size of Pluto were not of great concern. They could easily be seen in advance, and the Magellan's course adjusted to avoid them.

It was the thousands of smaller fragments that posed the real danger. Made up of frozen gasses and rock left over from the birth of the star system, their surface temperatures were near absolute zero. More importantly, their billion-year deep freeze meant that there would be no infra-red signatures to look for. Their soot-black surfaces would likewise render optical surveys equally futile. With the Magellan still moving at thirty thousand kilometers per second, a collision with even a fragment could be devastating. The new probes would at least map out the zones with the greatest concentration of debris, allowing them to plot the least risky passage through the belt. Radar scans and vigilant watches by the crew though would still be necessary to make it safely.

Kurt looked up as Jack walked in with George Palmer, the first officer. Palmer, a stocky, muscular man, stood a couple of centimeters shorter than Jack's two-meter frame. His straight posture and mostly gray crew cut hair spoke of his military background; his face, rigid as always, concealed any hint of his thoughts. Jack gave Kurt a quick hello, to which Palmer added a barely detectable nod of acknowledgement. Kurt responded with a smile and said, "Good morning. So are we ready to do some real work for a change?"

Before Jack could answer, Don Martinez followed them in saying, "I don't know about you, but I've been doing real work for a long time now." The slight edge in his voice didn't surprise Kurt at all. He was quite sure the chief science officer completely lacked a sense of humor, not to mention most interpersonal skills. Don was a short, high-strung man who always seemed on edge. His temperament had taken its toll on him though, giving him appearance of a man at least a decade beyond his fifty years. Kurt, however, didn't hold his attitude against him. He knew well that Don was under immense pressure today: even if most of it was self-imposed. Don was counting on the probes to settle once and for all, an argument that had been smoldering for decades but burst into the open over the past two years – whether there was intelligent life on Epsilon Eri-D.

There had never been any direct proof of the planet hosting an active civilization: only some very suggestive circumstantial evidence. Though the official motivation for the mission was to travel to the only life-bearing world close enough to visit, it never would have been funded without the serious hope of at least finding some evidence of an intelligent race. Two open questions in particular begged to be answered. First was the fact that at just under a billion years old, many believed the star system was too young to host the fully evolved biosphere that had been detected. The planet's atmosphere showed evidence of wide-spread complex life and photosynthesis: something that took the Earth over three billion years to achieve. Wishful thinking led some to even propose that an advanced race had terraformed the planet. That speculation would have remained on the fringes had it not been for the discovery of several unusual lines in its atmospheric spectra. The signals were too weak to be conclusive, but they suggested heavy, complex molecules: possibly even perfluorocarbons. These synthetic compounds certainly had no business being on an uninhabited planet. Adding that to the fact that decades earlier, serious papers had been written on using these very gases as a means to warm and terraform Mars was proof enough for Don. The on-going debate, however, stemmed from attempts to reconcile the atmospheric evidence with the lack of radio noise from Epsilon Eri-D. Though easily written off with the assumption that whatever race lived there simply didn't use radio waves for communication, it still ate at every member of the crew. The problem was that even at this distance, they still hadn't detected any communication at all from the planet – not even the weaker, indirect signals that would be the by-products of technology. The planet simply remained silent.

A few had proposed that the inhabitants were just too primitive to use radio. Don however had argued vehemently against this. And, Kurt had to agree; if those spectral lines were from heavy, synthetic compounds, then it required a certain level of technology. Others suggested that the aliens might not use radio based communications, a fact bolstered by the Magellan's use of frequency-modulated lasers to communicate with Earth. But this didn't explain the planet's total silence; there should be at least some sort of background electromagnetic emissions. Occasionally someone even revived the unpopular idea the alien civilization could be dead – either by their own hand or by some other catastrophe. Inevitably that proposal was quickly quashed and faded away. Even without the probes, they would know for certain in two months when they finally arrived at the planet. Kurt was quite sure, however, that the simple fact of not knowing was too much for Don; and two more months of uncertainty would be nothing short of sheer hell for the man.

"Verify probe statuses," Palmer called out.

Kurt paid him no attention until Palmer spoke again, too loudly to be ignored. "Lieutenant Commander Hoffman..."

"Yes...Yes, one minute," Kurt answered. He didn't care much for Palmer's use of his rank, but it was his way. A decade together on the ship, and the man still had trouble calling people by their first name. He shook the thought from his head and quickly brought up a status display on his hand-held terminal. "Nav-probes one and two are go; comm-relay probes one and two are go; and, planetary probes one and two are ready. We are set for launch."

"Good," Palmer answered. "Captain, we are ready."

"Alright, proceed with launch," Jack said.

Kurt looked around the table once before entering a command into the terminal. "Nav-probes one and two are in tube-one and ready...outer doors open...launch confirmed." A view from an exterior camera was displayed on the conference room wall. The probes with their propulsion stages resembled old, dome-capped, cylindrical ICBMs being launched from their silos. The image, though, wasn't as spectacular as a titan launch might have been. In place of flame was a short burst of compressed nitrogen that pushed the two probes with their unlit engines clear of the ship. Since the Magellan was constantly decelerating under the force of its antimatter drive, the un-powered probes rapidly fell away toward Epsilon Eri. Their engines would be ignited in just over a week, allowing them to get far enough ahead of Magellan to provide the necessary advance view. The data they radioed back would be critical for navigating the Magellan's path through the outer parts of the star system.

Palmer stared at his display and said, "Nav-probe trajectories are on target. No course corrections are necessary."

"Good," Jack answered.

Taking that as his queue, Kurt announced, "Planetary reconnaissance probes one and two are in the tube and ready for launch."

"Proceed," Jack called out.

Kurt touched the launch button again and the view-screen showed what could easily have been a replay of the nav-probe launch.

"Planetary probes are confirmed launched." The tone in his voice reflected the obvious redundancy of the statement.

"Trajectories look good," Palmer called out. "No course corrections are necessary."

"Comm-relay probes one and two are in place and ready for launch," Kurt said. These probes would move out about ten thousand kilometers to either side of Magellan, well clear of exhaust from the antimatter drive, enabling them to relay communications coming in from the other probes.

"OK, proceed with launch," Jack said.

Kurt issued the command and after watching the video feed said, "Launch confirmed." Shortly after they were away, each extended a long, spindly boom, and gracefully unfurled a large, mesh, dish antenna. A moment later they rotated according to pre-programmed commands, aiming themselves toward the other, now distant probes. Once stabilized, their engines ignited, allowing them to move out from the Magellan and keep pace with her. They only had enough fuel to match the Magellan's deceleration for about four weeks – just long enough to relay data from the fly-bys.

Kurt continued staring at the screen, only looking away when Jack asked Don to run a comm. test.

Don answered without looking up from his terminal, "Already on it." It took about a minute before Don spoke again. "Links with both comm-relay probes look good." He then worked at his keyboard some more before saying, "Nav probe one checks. And...nav probe two is good too. Transmission and reception are strong and clear.

"Planetary probe one is sending and receiving fine..." Don's voice trailed off. The pause that followed was just long enough for Kurt to begin growing impatient. Jack however broke the silence, "Don, what's the matter?"

Don ignored the question and typed furiously at his terminal. Jack's patience lasted barely a minute longer. "Don, answer me. What's going on?"

"Planetary probe two is unresponsive," was Don's barely audible reply.

"Are we getting its automatic beacon?" Kurt offered.

"No, nothing."

"Palmer," Jack said calmly. "Do we still have a reading on its trajectory?"

"Yes, sir. It's still falling toward Epsilon Eri at its initial velocity."

The room stayed quiet in deference to Jack. Kurt watched his friend look past the rest of them. It was certainly not the gaze of someone who was distracted.

"Don, anything yet?" Jack asked without looking at the man.

"Not a damn thing."

Then, turning to Palmer he said, "Prepare to ignite its engines. Let's see if we can slow it down and catch it as we go by." Without waiting for a response, Jack continued, "Computer."

"Yes, Captain," the machine responded politely.

"Prepare a line with a magnetic grapple. Use the emergency retrieval gear for the shuttles. I want you to try and catch probe two as we pass it."

"I will need a couple of minutes to prepare."

"Fine, it'll take at least that long before we catch up to it anyway."

"Palmer," Jack said.

"Yes, sir?"

"Ignite the engines."

"Ignition command sent," was the quick reply.

"Don, is there any confirmation signal?"

"No, still nothing."

"Palmer, what about its trajectory. Any change?"

"No, sir."

"Resend the ignition command. Computer, can we can get a visual?"

"No, sir. There is no line of sight. The probe is already behind the drive shield.," the machine answered.

"Damn," Jack said softly, his voice finally showing a hint of frustration.

Kurt watched Jack run his hands through his short, salt-and-pepper hair.

It was times like this where he thought he saw more gray than black in it – though it seemed to be more a sign of weathering than age. At fifty-six years, Jack was the senior member of the crew, but his athletic frame precluded any thought of him as a man past his prime. The intensity in his eyes said more about him than any wrinkle or gray hair. There was a strength behind his gaze that came from a man who was firmly in control, and who hated defeat of any kind. Kurt feared that though he was five years Jack's junior, he was the more aged of the two.

"Don," Jack finally said, "scan over a range of channels. See if the probe's broadcasting in some other frequency we haven't been monitoring."

"Monitoring channels..." Don said more to himself than in answer to Jack.

"Palmer, is there any change in trajectory yet?"

"No, sir. I've been doing radar scans via the comm-relay probes. I can see probe two, but nothing's changed."

Jack turned to Don, and asked, "Everything looked fine in the pre-flight, Right?"

"Of course!" Don shot back, not even trying to hide his irritation at being questioned about basic procedure.

Jack then glanced at each of them around the table and asked, "Any suggestions?"

"Just that we follow standard failure recovery procedures," Palmer said, "and set the computer to try reinitiating a link every twenty minutes."

The room was quiet again before Don said, "Programming for automatic re-initiation of the comm. link is set."

"Ok," Jack said as he stood up, "we've got two active comm-relay probes, two active nav-probes and one good planetary probe. This is why we have redundant systems. We're still in good shape. But, I want a full failure analysis report on this. We'll meet back here tomorrow at ten to look at the preliminary data from the nav-probes."

Kurt stood up, but stayed next to Jack as Palmer walked over. The first officer obviously had a question on his mind, but kept glancing over at Don who remained seated, staring at his terminal. "Do you think we should try building a replacement?" Palmer finally asked.

"How long do you think it'd take?" Jack asked.

"It shouldn't take more than a week to get a sensor package with appropriate imaging equipment together," Palmer replied. "Getting a propulsion unit might take longer."

Kurt answered without waiting for the question to be directed to him, "Definitely more than a week. The problem is we don't have any additional redundancy in the parts. Probe two was our set of redundant parts. We'll have to build an entire power unit from scratch. At best, it'd take at least two weeks."

"That would mean we'd be down to about two or three percent the speed of light before we could launch it," Jack said softly.

Kurt ran through the numbers and continued the thought, "It'd arrive only a week or so ahead of us. It might not be worth the effort."

"True," Palmer replied. "Plus, the comm-relay probes will have exhausted their fuel by then. They'll be too far out of range to relay any signals."

"Then we've got no real choice," Jack said. "We'll stick with one planetary probe."

"If there's nothing else, then I'm going to review the logs." Palmer said. As he turned to leave the room he added, "I'll check back with you in an hour."

"Good," Jack responded reflexively. He took a deep breath and walked to the doorway before turning to Kurt. "Well, at least it wasn't one of the nav-probes."

"True. We really won't lose much data because of this."

"Now how about that rematch you wanted?"

It took Kurt a full second to realize his friend was referring to the race they had the day before: five kilometers – four full laps around the habitat. Jack seemed to enjoy catching him off balance with the quick change of subject. "Only if you want a serious beating," he finally answered.

"I don't know about that."

Kurt noticed that as the conversation changed from dealing with the probe, Don got up and quietly walked past them. "You know, I did finish in under seventeen minutes a couple of days ago, so I won't be so easy on you this time," he said, prodding Jack some more.

"Yeah, but seventeen minutes in the equivalent to Martian gravity isn't much to brag about," Jack shot back.

All Kurt could do was shake his head and smile as they left the room. He knew better than to try to win this battle.

Chapter 3 – June 8, 2124

As was his morning routine, Jack sat in his living room sipping orange juice and reading the news from Earth. He skimmed an article detailing the latest economic battle between the European and Asian Unions, and caught himself wondering why he even bothered reading the reports. It wasn't that politics and economics bored him – quite the opposite. It was the fact that the news was over ten years old: the time it took for the signal, traveling at the speed of light, to reach them. The disagreement between the Europeans and the Asians had long since been resolved and likely relegated to the back pages of history. Administrations and who knows what else had come and gone. The truth was, it was all irrelevant. He knew why he read it. The dry report of activities back on Earth was one of their only connections to a distant home.

Jack paged back to the front of the news summary and stared for a moment at the date: February 20, 2119. It was nearly as irrelevant as the news itself – maybe even more so. All it served to do was represent one of the more unsettling aspects of their trip: an experience the crew coined as "lost time." Adding the ten-plus year journey for the signal to get to them meant that back on Earth it was sometime in mid-July, 2129. However, the ship's clocks read June 8, 2124. Just over five years were missing. Standard, text-book special relativity explained it, of course. But, reading about it was one thing: living it was quite another. The only way that Jack could digest the bizarre mix of dates was to fall back on an old, high-school example. Einstein called it the 'twin paradox.' Relativity said that since nothing could travel faster than the speed of light, then the passage of time itself was no longer a universal constant. Instead, the closer you came to traveling at the speed of light, the slower time passed for you with respect to the world outside your ship. In fact, according to Einstein's paradox, if you had a set of twins where one traveled at these relativistic speeds while the other remained on Earth, the twins would no longer be the same age when they reunited after the trip. The traveling twin would be younger. This effect, known as time-dilation, had been known for two centuries and confirmed countless times in experiments. Though Jack didn't have a twin back home waiting for him, it didn't make the effect any less real. The Magellan had accelerated for nearly seven and a half earth-years, reaching a top velocity of just over ninety percent of the speed of light. At that point, time was passing nearly three times more slowly onboard the Magellan than back home on Earth. Though they were now back to slower, sub-relativistic speeds, the cumulative effect of time-dilation had still taken its toll. Just under ten years had passed for the crew of the Magellan since the beginning of their trip, while their Earth-bound counterparts had seen fifteen years go by.

Jack tapped his display's menu-bar, closing the news report and brought up the day's agenda. At the top of the list was the morning status meeting. Unlike the typical tedious review of maintenance and prep tasks, this one would be interesting: today they would get their first look at data from the planetary probe.

He quickly brought his breakfast dishes into the efficiency kitchen, and headed back through his living room to the front door. Despite his rank as Captain, he had the same size, one-bedroom apartment as the rest of the crew. The only exception was for married crewmembers, who had an extra room. Space was limited, but the apartments weren't cramped. The mission planners had worked hard to strike the right balance between providing the amenities necessary to maintain morale, against the extraordinary cost of each kilogram carried on the Magellan. In the end, he had to admit, they did manage to achieve that balance.

Jack strolled out his front door and into the Garden: the largest open, livable space in the ship. Set in the midpoint of the globe that made up the habitat, it was four hundred meters across and took up three levels. During the mission planning stages, the psychological team had insisted on merging the fresh-food production and recreation facilities to create an open, Earth-like environment. Enough care had been taken that it truly felt as if he you were walking outside. Their one-story, shingled apartments formed a ring three-quarters of the way around the Garden, with the remaining quarter taken up by the two-story command building. With space at a premium, even the roofs of the apartments were covered with plants that were part of the food production system. The light blue-gray walls around the perimeter faded to the deep azure one would find on a clear day as they curved upward to the ceiling ten meters above. Diffuse lights ringed the Garden, giving the specter of mid-morning sunlight. With a temperature around twenty degrees Celsius, it was a perpetual spring day. The lights automatically dimmed in the evening, providing a 'night-time' that lasted a convenient eight hours.

Jack walked the short path across his front lawn to the main road. The yards were maintained by each apartment's occupant, providing a little bit of individuality. His own, however, was decorated with only a few, short, red-flowered shrubs. Though healthy, their arrangement reflected the fact that they'd been placed purely to break the monotony, and not out of any enjoyment of gardening. It was an almost austere sight when compared with his neighbor, an exobiologist named Alex Gilmartin. His carefully manicured array of flowers, ferns, shrubs and miniature trees gave the small area a lush, near-tropical feeling.

The road in front of him was little more than a one-lane, paved path that ran around the entire Garden. Though capable of handling the traffic of the occasional small, electrically powered maintenance cart, it was nearly always empty. Right now, it was perfectly quiet. Across the street, a small footpath led through the heart of the food production and recreation facilities. On the left was a golden field of hip-high, dwarf-wheat. Beyond it were small fields of rice, corn and other staples. Off to the right was the well-kept lawn of a multi-purpose ball field, followed by a cluster of tennis and handball courts. Beyond them lay a park, replete with small trees, shrubs, simulated stone paths and even a pond that doubled as a swimming pool. The psychological team, over Jack's objections, insisted on including this area so that the crew could escape the tension and technology that perpetually surrounded them. Though he wouldn't readily admit it, he was happy he lost that battle.

Continuing at a brisk pace down the center path, he glanced at a pair of robots harvesting the grain. The boxy, golf-cart size, silver-wheeled machines moved slowly through the rows of plants. Their long metal appendages, however, collected the grain too quickly for his eyes to follow. Despite their rapid motion, they made barely any noise – just a soft clicking accompanied by the hiss of grain pouring into holding bins. As he crossed an intersection with a second footpath that ran perpendicular to his, the wheat abruptly shifted to rows of corn. The planting was staggered to ensure a continual supply, resulting in the plants growing taller as he continued down the path. Near the end were stalks with sweet, mature ears, followed by a nearly bare plot peppered with seedlings. The path crossed the main road again, and ended at the glass doors of the brick-faced command building. In reality, the building was nothing more than a facade – just an entrance to the rest of the ship. Its appearance as a separate structure was simply to perpetuate the illusion in the Garden that they still had some semblance of a normal life.

Once inside, he made his way down a plain white corridor, identical to the dozens of others that wound their way through the rest of the habitat. Above the Garden, they led to laboratories, a computer center, as well as repair and other support facilities. Below were the maintenance corridors for the massive arrays of power units, superconducting magnets and other equipment that formed the core of the interstellar drive. Jack took an elevator up one level, and continued a short distance to the main conference room. Palmer, Don and Kurt were already present, prompting Jack to utter a quick, "Good morning," as he took his seat. "Since we're all here, why don't we get started? First, are there any pressing issues?"

Don spoke up immediately, "I've taken a look at our first atmospheric spectra from the planetary probe. Even though it's still two days out, I figured that we might finally get some answers regarding the strange spectral lines we originally spotted back home. The problem is, the spectra aren't consistent with an active civilization."

"What do you mean?" Palmer asked quickly, "that's something you said was beyond any doubt..."

"No...no, I'm not calling what I said into question. It's just that the details are confusing … that's what I mean. Back home, at ten light-years away, we could never get a good read on a lot of the trace components. Now that we're here, we have some good data, but it doesn't make a lot of sense. Basically, there are almost no short-lived compounds like nitrogen dioxide and sulfur dioxide, compared to the amounts of longer lasting synthetics. Of the synthetics, I've identified perfluoromethane and octafluoropropane, and have isolated a couple more that I still can't identify."

"Maybe the lack of regular pollutants means they're more advanced, or at least more sensible than us," Kurt interrupted, eliciting a chuckle from Jack.

Palmer ignored the comment and added, "Or, for whatever reason, they're unable to use the technological processes that pollute. This could mean there's no longer a civilization on Epsilon Eri-D, if there ever was one."

"That's not what I said," Don replied defensively.

"You can't just choose to ignore a valid possibility because you don't like it," Palmer shot back.

"Palmer, these compounds are definitely not natural. If anything, there's less doubt now about their purpose. Based on their concentrations, they are strong candidates for terraforming. I mean they've got a strong green-house potential, making them the ideal gases to warm up a world that might be too cold for liquid water. Maybe we've stumbled onto a work in progress here. We could be talking about a race able to engineer an entire planet."

"Then where're the energy signatures of technology?" Palmer pressed. "And what about signs of the machines needed to make these compounds?"

Deciding to put a quick stop to the emerging debate, Jack said, "We'll argue about what this means later. Don, how sure are you of these levels?"

"Very. Basically, from two days out, we can get close to the level of detailed analysis we'd have if we were in orbit."

"OK then," Jack continued, "what about our image resolution? Can we confirm anything visually yet?"

"No, not from this distance. The probes are still about fifty million kilometers out." Don paused as he quickly worked a calculation on his terminal. "We'd only be able to see features about one kilometer or larger."

"Which doesn't contradict what I said," Palmer added.

"It doesn't say anything either way." Jack interjected. "It's probably not so productive to spend time speculating based on this limited data anyway."

"Then why bring it up?" Palmer pressed.

Don glared at him as he answered, "I just thought it might be important to mention this. Anyhow, the probe will do a thousand kilometer fly-by in two days. Then, we'll have some detailed imagery to go with."

"Thanks Don," Jack said as he moved quickly to change the subject. "Kurt, how's our ETA at Epsilon Eri-D looking?"

"We finished the last of our main course corrections, so projections put us there in four weeks, on July sixth – our time."

They had just completed their passage through the Kuiper Belt, and Kurt proceeded to present their findings. Over ten thousand bodies had been catalogued; with the largest being a mammoth icy planet five times the size of Pluto. Its unexpectedly large collection of moonlets required a detour that pushed the arrival date out an extra two days. The only truly unexpected find though was that the Kuiper Belt ended some two times further from Epsilon Eri than the belt back home did from the Sun. Jack smiled on hearing this. Though there were still four weeks to go, it meant that they were already in the relatively clear space that was the main part of the star system. The crew would be spared a continuation of the round-the-clock watches and course corrections associated with searching for the hazardous, icy fragments in the belt. Though separated by centuries, Jack always thought of this duty as something they had in common with the lookouts on the ancient ships that sailed the icy waters of the North Atlantic. Those men had strained their eyes against the pitch black night, looking for icebergs that could wreak havoc on their vessels. Though his crew had telescopes and radar, their job was equally important and no less arduous.

Kurt finished with a status report on the various systems and the room fell quiet again. Jack gave the others a few seconds to pose any questions. When no one spoke up, he asked, "Don, what about our next targets and ETA's?"

Don stood up and quickly instructed the computer to display the familiar holographic diagram of the Epsilon Eri system. The lights dimmed and a bright, yellow ball representing the central star hovered over the middle of the table. Surrounding it were concentric, red ellipses tracing out the orbits of Epsilon Eri's twelve planets; the outermost curve swung within centimeters of Jack's face. There was some similarity to the Earth's system, in that the outer four planets were gas giants; though it included an unusual binary where a Jupiter-sized planet was orbited by another that rivaled Neptune in size. The hologram showed the massive orange and red striped globe moving along its orbit, with its companion, a muted cream-colored sphere, sweeping out an elongated path around it. The middle region of the system was more chaotic than back home. Two rocky planets, a Jovian, and two asteroid belts cluttered a region from three hundred million to three-billion kilometers from the star. The inner belt was undoubtedly made of the remnants of two terrestrial planets that came too close to one another; the outer belt though may well have been comprised of more pristine debris left over from the formation of the planetary system. The neighboring planets seemed to shepherd the two belts into their distinct regions. Further in toward Epsilon Eri was their target: Epsilon Eri-D. A near carbon-copy of Earth, it was only five percent smaller and sat one hundred and ten million kilometers from its sun. Its blue oceans and graceful white clouds called to them. Closer still to Epsilon Eri were the remaining four. Though all were roughly the size of Mars, they varied drastically in their environments. The furthest in was so close that it orbited its sun in only twenty days, leaving it with a molten surface. The next closest was an arid, baked world like Mercury, while the third held a stifling, dense atmosphere that might well be on its way to becoming a Venus.

Don started, "There's not much to say that you don't already know. Based on Kurt's data, we'll pass the outermost gas giant in four days. The other three Jovians, unfortunately including the binary, will be on the far side of the star system, so we won't see them on our way in. The only thing of real interest is the inner asteroid belt. We now know that it's very compact, and its inner edge is a little over a hundred million kilometers from Epsilon Eri-D – meaning it's easily accessible from the planet. When you take into account the fact that we, I mean humans, have only been in space for about a hundred sixty years, and already have some pretty sizable mining colonies in our belt, then there very well may be something to look for here. The reason that I bring this up is that our latest analysis of the planetary probe data shows that there are three nice sized dwarf planets in the belt that aren't far off of our inbound trajectory."

Don hit a couple of keys and their holographic map jumped to an enlarged view of the inner belt and the Epsilon Eri-D region. A band comprised of thousands of small, irregularly-shaped, yellow objects, arced across the table. A region of open space extended from its inner edge to the red curve of Epsilon Eri-D's orbit. The Magellan's planned course was a nearly straight white line that stretched from behind Jack in toward the deep blue globe of their target. Not far from their course, and nearly hidden in the field of yellow specks, were three red circles. "These circles identify the positions of the three dwarf planets. Their diameters range from 400 to 700 kilometers, and back home would be prime targets for mining colonies. If Epsilon Eri has a space-faring civilization, we should undoubtedly find something here. At very least they should have left their mark on these bodies.

"Since we've only just discovered them, we don't currently have any plans to look at them. However, I think that with a small course correction, we could take one of the shuttles over to the larger one. It's an opportunity we shouldn't pass up."

Don was right about the opportunity, but the real question was whether it would be worth diverting from their inbound course now, as opposed to visiting them at some other time, after they'd arrived at E Eri-D. Jack turned first to Don and said, "It's an interesting idea, but I'm not sure about slowing the Magellan down and navigating this behemoth in an asteroid belt." Before Don could protest, however, Jack turned to Kurt and asked, "Just to be thorough, do an analysis on this idea. See what it would involve in terms fuel, adjusted ETA and any risks to the ship."

Kurt worked at his terminal for a moment and said, "The only real issue I can see right now would be with slowing the Magellan down so that we can park it while the shuttles investigate the asteroids. We'd have to increase our deceleration by maybe ten or fifteen percent. After the mission's complete, we can run at high g's again to make up for lost time. Then taking into account..."

"Kurt," Jack interrupted, "Take your time and do a full work up on this. Let us know later. We don't have to decide right now."

Without missing a beat, Kurt continued, "What I meant was that running at higher deceleration might lead to some physical duress. I mean, with the resulting higher gravity on the ship, we'll all be effectively gaining about ten kilos."

"I see," Jack said thoughtfully. "Any comments?"

"You're not thinking of passing this up are you?" Don protested.

Palmer replied before Jack could say anything, "Don, you have to realize that this would just be an extra. Our main goal is to reach Epsilon Eri-D safely. This little trip you're asking will put the crew at some additional risk."

"This isn't sight-seeing..."

Jack put up his hand to stop Don's response. Turning to Palmer, he said, "We're not deciding anything one way or the other right now. Let Kurt do the work up. We'll also need get a clearer picture of how clean that region of space is, which'll require an additional review of the probe data. Once we've got all of the details, we'll consider it."

Jack allowed a few moments of silence to pass before asking, "Is there any other business?"

Kurt and Don answered, "No," in unison, and Jack took Palmer's silence to mean the same. "OK, we'll have our regular status meeting here tomorrow – same time. Don, let me know when you think you'll have some initial hi-res imagery from the probe."

Don answered with a quiet, "OK."

Jack knew that the next two days would pass interminably slowly as they waited for the probe's Epsilon Eri-D video feed. There were too many unanswered questions and too much time before getting those answers. But, there was nothing he could do about that. He looked over at Kurt who was now preoccupied with analyzing potential course changes and said, "I'll see you later."

Without looking up Kurt responded with something halfway between a wave and a mock salute. It was intended as much to acknowledge the 'good bye,' as to annoy Jack for saddling him with at least a half a day's worth of course and propulsion calculations. Jack just shook his head and followed the other two out, before heading down a separate corridor to his office.

Chapter 4 – June 9, 2124

The buzzing of the intercom cut through the dark, quiet room, piercing Jack's dreams before finally forcing him to sit up. Disoriented, he tried to focus on the clock on his night stand, but quickly gave up and barked, "Computer, time."

"Two thirty-eight a.m.," was the answer.

He grunted and said, "Lights on – low."

The noise continued as he looked at the communications unit sitting on the desk across from his bed. He forced himself to go to it and slap the "on" button. Palmer's voice immediately came in over the speaker saying, "Captain, we've got a problem with the planetary probe."

He suppressed the urge to chastise his first officer for waking him at this hour, but realized the uselessness of it. It would be out of character for Palmer to overreact and bother him about something that could wait. Plus, Palmer would actually view any outburst as a sign of weakness. "What's wrong?" he finally answered, matching Palmer's tone.

"We have a complete loss of signal from the probe as of zero-one-forty-five."

He asked the obvious, knowing Palmer had probably already checked it out, "Does it look like a comm. problem?"

"No, I've gone through all of the standard recovery procedures. I called you because I think that you'll want to see the final transmissions. I've taken the liberty of calling Dr. Martinez and Lieutenant Commander Hoffman as well."

Realizing he wasn't going to get any more sleep, Jack sighed and answered, "Thank you. I'll meet you at the command center in a few minutes." As he disconnected the comm. channel, Jack pondered Palmer's ever-present formalism. Never was there a, "Sorry for waking you," or casual "hello." Plus, it would have been a whole lot easier to simply call the others 'Don' and 'Kurt.' But, Jack thought, if that was the only thing there was to annoy him about the man, then he shouldn't complain.

He quickly threw on a T-shirt and pair of sweatpants, and headed out his front door. The Garden was dark but not pitch-black. Antique-style octagonal street lamps illuminated the road and footpath with a comfortable amber glow. He took in a deep breath of the "evening" air, and chose to jog down the path. It was as much to wake himself up as to get to the command building quickly. As he ran across the center of the Garden, he listened to the sounds of a summer evening – a combination of crickets and other assorted wildlife. Around a year into the voyage, someone had either gotten bored or homesick, and programmed the night-time routine to include this little bit of home. Nobody ever owned up to it, but the sounds of nature were so well received by the crew, Jack let it stay in the system.

It only took him a couple minutes to reach the building. Without breaking stride, he entered and jogged up a flight of steps, slowing his pace only at the end so that he could walk calmly into the conference room. Palmer was the only one present. "What've you got?" he asked as he headed over to the man.

Before he could answer, Kurt and Don entered. Don, flush from his own run over, said between breaths, "Let me see those images."

Palmer ignored him and said to Jack, "As I mentioned, at zero-one-forty-five, we experienced a total loss of signal from the planetary probe. All standard recovery procedures have been unsuccessful. Rather than say any more at this point, I think that it will be more productive to see the following replay of the probe's last transmission."

Jack took his usual seat across from Palmer. The large computer screen embedded horizontally in the table became active and displayed four separate windows, one in front of each of them. The view was black, prompting Jack to think that he didn't have any video feed yet. On closer inspection, though, he was able to discern a few white points that he assumed were stars.

Palmer began to narrate, "What you're looking at is the probe's navigation camera output at zero-one-forty-two. At this point, its main engines are directed toward Epsilon Eri-D, as it continues to slow down for today's fly-by."

The image remained fixed as the chronometer progressed forward to 01:43:00. Jack focused his attention on a pair of stars in the center, and for a moment, thought that he saw the image shudder slightly at 01:43:15.

"At this point, the probe has shut its engines off in preparation for a navigational maneuver," Palmer continued. "It should turn itself around, analyze an image of Epsilon Eri-D against the background stars to confirm its trajectory, and determine if any final course corrections need to be made. This routine is done twice per day."

The chronometer counted past 01:44:30, and as the probe began swinging around, the stars slowly moved to the left. Jack noticed that a new indicator on the lower right appeared, displaying the apparent angle that the probe had turned. At 01:44:55, it displayed 90 degrees: the halfway point in its turn. Abruptly, several white streaks cut across the field of view. At 01:45:01 the stars jerked hard to the right, then spun wildly. A moment later the window went black.

"What the hell just happened?" Don blurted out.

"I don't know. That's what we've got to determine," Palmer answered calmly. "The problem..."

"You can't be telling me that we've lost the probe?" Don interrupted.

"I'm not telling you anything. I've just shown you what we know so far."

"That's not..."

Jack cut him off saying, "Palmer, is there any way to get some telemetry on it?"

Before the first officer could answer, Kurt jumped in, "Not without directly receiving data from the probe. The comm-relay satellites can only echo what they receive. So, without a line of sight, we can't see it, nor can we do a radar scan for it. Basically, the engines and blast shield are in the way."

"Unfortunately, he's right," Palmer added.

"We can turn the Magellan," Don pressed.

Palmer started, "It wouldn't be any use..."

"What the hell do you mean? Remember, we lost the first probe during launch. We need this one!"

Palmer waited a second to be sure that Don was finished before answering. "Dr. Martinez, we're still over ten billion kilometers out. That means that the signal we just watched took a half a day to reach us. If you remember, we were supposed to receive the probe's fly-by data this evening. That means because of the twelve-hour delay in getting the signal, the probe should be passing Epsilon Eri-D right now; if it's even still in one piece. In other words, it's over. Anything we do now won't reach the probe until well after the fly-by is done. And we wouldn't even know those results until this time tomorrow.

"Captain, right now, I suggest of course that we keep listening in the unlikely case that we regain contact with the probe. But more importantly, we need to start looking hard at this last transmission to understand what happened. In about four weeks, we are going to have to travel through that region of space."

Jack looked over at Don, who was still stewing at being cut off. As they met each other's gaze, Don turned to Palmer and asked, "And, what are you suggesting about that region of space?"

"I'm just thinking that it's way too coincidental for us to lose the probe just before it encounters the planet."

"What do you mean...someone shot it down? You're the one who's been saying it's probably a dead world. Who'd be around to shoot at it?"

"I'm just saying that we have to look at all the possibilities. This seems like a plausible scenario."

Jack cut in before the argument could escalate, "I think that's enough guessing for now." But, as he thought about it a bit more, he saw the answer already there in front of them. "Wait a minute. Palmer, let's see those last frames again. Freeze on the one just before it began spinning."

Their displays again showed the sudden appearance of the streaks and then froze on the final frame. The image was pitch-black with a dozen narrow, gray and white streaks running nearly horizontally across the field of view. Jack focused on four that both started and ended within the frame. Without looking up, he asked, "The camera was at a right angle with respect to its trajectory, right?"

"Yes," Palmer answered.

"What was its speed?"

Palmer checked his terminal and said, "four hundred ninety thousand k-p-h."

"Computer," Jack said, "What's the effective shutter speed of the probe's camera?"

The machine answered with its customary, wordy, over-precise answer, "Each picture is taken by exposing the image chip to light for one hundred thousandth of a second."

"What was the camera's field of view at that time?"

The computer responded quickly, "For navigational purposes, it would have been using its wide angle lens, yielding a one hundred and thirty degree field of view."

Jack ran the numbers through his head, but was interrupted as Kurt called his name. Without looking up, Jack muttered mostly to himself, "We can prove right now whether something was shot at the probe." Continuing his conversation with the computer, he said, "Assuming these objects were non-luminescent, they would have been illuminated by the probe's lights. How far away would they have to have been, in order to show the observed brightness?"

"Without knowing the type of materials, I cannot answer."

"Assume standard asteroidal or lunar type debris."

"These objects would have been at most about 150 meters from the probe."

"I see where you're going with this," Don said with renewed interest.

Jack smiled as he followed up, "Now if the probe flew through a field of this type of debris, then based on the known camera angle, probe speed, and shutter speed, what length streaks would they make on the image?"

"Between one hundred fifty and two hundred percent of the width of the screen."

"Damn," Jack said softly as he stared at the obviously shorter streaks. "What if the material was metallic?"

"It would depend on the type of metal," the computer replied.

Frustration crept into his voice as he answered loudly, "Machined, unpolished."

"Based on the increased reflectivity, the material would be approximately four to five hundred meters from the probe. The streaks would then be fifty percent of the image width."

"So Palmer's right? It was shot down?" Don said with disbelief.

"No, this shows the opposite," Jack said calmly. "My calculation was based on the material drifting in space. If those were projectiles, they'd have had their own velocity heading toward the probe, in addition to the probe's speed – the streaks would have been longer. But, there's more that we can tell from this.

"Computer, using the width of the streaks, estimate the size of the particles."

"They range between five and thirty centimeters across."

"So you're saying it flew into some sort of debris field...wreckage maybe?" Kurt asked.

"That'd be confirmation that there's a space-faring race on Epsilon Eri-D," Don quickly added.

"Or there once *was* one," Palmer added solemnly. "But wreckage isn't the only explanation. We need to consider that it may have been placed there deliberately. It certainly destroyed the probe just as well as a projectile would have, plus static debris would be harder to detect."

"True," Jack replied, "but…"

"Sir, if I may," Palmer said, "I'm not guessing. I'm just suggesting that one possibility is that this is evidence of some sort of violent confrontation, or possibly a trap that was laid for us."

"What do you want us to do George – turn around and go home?" Don sneered. "It's not like we have a choice."

"Dr. Martinez," Palmer answered firmly, "I'm saying that we need to prepare contingency plans – nothing else."

"Palmer's correct," Jack said.

"Jack?" Don protested.

"We sent a single probe through this region of space," Jack said solemnly, "and it was destroyed in what I'll for now characterize as a debris field. We don't know how extensive that field is, nor do we know if there are other hazardous regions. That debris poses a serious risk to our ship."

The room was silent as Jack took a breath. He continued, "What was the probe's position when it was destroyed?"

"About ten-million kilometers from asteroid A832 – the largest of the asteroids that Don identified earlier," Palmer replied.

"Damn," Jack said softly. "Kurt, review the impact thresholds on the blast shield. Also, work with one of the pilots on a course adjustment that would potentially bring the Magellan into orbit near A832. We can't risk blindly going through that region at high speed."

"Sir," Palmer said, "I would recommend active scanning for the remainder of our inbound trip."

"I agree," Jack said. "Reinstate the same search rotation and protocols we used when traversing the Kuiper belt." Turning to Kurt, he continued, "What've we got that can see..."

"I'm already working on it," Kurt answered, "not much. We're still too far to see anything in detail. Maybe some telescope and radar scans will help, but the fragments'll be too small to resolve individually."

"I see," Palmer replied reluctantly.

"Let me know when you have the calculations done for the course adjustment," Jack said. "We'll see what other ideas we can come up with in the meantime. Otherwise we'll implement that plan out of an abundance of caution."

"OK," Kurt answered.

"Start on it in the morning. I think we all could still use a little more sleep." Jack stood up and walked over to Don who was staring blankly at the display. "I'm going to need your group to go over these images with a fine-toothed comb. Make sure my calculations are correct and refine them. Let's see what else we can learn from this debris."

Don gave a barely audible "OK," without looking up.

Jack watched him sit there for another moment before saying, "Don, do it in the morning with the group. Go get some more sleep right now."

He gave another "Ok," before reluctantly getting up.

Jack looked to Palmer who was already walking over to him.

"I still have night watch to complete," Palmer said. "I think I'll do it from here and look over this data a bit more myself."

"Good. I'll check in with you first thing in the morning." He started to walk out but turned back and said, "Palmer, thanks."

His first officer nodded in acknowledgement as he sat down to get back to work.

Jack followed Kurt out of the command center as Kurt said thoughtfully, "I see your point, flying through a debris field would definitely leave streaks on a picture. You even reminded me of a family ski trip in the Alps when I was a kid. I remember looking out the passenger window of my parents' car and trying to pick out the individual snowflakes; of course I couldn't – at a hundred forty k-p-h they were just long streaks of white."

"Something's still not right," Jack said mostly to himself.

"What?" Kurt replied. When Jack didn't answer immediately, he continued, "Are you talking about Palmer's paranoid crap? Like they planted this debris as a trap?"

"Think of it. Put yourself in the shoes of some aliens on Epsilon Eri-D who don't really know who we are. What would you think if you'd reviewed over a hundred and fifty years' worth of radio and television broadcasts from Earth?"

"Don doesn't think...."

"I don't care what Don thinks," Jack said firmly. "I am asking you what you would do in their shoes."

"I don't know."

"Yes you do," Jack pressed. "Be honest with yourself. It wouldn't be hard to conclude that Humans are an aggressive race. We've had world wars, regional battles, economic fights, oppression, just to name a few."

"So?" Kurt challenged.

"What I'm saying is that if you didn't want direct conflict with these uninvited travelers – us – then the logical course of action could easily be to try and avoid letting them know that you were even there."

"Jack, that'd be impossible. Think of it, you'd have to suppress all transmissions that might leak out."

"But, if you started immediately after receiving the first Earth transmissions of any real strength, broadcasts from the nineteen-fifties, then the last of your transmissions that inadvertently leaked out would have swept past Earth in the nineteen-seventies: long before any of the real radio searches for extra-terrestrial intelligence began."

Jack paused in the middle of the Garden and looked around at the quiet surroundings. Kurt however, broke the silence and said, "Come on. Are you saying this is all deliberate? The radio silence, the debris…"

"We've got to consider all possible scenarios."

"Maybe you should limit yourself to realistic ones, not stuff Palmer's dreaming up. I mean, if these aliens are more advanced than us – and they'd have to be in order to suddenly make a whole planet go radio-silent – then they must surely have known that it wouldn't hide them forever."

"But if this is the case, then it did buy them over a century's worth of anonymity; that is, until the lunar telescope array's spectroscopic analysis of Epsilon Eri-D's atmosphere in 2070. The problem now is that our approach is anything but a secret."

"So why stay silent?" Kurt asked.

"In their place I wouldn't want to give anything away yet. I'd review Magellan's data feeds from Earth to try and understand whether these humans were ambassadors or conquerors?"

"Really?"

"Yes, really. What I'm saying isn't anything brilliant or unheard of. In fact, it's the most prudent course of action. If you read Sun Tzu's, 'The Art of War,' you'd know that."

"A twenty-five hundred year-old book by an ancient Chinese general?" Kurt challenged.

"Yes," Jack said calmly. "Sun Tzu said that the key to victory lay in knowing your enemy's strengths and weaknesses, while telling him nothing of your own. From their point of view, destroying the planetary probe would postpone giving away anything about their capabilities and fits perfectly with this."

"So you're saying that they've somehow gotten access to and read ancient texts from Earth."

"Of course not!" Jack shot back. "But I'm sure any technological race would have developed their own analog to it."

"Then you're saying that they had to destroy the probe in some way that didn't make us suspicious. And making it look like an accident by having the probe run into a debris field would fit the bill."

"Almost..." Jack said, letting his voice trail off.

"What do you mean, 'almost'?"

"Using machined metal is sloppy – too sloppy for a well-planned action like this. I'd have used something natural like rocky material from the asteroid belt."

"So they were sloppy," Kurt answered as he threw his hands up dismissively.

"No Kurt, they weren't. One of my professors back at the academy had told me that whether you were playing a game of chess, or engaging in battle, never assume that your opponent made a mistake. The use of finished metal is just too big a mistake."

"So what do you mean? Do you or don't you think it was a trap?"

"I don't know. There're too many uncertainties."

"I told you pursuing Palmer's logic was a waste of time," Kurt said with a smile.

Jack ignored his friend and just glanced at his watch: it was already three-fifty-five a.m. He had allowed himself to run too long with this particular fantasy. They walked the last few paces to the ring road in silence before Jack said, "The problem is that without the planetary probe, we won't know anything for certain for a few weeks. And that means we're going to have to proceed carefully."

"Like you weren't going to do that anyway?" Kurt replied.

Jack just smiled; maybe his friend was right and this was all a waste of time. He turned toward his apartment and said, "I'll see you in the morning." He was sure Kurt had answered him, but he wasn't listening. He needed sleep. The next few weeks were going to be stressful and push the crew to the limit.

PART 2: EPSILON ERI-D

Chapter 5 – July 3, 2124

Jack stood in the center of the bridge, arms folded, staring grimly at the view screen. Palmer and Don flanked him as they silently looked on. The display showed the results of Kurt's latest radar scans – the first with enough resolution to pick out small particulate matter. Stretching out before them was a hazy yellow arc consisting of thousands of yellow specks – each representing one of the myriad of asteroids comprising Epsilon Eri's inner belt. That, however, wasn't the problem. A straight white line, depicting their inbound trajectory passed uneventfully through the belt; it was the presence of three, globular, green clouds that had their attention. The amoeba-like forms identified the boundaries of large debris fields that lay in their path and were near the asteroid A832. Each was a few hundred thousand kilometers across. Their presence, though, didn't require any emergency course changes; Jack had already chosen the cautious approach two weeks earlier when deciding to bring the Magellan into orbit near A832. If anything, the data proved he chose wisely. Once they had a full handle on the situation, they would be able to work their way around the obstacle.

"The positions of these clouds looks more than coincidental," Palmer offered. "Now that we've got better scans, it looks like they cover most potential inbound trajectories from Earth."

"The problem is," Jack replied, "Their coverage isn't complete." He pointed to a small but significant gap between two adjacent clouds and said, "If we wanted to, we could have adjusted course and gone right through here."

"Would you have risked it, knowing what you know now?" Palmer asked.

"Probably not. However, it's an awfully large mistake to make if you're laying a trap."

"Maybe they were pushing their tech to the limits just by setting this up. I don't think we could have done much better back home if we wanted."

"You're assuming they were sloppy or not very advanced. That's a big leap to make if you're still arguing that this is a trap," Jack said. They stared silently at the map for a few moments longer before he continued, "Don, were you able to identify the composition of the debris?"

"Not completely," Don answered. "I can tell you that the cloud closest to A832 is comprised mostly of typical asteroidal material. Maybe as much as seventy-five percent." A hint of excitement crept into his voice as he continued, "The remainder is definitely metallic. What's particularly interesting is the fact that the two clouds further out from it are mostly metallic debris. However, I'm unable to determine what type of alloys we're looking at."

"What do you mean?" Palmer asked abruptly.

"It's not really a problem since we're still two days out. The stuff's just too cold and made up of solid particles, so I'm unable to do a spectral analysis. We should get a better handle on it when we're closer."

"Were you able to get a read on the particle sizes?" Palmer asked as he continued staring at the screen.

"There's a wide range. A fraction are sub-millimeter grains, while others are in the five to thirty centimeter range that we saw in the last images from the probe. There's nothing bigger than a half meter across."

They stood in silence for a few seconds before Don added, "The strangest part is their shapes."

"Explain," Jack said.

"The radar signatures suggest that they're all rounded. I'm not sure what to make of it. They're not perfectly circular, but there are no sharp edges or anything. Like little globs or ellipsoids."

"Like it was from a molten cloud that condensed out there," Jack said softly.

"Say again?" Don replied.

"I've seen something like this before," Jack answered. "An automated mining ship back home in the main asteroid belt had its reactor go critical. It was carrying a couple tons of processed iron and aluminum on board when it blew. The explosion had a power in the tens of kilotons – enough to vaporize the cargo. When we went in to investigate, we found clouds of metallic condensate. Small metal beads had solidified from the vapor cloud."

"That explains it," Don said softly. "This could be the result of some sort of accident. That'd mean there's nothing nefarious here."

"That's a bit of a leap…" Palmer started, but was cut off as Don said, "What are you talking about? We're talking about clouds of metallic particles. You heard what Jack said."

Jack jumped in quickly to cut off the debate, "Before we start speculating, we need to get a handle on the extent of these debris fields and if there are any other hazards we haven't spotted yet. Palmer, we'll need detailed maps of this entire region. Find out where we can safely park the Magellan. We're only two days out from A832, so it's essential that we get this done asap."

"Understood," Palmer replied.

"Don, the proximity of these debris clouds to A832 probably isn't coincidental. Continue your analysis of the clouds, but also work with the others to look in detail at A832 itself. See if it was the source of this and what might have happened."

"We've already been working on that," Don said. "In fact, we may already have an idea about the source of the clouds."

"Go on, explain," Jack said with a hint of impatience.

"We calculated the mass of the one closest to A832 and then analyzed a preliminary map of the asteroid. It seems to have a fresh crater about the right size for creating a debris cloud of this size."

"Why just the near cloud?" Palmer asked.

"Mostly because of its shape and composition," Don replied. "If you look closely at it, it's more of an arc than a random blob. In fact, it looks like it's in the process of forming a ring around A832. This would be consistent with material blasted off of the surface from some sort of impact. The rocky material in the cloud also seems to have roughly the same composition as the asteroid's regolith."

"What about the others?" Palmer asked.

"Aside from being mostly metallic, their distance from A832 and the fact that they're symmetrical says to me they didn't originate from the asteroid."

Palmer voiced the obvious question, "From where then?"

"That, we don't know yet."

"Based on the inner cloud's shape and position, can you tell when this happened?" Jack asked.

"Only in rough terms," Don said softly. "Because we don't really know the dynamics of this system that well yet, we can only guess that it's in the neighborhood of a few centuries ago."

Jack looked at each of them as they stared at the screen in silence. There was a mix of emotions swirling around. There was no longer any doubt that they'd answered one of humanity's oldest questions: they weren't alone. However, this was hardly the time to celebrate.

"Sir?" Palmer said.

"Yes," Jack replied.

"In light of this, should we increase deceleration further to make sure we're a safer distance from A832?"

"Not quite yet. Let's see what the radar shows over the next few hours. We've still got a little time to play with."

"Yes, sir," Palmer replied emotionlessly.

Jack allowed another moment of silence to pass before asking, "Any questions?"

Don turned to him but didn't say anything.

"Don, what is it?" Jack asked.

"I'm still concerned about the lack of signal from E-Eri D – especially considering all of this."

"Let's just take it one step at a time. For now, continue your investigation into the source of these clouds."

Don answered with a reluctant, "OK."

Chapter 6 – July 5, 2124

Kurt stood by the service elevator door, tapped his comm. unit and called the bridge. "Jack, final inspection is complete. We are go for engine shut down."

"Very good," was the quick reply.

"I'll be up in a few minutes; Kurt out."

He looked back down the long, brightly lit, white hallway leading from the engine's primary power-conversion unit, and listened to the lonely hum of its transformers. Though the systems that controlled and fed the interstellar drive dominated the entire lower half of the habitat, only he and the three others in his engineering staff ever ventured down into this maze of maintenance corridors. In fact, he enjoyed referring to these twenty levels beneath the Garden as his catacombs. Today though, there was no time to appreciate the seclusion they offered.

Despite the accompanying tension, he welcomed the fast pace that had crept back into their lives over the past few days. The fact that they were now only ten thousand kilometers from A832 – the seven hundred kilometer diameter asteroid that was their current target – filled him a sense of excitement he hadn't felt since the Magellan's launch. Now there was one final maneuver to perform: steer the giant ship toward the planetoid, and shut off its great engines for the first time in the five years since turnaround at mid-point.

A tone announced the elevator's arrival; he took a deep breath as he stepped through its doors. His mind let go of the myriad of technical details that crowded his thoughts, and allowed the exhilaration of the moment to inch back into the fore-front of his consciousness. They even had a real mystery to investigate. Don's group had confirmed that one debris cloud did indeed originate from the asteroid's surface, while the other two were likely from some sort of artificial structures – possibly orbital processing stations. Based on Jack's memory of the mining disaster back home, Don had even put together what he described as the most likely chain of events here: one processing station blew up, with its scattered debris destroying the other one as well as whatever base was on the asteroid itself. There was certainly room for debate, but Kurt didn't really care that much. He was captivated by the fact that they'd actually found evidence of an advanced alien species. The mystery was: where were they now?

The elevator's arrival at the command level pulled him back to the present. He half-jogged the short distance to the bridge and tapped the door's "open" button. The hatch quickly slid aside, releasing a wave of commotion. Half a dozen simultaneous conversations blended into unintelligible noise. Maneuvering his way into the crowded room, it took Kurt a moment before he spotted Jack and Palmer at the central command console. They were deep in discussion with Janet Kinkade, the Magellan's primary pilot and navigator. Hovering in front of them was a detailed holographic image of A832 accompanied by a shimmering crescent – its half-formed ring of debris. The bright white line of the Magellan's trajectory dove in from the left, before gracefully entering into a high altitude orbit that stayed well clear of the debris field. Janet traced her finger along the white line as Jack and Palmer listened intently. Though he strained his ears, Kurt couldn't make out what was being said. He made his way toward them, but before he was within earshot, Jack looked up and called over, "Kurt, can you confirm that everything is ready for zero-g?"

"Yeah. I reviewed the all of the ship's main systems before checking the antimatter feed and hull-stress indicators. We're all set."

"Good."

Once the engines were shut down, there would no longer be any force pushing against the ship, thus removing their 'gravity.' This was the main source of work that had dominated his life for the past few of days. His tasks ranged from mundane reviews that ensured that all loose items were stowed, to the more critical analysis of hull compression and frame expansion models. Despite his rank as chief engineer, though, his work was basically done now. Nadya was the propulsion specialist, and would be running the show from this point forward. Aside from being Kurt's wife of fifteen years, Nadya was one of the top scientists in the field. In fact, the antimatter drive was in large-part her design. It had been said more than once that the Magellan was more a piece of Nadya and himself than Earth's first star ship.

Kurt scanned the oval room and the six workstations lining its perimeter looking for Nadya. It took a full couple seconds before he spotted her working with her assistant Pierre Tremont at the station furthest from him. They were completely engulfed in their work.

Kurt started turning back to Jack and Palmer, when Nadya caught sight of him and called out, "Kurt, I need you over here."

He navigated the crowd, and on reaching her said with a smile, "How may I be of service?"

Too busy to notice his attempt at humor, she answered flatly, "I need you to work on monitoring the power feeds as we begin shutdown. Watch the fuel rates." Pointing at a graph on her display, she continued, "We want them reduced at this rate. Also, I need an engineer to directly monitor hull stress. Claire's available isn't she?"

She didn't give him a chance to answer before she turned, located Claire at a nearby terminal, and without another word, jogged over to get her started on her new task.

"Two minutes until scheduled shutdown." The computer announced.

Kurt moved to an empty terminal and brought up a display of the planned power reduction rates. Instead of a hard shutdown, the engine thrust would be reduced slowly. The idea was to minimize the shock to the ship's structure. The graph in front of him specified the rate at which the antimatter flow would be decreased. Near the end of the process, the power of the magnetic fields constraining the stream would be cut back as well, lowering the reaction efficiency and reducing the thrust even further. A small red arrow at the top of the graph indicated the current fuel injection rate of two grams-per-second. Along the bottom was a timer counting backwards: it read one minute and thirty-six seconds.

The noise in the room subsided as people began concentrating on their respective tasks. The complexity of the shutdown procedure lay in making sure that as power was reduced, the magnetic fields focused the fuel streams symmetrically into the interaction zone. Even a minute deviation in either the matter or antimatter flow would result in an off-center thrust vector, and send the ship spinning.

The computer's announcement, "One minute until shutdown procedure commences," quelled the remaining conversations.

"All systems are ready," Pierre called out.

"Confirmed," Nadya said loudly, "we are ready. Computer, commence at zero count."

"Understood Lieutenant," the machine answered. During all formal operations, the computer reverted to using the crew's ranks and titles when addressing them. Kurt was sure that it was a deliberate, subliminal attempt to reinforce the command structure and the authority of the officer in charge.

"Five seconds…four…three…two…one. Shutdown process commencing."

Unlike engine ignition, the end of this countdown was anticlimactic. He heard and saw nothing. The only sign that anything was happening was the slow movement of the arrow down the curve of his graph: the flow rate was now down to 95%…90%…

Kurt searched his senses, trying to detect the feeling of his weight leaving him, but felt nothing. The seconds went by slowly, and the room was silent except for Nadya's periodic announcements.

"Thrust is down to eighty percent," she called out. A few seconds later she said in the same, semi-urgent tone, "Seventy percent."

Kurt could feel it now, there was definitely a difference. Between the loss of weight, and his own excitement, he felt a rush of adrenaline. The displays in front of him though, indicated that the rush was wholly unnecessary: everything was proceeding normally.

"Forty percent," she called out. Then, "Thirty percent."

A series of deep, resonating groans rolled through the ship as its beams, having been compressed under their own weight for years, finally began to relax. The eerie chorus of moaning metal nearly drowned out Nadya's subsequent announcements, and prompted Kurt to glance suspiciously at the ceiling and the walls. A primal part of him was hoping the ship would hold together. He knew better – the sounds were normal and the decompression was expected – but he couldn't suppress his slight anxiety. Finally, the noise subsided leaving them in a brief silence that was broken by the computer announcing, "Shutdown is complete. Hull integrity is nominal."

Kurt's feet begin to lift from the floor, prompting him to slide them into a pair of foot restraints.

"Janet, what's our position with respect to A832?" Jack asked.

"Seven thousand kilometers."

"And our relative velocity?"

As Janet worked at her terminal to calculate an answer, Kurt brought up a display of their course projections. The plan was to move to within four thousand kilometers of A832 and send a reconnaissance mission to explore the body. They were particularly interested in a crater he'd nicknamed 'ground-zero' – the likely location of the impact that created the orbital debris field.

"We're drifting toward A832 at six meters per second," Janet finally answered.

"Very good. Use thrusters to move us into a four thousand kilometer orbit." Jack paused for a moment, and then said, "Kurt, we didn't get much of a read on small debris orbiting A832 at low altitudes. Check on this."

"Will do," he answered.

"Nadya," Jack continued, "what's the status of the main drive unit?"

Kurt didn't listen to the answer as he initiated a series of active radar scans. At this range, the results were almost immediate. There was a strong echo from A832 itself, followed by a barely detectable secondary echo. He repeated the scans and confirmed the presence of a sparsely populated ring of scattered debris, and then called out, "Jack, the main debris cloud has a diffuse tail encircling A832. It looks like it covers an altitude from two to four hundred kilometers above the surface. Beyond that it looks clear. We should be fine with our planned orbit."

Before he could hear a reply, Janet announced, "Captain, I'm beginning the approach sequence."

Kurt felt a gentle tug to his left as Janet fired a set of rockets, rotating the ship to face the asteroid. A few seconds later there was an equally gentle tug to his right as a second burst stopped the rotation. Almost immediately after came a light, but sustained pressure pulling him to back to the floor; the ship's auxiliary engines were accelerating them toward their target. It wasn't anything close to a full Earth gravity, but it was enough that he was no longer weightless. As a challenge to himself, Kurt ran through a quick calculation in his head and estimated that the burn would last maybe fifteen minutes before the engines shut down and they coasted into orbit.

"ETA to A832 is seventeen minutes," Janet announced.

Smiling as he admired the accuracy of his guess, Kurt watched Jack rise from his seat and make his customary, short closing statement. "OK people, good job here. Let's plan on launching the recon. mission tomorrow morning at zero-seven-thirty."

Numerous conversations picked up again as the room slowly emptied. Once he had a clear path, he bounded over to Nadya in the low gravity. She looked up as she shut down the last of her command programs, and said with a smile, "Well, what do you think? Perfect as always."

"I don't know ... it sounded like there was an awful lot of hull stress at the end there." His response was answered with a light slap in the back of the head. She playfully pulled him closer and said, "So, it seems like we might actually have time for a normal dinner tonight."

"Sounds good, but it won't be anything gourmet. We're back to tubes and pre-packaged meals now."

"That's fine by me. It beats your cooking anyway." With that, she moved quickly out the door. Kurt shook his head and followed.

Chapter 7 – July 6, 2124

Jack leaned forward in the shuttle's co-pilot seat as he reviewed a map of their primary landing site. There were no obvious alien bases or other structures – a fact that resulted in a distinct drop in moral. The morning's surveillance photos showed a cratered plain littered with metallic beads of various sizes – likely debris from the cloud that A832's weak gravity had managed to pull back to its surface over the past couple centuries. The only object they spotted of real interest was a large piece of polished metal embedded in a crater wall. The obvious question burned in his mind: Was it only a fragment, or could it be part of a larger, buried structure? The answer was still unknown as the asteroid's high iron content prevented ground-penetrating radar scans from revealing anything beneath its surface.

The shuttle's external door closed with a hiss and a thud behind him, prompting Jack to steal a quick glance over his shoulder. Devon Roberts, the Magellan's junior pilot, was just climbing through the inner airlock hatch and sealing it. Immediately to his left was Masako Fukuhara, the ship's geologist, who quickly took her seat behind Jack. Devon made his way over and said, "I completed the pre-flight a few minutes ago – Janet'll be monitoring us from the Magellan, so we're ready to go when you are."

Jack glanced at his watch. "Five minutes early. I guess I'm not the only one anxious to get moving."

Devon answered only with a quick grin, climbed into his seat, and said, "Computer, is the shuttle bay prepped for depressurization?"

"Yes, Lieutenant."

Jack watched the young pilot flip through the control panel's status screens faster than he could follow. At forty-one, Devon Roberts was the youngest member of the crew. His mannerisms still showed signs of the brash, young, thirty-one-year-old that started the mission. His skills were among the best in the fleet, and having reached the rank of full Lieutenant at only twenty-eight, his career was assured. When Jack interviewed him for the mission, there was only one real question that he wanted answered: why give up a career that would surely make him an admiral by forty? The answer he got was short, but satisfying. Devon had given a dismissive flick to the gold bars on his collar and said, "Where's this really going to take me? In ten or twenty years I'll be stuck behind a desk planning missions that I'd rather be on. What's that compared to being the first people to go to another star system?"

Devon's appearance matched his youth. At an even two meters in height, his stature could only be described as athletic. His short-cropped brown hair showed no trace of gray, and his sharp facial features spoke of his English ancestry.

Devon checked the status indicators once more before quickly calling into the radio, "Janet, we're prepped for launch."

"You're go for launch," was the quick reply.

Devon gave Jack a quick glance, which was answered with a nod, and then calmly said, "Computer, depressurize the bay." There was the familiar rush of the air being pumped out of the chamber. A barely perceptible moment of silence passed before Devon spoke again. "Computer, open the outer doors."

A yellow warning light on the bay ceiling flashed, and two large, reinforced steel doors quietly slid aside. Beyond them lay nothing but pitch-blackness. Jack watched with approval as Devon took hold of the control stick and gently pushed forward, guiding them through the opening. They were immediately surrounded by darkness: their only light coming from the dim amber glow of the shuttle's controls. His eyes adjusted and a narrow band of stars framed by the black silhouettes of the Magellan's fuel tanks revealed themselves. They accelerated away from ship and soon the jeweled band of the Milky Way stretched out before him. Jack only had a moment to admire it before the shuttle banked right and a large, jet-black disk slid into view. Their approach from A832's night side hid any hint of the planetoid's nature; the globe simply grew, eventually filling his field of view. They dove toward the darkened surface, but saw nothing of it. There was no frame of reference – no way to judge how fast they were crossing the small world's surface. His only sense of motion came from stars rising in front of him.

Then, in the distance, the bright, thin crescent of A832's daylight side showed itself. Straining his eyes, Jack could just make out a jagged line of rough terrain on the horizon. The illuminated region grew slowly, tantalizing him with a barely discernable view of a gray, airless landscape. They descended further, and the swath of illuminated terrain broadened. Finally, his thirst for detail was quenched. A rugged collection of ashen craters lay ahead. Their far walls cast long, jagged shadows that stretched toward him, while their nearest edges climbed out of the darkness forming jeweled arcs. Barely perceptible streaks of beige gave the scene a hint of color. The terminator – the sharp line separating night from day – rushed toward them, and a second later they crossed into brilliant daylight. The asteroid's surface was painful to look at, forcing Jack to squint. As his eyes relaxed, he could see an endless, chaotic array of craters stretching toward the horizon; there were too many to count. Newer craters overlapped ancient impacts that likely dated back to the formation of the planetoid itself. The basins of each were filled with the rings of progressively smaller and smaller craters until his eye could only distinguish the features as dots. They continued on course, and the landscape changed. The cratered plain gave way to rows of rolling hills broken by sharp vertical cliffs. Soon they were passing over the rugged peaks of a small mountain chain, where Jack could see muted shades of yellow and brown mix into the lifeless soil below. He pulled himself away from the hypnotic scene, and forced his mind back on task. "What's our altitude?"

"Twenty kilometers. We're nearly at the site. ETA in two minutes," Devon answered.

The mountains were behind them now, and they were again gliding over cratered flatlands. The features grew, rushing by more quickly as they continued their descent. A silver glint embedded in a distant crater wall caught Jack's eye. It sparkled like a small diamond, in stark contrast to its dusty surroundings. They came up on it fast, and within a matter of seconds he was pulled forward by the pressure of deceleration. A moment later the pressure ceased and they were hovering no more than fifty meters away from the object. A mirror-like, metal fragment, maybe two meters across, was fully embedded in the base of a thirty-meter-high, ashen crater wall. His eyes were fixated on the rough-edged, square patch of silver, until a splash of color in the surrounding regolith caught his attention. Before his thoughts were fully formed though, Masako's voice broke the silence. "Do you see it? It's red, I mean really red!"

"I see it," he answered as he studied the ruddy patch of soil. "It doesn't belong here." Turning to Devon, he asked, "How close can you get us without kicking up any dust?"

Without answering, the pilot edged them closer before stopping about twenty meters away. Jack could see more clearly what at first he thought might have been an illusion. Near the base of the polished metal object lay several small pools of a deep maroon substance. They were perfectly smooth with rounded edges, and sat on top of the surrounding soil. Shimmering in the sunlight with crimson highlights, they seemed almost translucent. "It looks almost as if it flowed out from the edge of the metal," Jack said.

"I'd have to agree," Masako answered. "I'd love to get a sample."

"Devon, take us in," Jack said softly, "just try not to kick up too much dust around that stuff."

Jack leaned forward as the ground slowly rose up toward them. A light fog of dust surrounded the shuttle, but that was unavoidable in the one-fiftieth of a g that passed for gravity on A832. The altimeter read twenty meters, then ten.

They jumped back in their seats as dozens of small objects suddenly peppered the windshield. "Shit, pull up...pull up!" Jack ordered. The shuttle started rising as sanguine streaks slid down the glass. Before he could formulate any thoughts, there were more impacts across the side window. A fog completely engulfed them and turned distinctly red. "Engines off!" Jack barked.

Devon instantly obeyed, and the hum of the shuttle's engines ceased. They drifted slowly in silence as the asteroid's weak gravity struggled to pull them down. Nearly half a minute passed before they finally fell back to the surface, landing with only a slight bump.

"What the hell was that?" Masako called out.

Ignoring her, Jack simply said, "Devon, status."

Without turning to him, his pilot answered, "We took several light impacts across our bow, but no damage."

Jack didn't answer as he gazed out the window and only slowly became cognizant of what he saw before: the red substance was running down the windshield at a steady pace. He softly voiced his disbelief, "This isn't right."

Not hearing Jack's comment, Devon declared, "What's going on? I mean, look...it's a vacuum out there and there's barely any gravity, but it's flowing like water across a windshield. It should've either boiled off or frozen."

Jack paid little attention to the protests, and gazed deeper into the fog. Sunlight scattered off the tiny particles, creating a surreal ruby-laced mist that sparkled intermittently. The tiny red droplets mixed with the dust and circulated around them. Its ebb and flow brought to mind images of sand kicked up from the sea bottom in the surf, and swirling in its currents. Out of the corner of his eye he caught sight of Devon and Masako looking at him, waiting for a statement, or some sort of instructions. He decided they could wait a few moments longer, and instead chose to continue studying the mist.

It took only a few more seconds before Devon finally broke the silence. "Sir, I don't think this is going to settle down any time soon."

Jack smiled and said, "I agree."

"So, how long do you want to give it?"

"A little anxious aren't we?"

"No, it's just..."

"Don't worry, I'm not about to leave after going through all of the trouble of getting here. The problem is, I don't think the conditions are going to improve any over the couple hours we can afford to sit here."

"Captain, let me do a quick spectral analysis of the mist," Masako said. "It'll at least give us an idea of what we're dealing with."

"Go ahead," he answered as he stared out the window. It was difficult not to be mesmerized by the natural kaleidoscope gently circulating in front of him. His attention drifted like the streams of dust in the cloud outside. Eddies slowly unwound themselves, while other wisps curled into new vortices. He wasn't sure how much time had passed before Masako finally said, "This doesn't make any sense."

"Just give us a quick rundown."

"The problem is our equipment is too limited ... but the bottom line is I don't see any radiation danger, or any other hazardous readings. The spectroscopic results show two distinct components to the mist. The first is as expected: ammoniated clays, carbonates, iron and magnesium compounds, as well as water ice. All are common to this class of asteroid. The other component however is completely unknown. It does not have any spectral lines in any part of the spectrum. There is no out-gassing, or anything else that can be measured without directly retrieving a sample."

"You're saying it's inert?" Jack asked.

"Within the limits of the shuttle's equipment, it is completely non-reactive."

"Can you give an estimate as to when this will all settle down?"

"Not precisely. The lower limit would be on the order of days."

Jack rubbed his chin; the answer was what he had expected. He turned to look at both of them and asked another question whose answer was a forgone conclusion. "Shall we go for a walk?"

"I'll get the gear," Devon answered as he jumped up from his seat, and pushed his way across the five-meter interior of the shuttle.

Jack followed Masako to the rear of the shuttle and began donning his EVA suit. Though he was well aware of their equipment, he still felt a bit awkward as he pulled on the protective gear. The suits carried aboard the Magellan were a completely new design. Comprised of beige, Kevlar-coated tights, they were more like thick wetsuits than the traditional, bulky spacesuits he was accustomed to wearing back home. The truth was, the computer-controlled fabric was a marvel of technology. It automatically applied pressure as necessary to compensate for the harsh conditions outside, as well as had integrated heating and cooling systems. There was no loss in protection, and its increased flexibility was definitely welcome. His subconscious, however, longed for the familiarity and accompanying feeling of security that came with wearing a heavy, armored suit. Pushing the thought from his mind, he strapped on his environmental pack, donned his helmet, and asked, "Are you both ready?"

"Yes, sir," was the simultaneous, enthusiastic answer.

Jack squeezed by, stepped into the closet-sized airlock, and closed the inner door. It took only a few seconds for the airlock to cycle through. A green "open" button lit up when vacuum was achieved, at which point Jack pressed it without hesitation. The heavy, outer door unlatched with a deep, metallic clank he felt through the floor, and slid open.

Jack stepped out into the rusty fog without saying a word. The shuttle's flood lights tried to cut through the mist, but penetrated barely twenty meters: just far enough for him to make out the crater wall. The ground was covered with a fine, grey soil and was littered with a myriad of pebbles and rocks. Randomly interspaced with their rocky counterparts were dozens of dust-covered, metallic nodules. Their size and shape suggested that they were indeed the same material found in the orbiting debris cloud. Jack bent down, picked up a finger-sized nugget, and brushed the dust off of its silvery surface. It glistened in the light from his suit. As Devon exited the airlock and walked up next to him, Jack said, "Be sure to get a few samples of these. Make sure they're different sizes."

"Got it."

Jack admired his sample for another second before placing it in a storage bag. With an easy jump he launched himself toward the crater wall. The low gravity allowed him to reach a height of nearly three meters before he was pulled back to the ground. Bending his knees on landing, he absorbed most of the force, limiting his next bounce – the last thing he needed was an uncontrolled collision with a jagged rock. By the time he reached the wall, though, dozens of tiny red drops were running down his faceplate, obscuring his view. He reflexively tried to wipe them aside with his glove, but only succeeded in redistributing the fluid into new patters. His frustration grew as it took several more tries before he cleared an oblong area at eye-level.

Devon landed next to him, and as he fought to clear a window of his own, made the obvious remark, "This crap's a royal pain." On finishing his battle, Devon took a step forward, stared at a small maroon puddle, and gently kicked it. The fluid flowed with the same ease as water around his foot. A small amount near his toe followed the path of his boot upward, and continued in a long, slow, arcing trajectory away from them. "It's got no real viscosity – I didn't feel anything."

Masako joined them as Jack walked to an area shaded from the direct light of Epsilon Eri, and tapped at the sensors on his glove. The surface temperature read negative two hundred and forty-nine degrees Celsius: only a couple dozen degrees above absolute zero. Spotting a small pool of the substance hidden deep in the shadows, he probed it with his foot. The material flowed just as easily as had Devon's puddle, prompting him to say, "Damn, it's liquid even here."

Masako came over, pulled a screw driver from her tool belt, and crouched down next to the puddle. She gently stirred the fluid and watched it run effortlessly off the blade of the tool. "It behaves like a superfluid.

Maybe it was used as a lubricant or something," she said before scooping a small sample into a container.

"Good, stow that. Let's have a look at our metal artifact over here," Jack said as he led the way to the table-sized square of metal. Its surface was perfectly reflective – so much so that it had no color of its own. Jack detected a gentle curvature to its surface only through the slight distortion of his image. Reaching out, he lightly ran a finger down its side. It was hard and perfectly smooth. Turning to his companions, he said, "See if there're any smaller pieces around here – anything that we might not have seen in the photos."

They moved off in either direction as Jack crouched down to inspect the base where the metal met the asteroid's surface. He brushed away a small deposit of dust and found that the metal continued downward. As he started digging, he felt the cracking and crumbling of a fragile material. His helmet's light revealed several thin, fractured shards of glass lying in his freshly dug hole. The pieces were a rough, translucent gray-green, and filled with bubbles. It resembled volcanic glass – likely formed from the heat of an impact. Jack worked his way along the base, then up the side. It was the same all around. The artifact was completely embedded in the rock wall. Taking a small hammer from his tool belt, he broke off some of the crust covering the right edge of the object. His tapping progressed to hammering, revealing more and more metal buried beneath. He stopped only when he reached a layer of solid rock. Harder strikes failed to clear any more away, and he paused to take a breath and stare at it. The rock appeared to have been molten at some point, and solidified around the object. Impulsively, Jack swung his hammer lightly at the metal, striking it squarely. It left no mark. More forceful strikes were equally ineffective.

"Jack, I think that you'll want to see this," Devon called.

Jack looked around, but couldn't find his companion. His puzzled turns, led Devon to say, "Up here, sir."

Craning his neck upward, he spotted his pilot standing some thirty meters above at the top of the crater wall. "What is it?"

"You should see for yourself."

Jack groaned as he looked up the steep, near-vertical slope of the crater. After a quick search, he spotted an appropriate ledge about halfway up, crouched down and launched himself with a moderate jump. He rose quickly and immediately realized his misjudgment; he was going overshoot the ledge by several meters. His eyes scanned the nearly sheer wall above, looking for something to grab and control his ascent, and spotted two small protruding rocks. As his rise slowed, he reached for them, but they were just beyond his grasp. A moment later he hit the wall and let out a grunt. His ascent stopped, and he started sliding down. The sound of his suit scraping against the rock filled his ears. His descent was slow for the moment, giving him time to look around, but there was nothing to grab. Instead he slammed his hammer, point first, into the rock. It held, stopping his slide.

"You OK, sir?" Devon asked sheepishly.

"Yes," Jack answered, hoping he succeeded in hiding his frustration and embarrassment. There was a small crevice within arm's reach and he dug his fingers into it. A quick twist of his wrist freed the hammer from its hold. He drew a deep breath and with a sharp tug on the crevice, gave himself the speed he needed to finish his ascent. Landing gracefully next to Devon, Jack looked around and saw Masako walking along the upper rim about a hundred meters to his right. He glanced down at the interior crater wall before asking, "OK, what's so interesting up here?"

"Look across the crater."

Jack did as asked. At this height, they were above much of the cloud their landing had created, giving them a relatively clear view. Stretching about four hundred meters across, the crater was a near-perfect circle, indicating that the impact from which it was born was nearly head on. The rim's inner edge had a gentler slope than the one he'd just ascended, and met with a flat, rather unremarkable floor that was littered with rocks and boulders. A slight sparkle in the soil made him recognize the presence of more of the metal fragments. He scanned the edges, looking for larger artifacts but saw none. In the back of his mind he knew something else wasn't quite right.

Impatient to make his point, Devon broke the silence, "Notice that there's no interior cratering. And, off to the left here," Devon said as he pointed, "you can see our crater's wall overlays another, older one. This appears to be the youngest feature on the asteroid."

"By your tone, I take it you don't think this is a coincidence."

"No, and I'm not really happy with what this points to. I started walking around the perimeter like you asked, and found some smaller, embedded, polished metal fragments. I then thought I'd get a better view from up here. That's when I noticed the lack of internal cratering. Since the fragments are all embedded in the wall, it suggests that they were distributed by the impact. The pieces scattered in the soil likely fell back to the surface afterwards. If, as I'm guessing, the embedded fragments are distributed evenly all the way around, then the original structure was exactly at ground-zero. That would be much too coincidental to be a chance impact."

Jack gazed across the crater floor, looking for any sign of newer craters. But there were none: just a gray, moon-like sandy soil, with its collection of rocks, silvery nuggets and the occasional boulder. "How far around the rim did you get before you came up here?"

"Maybe five percent."

"Masako," Jack said, "what do you think?"

"Dev's guess isn't bad, but it's not an impact."

"What do you mean?" Devon asked with genuine curiosity.

"You're right, there is no interior cratering, so this is definitely the youngest feature on this asteroid. However, if you look at the shape of the crater floor, it isn't consistent with an impact."

"Explain," Jack said.

"Its structure is almost the opposite of what we'd expect. The height of the floor inside the crater is actually higher than the ground outside. In addition, the central region of the interior is lower than the floor near the rim. An asteroidal impact of this size should result in a crater floor that is lower than the outside terrain, but also accompanied by a raised central peak. Now, this crater's certainly not volcanic either. If I had to guess, I'd say some of its features are consistent with an explosive event of some sort, but non-volcanic in origin."

"So if the debris is evenly scattered around the entire crater wall, we could conclude that it was some central structure that exploded," Devon added.

"There's not enough data to conclude that yet," Masako replied. "The other possibility is that something like a large ship crashed here and exploded. Unlike an asteroid, it wouldn't have the mass to depress the entire crater floor. So it could yield the crater configuration and debris pattern we've seen so far."

"So what does this really mean?" Devon asked.

"I'm not sure. I mean it could be some sort of tragic accident that happened here. But I don't know."

"Let's hold off on the speculation for now," Jack said calmly. "Right now, I'd really like to get a sample of that metal. While I do that, I'd like you two to do a little digging. Get one of the drills and let's see how far the larger fragments extend beneath the rock."

"OK," Devon answered.

Jack took a couple steps back from the edge, then jogged back toward it, leaping at the end. He watched the outer slope of the crater wall pass beneath him, and admired the billows of crimson-tinted dust below. The ultra-low gravity gave him the sensation of gliding above the clouds rather than falling freely. It wasn't until several seconds had passed that it became apparent he was even moving downward. The clouds slowly rose to meet him, and again he was surrounded by the surreal fog. The ground became visible, and a moment later Jack landed in a crouching position, absorbing the landing. He figured the force of impact really wasn't much more than jumping off a chair back on Earth. Devon landed a few meters to his left and quickly headed to the shuttle to retrieve his equipment.

Jack returned to the large fragment, and looked for a suitable place to cut. The lower left corner's reflection showed slightly more distortion than the rest of the object. He hoped the stress that warped it had also weakened it. Bringing his face to within a few centimeters of the mirror-like surface, he searched for other defects: there were none. It was smooth and featureless, not even providing him with the slightest scratch on which to start cutting. He took a deep breath, withdrew a small power saw from his tool-belt, and pressed it against the spot with the greatest deformation. Its circular blade spun against the object, but failed to penetrate. Jack increased its speed, and pressed harder. After giving it more than a minute, he pulled the machine back and reviewed his progress: the surface remained unblemished.

"Devon," he called. "Bring me the laser cutter on your way back." He examined the saw's blade for damage and let the word, "Damn," slip from his mouth. The blade's once sharp, diamond coated teeth were nearly completely worn away.

"What's wrong?" Devon asked as he came up behind him.

Jack ignored the question, and said, "Let me have the cutter."

Devon handed him the meter-long device which could have easily passed for a thick bodied rifle. The bulk of the cutter was mostly an advanced power source that fed a high-energy laser beam capable of cutting through a half a foot of steel. Jack slung the normally heavy machine easily into position in the asteroid's low-g environment. "OK, stand back," he said as he flipped a protective eye-guard on the machine into position and pressed the trigger. A blinding, violet, beam of light, orders of magnitude brighter than the sun, leapt from the cutter's muzzle, striking the object's surface and reflecting immediately off into space. Thousands of secondary reflections from the tiny droplets in the fog bathed the landscape in a blazing purple glow. The visor was rendered useless – light stabbed at his eyes from all angles, forcing him to shut them tight. He held the trigger anyway, hoping to make some progress. At the count of ten, he finally disengaged the beam, and found himself standing nearly sightless.

Forcing back competing feelings of fear and frustration, he said in a measured tone, "Devon, I can't see a damned thing. How about you?"

"Nothing. I shut my eyes almost immediately after the initial blast, but it was too late."

"Masako," he called out, "what's your status?"

"Not good," she replied. "I looked in your direction out of curiosity when you started cutting and got a good eye-full."

He took a deep breath, but the frustration won out, and shouted, "Goddamn it!" Reaching forward with his hand, he found the crater wall, but it didn't do him any good.

"Captain, what's your status?" Palmer's steady voice called over the radio.

"Give us a few minutes here. It's just flash-blindness. Just a damned stupid thing for me to have done."

"You sure you don't need us?" he called back.

"No! standby," he answered with more sternness than he intended. He turned around and thought he could make out some ghostly silhouettes. Calling back in a conciliatory tone, "I'm starting to get some sight back already. Just...just give us some time here."

"Understood."

Time passed intolerably slowly. Jack tried forcing his eyes to focus on his surroundings, as if he could will his sight back. The action was of course futile, and he was relegated to letting nature take its course. He succumbed to an irresistible urge to move and do something, but after shuffling backward a couple of steps, he realized the foolishness of his actions. The last thing he needed was to fall blindly on some sharp piece of rock. The crater wall was visible now, but was little more than a fuzzy, black-and-white image. "How long has it been," he barked into his radio.

"Three minutes, sir," was Palmer's prompt response.

"Thanks," he answered, forcing a hint of appreciation into his voice. "I'm definitely seeing improvement here."

"Devon how're you doing?" he continued.

"I'm not blind anymore if that's what you're asking. But my sight's not going to pass any flight physicals right now."

"Uh-huh," Jack answered, only half paying attention. He was able to make out enough detail now to see that the cutter hadn't made any headway into the object; its smooth surface was completely unharmed. He stared at it a little longer as his sight improved – hoping to find at least the hint of a scratch, but there was nothing. The metal fragment seemed impervious to anything they had. Finally, he shouted, "It didn't do a damned thing!" Suppressing an urge to throw the cutter in disgust, Jack instead just took a breath and stepped back from the wall.

"Let me give it a try with my drill," Devon said. "It's got a diamond-coated bit."

"Knock yourself out," Jack answered, but stopped short of telling his pilot he thought it was useless. Devon crouched down near the spot on which Jack had been working and gracefully flipped the drill into position. As he started, Jack began walking around the perimeter of the crater. Though he chose the direction opposite to that which Devon had covered, it appeared just as his pilot had described. The wall was an amalgam of blackened solidified lava, fractured rock, compacted soil and other debris. Peppered sporadically throughout it were small fragments of the silver, alien metal. He picked at a couple pieces as he walked, but they were all firmly embedded in the wall.

He paused at a moderate-sized piece that was maybe a half a meter across, and dug at it with his fingers. The looser material near its edge fell away easily, but his fingers soon encountered solid rock. Jack once again hoisted the laser cutter into position, but this time aimed it squarely at the rock adjacent to the metal. The violet beam cut through the rock as if it were paper, effortlessly pealing it away from the buried metal surface. He carefully guided the beam downward and released the trigger as he reached the crater wall's base. The metal, unscathed by anything he had done, gently curved downward, and apparently continued deep into the ground.

Devon's voice came over the radio, "Captain, I haven't had any luck here."

Jack took a breath and said, "Masako, what's your status?"

"I'm back at the shuttle, it doesn't look like we have anything here that'll do any good."

He glanced at the clock on his glove and said, "It looks like we've been at this for over an hour. We're not gonna get anything else done out here today — not like this at least. Board the shuttle, I'll be there in a minute and we'll head back. Devon do you copy?"

"Affirmative."

Jack started at a brisk pace, but A832's miniscule gravity complicated things. Shuffling around the rim while examining the metal fragments was one thing; moving with a normal gait, however, meant that each step he took contained enough upward force to launch him a couple of meters above the ground. This was followed by a seconds-long wait as he floated back down before he could take his next step. Even turning a corner suddenly required deliberate thought — he had to gauge his trajectory and push off at just the right angle. True, each step covered better than five meters; it was just impossible to walk with a comfortable rhythm.

The shuttle lay only a few meters away now and he took a moment to focus his attention on his last two steps. The key was to ensure that he landed at the base of the craft rather than reaching it at some high-point in his arcing leaps. As he floated gently down to meet the exterior airlock door, he grabbed its handle to keep from rebounding away. Turning to look back, he saw Devon bounding toward him. The man was coming in high and way too fast. "Devon, watch..." he started but it was too late. He twisted away to shield himself from the inevitable impact, but instead was pelted with a spray of dust and rocks as Devon stopped himself in his tracks with a hockey skater's stop.

Before he could put together the words to chastise him, Devon said, "Uh, sorry sir. Didn't mean to get you covered in..."

Jack simply held up his hand to quiet him. Without another word, he opened the exterior door. As they climbed in, Devon was quick to change the subject and asked, "I know Masako said this was likely an explosion, but do you think it was deliberate – like an attack?"

"I don't know," Jack answered as he sealed the airlock and started the decontamination cycle. Several high-pressure gas jets roared around them, blowing even the finest dust off their suits. This was followed by an equally loud set of pumps removing the gas and debris from the airlock. A few moments of silence followed while the computer scanned them for any residual contaminants. Finally, there was the hiss of air being pumped back into the chamber. "If this was a strike," Jack continued, "then who did it?" A green light on the inner door flashed, indicating that they had achieved atmospheric pressure, but Jack's mind had wandered. If this was the result of some attack, then what were they walking into? The only thing that gave him any solace was the fact that whatever happened here, happened a long time ago. "But how long ago?" he muttered to himself.

"I was wondering that too," Devon said, as if he had anticipated the question.

Jack stared at the green 'proceed' light, but didn't see it. His mind still labored to make sense of it all. "There's too damned much we don't know," he said as he finally opened the inner door and removed his helmet. "Hell, we don't even have any idea what that metal is out there – or, if it's metal at all."

Devon opened his mouth but Jack cut him off. "Think of it. We literally couldn't scratch it. Whatever it is, it's a hell of a lot more advanced than anything we've got. I can't even imagine how we'll come up with a way to figure out how long it's been out here!"

Devon finished removing his suit, and began stowing his gear. "Well, whatever it is, I'd bet that it's been out here for at least a few centuries."

"Maybe longer," Jack answered. "Let's let Masako and Don do a more detailed analysis."

"What do you think this means for E-Eri-D?" Masako asked hesitantly from her seat.

Jack didn't want to lead them on, but neither did he want to quash their hopes altogether. "My gut tells me there's no threat there. If there was, they'd have done something already." He drew a breath before continuing, "It's the same mission as before, except that we now know there is or was intelligent life here. We're going to be the first humans to walk through an alien city. Even if they're not there anymore, think about just being able to sift through their ruins and maybe even their libraries. Whatever we find, it'll be unmatched by anything in all of human history." As Jack and Devon took their seats in the cockpit, Jack hoped his words at very least masked his own disappointment.

Devon activated the shuttle controls and prepared for ascent. Jack hit the comm. button, and said "Magellan, we are preparing to return."

"Understood," Palmer replied.

"Good, Shuttle-one out."

Chapter 8 – July 7, 2124

Jack stood quietly in the lab as he watched Don carefully pick up a small metallic nugget from the sample tray. The scientist held it up to the light before turning to him and saying, "It's truly amazing. We've developed the technology to travel to another star system, but I still cannot give you any details about this stuff's composition."

"How's that possible?" Jack asked.

"We just don't have the equipment on the Magellan to do the analysis. My best guess at this point is that it's some sort of super conductive material with an extraordinarily high critical temperature and critical field strength – way beyond anything we've even theorized."

"Don, explain what you mean," Jack pressed.

"It's perfectly reflective in all wavelengths – which can't really happen in nature. I mean if you extrapolate some of our theories, then maybe a special type of superconductor could do this. But more importantly, since it's perfectly reflective I can't really probe its structure. I've tried subjecting it to high temperatures and magnetic fields to break it out of this state, but haven't succeeded. Hell, I can't even determine if it's truly metallic or ceramic, or something completely different. It is a low density substance, so it's not based on any of the compounds we use for high-temp superconductors, like copper oxides. Its extreme strength says that it's got a very tight crystalline structure. However, I haven't even been able to cleave a section off of it to start seeing the nature of this structure. The next step would be to try X-ray diffraction or even neutron diffraction, but we just don't have that type of apparatus on board – it's not something you typically bring along on any type of off-world mission. Give us a month's time and maybe we can adapt some of our equipment to try X-ray diffraction. Other than that, I just don't know."

Jack stared at the nugget for a moment before saying, "That piece has obviously been exposed to some extreme conditions – I mean its shape says that it's definitely been melted. So how can it still be superconductive?"

Don turned to look him directly in the eye and said, "Jack, that's the problem. I've got no damn idea. Based on our...I mean humanity's understanding of solid state physics, this shouldn't be possible. But, here it is."

There was a moment of silence before Don continued. "I just don't know what to say. I mean on the one hand it's all truly amazing. Here we have evidence of technology well beyond ours. But it's just collections of debris and rubble."

"I know. Do you have any guesses about the original structures?" Jack asked.

"I had Masako review some detailed maps of A832 we took from orbit, and they failed to show any structures that survived whatever happened here. We looked at the masses of the symmetrical clouds and estimated that each contains on the order of fifty thousand metric tons of material. Assuming that each came from a single space station or ship and that there's no missing material, we're looking at something quite large. By comparison, the Magellan's fully fueled mass was only thirty thousand metric tons."

"I'm well aware of the Magellan's specs," Jack said.

"I know," Don replied. "Umm...the structure on the asteroid's surface, however is a different story. I can't really estimate how much material is or was there. We still can't even tell if it was a surface base that exploded or something like a large ship that crashed there. As you know, the larger fragments were embedded in the crater, and it seems very likely that there's more material buried beneath the surface. So all that I can say is that it was probably larger than the lunar polar colony which has about a hundred people. The bottom line is – we've got nothing intact to investigate or piece together."

The room remained silent as Jack digested their findings. Before Jack could formulate a response, Don continued, "On the one hand, it might make sense to search the other large asteroids in this region. However, I think it would be much more useful to go directly to E-Eri D; it is the home of whatever civilization was out here in these asteroids."

"Searching the other asteroids right now isn't possible anyway," Jack replied. "The Magellan isn't suited for short trips – it's too large and has poor maneuverability. On top of that, we'd be going too slowly to use the magnetic scoop to harvest any interplanetary hydrogen, so we'd eat too deeply into our fuel reserves by making one or two more small trips here. Anyway, we can always take a shuttle back here once we've set up base camp on the E-Eri D's surface. There will be plenty of time for that down the road."

Don just nodded in agreement before Jack continued, "Were you at least able to make some progress with the fluid sample?"

"No," Don replied, and said nothing else.

Frustration crept into Jack's voice as he pressed, "You've got to have figured something out."

"Nothing meaningful. It's red. Its viscosity is near zero. It's vapor pressure appears to be zero. It seems to be completely inert. And, there's no way in the world it's natural."

"You're not being helpful," Jack shot back.

"Don't you think I'm frustrated too? We've spent two days here and aside from what I just said, I can't tell you anything else about it." Don took a deep breath before continuing, "At this point, it looks like all of our answers will be on E-Eri D. We should start heading there right away."

Jack simply nodded and said, "There's a problem with that too…"

"What are you talking about?"

"Palmer and Devon completed their remote scans of the system; they found at least two more debris clouds near the planet."

"So, how does that affect us?"

"One's about the same size and composition as the metallic clouds here in the asteroid belt. It lies in our path, so we'll need to make some course adjustments."

"That's not too hard," Don said dismissively.

"The other cloud's tougher to pin down. It's closer to the planet – possibly where we were going to park the Magellan. However, the clouds out here in the belt are interfering with our readings. We may need to pull out to some empty region between the belt and E-Eri D to re-evaluate things."

"I don't see why we need to do that," Don said with an edge. "We'll get a better read on it once we're closer. I mean how hard could it be to adjust our course en route?"

"Don," Jack said calmly, "it's one thing to find clouds here near the asteroid. They're close to one another, and like you suggested, it might even be possible that a single event caused this. It's another thing to find signs of wreckage tens of millions of kilometers away. That's a much more ominous sign. Palmer wants to analyze the situation further before we decide how to proceed – and I have to agree, it's a smart move."

"Jack, what are you talking about? You can't just give in to Palmer's paranoia. It's not like we can abort our mission."

"I'm just saying there's no harm in being prudent with our analysis. Let's take our time and make an informed decision."

"It's one thing to be cautious," Don replied, "it's another to sit around doing nothing just so you can say you slowed things down. It's a waste of time; we're not going to learn anything else here. Even if we leave right now, it'd still take us several days to get there – plenty of time to be prudent and *analyze* the situation."

"You make a good point," Jack said in an attempt to appease him. "Let's go over all of this when we meet later and plot our actual course."

"Jack, I can tell when you're just paying me lip service," Don said with an edge creeping into his voice. "But, listen to me; there's no point in just sitting still. If we don't have the fuel to examine the other asteroids in this belt, then we need to go to E-Eri D. We're not going to learn anything else useful just sitting here."

Jack patted Don on the back and said, "I know it's frustrating, but you are doing good work here. Just bring all this up when we sit down together later." He headed for the exit, expecting Don to continue the debate, but the scientist stayed curiously quiet. As he left, Jack felt obligated to add, "See you later Don."

"Fine," was the half muttered reply.

Chapter 9 – July 13, 2124

Kurt pulled his chair in to the table as he and Nadya sat down for what would be their last normal meal for the foreseeable future. The Magellan had spent three days accelerating away from A832, threading its way through the debris fields, and was now in its third and last day of deceleration as it neared Epsilon Eri-D. In a few hours, they would shut the main engines down and park the ship in orbit near the planet, heralding the start of round-the-clock shifts that would mark the beginning of their real mission. For now, though, Kurt was content to lean back and enjoy the aroma rising from his plate of chicken parmigiana – one of his favorites. It was also one of the few meals he was capable of cooking competently.

Nadya took her first bite and said, "Not too bad for lunch; it'll do."

Kurt ignored the comment and began eating slowly.

"So, tell me the truth," Nadya said. "Do you think Jack would've relieved him of duty if he kept it up?"

"Who, Don or Palmer?"

Nadya laughed. "Don of course. We all know Palmer wasn't doing anything out of the ordinary – he's just a jerk. But Don...the man was actually one step short of inciting mutiny."

Kurt took another bite of his chicken; it was much more pleasant than replaying the argument from a few days ago. Don had presented their findings on the asteroid mission, and reported that they still had no idea about what was going on. They were unable to identify the red fluid, or any meaningful details about the metal fragments in the clouds or the crater. At that point Palmer stepped in and tried to convince Jack to delay in their approach to E-Eri-D. To say that it drew a fierce response from Don would be an understatement.

"Well? Don't avoid the question," Nadya pressed.

"Depends on how you look at it."

"What? You agree with him?"

"No," Kurt said incredulously. He took a moment to mop up some sauce with a piece of bread before continuing, "Don's wrong of course. But think of it – he's just over anxious. The way he sees things, he's finally about to start his real job. Jack's wanting to push out our ETA by a few days was just a bit much for him. Especially since, as Don saw it, taking the slower, cautious approach to E-Eri-D was just to appease Palmer's paranoia."

Nadya's blank stare told him to continue, "Think of it; he's been waiting for this for a decade. As far as he sees it, he's just been biding his time with his ship-board research. On the other hand, we...I mean Jack, you, me and the rest of the command and engineering staff...we've been doing our primary job: flying and running the ship. As far as Don's concerned, he's been doing busy work. I just don't think he can stand any more waiting. In a sense I can't really blame him for that. It's just that he doesn't have a clue about how to get that across."

"I don't know. It sounds more like you're trying to make an excuse for him. It's pretty obvious to me it's a power play. He's the chief science officer. Once we touch down on E-Eri-D, we will be fully in the science phase of the mission. He figures he'll be in control. Plus, you and I both know he's never been happy taking orders from Jack or Palmer. This little scuffle was his way of saying he'll be running the show soon."

"Come on. Jack'll still be in command of the mission – it's not like Don's going to be our boss. Don'll just be coordinating the research. Anyway, how can you say arguing with Jack over our approach trajectory means this?"

"Jack relented didn't he?"

"That's not the point."

"But it is," Nadya pressed. "Jack overrode Palmer and returned to the original approach vector. That's what Don wanted – to show the crew that things would be adjusted to meet his requirements."

Kurt wasn't convinced, and picked at his spaghetti as he tried to formulate a response. Nadya spoke first though. "Listen, I'd have agreed with you if Don didn't start pushing the issue that the whole science staff agreed with him. You know, us versus them. Like he'd been discussing this with them behind Jack's back, and had their backing to go up against him."

"I don't think he did that," Kurt protested.

"I don't either. But the point is, he didn't have to. He chose this little battle carefully. You know that even if they don't all agree with Don on everything, they're just as anxious as he is to get to E-Eri-D. So, I'm sure they didn't mind Don pushing that point; nor did they see the point in disputing his assertion that they, the science staff as a group, were united behind him. Then add to that Don's saying that Jack was arbitrarily dictating terms..."

"Yeah, but that's when Jack started putting his foot down."

"Barely. Don still got what he wanted."

"I don't know," Kurt said as he finished his last piece of chicken. He got up, as much to end the conversation as to clear his plate, and said, "I just don't know. I think this speculation is as pointless as Don fighting over shaving a few days off a ten-year trip. It's not going to make a bit of difference in the end."

Kurt walked into the kitchen without waiting for an answer, and rinsed the remnants off of his plate into the food recycling unit. The machine hummed as it began breaking the scraps down into their basic organic compounds, producing an unappetizing paste that would ultimately be used to fertilize the ship's crops as well as grow synthetic meat. The thought stuck in his mind for a split second before he dismissed it. To the best of his recollection, simulated chicken tasted just like real chicken back on earth.

He returned to the dining room completely distracted by food recycling when Nadya asked, "Do you think the science staff trusts Don?"

"Huh?"

"Do you think they trust him?"

"That's tough to say," he answered softly. The eight-person science contingent was a diverse, international group from several different disciplines. To lump, biologists, planetary scientists, a botanist, an archaeologist, and a linguist together, and think of them as a coherent group seemed futile.

"Well, what about Alex?" Nadya asked with some impatience, "he spends enough time with you and Jack."

"True, but the problem is, I don't think that he even notices anything that's going on. He's a workaholic. When he does come up to breathe from his research, yeah he'll go for a run with Jack and me, or play some tennis. But he never says a word about the others. He'll either tell us about his newest experiment or talk about the latest baseball game he watched on the feed from Earth. And, that's even after I've reminded him again that the game's over ten years old."

Nadya pondered the point before saying, "I guess that's true for most of them."

"And most of us in engineering too," Kurt added. "Face it we're all a bunch of geeks."

"Speak for yourself."

Kurt chuckled as he activated a computer display in the corner of the living room and brought up his afternoon schedule. "Anyway, it's almost one-thirty and I'm supposed to meet Janet and Devon up in the IPV." Formally known as the Inter-Planetary Vehicle, the IPV would be their home and main source of transportation until they set up base camp on Epsilon Eri-D. The cramped craft was traditional in terms of spaceship design. Its smaller dimensions made it much more maneuverable, as well as capable of landing on the planet's surface. "The pilots want to do a complete walk-through of their craft before we start using it. What've you got planned?"

"I'll be up that way too, but later on. Pierre and I need to test the propellant feeds and discharge grates on the IPV's ion engines. Maybe I'll see you then. Otherwise, I'll be back here a few hours after engine shutdown – maybe around seven."

"See you later then," Kurt said as he headed out the front door. Jogging at an easy pace toward the control center, he took in the bright daylight with its light breeze as if it were real. These were vastly different surroundings compared to those that waited for them aboard the IPV. Gone would be the comfort of apartments and walks in the garden. Instead, he and Nadya would share a room barely big enough to hold a bed, desk and dresser. Then again, it really was a small inconvenience once he took into account the fact that a few weeks down the road they'd be walking freely on Epsilon Eri-D, in real sunlight, and breathing real, fresh air.

Kurt reached the command center and walked directly to a waiting elevator. "IPV bay," he said. The elevator accelerated quickly to the top level. A moment later it slowed, letting him out into a short, stark-white corridor. A few meters ahead lay an airlock; its inner and outer doors were set in the open position to facilitate the ferrying of supplies to the craft. Kurt stepped through the narrow passage into the IPV's equally narrow corridor. Its walls were lined with uniform, gray plastic panels. The pattern was interrupted every few meters by doors for storage cabinets or entrances to other compartments. A continuous line of white lights ran along the top of the walls, adjacent to the white, rubber coated ceiling. The floor was charcoal gray and made of the same surface as the ceiling, making it easier for one to push their way down the corridor in zero gravity. At not quite fifty meters in length, the IPV had just barely enough room to house its eighteen crewmembers, and provide them with the rudimentary lab facilities required of a field operation. The only additional equipment it carried were two small, three-person shuttles, intended more for use as runabouts than anything else.

Kurt continued down the narrow hallway until he came to a small ladder. Climbing it to the IPV's upper level, he followed the corridor a few meters further to the bridge. The dimly lit, circular room was a little over five meters across, and packed with control panels and workstations. He figured that it could fit maybe eight people before they'd get in each other's way. The room's gray walls were interrupted frequently by the bright colors of computer displays, which contributed the majority of its lighting. A low ceiling hung only a few centimeters above his head, giving him the urge to duck with each step he took. Kurt looked across the room, past the captain's command chair, to the two forward-facing pilot's stations. Janet and Devon were working intently and hadn't noticed his arrival. Walking closer, he overheard them discussing their recent test of the navigation system. After a few more seconds of eavesdropping, he said, "So, how're the systems checking out?"

Neither appeared startled by his sudden statement. Janet simply turned and answered, "Everything looks fine so far."

"How long have you two been at it?"

"A couple of hours now," she admitted. "We decided to get an early start on things here."

"So, is there much left to go over?"

Devon answered this time, "Not really. Nav-systems were the last of the internal systems to check besides propulsion. And Nadya's going to do that later."

"Good."

Janet looked to Devon, and said, "I'm ready for the walk-around if you are."

"OK, let's go have a look."

Kurt let them lead the way off the bridge and then up a ladder that ended at a circular hatch in the ceiling. He climbed through it, into a small airlock above and locked the inner and outer hatches into "open" position, before continuing out onto the IPV's smooth outer surface. Kurt felt dwarfed as he turned and looked back across the IPV's white, delta-shaped body. The craft stretched out over half a football field in front of him. The bay-ceiling hung only a couple of meters above his head, accentuating the fact that he was standing nearly ten meters above the bay floor. His eye followed the broadening shape of the craft back until it ended abruptly at the engine housing. There was no tail. Its lifting-body design required only two short wings that were mounted most of the way back. They extended outward only a few meters before bending up and ending at his eye-level.

Janet and Devon joined him on the outer surface, and walked to the back of the ship, carefully studying its condition with each step. Janet led the way down a ladder embedded in the aft structure between two of its engines. Once on the bay floor, Kurt looked back up and admired the massive, silver mesh grates that spanned the width of the IPV and made up the outer surface its ion engines. Tens of millions of volts would pass through them, helping accelerate ionized xenon gas out into space at nearly the speed of light. The relatively small but high-speed wisps of gas would provide the thrust necessary to move the ship efficiently between the system's planets. He trailed the pilots at a polite distance as they continued their inspection. The white surface he had admired from above continued down the curved sides of the IPV before ending abruptly at its black underbelly – not too different from the space shuttles from a century ago. Kurt walked beneath the left wing, and watched as the IPV narrowed while they made their way toward its rounded nose.

Devon took a moment to inspect the front landing gear, while Janet stopped for a second look at the elevons on the ship's right wing. He knew they were in good shape from his own inspections a day earlier, but it was the pilots' prerogative to do the final inspection and make sure they were comfortable. He opened his mouth to ask Janet if she'd found anything when the Magellan's warning buzzers cut through the air with a harsh, abrasive tone. He froze in his tracks. An automated voice announced, "Warning, emergency course change. Prepare for high-g deceleration. Deceleration of two-point-five g's to commence in thirty seconds. Take the necessary precautions." The message began repeating itself.

His stomach dropped as he quickly scanned the room and spotted Devon sprinting for the ladder. Within seconds, the pilot was on top of the IPV, heading for the airlock they'd just used. Kurt knew he'd never make it up in time, and looked around the bay for other options. "The rear access hatch," he said as it flashed into his mind. "Janet, over here!" he called out, and ran for the portal embedded in the floor near the rear of the bay. She started to follow, but stopped and instead made a run for the ladder Devon had just scaled. Kurt stopped in his tracks and shouted, "Janet, No! This way, there's not enough time."

"Ten seconds until emergency course change. Take all necessary precautions," the warning system announced.

"Janet!" Kurt shouted again, but she didn't answer. He couldn't tell if she heard him, and took off in her direction. She wasn't halfway up the ten-meter ladder when he reached the rear of the IPV and screamed, "Get down! You're not going to make it!"

Janet paused and looked back at Kurt.

The computer announced, "Four, three…"

"Jump now!" he shouted at the top of his lungs.

She stared at him. Fear filled her eyes as the computer's count reached one. "High-g maneuver commencing."

The Magellan shuddered as the engines kicked in to full power. Its super structure whined under the increased force; deep, resonating groans echoed around them. The pressure grew too fast, throwing Kurt backwards. He hit the floor hard, forcing the wind from his lungs. Gasping for breath, he began to panic before his chest muscles recovered enough to allow him to gulp in breaths of air. Reflexively he struggled to sit up, but the weight was too much. The best he could do was to lift his head slightly. He searched for Janet, but the ladder was empty. Pain gripped his head, and forced him to lie back down. The groaning and creaking slowly subsided as the Magellan's beams and support struts reached a new equilibrium.

The computerized voice announced, "Deceleration will continue for eight minutes. Take appropriate precautions."

"Precautions," he spat with disgust. He forced his head up again to look for Janet, and spotted her collapsed form on the floor. "Damn it!" he shouted. It took all of his strength just to roll onto his belly and get up onto his hands and knees. Laboring under the weight of more than two people, he crawled to her, calling, "Janet, can you hear me?" There was no response; she just lay there motionless.

When he reached her, he rolled her onto her back, and found a stream of blood running down the side of her face. He followed the blood trail up to her scalp: there was a small gash under her matted blond hair. Struggling to support his weight, he leaned over her face and checked her breathing: it was labored and shallow. "Computer!" he shouted.

"What is your status, Lieutenant Commander Hoffman?"

"Not good. Janet fell about five meters under two-and-a-half g's. She's unconscious and at very least got a concussion. There's a gash on the side of her head, maybe a skull fracture too." Kurt thought about her fall – the equivalent to a four-story fall in Earth gravity, and added, "There're probably other broken bones too."

"I am informing the Captain."

"Good. How much longer until the engines shut down?"

"We'll have zero g in six minutes. The captain wants to know your status."

"I'm just bruised a bit and have a nasty headache. Janet's the one to be concerned about. We've got to get her to medical."

There was a short pause before the computer answered, "The captain says not until we're at zero-g. It is too dangerous to try and move her now."

"Damn it, that's not good enough."

"I'm sorry Lieutenant Commander, but..."

"Put me through to Jack," Kurt shouted impatiently.

There was only a brief pause before the computer responded, "Go ahead."

"Jack, what the hell's going on up there? Janet's in bad shape down here."

"Kurt, you've got to hold tight for now. There's nothing that we can do. The sensors picked up a gravitational anomaly around E-Eri-D and the computer determined we had to abort our approach immediately."

"What do you mean an *anomaly*?"

"We'll talk about that later. Where's Devon. I'm going to need a pilot up here asap."

"We were on the floor of the IPV bay when the warning sounded. He made it back into the IPV, but that's the last that I saw of him."

"We'll check in here for him. As for Janet, I don't want to move her under these conditions. From what the computer relayed to me, it sounds like she's stable enough for now."

"Jack, she's bleeding from the head. I'm only guessing that..."

"I know Kurt. But unless she's in full cardiac arrest, moving her will only make things worse."

Kurt wanted to argue, but reluctantly answered, "OK." The increased weight was starting to overwhelm him, and he gave in and lay back down. "What about Nadya, and the others?" he asked.

"She's OK. Most everyone else has checked in with little more than bumps and bruises," Jack replied.

Kurt breathed a sigh of relief while Jack continued, "I'll tell Helena to get over to you as soon as we're at zero-g. I'll check in with you then."

Kurt didn't want to wait that long for the ship's doctor, but there was no choice. He lay still for a few seconds but the throbbing in his head kept him from resting. He ran his hand along the back of his own head, searching for the spot from which the pain emanated, until his fingers found a bump near the base of his skull. As his hand explored the area around it, he realized that his hair was wet. He yanked his hand back, and saw that it was dark red with his own blood. "Computer!" he shouted, "how much longer?"

The machine answered in its eternally calm voice, "four minutes and thirty seconds."

"Damn," he said softly. He tried to sit up again, but his strength failed him and he remained pinned to the floor. The room started to move around him; his hands went numb and he felt nauseous. He struggled to focus, and tried to call the computer, but couldn't summon the strength to utter a sound. The numbness spread across his body and face, then there was only blackness.

Chapter 10 – July 14, 2124

Jack settled into his chair at the oval conference table and looked across at Palmer and Don – the only others in the silent room. Each was fully engrossed in their work, giving him a chance to clear his mind. Exhaustion took hold, though, and made him acutely aware that this was the first chance he'd had to sit down in the past six hours. It felt good. As quickly as his body recognized its need for rest, his mind overrode it. There wasn't any time for this. Their frantic work since deceleration only resulted in achieving a semi-stable position around Epsilon Eri-D and its mysterious, massive companion. He drew a deep breath; part of him regretted that his break would end now by his own doing when he started the briefing. "Gentlemen, shall we begin?"

Don looked up quickly and responded, "OK, well I've had the entire science staff working on trying to understand what this object is. We've done comprehensive observations across the entire E-M spectrum, radar scans and gravitational mapping, and unfortunately don't have much yet. The best that I can do for now is show you our latest images, and give you some rudimentary data on the object." He pressed a small indicator on his computer panel. The lights dimmed and a hologram appeared above the center of the table. Jack had seen two preliminary, low-resolution images earlier in the day, but this was much sharper, and was stunning in its simplicity. Floating in front of him was a short, thick, polished, metal tube flanked by two loops of silver. Their centers were aligned along a common axis, their curved surfaces were completely featureless and perfectly reflective. Each was separated from the other by a distance that was a few times its diameter. The image rotated in front of him, and he could see the background stars showing through the centers of the outer rings. The tube though seemed opaque; its center looked solid and pitch black. Their plain forms prevented him from gaining any feeling of their true size or nature.

Don continued, "What we've determined so far defies logic. First, as we already know, it is located in Lagrange point two, our original target location. Actually it's not truly a Lagrange point anymore since the mass of the object has actually changed the dynamics of the entire system, but it is a rough equivalent to L-2; we can get into that later. The structure is large. The outer rings are located one hundred kilometers away from either side of the center tube, and each is twenty-five kilometers in diameter. Even on close inspection with our on-board telescopes, they show no discernable surface features – just perfectly smooth, reflective metal. The outer rings are massive, but nothing unexpected for their size. Each is about ten-to-the-seventeenth kilograms, or about the mass of a small asteroid.

"The center one is..." Don drew a deep breath, before continuing, "I don't know. It's just damned impossible."

Palmer barely let a second pass before he asked impatiently, "What're you talking about?"

"It too is twenty-five kilometers in diameter and it's about twenty-five kilometers long – basically a little bigger than New York City. But, that's not the problem. Its mass reads as nearly five-percent of an Earth mass; we're talking over four times the mass of the Moon. That's tens of thousands of times more massive than anything that size has any right to be."

Jack stared at the surreal tube and asked, "Are you sure?"

"Yes. Positive," he answered. "That's what wrecked our approach here. The L-2 point you know is a balance point between gravitational fields of E-Eri-D and its parent star E-Eri..."

"Yes...yes, go on," Jack said.

"Well, this thing's sitting right in it. More importantly, its seemed to have created a gravitational well collecting all sorts of debris into this region of space. The presence of the debris is what forced our course change. The object's so massive that as we began adjusting our approach for our originally planned orbit, we started falling towards it. The mass was easy to calculate by the rate it was pulling us in."

"What the hell's it made of?" Jack asked.

"It's impossible to say." Don answered. "If it's actually a hollow cylinder, then its density would exceed that of a white dwarf star and start approaching the type of matter found in collapsed stellar remnants like neutron stars."

Palmer raised a finger and opened his mouth to ask a question, but Don presumed he knew what was coming, and preemptively answered, "When our sun dies, it'll basically run out of fuel and leave behind an extremely dense core – that's a white dwarf. It's a hundred thousand times denser than lead. When a much larger star goes supernova, the force of the explosion can compact the core into a neutron star or possibly even a black hole. So, imagine the mass of our entire sun, packed into something the size of New York City. That's how dense a neutron star is. In this case, the cylinder's matter is hundreds of times denser than a white dwarf and is starting to approach that of a neutron star – well beyond any natural material known to man. Hell, our theories can't even explain how this can even exist!"

"That's not what I was going to ask," Palmer said calmly. "Are you sure about these measurements?"

"Of course! I didn't believe it the first two times we got the readings. It took two more for the meaning of all this to sink in. It's amazing...I mean whoever built this can engineer planetary masses. Think of what we can learn from them."

"I think it's a little early to talk about making contact," Palmer said. "In fact, the prudent course of action would be to back off a bit."

"What the hell are you talking about? This is more than I could've dreamed of."

"Don't you understand?" Palmer shot back forcefully. "By your own estimation, the civilization that created this can engineer matter that nature can only make via the explosion of a large star. We're nothing compared to them. We've got to move off before we're spotted and..."

"You idiot," Don sneered. "If they can build that, they probably knew we were coming before we even got past Mars back home."

"Enough!" Jack said. "We're not going to have any of this crap. Palmer, if they're even still around, they know we're here; that's a safe assumption. Don, let's not jump the gun. Let's just figure this out and take it one step at a time."

There was a short pause before Palmer calmly said, "OK, then. What does it do?"

Don threw his hands in the air and said, "I haven't the slightest idea."

The room stayed silent as they studied the image. Jack found himself feeling a strange combination of awe and frustration – the same frustration he felt on A832. Don was right; this was beyond anything they could have hoped for. Evidence of a civilization far, far more advanced than humanity. The problem was, it was so much more advanced that he couldn't even fathom what any of it was. Of course there would be time to investigate, but right now his gut was filled with a loathsome feeling of helplessness. "Are there any signs of energy or any sort of activity?"

"No power. At least nothing we can recognize. Our radar scans of the central tube did show something else unusual though. It might be spinning – spinning very fast."

"You can't tell?" Palmer asked.

"There aren't any surface features to watch go round. We just saw a very strange distortion of the radar echoes. Rapid rotation is the most likely explanation. More observations will tell us for sure."

"What else do you have?" Jack asked.

"Nothing more on the object, but we've already found some structures on the planet."

The holographic display changed to an orbital view of Epsilon Eri-D's western hemisphere. The southern half was dominated by a deep cerulean ocean speckled with bright white cloud systems. In the north was a large, beige, continental mass bearing a strange resemblance to Australia. Its eastern edge, however, tapered off into a chain of large islands that eventually curved southward and back on themselves, forming an equatorial sea reminding him of the Caribbean.

"We found what appears to be a city right about here." Don said. On cue, a red circle appeared in the eastern extremity of a peninsula leading to the island chain. "I'll magnify as much as I can, but remember that we're still four million kilometers out: About ten Earth-Moon distances. Our resolution will be limited to about a hundred meters."

The image zoomed in to show an aerial view of a tropical coast line. The interior was a rich, dark green from lush vegetation. A thin, white line of sandy beaches separated the forest from the surrounding shallow, teal waters. Away from the coast, the waters changed to the deep blue of an open ocean. Jack scanned the forested landscape for Don's "city." Not far inland he spotted a single gray structure, maybe the size of a golf ball on this scale. It was surrounded by a mottled black and gray ring which he assumed to be smaller buildings. Leading radially outward in several locations were hints of straight lines that cut into the vegetation before fading away. Maybe roads – he wasn't sure.

Don continued, "The central structure is a single dome about fifteen kilometers in diameter and maybe two kilometers tall at its peak. It's surrounded by what we believe are buildings, but at this resolution we can't be sure. I'm hesitant to say this, but our best image enhancements suggest that these may well be in ruins. However, I'm not really convinced of that considering that the Dome itself is intact. In any event, we'll know for sure once we're closer. The radial lines may be roadways or some sort of transportation track. There are no signs of power, transmissions or any other activity."

"Are there any other structures? Smaller ones elsewhere?" Palmer asked.

"Nothing big enough for us to see at this distance. But, there is another continental mass that we haven't examined in detail yet. It'll rotate into view in about four hours."

Don continued with his description of the planet, but Jack only half-listened. Part of him wanted to know everything possible about this new world, but there were too many other things battling within him for attention. Most important was their recovery from the emergency deceleration. Not all of the damage reports were in, and he still needed to check on the injured. It appeared they had gotten lucky – there were only four injuries, with Janet being the most serious. Equally important was determining where to park the Magellan. An orbiting debris field and the alien object precluded keeping the ship in a close orbit. Plus, they still had to further stabilize their current position, not to mention a dozen other tasks that needed attention.

Don stopped talking and Jack reflexively answered, "Thanks Don." The scientist's perplexed look made him think that either he'd been expected to answer some question he hadn't heard, or that Don wanted to continue. It only took a split second to determine that whatever it was, it didn't matter. "Do we have any updated injury reports?" Jack asked.

"Nothing yet sir," Palmer replied.

"Damn it, what do you mean? It's been over four hours since her last update." He activated the comm. and said, "Helena, respond please."

As he waited for an answer, he calmed himself and spoke again to Palmer. "We'll go over the Magellan's orbital position and damage reports in a minute."

"Actually," Palmer said, "we only took minor damage. And, nothing at all to our main systems."

"Good. We can..."

"Jack, Helena here."

"Yes, is there any update on your patients?"

"I was going buzz you in a few minutes with it anyway, but now's just as good. Kurt's basically OK. I've confirmed that his concussion was very minor. I just gave him the go-ahead to return to duty. Also, I finished checking out Claire and Masako. Nothing broken – all they had were some bruises from falling equipment..."

"And Janet?"

"She's another story, Jack. She's not in good shape. She sustained a skull fracture, several other broken bones, her left lung was punctured and she's in a light coma. It took some work, but I've stabilized her for now."

"Shit," Jack said under his breath. "Beyond stabilizing her, what do you think?"

"There are some complications due to our situation. Because we're at zero-g, I've been having trouble removing fluid from her lungs. Plus, I had to put her in a pressurized suit to get better control of her blood flow. I don't think we're going to lose her. But with the coma, I don't know what sort of neurological damage we're dealing with. I'll do my best, but I just can't promise anything. I'll keep you informed of any developments."

"Thanks Helena."

The idea of losing one of his crew ate at him. Of course he knew that there would be fatalities on a thirty-year mission like this. But not like this – not so early. Helena's confidence about Janet surviving didn't matter: permanent brain damage was nearly the same as death. He tried to pull himself away from exploring the morbid possibilities but couldn't. The crew was his responsibility. There should have been some way to see this coming – to see the object at L-2 in advance and avoid the maneuver.

He forced his mind back to the present and noticed that the others were waiting for him to speak. "OK, Palmer did you finish an orbital analysis with Devon?"

"Yes," his first officer answered. "As you know, the main problem is that presence of this alien object has changed the gravitational nature of this system. In short, it's occupying what was L-2 and has destabilized the positions near here. Basically, if we tried to orbit in this region, we'd have to run engines periodically to correct for gravitational influences from the object. Normally, that wouldn't be a big problem except for the fact that the Magellan isn't designed for periodic small maneuvers. So parking it here is impractical. Further in toward Epsilon Eri-D are several stable regions where we might consider orbiting. But, there is an extended debris field that occupies that region of space. The risk of impact from some random piece of material is relatively small. However, the consequences of what would happen if it pierced one of the antimatter tanks would be catastrophic. That rules out orbiting the Magellan there."

"So where does that leave us?" Don asked.

Palmer ignored him and looked directly at Jack as he continued, "At this point, I recommend parking the Magellan in a planet trailing orbit at a distance of about ten million kilometers. There is one drawback to this. The Magellan will be too far from Epsilon Eri-D for repeated trips using the IPV – we'd run out of propellant too quickly."

"So the Magellan would be stable," Jack said, "but we'd have to transfer the crew to the IPV a few weeks early – before we've found a suitable location for base of operations on the surface."

"That is correct," Palmer replied. "We would still travel back to the Magellan periodically for supplies – maybe every ten days or so. And, of course we'd maintain a data link to its communications and computational resources."

Jack looked to Don who was nodding silently in agreement. The idea was sensible. He swiped at the comm. button and called, "Helena, are you still there?"

"Here, Jack."

"It looks like we're going to have to move up our timetable and begin moving to the IPV now. No one will be staying behind on the Magellan. Can you move Janet?"

"I'd rather not."

"How long do you need before we can move her?"

"It's not a matter of how long. While she's in the coma I'd rather keep her here."

"How long are we talking here: days or weeks?"

"As long as it takes," she answered calmly.

Don spoke up, "Are we talking about putting the whole mission on hold while..." He stopped when Jack raised his hand to him. "Helena," Jack continued, "will there be any risk to moving her to the IPV?"

"Jack, I'd feel more comfortable..."

"This is not a matter of comfort. The bottom line is that we can't move the crew onto the IPV without our primary doctor. That means in order for the mission to continue, we're going to have to move her. The only thing that'll keep me from doing this is if you tell me that the move will endanger her. Are you telling me this?"

There was a short moment of silence before Helena answered, "No. The sick bay on the IPV will be adequate, and if we're careful the move won't hurt her."

"Good. Let me know if you need anything at all."

Jack abruptly disconnected the comm. and turned back to Palmer. "I'm going to have Kurt coordinate the move along with all of the supplies. I want you to work with Devon and finish plotting the orbit for Magellan. Also, get a parking orbit mapped out for the IPV. We'll plan on staying in orbit for at least a couple of weeks while we run reconnaissance missions with the shuttles."

"Yes, sir," Palmer answered.

"Don," Jack said, "You and I are going to review all of the planetary data we have so far. I want to get a good picture of what to expect before I take a team down for our first landing."

Jack looked back over to Don who was staring intensely at his display, and said, "Don?"

Don looked puzzled for a moment, and then replied, "Yeah...that sounds fine." His voice trailed off as he looked back down at his display.

"OK, let's proceed," Jack said.

Palmer left the room as Jack pushed his way across to Don's chair. Don was staring at a set of charts on his terminal. Jack gave him a moment before asking, "Any problem?"

"No, actually everything looks good. I'm just reviewing our latest measurements of Epsilon Eri-D's atmosphere. It's as all of our long-range spectra said – nearly a carbon-copy of Earth. Just a little less Oxygen and a little more Carbon Dioxide and Nitrogen, but nothing that would stop us from breathing it."

"So, what's the problem?"

"Well, it looks like a perfectly good planet. It's just ... I don't know."

"What aren't you telling me?" Jack asked, deliberately keeping any hint of impatience out of his voice.

"Nothing."

"That's not true, now explain. Or should I assume that you weren't telling us the whole truth about the image of that city."

Don's quick look up confirmed his suspicion. Jack waited though, letting the silence force Don to answer.

"Jack, it's just that we're too far out to know for certain."

"Don, I need to be able to rely on your judgement, so you need to tell me everything. Otherwise, we will have a problem."

"They're ruins," Don blurted out. "At least I'm better than ninety percent sure. I just wanted to be perfectly certain before I publicly announced something like this."

"Or, before you admitted it to yourself?" Jack asked with a hint of empathy. "Keep in mind, this is what we expected after finding the wreckage in the asteroid belt."

"I guess I was still hoping. I just don't understand why it's like this."

"That's part of what we're here to find out. Think of it, regardless of whether there's anyone left down there, we're about to explore an entirely new world, not to mention see the first definitive proof ever that there are other intelligent races out here. This is nothing short of the most amazing thing any of us could ever have dreamt of doing."

"I know." Don looked away from him, but then perked up as he quickly added, "Jack, there is one other thing that I noticed."

"Go on."

"The more I look at this, the more it looks like a colony."

"How do you mean?"

"Well, we have a single, small city-like structure, but there's nothing else. No other signs of civilization, nor any signs of less advanced construction. A city should be an amalgam of buildings from different times as the civilization learned and advanced. Look at New York. Even leaving historical buildings out of it, it's still a mix of structures built at different times over nearly two centuries. This place here looks like it was done in one shot."

"We still haven't seen what's on the other side of the planet," Jack said, playing devil's advocate.

"True, but at their apparent level of technology, they should be spread across the globe. There's something else going on here. I want to know more about them." Don took a breath and opened his mouth as if to continue, but said nothing.

"You want to go down on this first landing," Jack said.

"Yes, of course. I thought that went without saying. The truth is, I was a little surprised that you said you were going to go."

"Captain's prerogative," Jack answered with a smile. "I want to speak those words that'll go down next to Armstrong's 'One small step for a man' line." He watched Don's face start showing a hint of disappointment, and said, "But, it would only be logical to take the chief science officer with me. Palmer and Kurt can take care of the IPV while we're down there."

Don allowed himself a smile as he asked, "When do we go?"

"As soon as we get the Magellan in a distant stable orbit and we get the IPV back here – probably tomorrow morning. So we'll need to set aside some time soon to go over your data."

"I'll get everything we need together now," Don answered with a hint of enthusiasm.

"Good, I've got a lot of other matters to attend to in the meantime."

Chapter 11 – July 15, 2124

Jack stood with his back against the wall of the IPV's small sick bay, and watched as Helena carefully checked the tiny silver sensors on Janet's forehead. White bandages covered most of her scalp, allowing only a few locks of her short, blond hair to show through. Her face was peaceful, as if asleep, but her pallor said otherwise. Several thin wires emerged from the beige sheet that covered her, and ran up to a monitor. Helena periodically glanced at it, tempting Jack to ask what she was seeing, but he knew better than to interrupt. To distract himself, he studied the computer readout, but it told him nothing more than he already knew – her vital signs were stable and she was still in a coma. Frustrated, he pulled his attention away from the display and looked around the bright, beige and white room. It was barely large enough to accommodate three patients and accompanying support equipment, giving it a perpetually crowded feeling: a fact that became apparent again as he stepped aside to let Helena move around and check another monitor. She then used a small, stethoscope to listen to her patient's chest once more before looking up at Jack. "Well there's some improvement. She's still comatose, but her lungs are clearer and her pulse and pressure are staying stable."

"So what does that really mean?"

"It means that we're headed in the right direction. The longer she had problems with fluid and her B.P., the more likely we'd have problems bringing her out of the coma. This is going to take time."

"Have you thought about direct neural stimulus?"

"I'm not comfortable about using that without knowing more about any potential damage to her brain. Letting her come out of this at her own pace is the best way."

"But what about..."

Helena cut him off using a gentle tone, "Jack, I know you want to somehow fix this, but there's nothing you can do right now. And don't second guess yourself. There was no way to prevent this. You had to approve the maneuver. It saved the ship and who knows how many other injuries and lives. Now let me do my job here, and everything will work out."

Jack didn't want her making excuses for him, and simply replied, "How long do you think it'll take?"

"Maybe a few weeks, maybe longer. I can't say."

Devon's voice came in over the comm., "Captain, we're at five minutes before orbital insertion."

"Thank you." Turning to Helena, he said, "I've got to head back to the bridge. Let me know if anything develops."

"Of course."

Jack gave himself a good push and glided into the dimly lit hallway. A quick kick against the wall sent him down the narrow passage. Its close dimensions allowed him to grab and push off of either wall without having to zigzag unnecessarily, making it easier to traverse in zero-g than under normal gravity. The only navigational challenge occurred as he passed Maurice Traynor, their computer tech, who was heading toward the stern. Deep in thought, Maurice barely seemed to notice him, and just pushed down to slip by underneath. Jack awkwardly yanked his legs up, barely in time to avoid contact. He turned quickly to make sure Maurice was OK, but the man was already heading out of earshot. Jack just shrugged to himself, turned and headed back toward the nose of the ship. As he reached the corridor's end, he grabbed onto a ladder leading to the upper deck. There was no need to climb it; the ladder served merely as a convenient hand-hold on which to pull as he launched himself upward. After that, there was only a short, straight passage before he reached the bridge.

The room was lit more by the light from a dozen computer displays and the bright image of Epsilon Eri-D on the main view screen, than by the dim lights lining the ceiling. Jack glanced around and quickly took note of who was present. Devon was seated at the right-side pilot's station near the front of the room; Palmer, Don, Kurt and Nadya were seated at four of the six workstations that lined its perimeter. Though he hadn't said anything, Devon seemingly sensed his presence, turned to look back at him, and said, "Everything is go for orbital insertion in three minutes and twenty seconds."

"Good." Jack glided over to his command chair, before saying, "Are all data links back to the Magellan in place?"

"Yes, sir," Devon answered. "I also double checked the relays that'll be sending our signals back to Earth. Everything's set."

"Very good." He looked down at a small hand-sized computer display attached to his armrest. It depicted the IPV's approach to Epsilon Eri-D via a cryptic schematic. A light blue ellipse encircling a blue globe indicated their target orbit; a yellow line entering from the left, represented their approach.

"Three minutes until orbital insertion," Devon announced. "Engine burn commencing in ten seconds." The room stayed silent until Devon spoke again. "Three…two…one, burn commencing."

A barely audible hum started, and slowly grew until the ship was filled with the drone of high-power transformers feeding the ion engines. Jack was pressed back into his seat by the acceleration.

"Engines are operating nominally," Devon called out over the din.

Jack looked up at the view screen, which was filled with the northern hemisphere of Epsilon Eri-D. Centered on it was the oblong continent he'd seen earlier. It contained the only signs of civilization they'd uncovered so far. The dusty beige tones of a great desert dominated the western two-thirds of the continent. A line of rugged, dark gray mountains peppered with snowy peaks bordered the arid region, separating it from the plains and tropical coastal regions that lay to the east. Off shore, past the shallow, teal waters, was a swirl of thick, white clouds: a tropical storm system was trying to take form.

The noise from the engines subsided, and the feeling of weightlessness returned. "Burn concluded," Devon said in a normal tone. "We are now in a synchronous orbit over the continent." Devon continued his announcement by reading off their longitude, latitude and other relevant data, but Jack's attention was still fixated on the planet in front of them. The world was as close to a carbon copy of Earth as they would ever find. It was ninety-five percent of Earth's size. Though it was a full one-quarter closer to Epsilon Eri than the Earth was to the Sun, this was balanced by the fact that Epsilon Eri was a cooler star. Jack marveled at this coincidence, since it resulted in Epsilon Eri-D having nearly the exact same climate as back home. In fact, Don's preliminary data showed the planet's average temperature to be eighteen degrees Celsius, just two degrees warmer than Earth. Its surface was even mostly covered with water. The only real difference was its age. Epsilon Eri and its planetary system were three and a half billion years younger than the Earth.

Jack's train of thought was interrupted as Devon said, "All systems are stable." And then in a lower tone, "Will you be prepping the shuttle for immediate departure?"

Jack smiled at Devon's unsuccessful attempt to hide his disappointment at being excluded from the first landing party. Unfortunately, the small runabouts that passed for shuttles on the IPV held only three people. He answered calmly, "Yes, I'll be heading down to the shuttle bay in a minute." Turning to Kurt, Jack continued, "I'd like you to get the mapping and communications satellites deployed as soon as possible. Let's see about getting a good overall picture of this place. Once that's done, we can start thinking about plans to land the IPV."

"I should be able to have it done within the hour," Kurt answered.

"Good," Jack replied. He went over to Don and said, "Helena wants us to stop by sick bay for the gear before we go down."

"OK. I'm ready when you are."

Turning to Palmer, who was now standing by his side, Jack said, "Palmer, the ship's yours."

Palmer replied with his standard, "Yes, sir."

Jack quickly headed off the bridge with Don following close behind. When they reached sick bay, Helena was standing in the doorway talking with Alex Gilmartin, the exobiologist that would be accompanying them on the landing. Seeing them, she turned and said, "Good, you're here already. I won't have to go over this twice."

"Why, what's going on?" Don asked.

"Nothing big Don, I just want to go over the bio-contamination protocol and talk about the modifications that I've made to the suits. Since you'll be landing in a tropical climate, you won't need the insulating and climate control layers. Basically, all you'll be wearing is the equivalent of a biohazard suit. The outer layer has the new coatings we came up with. Basically, they're so frictionless that even pollen and dust'll slide off of them. But despite that, I still want you to take the same precautions you would have with the old suits: decontaminate in the airlock, and seal the suits in there before returning back here. The only things from that planet I want coming back on this ship are your sealed samples so I can prep the necessary serums."

Jack took a neatly folded, olive-green suit from her. It shimmered in the light and felt slippery to the touch, even more so than silk. He then picked up a flexible helmet, which on closer inspection looked more like a hood than anything else. It had a clear, plastic face plate in front, and translucent green sides. A small camera and light assembly, no larger than a half-dollar, sat just above the face plate.

"No hoses or air supply?" Don asked.

"No," Helena answered, "Since the atmosphere checked out so well, I decided to go with a five-angstrom molecular filter on the hood. The sides and rear of the hood are actually a nano-mesh that won't let anything through larger than Oxygen and Nitrogen molecules."

"So we'll get to breathe fresh air," Jack said, emphasizing the "we."

"Don't push it," Helena shot back. "I could still change my mind and make you breath the bottled stuff. Anyway, before I let you go, I want you to pay particular attention to the neck seal around the hood." She took the one from Jack's hands and flipped it over. "You'll need to make sure it fits tightly against the plastic neck ring on the suit. The suit's fabric has embedded electronic sensors and transducers to ensure a perfect seal, as long as there are no large folds or gaps. So check each other to make sure that there aren't any."

"Understood," Jack said as he took the hood back.

"And one more thing, get samples of everything. The audio and video recorders will be running the whole time, so make sure that when you get a sample, I can see the bottle or bag number before you put it away. I'll need to correlate them with the images of the environment that you took them from."

Jack pulled the suit on over his clothes, tucked the hood under his arm, and asked, "Are there any questions?" Alex and Don just shook their heads. Shrugging his shoulders, he looked back to Helena and said, "OK, I think we're set. We'll see you in a few hours."

The airlock to the shuttle was only a few meters down the hall. Jack led the way in silence, looking back only as he climbed into the small vehicle. It seemed that they were all completely engrossed in their own thoughts. The cabin was cramped to begin with, and most of what little space it did have was consumed by stacks of sample cases. He pushed himself toward the front of the craft to make room for the others, but found that it was easiest just to immediately climb into the pilot's chair. As Don glided into the seat next to him, Jack turned around and said, "Alex, you want to seal that..." but stopped as he saw that Alex was already locking down the inner shuttle door.

The scientist finished what he was doing and answered, "What? You think I want to waste any more time up here?"

"I should've known better. Computer, are all systems ready?"

"Yes, Captain."

"Depressurize the shuttle bay and open the outer doors."

There was the tell-tale rush of air being pumped out, followed by the computer announcing, "Bay doors are open, sir." Jack's view out the cockpit window, however, told him nothing. The shuttles were docked nose-first to the IPV, and launched by backing out of either a port or starboard hatch near the rear of the vehicle. As a result, all he saw through the cockpit was an inner corner of the shuttle bay. "Rear view," he said.

The cockpit window darkened quickly as an embedded LCD matrix charged. A second later he had a clear view from the aft camera: A line of ivory clouds drifting over a deep blue ocean below was framed by the open shuttle bay door. Jack took the control stick in his hand and gently pulled back. The shuttle bay disappeared and the curved edge of the globe set against the black backdrop of space came into view. Sunlight glistened off of the inviting alien ocean. Hanging peacefully above the deep blue water were the bright white wisps of a distant cloud formation. They broadened and curved southwards, making up a storm system on some frontal boundary. Jack stayed focused, though, and said, "Front view." The image disappeared as the window became transparent again. The delta-shaped IPV lay in front of them, its bright spotlights emanating from the open, starboard bay door. The craft grew smaller as they slowly drifted away, becoming little more than a triangular toy floating in a black sea. He pushed left and forward on the stick, and the shuttle turned quickly toward the planet, beginning its descent.

At first it felt as if they were stationary, suspended high above the ocean below. The engines rumbled but they made no apparent headway. Jack glanced to his right and saw Don staring silently out the window. No one said a word as they watched in anticipation. The amber hologram of the ship's instruments floating to his left gave the only indication that they were on course. Their altitude was dropping and had just passed the 4,000 kilometer mark. Their speed was now under twelve thousand kilometers per hour. The deep blue of open ocean, leading up to the northern continent's arid western landscape dominated his field of view. As the minutes passed, their downward progress became visible. The curve of the planet's surface flattened, and the blue haze of an earth-like sky began to surround them. He had to look nearly straight up to still see the blackness of space. The computer adjusted the shuttle's attitude, pitching its nose upward in anticipation of the scathing heat that its underbelly would soon absorb. His only view now was out the side window, where he saw the western coast of the continent pass beneath them: its great desert stretching out ahead. They were low enough now that the approaching snowcapped mountains appeared as more than just rough patches on some detailed map. Jack tried focusing on them, but the air was growing thick, and an iridescent orange glow began to obscure his view. Equipment rattled as they plowed into pockets of thicker and thicker air; yellow-orange flames from the super-heated gasses outside illuminated the cockpit in an eerie glow. His weight quickly returned and passed his normal ninety kilograms. Within a minute, two and a half g's of deceleration pressed him deep into his seat. Breathing required a conscious effort. As the ionized cloud surrounding them intensified, the windows turned opaque and Jack was forced to watch their progress on the instruments projected onto the now dark surface in front of him. They were at fifty kilometers and traveling just under eight thousand kilometers per hour. Another two minutes and they'd be through the rough part.

The seconds passed slowly as Jack longed to gaze upon this new world. He searched his senses and finally felt what he was anticipating: his weight was starting to drop. They were still cruising at Mach four, but had shed most of their excess orbital energy. The surrounding plasma dissipated and the windows turned transparent again, revealing a deep, azure sky. A glance out the side window showed that they were just passing over the eastern coast of the continent. Their altitude was down to seven kilometers and their speed to Mach three. It was time to begin their approach to the city. Jack banked the shuttle right and Don immediately drew a deep breath, drawing Jack's attention. Outside Don's window was a string of tropical islands set in a shallow sea – their white sandy beaches contrasting against the turquoise waters. Even at a few kilometers up, he could easily make out submerged shoals and reefs.

Jack completed the one hundred eighty degree turn to head back toward the peninsula. As they went subsonic he angled the shuttle's nose down to complete their descent. The pristine coastline filled their view now and was all consuming. There wasn't enough time to take it all in, though, before they suddenly sped over a line of surf crashing on a beach. In an instant the landscape changed to a lush tropical forest. The vegetation, blurred by their speed, was a continuous, textured green carpet below. Moments later, rolling verdant hills rose up from the coastal plain. Occasional breaks in the forest canopy revealed small inland lakes and rivers. Somewhere deep inside him, came an urge to ignore their mission and simply set the craft down beside one of the lakes. He just wanted to step outside and feel the fresh air and sun on his skin: to hear the natural trickle of a near-by stream.

Reluctantly, Jack suppressed the desire and said, "Computer, superimpose target map." The view directly in front was instantly spoiled by iridescent yellow lines of longitude, latitude and other terrain markings. A small red arrow hovered in the distance, indicating the position of their target. He adjusted course slightly, moving the arrow so that it lay directly in front of them, and read the distance to the city aloud for Don's and Alex's benefit: "Our target is approximately fifty kilometers further up the peninsula. ETA is five minutes."

Time passed quickly as he relaxed again and watched the fertile landscape pass beneath them. An ancient mountain chain peeked out of the haze in the distance; its smooth, weathered slopes reminded him of the Appalachians back home. A moment later, the large silver dome of the city came into view, rising above the surrounding forest. Even at ten kilometers away it was an imposing structure, towering above all that surrounded it. As they closed on it, the thick vegetation below ended abruptly, replaced by the blackened ruins seen from orbit. Row after row of nearly identical, hundred meter-long, concrete buildings passed beneath them. Their roofs were long gone – their walls ending in jagged, singed edges. The dome now loomed before them. Jack slowed to a stop and engaged the vertical thrusters so that they could hover and look for an appropriate landing site. The orbital view showed a promising area near one of the tracks that stretched away from the city into the forest. He banked left, and guided the shuttle slowly along the dome's perimeter. Piles of rubble filled most of the buildings and the streets between them. Plant life had thoroughly invaded the city, growing freely in and around many of the structures. Scanning the area, Jack spotted the clearing and announced, "We'll set down here."

The thrusters kicked up some dust and debris as he called out, "Ten meters. Five meters...three..." Leaves and dirt swirled around them as they touched down with a gentle bump. "IPV, this is shuttle one," Jack said into the comm.

Kurt's voice came in over the speaker, "We read you."

"We've set down in a clearing near the south-eastern edge of the dome."

"We've got you on satellite view."

"Good. We'll commence external reconnaissance shortly."

"Understood."

Jack did a quick post-flight check of the instruments. Everything looked good, and he powered down the engines. He picked up his hood and a small tool bag, and said, "Ok, let's seal our suits and test the comm. links." The hood slipped on easily enough, but it took a moment to run his thumb and fore-finger along the neck ring and get a good seal. "Don, can you hear me OK on this."

"Yeah, you're coming through fine."

"OK. Do me a favor, check my neck seal, I'll check yours afterwards."

"Hey, what about me?" Alex chimed in.

"Well, I guess that means your comm. unit's working," Don answered with mock disinterest.

"No, I mean my seal."

"I know what you meant," Don said with a hint of annoyance, "just a moment. Jack, yours looks good. Now turn around Alex."

Jack checked Don's seal before opening a small compartment near the airlock. He withdrew a pistol and holster for each of them. Before he could speak, though, Alex said, "Guns? Really?"

Jack calmly replied, "Its only for use in case we encounter any aggressive animal life. If you look closely at the top of the handle, you'll see it has settings for lethal and nonlethal ammunition. If we need to scare something off, use nonlethal and it will fire a rubberized projectile. If someone's life is in imminent danger, you can use the other setting to fire a hardened metal round."

"Understood," Don replied.

"Any questions?" Jack asked as he tried to squeeze by to get to the airlock. Alex though was in his way and already reaching for the door, prompting Jack to ask, "What do you think you're doing?"

"What do you mean? I was just going to get off this ship and make room for you."

"Yeah right. Like I'm going to let you be the first person in human history set foot on an extra-solar planet."

"Well," Alex said as he stepped aside, "you can't blame me for trying."

The radio came to life with Kurt's voice, "Hey guys, you might want to be a bit more serious in there. This is all going on direct feed back to Earth. It's sort of a historic moment you know."

"That's right, spoil the fun," Jack answered as he stepped into the air lock. "You're just pissed because you're up there and we're down here. Anyway, it'll be over a decade before they hear any of this." Jack sealed the inner hatch behind him. "And, by the way, what do you mean, 'sort of' a historic moment?'"

"Well, you know..."

"OK, I'm in the lock and getting ready to exit the vehicle."

Kurt's voice took on a more serious tone as he said, "We're getting a clear feed of all your signals."

Jack took a deep breath and opened the outer door. Sunlight shined in on him – the first he'd felt in years. Its warmth was comforting and he was tempted to just close his eyes and soak it in. Instead, he stepped onto the threshold of the door, and took another deep breath. It was bright, and it took a moment for his eyes to adjust. They had landed in a clearing that was maybe thirty meters across, and surrounded by the crumbling gray cement walls of long abandoned buildings. Small trees and brush grew from the myriad of crevices and openings in the ancient construction. "I'm not going to challenge history here," Jack said solemnly. "I think that it's better to pay tribute to those who went before me and echo their words. This is one more small step for a man, and another giant leap for mankind." He climbed down the short ladder that led from the airlock door, and stepped onto the debris covered soil. The ground crackled with the sound of dried leaves and twigs. Looking around he said, "It is truly a beautiful day here. The light from Epsilon Eri is a bit oranger than the sun; it makes it feel like it's early evening despite being close to midday. The sky is a deep almost violet-blue. I feel like I could be back on Earth, as if it was late afternoon somewhere in the tropics. The temperature is warm – a comfortable twenty-seven degrees Celsius."

He took a few steps away from the shuttle, and continued, "I seem to be standing in the middle of a wide, but debris-covered street. There are buildings all around, but they're all damaged and long since abandoned. Their walls are cracked and show scoring – maybe from a fire. It looks old though, like this happened a long time ago. There's also a lot of plant growth around – weeds, small trees." He walked over to a small group of bushes that stood at eye-level. Each had a cluster of fern-like leaves growing from the top of its meter-high trunk, and reminded him of palm trees.

As Don and Alex caught up with him, Alex took a leaf gently in his palm and said, "It's much more like Earth vegetation that I would ever have imagined." He touched the trunk and said, "Whoa," as he pulled his hand back. "That was weird." He poked it again and said, "Damn, it's definitely not wood. Feel it."

Jack ran his gloved hand along the side Alex just touched. The khaki surface was leathery to the touch, and gave way easily as he pressed his fingers against it. Pushing a little harder made the entire plant bend. "It feels almost like skin and flesh," Jack said.

"Yeah, and look at this," Alex said coaxing Jack closer. "Its surface is covered all over with this stuff."

Jack looked closely. Hundreds of thin, rubbery needles grew out of the trunk, extending about a centimeter from the surface. There weren't enough to fully cover it – just enough to be noticeable.

"Oh man this is wild!" Alex called out.

Jack watched what the scientist was doing and followed suit, running his fingers up and down the plant's 'skin.' After each stroke, the needles rose toward his hand and then after a second, lay back down.

"I take my comment back about being similar to Earth."

"Is it animal or plant?" Don asked.

"Maybe something in between," Alex answered. "It's sure as hell unlike anything I've seen before."

Jack walked toward a doorway in the nearest of the ruined buildings. At three meters wide and three meters high, it suggested its former inhabitants might have been somewhat larger than humans. The interior floor was covered in rubble. Weaving its way through the rocky fragments were a dozens of rust-colored vines, each sprouting olive green ferns every few centimeters. The rubble had the appearance of broken concrete, but when kicked, the fragments moved much too easily. He reached down and picked up a chunk about the size of his chest: it weighed barely five kilos – a similar sized piece of concrete should have been at least ten times heavier.

"What is it?" Don said, coming up behind him.

"It's some sort of light weight structural material. Definitely not cement-based."

"I can see that," Don said as he picked up two smaller fragments. While rubbing them against each other he said, "They don't seem to crumble. I wonder how strong this stuff is?"

Jack pulled a small hammer from his tool pack, placed his piece on the ground and struck it near the edge. His hammer bounced back without marring the material. He struck it harder, but again had no effect on it. "Well, it's definitely got some strength to it." He looked around, found a palm-sized chunk and placed it in a sample bag.

Jack turned to leave but saw Alex staring at Don's boot.

"Don, don't move," Alex said.

Don reflexively tried to turn toward Alex, but nearly fell over: his foot was tangled in several finger-thick vines. "What the..." Don started.

Alex cut him off, saying, "Stay still for a moment."

Don obeyed as the three of them watched the vines slowly move along his boot and leg. They crawled at a snail's pace, barely moving a couple centimeters in their few seconds of observation.

"Can you get it off me please?" Don asked with a hint of urgency.

Alex crouched down, took a small metal probe from his pack and poked the nearest vine. It withdrew at a slightly quicker rate. He carefully pulled and tugged at the others on Don's foot causing them to follow suit and retreat toward a small opening in the rubble.

As the last one let go, Don took a quick step back toward the door and said, "OK, that was a little gross."

"It's definitely predatory," Alex said. "It means there must be other, more mobile, animal-like life here."

"That makes sense," Jack said while looking more suspiciously at the various alcoves in the rubble.

Alex retrieved a small set of scissors from his pack and said, "I'm definitely going to want a sample of this thing." He leaned over the end of a thin vine, and carefully snipped off a six-centimeter segment. Instantly, the remaining vines around them shot back into the rubble.

Don jumped back as he asked, "OK, what the hell was that?"

"I don't know," Alex replied. "But, their uniform reaction says that they're all part of a single, larger organism." He stood up, looked around once more and said, "I'm definitely going to have a hell of a lot of fun here."

"Biologists!" Don said with mock disgust.

"Hey, at least I'm not running away from every little thing that moves,"

Alex shot back.

Jack rolled his eyes as he led the way out of the ruined building and calmly said, "Keep your eyes open. This is untamed wilderness – we don't have anything like this left on Earth." Looking up at the dome wall that loomed nearby, Jack continued, "Let's move on. Kurt, are you reading us clearly?"

"Yes. We've got a good clear audio and visual signal."

"Good. We're going to scout out the region around the edge of the dome."

In contrast to the surrounding ruins, the dome seemed intact. The surface of the gargantuan structure was windowless, and made up of countless, dull-gray, square panels that were each several meters across. There was no sign of ornamentation, just endless rows of panels. The wall rose vertically at least a hundred meters before curving out of sight. Jack tapped the nearest square and it felt solid – maybe metal or some type of stone. Its smooth face should have shined in the sunlight, but countless years of weathering left it dull and stained. The gaps between adjacent panels were filled with grime and some type of moss-like substance. There were no cracks, though, or any other signs of physical damage.

A rustling sound in the nearby trees made Jack spin around. He kept his hand on his holster as he scanned the area, but nothing revealed itself. "Let's stay together," he said quietly. A look to his side told him the statement was completely unnecessary: Don and Alex had already moved to within a couple meters of him.

They continued along the perimeter of the dome at a slow pace; the only sound was the crackling of dried leaves underfoot. The dome wall seemed completely uniform: just a continuous progression of dull-gray panels. Clusters of trees and brush grew between the ruined buildings to their left, but stayed an even twenty meters from the structure's edge, giving them a clear path along which to walk. Jack reasoned that just beneath the debris on which he was walking must be a hard surface that was impenetrable to their roots. Looking back to the tree-line, he noticed that nothing grew taller than about five or six meters.

A louder rustling sound emanated from within the brush. Jack stopped in his tracks, this time unbuckling his holster flap. Something caught his eye as Don called out, "Jack. Did you see that?" There was definite movement about twenty meters to his left – right along the base of the tree line. Alex ventured forward with his hand nowhere near his weapon, causing Don to say, "Alex? Really?"

Jack took the statement as his cue to step forward and say, "Alex, stay back for a second."

"Fine," Alex replied with a shrug.

The rustling grew louder; the dried leaves at the edge of the brush began shifting as if something was moving just beneath their surface. Jack slowly withdrew his pistol but held it at his side. Whatever was burrowing underneath was making its way toward them in random fits and starts. Though they remained hidden, the moving leaves suggested that there were three or four small creatures. Jack relaxed his grip on the gun as he realized that they couldn't be any bigger than a squirrel. He crouched down, picked up a small rock and lightly tossed it in front of the nearest one. All movement suddenly stopped. He tossed another toward the same spot. Before it hit the ground, four shiny black creatures shot out from the leaves with blinding speed and disappeared into the tops of the trees.

"Damn they were fast!" Alex exclaimed.

"Did they fly?" Don asked with a hint of nervousness in his voice.

"No, it was definitely a jumping motion," Alex answered. "Though it was a pretty powerful one at that." Alex walked toward the spot where the rocks had landed and continued, "I'll review our video recordings later of course, but it looked like they had exoskeletons – maybe not too different from insects back home." He poked around the leaves with a stick and said, "I'm definitely going to have to collect some samples of them."

Jack watched the tree tops for a moment longer before saying, "OK, let's keep going." The landscape was remarkably uniform as they made their way along the dome's perimeter: more rows of grey panels to his right, and a mix of crumbling structures and vegetation to his left. As they reached the one-kilometer mark from their shuttle, Alex said, "It's surprisingly quiet. There're no signs of anything analogous to bird calls or insect noises. It suggests the animal life here hasn't evolved very far."

"We did suspect that the biosphere here would be more primitive than Earth's," Don said.

"True, but this plant life looks very complex," Alex replied. "Especially the moving samples we saw back near the shuttle."

"If the place was terraformed, they might have engineered the environment to suppress more aggressive species," Don offered. "Animals do tend to be much more aggressive than plants."

"It depends," Alex said with a smile. "The vines you found back in those ruins got you running. So I guess they weren't all that passive."

"Shut up," Don said, with a hint of embarrassment. "I didn't run."

They continued for another few moments in silence before Alex pointed ahead and said, "Jack! Over there, I see something." About a hundred meters away was what appeared to be a hand rail. It started about ten meters from the dome and went straight to the wall.

"I see it," Don said as they walked cautiously in its direction. "It looks like a railing."

Two parallel sets of metal tubing were supported about a meter off the ground by evenly spaced posts. Jack could easily imagine them flanking some grand walkway. Any trace of pavement though was no longer apparent as the ground was uniformly covered with soil, small plants and dried leaves. At about three meters from the dome's edge, the railing angled downward, connecting with the wall just above the ground. There were no steps; however, the ground did slope slightly at the end.

Don kicked at the soil near the wall's edge. "It looks like it's been abandoned for quite some time."

"But how long?" Jack responded. A large panel, lighter in color than the others, was centered between the handrails. It seemed safe to assume that it was the door. He pushed at it, even though he knew it wouldn't do any good. The wall didn't budge. There was no apparent control panel. Jack dug his fingers into the gap between it and the adjacent wall, scooping out finger-fulls of grime, but didn't uncover any buttons or other hints about how to open it. The answer was in front of him but where? Taking a small shovel from his tool bag, he began digging at the base of the path. The soil was dark and fertile, similar to peat moss. Alex quickly joined him. As they progressed downward, the earth became heavier and more compressed, evolving into a thick layer of clay that took some effort to remove. Within a few minutes though, they found the hard, stone floor that lay beneath. Its thirty-degree slope matched the adjacent railing.

They kept digging until they cleared away most of the debris from the base of the door. Jack stepped back while Don crouched down, examined the strata lining the side of their excavated path, and said, "The layers are distinct, and seem like natural deposits, except for this thin, black layer coating the stone."

"It looks like soot," Jack offered.

"I think so too. Maybe evidence of a large fire." Don scraped a sample into a small container, and then without a word walked back to level ground, picked up a shovel and started digging.

Jack joined him and asked, "What are you looking for?"

"That area's about eighty or ninety centimeters deep, but that's a recessed ramp leading to a wall. Debris could easily accumulate there from wind and storms. I'd like to get an idea of how deep it is here, away from a windbreak." They hit bottom about a thirty centimeters down. Don knelt down to examine the side of their new trench, and said softly, "The layers look the same…just not as thick over here."

"So, how long do you think it took for all of this to accumulate?" Jack asked.

"It's tough to say. I'd need to know a lot more about the weather and geologic history of this area."

"I mean roughly, Don. Are we talking decades or centuries here?"

"I can help you with the weather part," Alex offered. "All you have to do is look at the plant life here." He took a broad leaf in his hands from a nearby dwarf tree and tore it. "It's no stronger than a palm leaf back home. That means to me that the worst storms here can't be much more severe than what we have in the Caribbean. That should at least help you estimate the maximum rates stuff could be blown in and deposited."

Don nodded in agreement. He poked a bit more at the lower layers, before climbing out of the trench. "We're talking centuries here. Maybe two...maybe ten, I can't say for sure..." his voice trailed off. He then muttered something Jack couldn't quite make out.

"Say again Don."

"Nothing." Don took a few steps away before adding, "It's just that this really seals it. There's no one here."

"Come on," Alex said. "You've got to admit that we've known that for a while already."

"I know it doesn't make any sense. It's just that...I was still hoping that we'd find someone. A survivor, I don't know."

"Let's just focus on what we have here." Jack pointed to the dome and continued, "First, let's find a way into that."

"I guess I could try an ultrasound of this area" Don offered, "just to see what's under this dirt and confirm that there's a void on the other side of that panel – you know, see if it really is a door."

"Good." Jack stepped back as he watched Don retrieve the equipment from his pack. There really wasn't much to do: the ultrasound device was no bigger than a lunchbox and connected wirelessly to Don's computer.

"I'll start over here," Don said as he placed the device on the soil near the edge of the railing. He activated the machine; a split second later a black cloud of dust rose from the surrounding soil. Don took a stepped toward it, but jumped back as the cloud moved directly toward him. "Jack? What the hell is this?" he said as he backed away. The cloud quickly caught up and surrounded him. "Jack?"

"Stand still," Alex called out. "It's behaving like a swarm. They're probably analogous to insects back home."

Don ignored him and started swatting at the creatures.

Alex shouted again, "Don, just stand still for a moment. Your suit'll protect you."

As Don finally stopped flailing, Alex calmly walked over to the ultrasound unit and said, "It looked like the high frequency output from this thing disturbed them." He picked it up, pointed its base at Don and walked directly toward him. When he came within a couple meters, the cloud slowly backed off. Alex stepped closer while waving the device with outstretched arms; the creatures quickly dispersed, seeking refuge in the near-by brush.

Don backed away from both the railing and the brush and said, "What the hell is all of this?"

"It's nature Don," Alex shot back. "The world isn't limited to the dry equations you use in physics and planetary science."

Don replied with a frustrated grunt as he tried to dust off anything that might have stuck to his suit.

"They were too small to see individually," Alex said as he stared longingly into the tree line.

"What?" Jack said.

"The creatures in that swarm. That was definitely insect-like behavior, but they were much smaller than back home." Alex took a look around before continuing, "Don, come here, I want to get a closer look at your suit."

"Sure," Don replied as he stepped toward the man.

Alex leaned over him with a flashlight, and carefully inspected the folds in the near-frictionless fabric. "It doesn't look like anything stayed on you. But we should thoroughly decontaminate your suit."

Jack nodded in agreement as he called into his radio, "Kurt, have you been getting all of this?"

"Yes, it seems like it was a good idea to bring Don along as bait."

Jack chuckled as Don muttered, "Shut up. I don't think you'd do any better down here."

"Anyway," Kurt said, "I thought I'd let you know that you've been out of the shuttle for an hour and a half, and you're over a kilometer from the landing site."

"I was already thinking about that," Jack replied. "It's time to head back. In any event, we're going to need some more equipment before we can start excavating around this area."

"I'm going to want to leave some cameras and other monitoring equipment out for a few day-night cycles, for when we come back," Alex said. "I'd like to get a better idea of what goes on here when we're not around stirring things up."

Chapter 12 – July 16, 2124

Kurt stared intently at Alex's array of biological samples while the others filed into the lab. Each specimen was carefully sealed in a petri dish-like container, with all of them held in an air-tight glove box. Twenty in all, the specimens were obviously arranged in some sort of order – though the reasoning escaped Kurt for the moment. No sample was larger than a few centimeters across, and all looked to be at least somewhat plantlike – except for the ones he assumed to be soil samples. Don walked up next to him and said, "Dried bits of plants and dirt – exciting, isn't it?"

Kurt had a wise-ass comment to shoot back, but held his tongue as Helena, Jack, and Palmer entered. They immediately moved forward, forcing Kurt to reluctantly take a step back: there was only so much room in the lab. Don joined him in the second row as Alex started speaking.

"Ok, so these are our first samples. Keep in mind that all I did was collect a few representative specimens during our excursion yesterday; so, this is far from the detailed study that we'll be doing over the next few weeks. Helena has a portion of each as well – that should allow her to start looking in greater detail at any threats, potential allergens and other issues that we'll face."

"Keep in mind, that'll take some time to figure out," Helena added.

"True," Alex continued. "So, for the time being, please don't ask me for any real details either. Let me start by just summarizing some of our findings. First, and probably most interesting, life on Epsilon Eri-D is much more similar to Earth life than I thought possible. It is cellular based, where their cells use a variant on DNA. We still have work to do, but it actually looks like they use the same amino acids and base molecular structure that we do. In retrospect, this shouldn't be that much of a surprise since the environment here is so close to that of Earth. What it does mean, however, is that we should likely be able to synthesize the necessary serums and vaccines to let us roam free on this world.

"Now, of course, there are some significant differences. The first one that caught my eye is that the difference between plant and animal life here is not quite so distinct. All of the organisms I've sampled so far have a variant of Chlorophyll, but lack cell walls and seem to have structures that allow for mobility. I wouldn't call them true muscles. But, as Don was able to demonstrate, these organisms were able to move in a controlled manner toward him and just as quickly retreat when they were threatened."

"He's just not going to let that go, is he?" Don muttered to Kurt. "Doesn't he realize I'm the one who makes his duty assignments?"

Kurt smiled and said, "But he's a scientist. You know how they are: they don't have a clue about how to deal with the people around them." He paused for a split second to let his words take hold before continuing, "Oh, but wait, you're one of them too, aren't you?"

"You better watch what you say," Don shot back with a smile. "Remember, Jack was one of us *scientists* too. I'll tell him what you just said – and maybe add an extra detail or two just for a little effect."

"Kurt, did you hear what I asked?" Alex said.

"Sorry, just discussing some technical details here with Don." Don shot him a dirty look as he continued, "What did you need?"

"We observed some very small, airborne creatures. I'm betting they're insect-like. I'll need you to put together a small sampling device to catch some of them. I was thinking of something along the lines of a low power vacuum with a filter to catch them."

"No problem," Kurt replied.

"Also, we found that some of the life here is particularly sensitive to high-pitch noise – stuff in the ultra-sound range above thirty-kilohertz. Could you piece together a couple of variable pitch speakers with triggers. I was thinking they might be useful as a non-harmful repellant of sorts."

"Not a problem either," Kurt said as he noted the requests in his hand-held computer. "When do you need them by?"

"We'd like to head back down tomorrow morning. Can you have them ready by then?"

"I'll do my best."

"Good," Alex said. "As I was saying, the plant-like life here has some similarities to animal life back home, but there are differences. For one, the metabolic rate of the cells I analyzed from Don's vine is much faster than that of a typical plant. I honestly don't think photosynthesis, or its analogue here, is capable meeting all of its energy requirements. This would explain the organism's predatory behavior: it needs some external source of energy." Alex pointed to the dish containing the vine sample and continued, "You'll notice the maroon fluid that's oozed out of it. It's less viscous than sap, and is probably the core of a more advanced circulatory system. This small fragment doesn't tell us that much, but the behavior we observed when I cut it suggested that it was part of a much larger organism. I'm willing to bet that its main body has some sort of pumping organ, along with other organ systems. I'm not sure how centralized all of it will be, but it should be really amazing to investigate."

"Alex," Don said.

"Yes?"

"Will you be sending around a written report of all of this for us to read?"

"Definitely. In fact, it'd be a great way to get some feedback in terms of what we want to do next. There is literally a myriad of opportunities here – I'm really not even sure where I want to begin."

"That's a good idea," Jack said. "For now, why don't we stick to the information most relevant to preparing for our next surface mission."

"OK," Alex replied. As the scientist started talking, Kurt leaned over to Don's ear and whispered, "Pretty slick. I guess you were getting a little bored?"

"I can skim through most of that stuff later," Don answered. "All I really want to do is get inside that dome."

"Listen up please," Alex called out in a slightly raised voice. "Because these organisms show advanced predatory behavior, and because none of the potential prey have shown themselves, I think it would be wise to be very cautious when we're down there. To put it simply, the prey is hiding for a reason. We don't want to stumble into anything dangerous."

"A wise precaution," Jack replied. Turning to his first officer, Jack continued, "Palmer, I understand that you've been working closely with Masako about the alien object in orbit?"

"Yes, Lieutenant Fukuhara's planetary science background was the best match for this. We have spent a reasonable amount of time observing the object, but have only come up with more unanswered questions. I think I'll let her explain."

Kurt turned as Masako started speaking from the back of the lab. "First, we were able to refine the estimates of the masses of the rings. The outer rings are identical. Each has an inner diameter of twenty-five kilometers and a circular cross-section with a thickness of one kilometer. We now estimate their masses to be three times ten-to-the-seventeenth kilograms which as Don reported earlier, is in line with the mass of a small asteroid. The central ring is still puzzling. It too has an inner diameter of twenty-five kilometers. We have refined our estimate of its mass to a little more than five percent of an Earth mass or three-point-two times ten-to-the-twenty-third kilograms; in other words, this seemingly small object is four-and-a-half times more massive than our moon. What's particularly interesting is that these measurements mean it's made of some entirely new form of matter. Something we've never even theorized. We're talking about matter over ten-million times denser than lead. So in short, I've got no idea what it is."

"Were you able to solve the ring-position problem?" Kurt asked.

"Actually yes," Masako replied. "That was one of the few answers we were able to come up with. For those who don't know, the problem we were dealing with is that the gravitational field from the central ring is so strong, that it should have pulled the outer ones into it. However, we found what appears to be an elegant example of celestial engineering. The whole object, outer and inner rings, are spinning on an axis perpendicular to its central axis. Basically, the outer rings are orbiting the central one – but the central one is spinning as well, so that they maintain their alignment. They make one orbit every seven-point-four minutes. That's what's keeping them in a stable, aligned configuration. Unfortunately, that's about all we've been able to learn so far."

They stood in silence until Palmer said, "At this point, we're not really sure how to even study it." Palmer waited a moment for comments and continued when the room remained quiet. "We were, however, able to completely map the debris clouds. Our best guess is sort of obvious: they're what's left of an orbital structure or ship. However, the particles themselves seem remarkably uniform. Like the ones near the asteroid, they're comprised of some sort of metal. The individual pieces seem rounded, and range from centimeter-sized to chunks a half-meter across. But there's no sign of any actual fragments of larger structures: No broken up hull, solar panels or anything at all.

"The main debris cloud is in an orbit that trails the massive rings like a tail. We found a second, more diffuse cloud in lower orbit near E-Eri-D. We were aware of part of it when we plotted your course to the surface. It looks like it's part of a larger cloud that's really more like a ring around the planet. The center of the distribution is about a thousand kilometers above the planet's surface. Now that we've mapped it, it'll be easy to stay clear of it."

"Good," Jack replied. He looked once around the lab before asking, "Are there any questions?" When no one answered, Jack said, "OK, then we'll proceed as planned. Alex, Don and myself will conduct a second surface mission tomorrow. Hopefully with the appropriate equipment, we'll be able to get into the dome. Once we have a better handle on the environment down there, we'll start regular daily trips to the surface.

As the others nodded in agreement, Jack said, "Palmer, I have something else I want you to do."

"Sir?"

"We need to get more information about the orbiting object. Do you want to take shuttle-two in for a closer look?"

Though he looked for it, Palmer's face didn't show a trace of emotion. The man just answered. "Yes, sir. May I choose who I take with me?"

"Who do you want?"

"My first choice is Masako."

Jack looked to Don and asked, "Any objections?"

Don rubbed his chin before answering. "As before, her background in planetary science should be well-suited for this. And Palmer, your engineering training should make the two of you a good team, but I don't know how much engineering knowledge will help with analyzing this thing."

Jack knew Don wasn't trying to be condescending, and couldn't tell what Palmer made of the comment. He gave them a second before saying, "I'll take that as an approval."

"Yes," Don said quietly.

"Palmer, with Devon being our only available pilot, I'm going to need him for the IPV, which means you're going to have to fly this one yourself."

"No problem, sir. I'd like to get an early start on this. Maybe at zero-seven hundred."

"Do you think you can be ready by then?"

"It's only nineteen forty-five, so if we get started immediately, yes."

"Ok, proceed," Jack said with a smile.

Chapter 13 – July 17, 2124; 11:00:00

Jack stepped out of the shuttle airlock into the bright sunlight. Even though it was still morning, ship-time, the sun was already well past midday on E-Eri-D giving them only three hours to work before sunset. They would never actually be able to get into sync with the planet's day-night cycle: its sixteen-hour day was simply too short. For now, though, it didn't matter. Jack just stared straight ahead at the dome's wall. Its mysterious railing and possible doorway called to him. He picked up his equipment bag and walked slowly across the leaf covered ground, stopping about a meter from the wall. Its dull-gray, square panels stretched away in either direction: the large lighter one they assumed to be the door stood in front of him.

"Jack," Don called. "Do you want to use Kurt's device to clear this area of any those insect creatures while I setup my equipment?"

"Coward," Alex said mostly under his breath.

"I heard that," Don shot back.

Jack just ignored them and said, "Just stay back for a minute." He pulled a black, palm-sized box from his bag. The front had the mesh covering of a speaker while its back had a handle and a small computer display. According to Kurt, all he needed to do was hold it in the desired direction, choose a volume setting and press the activate button. It seemed simple enough, but

Jack still chose to hold the device carefully at arm's length. Positioning himself with his back to Don and Alex, so that any escaping creatures would head away from them and the shuttle, he pressed "activate."

The frequency was high enough that they heard nothing, and initially, nothing happened.

"Is it working?" Don asked.

Jack lowered his arms as he opened his mouth to answer, but stopped as the soil in front of him began to stir. He held the device in position for a second longer but nothing else happened. Pointing it to his left and right had a similar result – some motion beneath the leaves but little else. He turned up the volume and reflexively stepped back as a diffuse, black cloud shot out from the ground. It behaved as if it were a single organism. Hovering a few meters away, it carefully kept away from his speaker. Each time Jack stepped toward it, the cloud backed off an equivalent distance.

"It doesn't seem to want to leave," Alex said.

Jack turned the volume control up to maximum and the cloud quickly dispersed in all directions. Aiming the device back to the ground didn't result in any more movement. Jack walked slowly back across the area in front of the door, sweeping the device back and forth, but found nothing else.

"I guess you cleared out their hive or nest," Alex said. "There might not be any others right around here."

"Ok," Jack answered while eyeing the ground suspiciously.

"Still," Alex said, "I think we should keep that thing on while we're working here. Let's convince them not to come back for now."

"Good idea," Jack replied as he placed device on the ground, facing away from the wall.

"Jack," Don called. "Can you come over here and help me with this?"

"On my way." Don was in the middle of setting up an array of sensors that would hopefully give them a hint of what lay behind the wall.

"There," Don said pointing to the ground in front of him, "hand me the radar unit."

Jack did as asked.

"This should hopefully penetrate these walls and give us a hint of what's in there.

"Guys," Alex called out.

"Just a minute," Don answered as he focused on setting up his gear.

"I think you'll want to see this," Alex persisted.

Jack turned to see Alex crouching by the base of the wall.

"What is it?" Jack asked.

"Look for yourself."

The man could be frustrating when he wanted to be, but Jack obliged and stepped down into the trench they had dug the previous day. Craning his neck to peer over Alex's shoulder, he finally saw what had caught the scientist's attention. Beneath the railing, right up against the side of the wall, was the faint outline of a small square cover plate about thirty centimeters across. Alex carefully brushed away the remaining dirt that clung to the seam.

"Jack, I need you guys out of the way if I'm going to take a..." Don started, but cut himself off when he realized no one was paying attention. "What's going on?"

Jack didn't answer. Instead he took a large screwdriver from his tool pouch and forced its blade into the seam. The cover plate popped off with surprising ease, revealing a shallow, recessed cavity containing a single large handle.

"What do you think?" Alex asked.

"What'd you find?" Don asked as he jumped in behind them.

Jack just smiled, grabbed the handle firmly and pulled. It moved smoothly. The soft hiss of a hidden hydraulic piston was followed by the sudden, heavy clank of an unseen metal latch. They backed off a couple of steps as the large panel before them slid into the ground, hitting bottom with a deep resonating bang. In front of them lay a long, dark corridor, as broad and tall as the three-by-three meter door that just opened. Jack flicked on his flashlight, but the passageway extended beyond the range of its beam. The walls and ceiling were lined with a deep charcoal metal or stone, polished to a high gloss. The floor might have been the same substance too, except for the fact that it was uniformly coated by a thick layer of dust or dirt. "Kurt, are you getting this?"

"Yes, there's a little static, but we see it."

"OK, we're going to go in a bit and look around."

"Understood," Kurt replied.

Jack led the way. There were no markings or even any patterns along the walls: just a smooth, uniform, dark-gray surface. They proceeded slowly — the only sound was the shuffling of their footsteps and their echoes off the hard, alien walls. After walking nearly half the length of a football field, the corridor curved gently, and they lost the last of the sunlight that had been at their backs. The beams from their flashlights were so completely consumed by the all-encompassing darkness that it took them a moment to realize when the passage had become straight again. They continued until the surrounding walls and ceiling suddenly disappeared: they were at the entrance to a mammoth, open chamber. Jack stood at the threshold, and surveyed the area with his light. The air was thick with dust, keeping him from seeing very far. Directly in front were three large objects — machines of some sort. Each was the length of a small truck and the better part of two stories tall. They were covered up to eye-level with dull, silver sheet metal, while the upper portions were a complex array of coils with interconnecting pipes and cables. They seemed to resemble turbines he'd seen used for power generation – however, he knew better than to start blindly guessing as to their actual purpose.

Jack walked slowly to the nearest one and saw a jagged, half-meter wide hole about waist-high in its paneling. He brushed away the centuries of dust that clung to its side, exposing charring along its sharp edges. Shining his flashlight into the hole revealed a fused mass of melted plastic panels. "Don, take a look at this."

Don came up from behind followed a second later by Alex. The two peered in for a minute before Don stepped back and said softly, "I'm not sure I like what I'm seeing here."

Jack had the same misgivings, but thought better of agreeing aloud. Instead, he reached into the hole and gently tugged on one of the plastic boards that protruded from the melted mass. It snapped off without any effort. The rectangular shard was as large as his hand and covered in a thick coat of gray dust. He took a can of pressurized nitrogen from his pack and blew off the dust. The wafer thin piece was translucent teal and shimmered under their flashlights. Bringing his face close to its surface, he could just discern a finely etched pattern of lines running its entire length. It reminded him of a circuit board, except for the fact that the patterns were more like groves than lines of metal.

Alex walked off to his left before shouting, "Jack, over here!"

Jack whirled around as much from surprise as curiosity and looked blankly at the man, until he took Alex's unbroken gaze across the room as his cue. At the end of Alex's dusty flashlight beam was the dull surface of an adjacent machine. Centered in its side was another jagged hole, nearly identical to the one by him. Jack stepped toward it, but caught his foot on something, inadvertently kicking it across floor. The object skidded away with a hollow sound. Jack's eyes reflexively followed the noise, trying to find it in the darkness, but it was gone. He then glanced straight down at his feet. There lay a pile of debris shrouded in dust and spread across a couple of meters of floor. The collection of cylindrical objects numbered at least a few dozen and were of varying sizes. The ends of a few curved upward, protruding from the blanket of dust, showing themselves to be a pale, lifeless yellow. Without thinking much, he pushed at one with his toe. It was light and slid easily, dragging several other pieces with it. The last one in the chain, though, made him stop. Before he could translate his gut feeling into a thought, Don jumped back, shouting, "Damn it Jack, is that..." but stopped – his voice trailing off as he regained his composure.

Jack looked down at the large, hollow, oval mass. It lay motionless with both eye sockets staring at him. Alex, who hadn't so much as twitched during the commotion, stepped forward and calmly crouched down by the pile of bones. Without a word, he carefully brushed the dust off the skull, picked it up and examined it at arm's length. Its elongated shape was animal-like, though its cranium was definitely larger   than a human's. The two large eye sockets were set wider apart than a man's. There was no obvious nose, and the mouth area seemed toothless.

Don shined his light at the bones strewn in front of them. Now that there was context, it was obvious that it was a complete skeleton. Jack was a little surprised by its similarity to terrestrial animals. A spine, ribs, and four appendages were easily recognizable. The creature was about two and a half meters long and seemed in near-perfect condition except for something by the ribs.

"Jack? Do you …"

"Yeah I see it," Jack answered, not waiting for Alex to finish his question. There was a hole in the near side of its ribcage. The edges of the broken bones were singed and looked almost as if they'd melted. "Kurt, I assume you've been listening in on all of this. Can you make out what we're seeing on the video feed?"

There was no answer. "IPV, do you read us?" Jack called.

More silence followed.

Don looked around the room and said, "The metal in these walls could be blocking our signal. At least we're recording all of this – they can review it when we get back."

Jack wasn't satisfied with the answer and said again, "IPV, do you read us?"

"Hey, there's another body here," Alex called. Jack turned and followed Alex's flashlight beam across to the adjacent machine again. Lying beneath its hole was another skeleton.

"What the hell went on here?" Don asked loudly.

"I don't know, but we can find out later. I want to head back out and restore contact with the IPV."

"Not yet," Alex said as he walked deeper into the chamber.

"Not now," Jack said calmly. "We can come back later."

"You can't be serious. Look at what we've found!"

"Alex…"

"Come on! Let's at least get a broader view of what we've found. Just a quick walk-around – something we can review when we get back to the IPV. Besides, a few more minutes isn't going to kill anyone."

The truth was, he didn't want to leave yet either. His desire won out over his subconscious concerns and he said, "OK, but let's do this quickly.

We'll split up – one of us down each side, the other down the middle. Go only a hundred meters, no further. I want to meet back here in ten minutes."

"I've got the center," Alex said as he disappeared into the pitch-black cavern.

"Alright then, I'll take the left. Don, you've got the right," Jack said. He walked slowly, keeping the charcoal-gray wall to his left. There were more rows of machines, all identical to the first ones, creating neat aisles that went on as far as he could see. It wasn't until he was five rows in, that he saw another body. As before there was a single blast hole in the device, and a crumpled skeleton lying beneath it.

"I've found two more bodies over here," Alex said over the comm. link.

"Three here," Don responded. "They're all the same. A single shot for each."

Jack kept walking. After the sixth body he stopped counting, and instead tried to look for something different from the surrounding monotony – some clue as to what might have happened. The darkness and uniformity of the surroundings made it tough to judge distance, so he resorted to counting his paces. Around seventy paces in, he came to a wall and had to make a right turn to continue.

"I've reached a wall," Don called over the comm. "There's no door here but..."

Jack let a few seconds passed before he said, "What Don?"

"You've got to get over here. I've found something."

"What?" Jack pressed.

"Just get over here."

Jack walked back the way he came, looking down each row for his science officer. It wasn't until he was nearly back at the entrance that he saw the dim glow of Don's light in the distance. He picked up his pace as he headed toward it. When he finally reached him, Don didn't even glance at him. He just said, "They were slaughtered. They never even had a chance."

The wall in front of them was covered with dozens of charred blast marks. The floor was littered with bones – too many to count. He couldn't even estimate how many bodies were there.

Alex came up from behind and said, "What the...were they...," but stopped as Don answered his unspoken question: "It looks like they were herded over here and executed."

Jack glanced around them and said, "I agree. It doesn't look like they even put up a fight."

"How can you be sure?" Alex asked hesitantly.

"Look at the machines and walls behind you. They're undamaged.

If…whoever they were had fought back, they'd have shot at their attackers in this direction. I'd expect to see some damage here. There's nothing."

"This isn't right," Don said softly.

Jack allowed them another minute before saying, "OK, don't touch a thing. I want a full team in here to document this properly. Let's get back outside and re-establish contact."

Alex didn't protest this time and just started slowly back toward the entrance. As they walked, Jack looked over the room's walls and machinery. There were no other signs of violence. Nothing had been ransacked. They continued back through the entry corridor, and as they rounded the final bend, his eyes were stung by the bright sunlight from the distant door. There were a couple quick bursts of static from the radio, and then a barely intelligible voice came through.

"…one team, this is IPV, please respond. Shuttle-one team…"

It was Kate Stewart, one of the mission's communications engineers. Jack quickly replied, "IPV, we read you."

She left the comm. link open, allowing him to hear her say, "Kurt, I've got him."

A second later, Kurt's clearly stressed voice came over, "Jack, where the hell were you?"

"In the structure – I told you we were going in. What's going on?"

"Damn, you don't know. We lost contact with shuttle-two about twenty minutes ago. There was short burst of gamma rays from the object and then we just lost them."

"Do you have them on sensors?"

"No, nothing."

"What's your status?"

"We're holding our current orbit, but were about to land the IPV and start looking for you."

"What about their transmissions before you lost contact? Was there any sign that they were in trouble or…"

"Nothing, Jack. I've been through this a dozen times…" Jack could hear Kurt stop and take a deep breath. "Sorry Jack. No, there was no sign. We just had a clean data stream and then all contact ceased."

"OK, ready the ship for departure to the object. We'll leave as soon I get the shuttle back aboard. Jack out."

Chapter 14 – July 17, 2124; 15:05:00

Kurt leaned forward in the command chair and ran his fingers through his hair. This was not where he wanted to be – not in Jack's seat. Anything else would be preferable, even cleaning the grime off of the bio-matter recycling units during a maintenance shift. He glanced impatiently at the command console. Its upper corner read, 15:05:00, 17 July 2124. It would still be another half hour before Jack's shuttle returned and he could finally relinquish this post. Just to keep from dwelling on it any further, he turned to the communications station to his right. "Kate, any more luck with the adjustments you made?"

"Still no response," She replied without looking up. "The mods are online and working. It's just that there's still no signal from them." Unwilling to let her statement end so pessimistically, though, she continued, "But there's still one more thing I want to try. I'm betting that there might have been an EMP associated with the gamma burst; that could've knocked out all of the shuttle's systems. As a last resort they might try to contact us using the short-range comm. unit in an EVA suit. We just need to squeeze a bit more gain out of this and we should be able to pick even that up."

"Good, let me know what you get," Kurt answered reflexively. He was instantly self-conscious of how much his response sounded like something Jack would say. The last thing he wanted was to seem like he was pretending to be something he wasn't. The bottom line was that two crewmen were missing on his watch. Something that he was sure wouldn't have happened if Jack had been onboard.

"Lieutenant Commander Hoffman."

It took a split second for him to realize that the computer was calling him. "Yes, what is it?"

"I have just completed processing all of the data that was transmitted from Shuttle-two before loss-of-signal."

"Good...good, is there any sign of what happened?"

"Nothing quantitative, sir. I can integrate it into a VR playback for you. You might find that helpful."

"Yes, good idea. Thank you," Kurt answered, though he was not completely sure of what he wanted to do. It was just easier to accept the computer's advice. He pulled a pair of opaque glasses from a compartment in the command chair's armrest, put them on, and then carefully placed a couple of tiny speakers in his ears. "OK, begin playback."

"From what point would you like to begin?"

"I don't know...let's try the last ten minutes."

The dark mask of the glasses abruptly switched to an all-encompassing view of the shuttle's dim interior. He was standing behind the pilot's and co-pilot's seats and could see the backs of Palmer's and Masako's heads as they stared out the cockpit window. Directly in front lay a silver torus: one of the object's outer rings. It was thin, like a bracelet suspended against a black curtain. They were still far enough away that it didn't quite fill his field of view. Its elliptical appearance told of Palmer's cautious, off-axis, approach vector. The ring grew though as Palmer brought the ship in, and soon Kurt found himself gazing at the thick, silver arc of its upper left quadrant. They continued their approach in silence, and the curved surface grew flat, transforming into a metallic plain stretching out before him. Its reflective surface was so perfect that it became difficult to discern whether they were hovering above some massive metallic object or just floating in open space. The surface only manifested itself through a slightly grayish tint at the reflection's edge.

Masako broke the silence. "I don't know what we're going to gain from another close pass out here. I really want to see the central cylinder up close."

"Too dangerous," Palmer muttered. "Like I said before, we're going to take this slowly and carefully. Besides, even here we're experiencing some significant tidal forces. If we get too close to that one, it could rip us apart." Palmer adjusted his course, and in an attempt to appease his shipmate, said, "Why don't we try a touch and go on it this time. If that goes well, then we can try setting down on it."

Masako's interest was sparked. "I wouldn't mind trying to find out what it's made of. There's no reason..."

Palmer, though, was clearly ignoring the response and cut her off, saying "Fifty meters and closing."

Kurt gazed back out the window, captivated by the growing image of their own reflection – he could have sworn they were simply approaching shuttle-one for some sort of rendezvous.

"Thirty meters and..." Palmer's voice trailed off as he suddenly started working intensely at the controls.

Kurt watched with disbelief as he realized that the man was actually increasing thrust toward the object. The ring, however, still lay in front of them, unchanged.

"I'm encountering some sort of resistance. It's almost like it's holding us back from the surface. Increasing thrust now to fifty percent."

Kurt hung on those words for the few seconds before Palmer announced, "No progress – we're at twenty-nine point five meters. Do you detect any energy readings?"

"Nothing."

"I'm going to move us transversely. Maybe we can find a region elsewhere that'll let us set down." Barely a minute passed before Palmer announced, "Still nothing. I'm increasing thrust to seventy percent." The ship's normally silent engines began to hum under the strain. "Altitude still..."

"Something's wrong...engine temps are rising fast," Masako called out with some urgency.

"Understood," Palmer replied. A warning buzzer cut through the air, an automated voiced announced, "Engine temperature approaching critical."

Palmer silenced the buzzer, saying, "Ok, I'm reducing power."

Before he could act though, the voice announced, "Temperature past critical, emergency shut down commencing."

The engines' hum ceased abruptly. In the same instant, they shot away from the ring's surface as if someone had released a giant spring. The once smooth silver plain regained its curvature, and Kurt found himself staring at a quickly receding segment of the ring. Reflex took over and he dug his fingers into the command chair's armrest to brace himself.

"I've got no power available," Palmer called out, his voice cracking under the strain. "We're heading for the far side of the ring." Palmer typed frantically at the control terminal as the computer announced "Warning, course change required. Impact in twenty seconds."

The sky outside became filled with an eerie blue-green glow. The computer announced, "Impact in ten..."

Its voice cut out and the playback ended.

"Damn it!" Kurt said loudly as he pulled off the glasses. Kate looked up at him in surprise. "Sorry," he said in a subdued tone. He regained his train of thought and continued, "Computer, show me the shuttle's path during that last minute."

The small terminal on his armrest displayed a head-on view of the three rings. A red dot marked the shuttle's position as it slowly inched its way toward the inner surface of the near ring. "OK, this must be when he increased thrust," he said softly to himself. The dot held its position for a few seconds, and then shot outward across the ring. As it reached the midpoint, it disappeared. "So it didn't hit," he said aloud.

The computer responded to Kurt's rhetorical statement. "There is no evidence to support that conclusion, sir. This just represents our loss of signal. At that point all sensors were overwhelmed by the gamma burst. The shuttle could have continued along its trajectory and struck the ring."

Kurt wasn't even willing to entertain that notion. "Is there any evidence of an impact?" he challenged. "Any sign of debris?"

"No, sir. The gamma burst saturated our sensors. Since they came back on-line, we have not found any trace of them."

"Then why are you suggesting that they hit?"

Kurt only realized he was shouting when he finished his sentence. Though it was only a machine, the computer knew better than to respond this time. The problem was, the lack of any sign of shuttle debris was hardly evidence of their being alive and well. He took a deep breath and made a deliberate effort to calm himself. "How long until shuttle-one's aboard?"

"Ten minutes until docking." If he didn't know better, he'd have thought the computer's tone was almost apologetic. That and the continued silence on the bridge made him further regret his outburst. He abruptly got up and said, "I'm heading down to propulsion. Let me know if anything comes up."

Devon looked back at him from the pilot's station and gave him a quick "OK."

It took a few minutes to wind his way through the narrow corridors to engineering. As he reached the stern, the hallway widened to accommodate the control station for the IPV's fusion reactor. The junior member of his engineering staff, Claire Hughes, was working intently at one of its screens, and gave him a quick, "Hey Kurt." He answered with a polite, "How's it going?" and then watched over her shoulder as she reviewed reactor output models.

"I'm looking at different ways we can power up the main discharge plates," Claire said. "Nadya thinks we can get a hundred ten to a hundred fifteen percent out of the engines. That'd cut the run over to the object to just over an hour. The catch is making sure we don't burn anything out."

Kurt nodded in approval. "Where is she anyway?"

"Last I saw, she was working up top in there," Claire said as she gestured to her left, toward the closed bulkhead leading to the propulsion room. "She drafted Maurice into helping her replace one of the xenon infusion valves."

"Maurice?" Kurt said in dismay. The man could work marvels with computer code but was about the last person he'd expect to see getting his hands dirty with actual hardware.

"Yeah, I was surprised too. But, no one else was around and she needed an extra set of hands."

"Thanks." Kurt swung open the heavy blast door that helped isolate the propulsion section from the rest of the ship. After climbing through, he reflexively sealed the hatch behind him. At twenty meters across with a seven-meter high ceiling, the room was technically the largest single open space on the IPV. However, only a small percentage was truly open. There was barely enough room to take four or five steps across the gray, anti-static floor before reaching a floor-to-ceiling array of cables, pipes and catwalks. There, countless bundles of multi-colored wires snaked their way up and down a metal framework, before diving deep into the innards of the engine assembly. The semblance of chaos masked the true sophistication of this several-meter thick layer of machinery: every last wire had been carefully placed to help transform and regulate the megawatts of power required by ion drive. The hazardous nature of this high-voltage mass was challenged only by the rows of large, bright-green xenon cylinders that lined the wall behind him. Though the xenon that served as their propellant was inert, the only way to store an ample supply was to keep it pressurized in these tanks at hundreds of thousands of atmospheres. Kurt chose not to think about what even a small puncture would do to the ship.

He scanned the room until he spotted Nadya in the far left corner of the ceiling working with Maurice on a propellant transfer pipe. Kurt grabbed a railing for leverage, and gave himself a moderate push in their direction. Neither noticed him approach. Maurice was carefully holding a valve in position as Nadya laser-welded it onto a feed pipe from a near-by cylinder. Kurt caught a hand-hold in the ceiling, and watched from a distance. Every few seconds Nadya paused and used a small probe to check for weak spots. The high pressures of the xenon gas demanded that the welds be near-perfect. He turned away from the bright blue light as she began welding again, and only realized she was done when she said, "This looks good enough. I didn't like the readings I was getting earlier."

Turning back to her, he asked, "What, you found a crack?"

"No...no, nothing that bad. I did a quick pressure test before, and this valve showed some vibration. If it got just a little worse, there'd be a risk of a crack forming. The last thing I'd want to do is to tell Jack he'd have to shut his engines down in the middle of some maneuver."

Nadya looked over to Maurice, who was not so subtly taking quick glances down at the exit hatch. She let him off the hook, saying, "Thanks for the help."

"No prob," he answered and launched himself toward the door. Kurt just shook his head as the man exited the room.

"I think he's getting weirder," Nadya said while stowing her tools in an equipment bag. "He barely said two words to me the whole time we were working here."

"I know what you mean. We've been together what, ten years on this mission, and I can't say that I know him."

Nadya led the way back down to the floor. "I sometimes wonder why he's even here."

"He was Palmer's pick."

"I know that. It just doesn't seem like he fits."

"I just know that he served with Palmer on Ganymede station. Jack told me Maurice even saved Palmer's life when a drilling platform depressurized. I guess Palmer felt he owed him."

Nadya answered with a quiet "Hmmm" as she placed her tool bag in small compartment by the hatch.

Deciding he'd had enough of that subject, Kurt said, "Claire says you think you can push the engines to a hundred fifteen percent."

"You know they're rated up to that."

"Of course. But did you ever push them that high during trials back home?"

"Yeah."

"OK, for how long?"

There was a distinct pause before she answered, "About thirty seconds. I didn't see any point to pressing any harder during testing."

"Alright, how about the xenon then?"

"It's going to eat up a good deal of the stuff. But..."

"But?"

"Let me finish," she answered with some agitation. "I checked the spectra of E-Eri-D's atmosphere. It's got trace amounts of it – about fifty percent more even than Earth. We'll be able to filter enough out to refuel."

"Lieutenant Commander?" the computer's voice called out.

"Yes, what is it?"

"The captain's on final approach. He'll be on board in about five minutes."

"Thank you."

The machine continued, "The captain asked that you meet him in the conference room. He wants to be briefed as soon as he gets aboard."

"Got it." He turned to Nadya and said, "Well, it looks like you finished just in time."

"Like there was any doubt?" she shot back with a smile. "And, Claire should be about done with her analysis, so we'll be able to charge the plates right away. Tell Jack we'll be ready to move as soon as he gives the word."

Kurt was halfway out the door when Nadya called back to him, "Ask Claire to come in here as soon as she's done out there, will you?"

"OK." He sealed the hatch behind him, and tuned to Claire who was still busy at the reactor control panel. He opened his mouth to relay Nadya's message but didn't get the chance.

"Don't worry, I heard her. I've got one more simulation I need to run, then I'll go in."

"Thanks." He started down the corridor, then stopped for a second to let his eyes adapt. Though normally adequately lit, the hall seemed dark compared to the brightly lit engine room. He took advantage of the pause to tap his comm. unit and say, "Bridge." It beeped in response and he continued, "Kate, Kurt here. Any updates on raising Shuttle-two on the radio?"

"Sorry, but no. The adjustments worked. I'm getting the amplification I thought we needed but we're not getting any signal. It's like they're not..." Her voice trailed off.

Kurt gave her a second before answering. "I understand. Just keep trying."

All Kate managed was a subdued, "OK."

He disengaged the comm. unit, and stopped himself from shouting the few choice words that formed in his mind – it wouldn't do any good. Instead he just pounded the wall lightly. He didn't want to go into the briefing and tell Jack the shuttle was still lost. There was no reason to be afraid of Jack's reaction. It wasn't his style to lay into people. Deep down, Kurt knew the real source of his fear: he still didn't want to admit that any of this was even happening. Stating it outright to Jack meant it was real. It took a deliberate effort to push the self-doubt from his mind before heading down the corridor at a brisk pace.

The conference room was just off from the bridge – at the opposite end of the ship from engineering. At very least he wanted to get there, and have everything ready before Jack arrived. He turned down the last stretch of hallway as Devon's voice cut through the air on the ship-wide intercom, "Attention. We will be engaging engines at full power in three minutes. Please prepare for acceleration."

Kurt ducked into the room and the lights automatically flickered to life, revealing a simulated pine-paneled room just large enough to hold its two-meter wide, round table, and the eight seats that circled it. He stared momentarily at the table's fake wood trim, a match to the surrounding walls, before strapping himself into the nearest seat. Using the embedded computer console in front of him, he brought up a schematic of the Epsilon Eri-D region. It was a simple diagram with the orbits of Epsilon Eri-D and the object marked with thin, blue arcs. He traced a line between their position and that of the object, and entered an engine thrust parameter of one hundred fifteen percent. The system responded with an estimated trip time of fifty-nine minutes: shorter than he expected, but longer than he wanted.

Kurt looked up just as Don and Jack entered the room. Jack gave him a quick nod before sitting down and activating a comm. channel. "Devon, we're ready now. Engage engines."

"Yes, sir," was the pilot's quick response. Devon followed with a ship-wide announcement. Immediately after, the force of the engines pulled Kurt into his seat.

"Alright," Jack started, "tell me exactly what has happened."

Kurt began with a detailed narrative, starting right from when Jack left for Epsilon Eri-D. He was tempted to edit out unnecessary details, but decided that it'd be better to include everything: even his own personal thoughts, as well as reviews of every bit of data he'd seen. Jack would be the better judge of what was relevant. At times Jack's tone showed some barely-suppressed impatience. Kurt, however, knew better than to take it personally. His friend's anger wasn't at him: it was at not being on the bridge when they lost contact with Palmer. The meeting continued uneventfully until Devon announced that they had reached a stationary position near the object.

Jack responded to the announcement saying, "Good, hold position at one thousand kilometers from the ring where shuttle-two was lost."

"We're there now," Devon answered.

Jack cracked a slight smile at his pilot's prescience, and replied, "I'll be on the bridge in a minute."

Kurt straightened up when Jack abruptly stood, turned to him and said, "I want you to work closely with Don on an analysis of this thing. But, you'll also need to keep a close eye on the ship's systems. I don't want to get caught in whatever happened to them, so if you see even the slightest sign of anything unusual…"

Kurt simply answered, "Got it," and followed as Jack led the way to the bridge. Jack took his seat and started giving directions to Devon, while Kurt followed Don over to his station.

In a low voice, Don said, "From what you described, I don't expect there to be much for us to analyze. At least not much more than what you've already done."

"You're probably right," Kurt answered. "Though, in this case, I wouldn't mind it at all if you found something I missed. You know, solve this mystery right away and get those guys back safely."

Don answered only with a half-smile, and directed his console to bring up shuttle-two's transmitted data logs.

Kurt continued, "I went through their scans a bit. They weren't even able to show what that thing's made of. The problem is, I don't think we've got any equipment on board the IPV that'll do any better." As Don paged through the data, Kurt looked up at the main view screen. The broad silver arc of the near ring dominated the fore-ground. Behind it was the thicker central ring, with its opaque, black center. When he looked back to Don, the scientist had switched to actively scanning the alien device with the IPV's instruments.

"I'm not getting any readings on it at all. Nothing. And we're talking about radar and full-spectral analysis," Don announced.

Jack turned and asked, "Nothing at all?"

"Nothing. I'm repeating the full range right now: Visible, UV, IR, X and Gamma ray. It's perfectly reflective across the board. There's not the slightest bit of absorption or anything."

"What about the central one?" Jack asked.

Kurt watched Don's fingers fly across the keypad as he re-aligned the sensors. When the first readings were displayed, Don quickly cleared them and tried again.

Jack's impatience showed as he said, "Don?"

"Give me a second. We're closer than before so I want to be sure…"

"What do you mean?"

"The outer surface is just like this ring. Everything I throw at it gets bounced back. But the middle is different. It's like there's nothing there."

"It can't be empty," Kurt protested. "Then we'd see the stars on the other side."

"No, you don't understand. I'm getting nothing back. On the screen, in visible light, it's pitch black. That means, it's absorbing everything. What I'm telling you is that its doing that at all wavelengths. Long radio all the way out to Gamma. I'm not getting the slightest bit of reflection back at all. Nothing solid in this universe absorbs everything and emits nothing. Hell, that'd violate the laws of thermodynamics! The only way that I'd get readings like this is if it were hollow – but that's obviously not the case since we can't see through it. It doesn't make a God damned bit of sense!" Don was practically shouting by the end.

Jack answered in the same calm tone he always used, "Do you see anything unusual at all from the reflected spectra from the outer surface?"

"Nothing…well, there's a strange bit of skewing of the wavelength distribution. But that could easily be explained away due to the gravitational effects. Remember, we've got a planetary mass here compacted down to only a couple dozen kilometers. Or, it could be rotating – like what we were thinking before."

Jack politely rephrased his question, "Don, is there anything that will help us find out where that shuttle is?"

"No, nothing. I am picking up some of the metal nodules from the alien debris cloud, but not even a hint of anything that I would classify as shuttle debris."

Kurt watched silently as Jack just stared at the main view screen. He wanted to add something to the discussion, but there really wasn't anything he had to say. The bottom line was, Kurt still felt fully responsible for the shuttle's loss. Jack finally broke the silence, saying, "Devon, bring us closer and take us across to the other side of the near ring. We'll start our search from there. Plot a standard-grid search pattern."

A wave of apprehension twisted in Kurt's gut. He didn't know why, and futilely looked to the view screen, searching for an answer.

"Don," Jack continued, "scan every inch of that thing while we do this."

Kurt knew they had to stop, but hesitated. As they approached the half-way point, it felt like he was looking down the barrel of a gun. A wave of nausea shot through him as the image became awash in the same blue-green glow he'd seen in the VR playback. "Jack! Get us..." He wanted to get the rest of the words out, but couldn't. The room appeared to flex and bend around him, like he was looking through water. Everything, even the people around him started pulsating. The ripples of distortion coalesced into a wave that swept toward him. Before he could react, he was thrown from his seat against the rear of the bridge. Pinned against the wall, he struggled to breathe and grew dizzy. The sounds of glass and metal crashing around him were deafening. He tried to push the fear aside and understand what was happening, but slowly the din, and everything around him, faded away.

PART 3: G3-ALPHA

Chapter 15 – July 17, 2124; 22:00:00

Jack was surrounded by darkness and silence, and only slowly became cognizant that he was on the bridge and power was down. He turned his head to regain his bearings but a sharp pain cut through his shoulder, forcing him to stop. It took a deliberate effort to gather the strength to ignore the injury and look around. Nothing was moving, save for a few drifting shards of glass and metal that sparkled slightly in the dim, red, emergency lighting. They mixed with the long shadows of the darkened bridge, making it difficult to discern what had happened. Fixing his gaze toward the front, he was finally able to make out the silhouette of Devon's unconscious form still strapped in the pilot's station. Kate was drifting not far to his right, near her terminal.

"Devon," he called not too loudly. There was no answer and he repeated himself with more urgency, "Devon! Kate! Can you hear me?"

Again the bridge remained silent. He withstood another sharp stab of pain as he turned quickly toward the rear. Kurt and Don were floating near the access door. "Kurt!" he shouted. Frustrated, he hit the ship-wide intercom button and called out, "This is the captain. If anyone can hear me, please respond immediately." The echo of his voice from the ship's speakers quickly faded, and the room was silent again. He consoled himself with the thought, 'At least we've got some power.'

The stillness broke as a response came in over the comm., "Helena here, Captain."

Jack didn't bother hiding his relief as he answered, "Thank God. What's your status?"

"We got banged up pretty good. Right now it's just myself and Maurice here – not counting Janet. What the hell happened?"

"I'm not sure yet. I'm going to need some help up here though. It looks like everyone here's unconscious."

"Give me a couple of minutes."

"Thanks. Bridge out." Jack unstrapped himself and carefully pushed his way through the debris toward Kurt and Don. They were breathing, and to his relief both men started stirring when he touched their shoulders. He spun back to the front as Devon grunted, and muttered, "What the hell?"

"You OK?" he called.

"I don't know, I guess."

Jack momentarily left them to their recovery, and said, "Computer, I need a report of hull integrity and all other critical components now."

He was caught off guard when there was no response. The computer system was powered by its own separate, shielded grid, and should have stayed active. He repeated his request, but again there was no answer. "Maurice, are you still there?" he called.

"Yeah?"

"I need you to get the computer back on line."

"What's wrong?"

"I asked for an update, but got no response."

"Hmmm, might be the receivers, though the surge protectors might have been triggered as well."

"OK, whatever it is, I need it fully functional asap." Without pausing, Jack typed in the engineering channel, and said, "This is the bridge, respond please."

"Nadya here," was the quick reply.

"What's your status?"

"I've got one nasty headache, and Claire's unconscious. Don't know if I was too. Anyway, the reactor's in safe mode, so it'll take me a few minutes before I can get main power back on line. For now, all we've got is battery power for life-support, comm. systems and the like. What's going on?"

"We're not sure yet. I'll let you know once we know something. Just let me know as soon as you're ready to get main power back on line."

"OK."

Jack took another quick look around the bridge and met Devon's questioning gaze. Gliding over to his dazed pilot, he asked, "How're you holding up?"

"I'm fine," Devon answered, though his tense expression hinted that his pilot wasn't being completely truthful. "How long was I out?"

Jack reflexively looked to the clock over the main view screen, but like everything else, it was blank. He then glanced at the antique watch he wore on his wrist – a gift from his grandfather before the Magellan's launch – its hand wound springs would have been immune from any power surges or E-M pulses. It took a deliberate effort though to angle his arm and get enough light on it to read its dial. Then in disbelief he read it again, and softly muttered, "Damn."

"What's wrong?"

"It's ten – we were out for over six hours." He quickly turned to Kurt, who was now hovering next to him, and said, "I need you to get me a full damage report. Check every bulkhead."

"I'm on it."

"Don, go help Helena. Do a room by room search for injured. Make sure everyone is accounted for."

"OK."

Jack watched the two exit the bridge before returning to his seat. As he leaned back, the lights flickered to life. A moment later there was the welcome hum of circulation fans and other equipment coming to life as main power flowed back through the ship.

Nadya's voice came in over the comm., "Jack, we're back up and running, but it'll take a little time for many of the systems to fully re-initialize."

"Very good. How about the engines?"

"I don't know yet. I'll call you back in a few and give you an estimate. Engineering out."

"Devon," Jack said, "try and get an accurate fix on our position. If we were out that long, I want to know how far we've drifted. Also..."

A warning buzzer cut him off. Jack waited for the automated announcement that normally followed, but there was none. A wave of frustration hit him for a split second before he realized the buzzer meant at least some of the computer's functions were on-line. He'd just have to find out what was going on the old-fashioned way. His terminal displayed two words in bold, amber letters, "Communications Error." Touching it yielded the message, "Error Code 165A."

"Kate, what's a 165A?"

"You sure about that?"

"Yeah."

"It's the data link with Magellan – it's down."

Though the crew had fully moved over to the IPV, the Magellan still served as a communications hub and storage facility for supplies. There was even a contingency plan to move back to the Magellan if a proper base camp couldn't be established on Epsilon Eri-D. As a result, the IPV maintained a perpetual data link with the Magellan. "Devon, after you get our position, check our antenna orientation."

"I'm having a problem with that, sir."

"What, the communi..."

"No, our position. I'm getting terminal errors on the nav-system. It won't re-initialize."

"Can you by-pass them manually?"

"No, these are hard stops. It won't continue with the startup program."

"What're we talking about here, hardware or software?"

"I know where you're going with this, sir; but I've done those checks already. The problem is that I can't tell. It just says that it's unable to validate reference stars. It could mean one or more of the external cameras is down, or that it's having problems with the on-line charts."

"It could be the latter since the main computer's still off-line," Jack offered. "But first see if you can get an image directly from each of the nav-cameras, and verify things manually."

"OK, I'll let you..."

"Jack!"

He spun around to see Kate staring at him from her communications terminal. "What've you got?"

"The locator beacon from Shuttle-two. I've got a signal"

"What? Where?"

"I can't tell without linking to the nav-system."

"Damn! Are they transmitting anything?"

"No, I'm just getting their beacon."

He resisted the urge to shout the obvious and tell her to get him a signal. Instead he took a deep breath and stared ahead at the main view screen. Though it was blank, he didn't break his gaze. There had to be a way to get something more. "How strong is it?" he finally asked.

"It's tough to tell. It sounds like it's fading. Wait..."

Jack allowed only a couple seconds to pass before he asked, "What?"

"It's gone." Her statement was so sheepish, that he almost wanted say that it was OK, but it wasn't. The bridge stayed silent, waiting for his response. Instead he continued staring at the screen. His mind raced through likely causes and recoveries, until it finally latched onto a possibility – a failure in their antenna or amplifiers – and asked, "Do you think it's a receiver problem, or did it stop broadcasting?"

"I don't think it stopped transmitting, but I can't say for certain."

"What makes you think so?"

"If it'd stopped, I would've expected it to just cut out. This thing just faded away."

It was better than nothing, but there was no sense pursuing this for now. Kate would let him know when she knew more. He immediately jumped back to their nav problem, and asked loudly, "Devon, do we have an external video feed yet?"

"No, sir."

"God damn it! I don't like flying blind." He pounded his intercom button and shouted, "Maurice, respond please."

There was no immediate answer. He looked around the bridge, but no one met his gaze – they all had their heads buried in their terminals. Though he knew that only a few seconds had passed, the wait since his call was too long. He raised his hand to hit the intercom button again, but stopped as an answer finally came through.

"Maurice here. The computer's still not on-line. It'll take..."

"Forget about it for now. I need the nav-system up immediately."

"That'll take some time too."

"We don't have any time. Whatever it takes, get it up asap!"

There was no immediate answer, prompting him to ask, "Maurice did you hear me?"

"Yeah. I'll let you know when I've got something."

Jack disconnected the comm. channel as calmly as he could, and asked aloud, "Can anyone tell me what the hell is functional around here?" He didn't expect an answer; it was as stupid question. He just leaned back in the silence that followed. Sitting still even for a few seconds, though, was too much and he called down to propulsion. "Nadya, what's your status?"

"Not bad. We've already got full use of the maneuvering thrusters. But it'll be another ten minutes before I can begin charging the main drive."

"Good, was there any damage?"

"None that I've found so far. It looks almost like we had a massive power surge that tripped all the breakers. All we're doing down here is resetting relays and cut-off switches."

"Excellent. Let me know as soon as we can move. Jack out." Without pausing, he activated the main intercom again and said, "Don, respond please."

A second later his science officer's voice came through, "Don here."

"What's your status?"

"So far so good. I just met up with Helena, and we've got everyone accounted for. Most people just kept dialing into sick bay, reporting their loss of consciousness – it made tracking them all down much easier. Hold on, I'm gonna put Helena on."

"Jack?" she said.

"How're we doing Doc?"

"So far nothing worse than a few bumps and bruises. Claire was banged up the worst, but I don't think she has a concussion. I'm at a loss as to why we were all out so long. I am going to do some tests on a few people – just some spot checks."

Before he could answer, Kate interrupted again, "I've got them again, Jack."

"Helena, carry on. I'll get back to you. Kate, what've we got?"

"Just its locator beacon again. It's weak but getting stronger."

"No regular communications transmissions?"

"None. But, the beacon can give us a rough status."

"How so?"

"It's triggered in one of three modes. Each tells us something about the amount of damage the shuttle sustained. For example, there's a mode that would tell us if the cabin depressurized and there was no life-support." She paused for a split second, realizing the conclusion that could be drawn from her comment, and continued quickly, "But, that's not the case here. This one says the crew compartment is intact: just that there's no power. Maybe similar to our own situation."

"Good. How's the signal now?"

"It's holding steady. I just...wait..."

Kate had a habit of completely immersing herself in a problem, and forgetting about everything else around her. He knew she didn't realize she'd left the rest of them hanging on her unfinished thought, and gave her a few more seconds before finally asking, "What is it?"

"I don't get it. It's getting fainter again. If it's like before it'll be gone in a few more seconds."

Jack chewed on his lower lip for a moment before saying, "It's cyclic."

"Yes."

Devon interjected, "I think I know why. Give me a second to get the main view screen on line. I've got a video feed from one of the nav-cameras."

The screen display came to life, showing a field of stars, slowly slewing past. Jack was transfixed by their leisurely movement from left to right. "So, we're spinning," he said softly.

"Yes, sir."

The bright light of a sun entered from the left, quickly saturating the camera for a moment before the automated filters kicked in. They watched in silence as the star's disk made the same slow journey across the display.

"OK, so we've got E-Eri there. I should be able to have us stabilized in a moment," Devon said.

"The spin explains our signal loss," Kate added. "Our antenna's been rotating into and out of alignment with the shuttle."

The star moved out of view, and as the filters disengaged, the star field returned. Their march slowed until they finally stopped, and Devon said, "There, got it."

"What's our position and speed?" Jack asked quickly.

"I can't tell yet. I need more than just E-Eri. Let me get some references first."

"Kate," Jack said, "While he's doing that, see if you can get a fix on the shuttle."

"Already on it. Devon, can you bring us back another forty-five degrees away from E-Eri. Stay in our horizontal plane. I think that'll point us roughly at the shuttle."

The stars crawled across the screen again. After a few seconds they began to slow as Devon was completing his maneuver, when Kate called out, "No Dev, go a little further. It's still getting stronger."

"I don't have anything visual yet," Devon said.

"A little further...there, stop."

"I see it," Devon called out. "Jack, I've got radar contact. Five degrees to port, elevation fourteen degrees, distance fifteen thousand kilometers."

"Kate," Jack said, "still only the beacon?"

"Yes, but its origin matches Devon's radar contact. That's definitely them."

"Now we've got to get there."

"I'll need the nav-system on line before I can plot a course," Devon said.

Jack activated the intercom and called, "Maurice, respond please."

"I'm here," was the surprisingly quick answer.

"How're we doing down there?"

"It's checked out. There's nothing wrong with the navigation software."

"Was it operating properly before?"

"Best that I can tell, yeah."

Jack looked up to Devon's waiting gaze, and said, "Reset the initialization program. Maybe it needs to start from scratch."

Devon went straight to work at his console without answering. Barely a minute passed before he muttered something under his breath and spun around to face Jack. "I'm still getting the same fault."

"Damn it all," Jack said as he slapped the comm. button again. "Maurice, you still there?"

"Yeah. I've been following it from down here."

"So what the hell's going on?"

"I don't know. Everything's running right. I can see the video data going in, and the pattern matching routine's starting up."

"And then?"

"It's not getting a match."

"I can see that," Jack said abrasively.

Maurice continued, "What I mean is that up until the fault, everything is running as programmed. The video feed is being properly converted into a comparison matrix. The program then goes through the matching routine, but doesn't get any hits."

Jack had a less than civil response on the tip of his tongue, but held it. Forcing some level of composure into his voice, he just said, "Stand by."

He stared momentarily at the display screen attached to his armrest, and noticed a shadow being cast across it. He turned around to find Don hovering just behind his chair.

"How long've you been there?"

"Only long enough to see that we have a navigation problem. I finished the crew check with Helena and thought that I could be of more use up here."

"Good. I was just thinking that since we can't get the system on line, why don't we start from the beginning? See if you can use one of the ship's telescopes to identify the position of E-Eri-D with respect to us. Then work backward from there and derive our position."

"I'll get on it right away."

As Don headed to the science station, Jack said, "Devon, I want you to fly us to the shuttle."

"But the nav..."

"Don't worry about using computer guidance. Just, do it manually. We don't have the time to sit around waiting for this thing to get fixed."

"OK, give me a few minutes to get a couple of relative positional fixes, and we can get under way."

He flipped the intercom switch again, and called, "Maurice?"

"Here."

"For now, skip the nav-system. Just work on getting the main computer systems fully on line."

"I've already started on it. I should have it back in a few more minutes."

The bridge was silent again. Jack looked around and watched as everyone was fully engulfed in their tasks. It gave him a welcome moment to organize his thoughts. They only had two simple, but urgent goals: Get to the shuttle, and get their nav-system on line so that they could get back to Epsilon Eri-D. With any luck, Palmer and Masako were OK and just stranded on a disabled ship. For a split second he played devil's advocate with himself and wondered if his last thought was just wishful thinking – it didn't matter. Right now they had to focus on rendezvousing with the shuttle and pulling it into the bay. He leaned back and a wave of fatigue washed over him and dulled his senses. He quickly shook it off, but then grew frustrated with not having an active role in these tasks. His mind was still locked into the sense of urgency: sitting idly was unacceptable.

The sound of Devon's voice provided a reprieve as he announced, "Prepare for engine ignition in thirty seconds."

"How much power do we have?" Jack quickly asked.

"Nadya said I can run them at full throttle if I want. So I plan on doing just that. Figure on an ETA of thirty minutes."

"Excellent," he said quietly.

Devon used the ship-wide intercom again to announce, "Ten seconds to ignition."

After a short pause, his pilot counted the final three seconds aloud. At zero, Jack heard the hum of tens of millions of volts coursing through the IPV's powerful ion engines. Barely perceptible, high-frequency vibrations tingled his senses as the ionizing grates charged. He felt the gentle, but building pressure of acceleration push him into his seat. It would take a good minute or two for the engines to reach their full thrust, but he was relieved that at least they were moving. His mind raced again: there was more that needed to be done. He became acutely aware of how little he actually knew of the ship's status, and called into the intercom, "Kurt, respond please."

It took a few seconds before he heard the reply, "Kurt here."

"Do you have a damage report yet?"

"I just completed a walk-through inspection of the ship, and was about to call you. Surprisingly, we're in pretty good shape."

"What do you mean, 'pretty good'?"

"There are no hull breaches, and most ship functions are operating properly. We've just got some minor damage. Basically, anything that was loose got tossed about a bit."

"That's all?" Jack said, realizing only after the fact that he sounded a bit too shocked.

Kurt took it in stride though, saying, "Yeah, that's why I said 'surprisingly.' Anyway, the problem is, we still don't know what happened."

"Can you make any guesses from what you've seen?" Jack allowed Kurt a few seconds to think it over before offering, "What you've said seems consistent with sudden deceleration like from an impact."

"Yes and no. The problem is that the hull shows no damage at all."

Jack replayed the last few seconds before he blacked out in his mind. "What about sudden acceleration?"

"You'd get the same damage I saw, but you'd need something to push...or pull us pretty hard to get that. I don't see what could have. What makes you think that?"

"I vaguely remember being thrown pretty hard into the back of my seat. How about you?"

"I'm not sure. I remember the green light outside. And ... it's pretty fuzzy from there. I think I might have been thrown backwards too. Then nothing else till you woke me. But I'm not sure I'm buying into something suddenly pulling us in toward it. Wait a minute, Maurice's trying to get my attention."

Jack waited a few intolerably long seconds before Kurt's voice came back on the comm., "He says the computer's fully back on line. Give it a try. I'll check back with you later."

Jack disconnected the comm. link and said, "Computer?"

"Yes, Captain?" was the polite reply.

"What information do you have on our current situation?"

"I only have a partial understanding of our status. There is an approximately six-hour gap in my memory records, which is disconcerting."

"Welcome to the club," Jack quipped.

Though the machine's programming allowed it to seem almost human at times, its lack of response told Jack it still didn't understand the irony. He continued, "We'll address that later. Right now the nav-systems are down. Review Devon's logs and see if you can explain the errors he's been getting."

There was a barely noticeable pause before the computer replied, "I am unsure. The most probable answer is that some of the archived data was corrupted."

"What do you mean?"

"The routines that compare the observed star fields with our stored maps are unable to make a match. I've reviewed the performance of the code and it is running a proper comparison of the stored map data with the images from the three external nav cameras. Since its are not getting a match, and the cameras are operating properly, then there must have been some corruption of the archived data."

"How is that possible?"

"I know of no likely cause. I can take some of our astronomical data and re-process it into chart format. It's highly unlikely that it too would have been corrupted."

"Good, proceed."

"It will take a few ..."

The machine's answer was cut off, as Don shouted, "Jack!"

"Just a minute."

"No, I need you to see this now."

He spun around in his chair, and answered with an exasperated, "What?"

"Look up on the main screen."

Jack obliged. A massive, dark globe shrouded in clouds lay before him. Thick bands of steely grays mixed and swirled with adjacent bands of browns and reds, reminding him of Jupiter. But, the colors were wrong. These were dark like smoke, and had an air of in-hospitability about them. He studied the alien world more closely, and was able to make out a couple spots near the northern pole where the atmosphere thinned to a haze. The small breaks in the cloud-cover revealed glimpses of an even more shocking surface. Its dull, blue-gray sheen, was distinctly metallic, and was covered with geometric patterns so detailed his eye couldn't take them all in. Groups of straight, parallel lines ran for hundreds of kilometers before intersecting sets of concentric circles that must themselves have been tens or hundreds of kilometers in diameter. Jack strained his eyes, but was unable to discern any individual structures and assumed they were just too far away to see. It felt as though he was just able to steal a glimpse of some beautifully etched metal sphere. The scene was nothing short of hypnotic and he had to fight to pull his attention away. "Don?" he said softly.

When there was no answer, he turned to the station behind him and saw his science officer transfixed by the image. "Don! What the hell am I looking at?"

"I'm at a loss here."

"That's not an answer." He took a deep breath and said, "That's not Epsilon Eri-D."

"No, it isn't."

"How big is it? Is it one of the large asteroids with a hell of a large colony?"

"I don't think so. My grav readings show it to be larger than E Eri-D by about ten percent."

Jack stared at the man and asked abrasively, "How many Earth-sized planets are there in the E Eri system?"

"Aside from Eri-D, none within thirty percent."

"Since this obviously isn't E Eri-D, explain how it could have been missed?"

Don just stared blankly back at him. Jack continued, "Is there any chance the lunar telescopes or our probes could've missed this?"

"None. They're all quite capable of seeing things down to large asteroids."

"But obviously we did," Jack shot back.

Don looked back down at his workstation. Jack assumed the man was hoping to escape into his data, and decided to let him do so for the moment. The escape was short-lived though, as Don said, "Jack, it gets stranger. Look at this."

On cue, the main display changed. The drab disk was replaced by a sphere awash in brilliant colors. Don said, "This is an infra-red view of the planet. I've used the standard artificial color assignments. Violets and blues are cool regions and reds are hot. Deep violet here represents roughly room temperature at twenty-five degrees C; bright red is about a hundred and eighty degrees, and white is over two hundred."

Jack began to take in the patterns. The planet was evenly peppered with small white circles. Each was surrounded by a thick red region that then faded through shades of orange and yellow. Before most could fade to something close to room-temperature, they butted up against adjacent hot zones. The only area that had a few small regions of blues and violets was the northern polar zone. "It doesn't look very hospitable at all," he said softly.

"No, it doesn't," Don agreed.

"What about those structures we saw in the visible image?"

"It does appear to be technology on a scale we've never imagined, but I can't begin to understand why they'd build it here."

"I'm guessing that the cooler regions here match up with the breaks we saw in the clouds," Jack said. "Can you magnify the image?"

"Not at this distance," Don answered.

The bridge was silent as Jack mulled over the options. He quickly pushed aside his curiosity, as there was a more pressing issue. "There'll be more time for this later. Devon, what's our ETA to the shuttle?"

"About twenty more minutes."

"Don, I need you to get back to determining our position using E Eri-D. Find it, and get the nav-system fully updated. Follow up with the computer's results using the astronomical database. After we get that done, and retrieve the shuttle, we can investigate this place further."

Don answered with a slightly disapproving "OK."

Jack activated the comm. again and said, "Kurt, meet me by the shuttle bay. Helena, meet us there too in case there's a problem." Without another word, he got up and left the bridge.

Chapter 16 – July 17, 2124; 23:30:00

Jack drummed his fingers anxiously against the shuttle bay bulkhead. The IPV had reached the shuttle on schedule, however bringing the unpowered vehicle aboard proved to be a delicate and agonizingly slow task. He watched as Kurt carefully manipulated the IPV's robot arm – he was in the final stages of setting the craft down in the bay. The hatch would be open in only a few more minutes, but Jack was still frustrated by being so close, yet unable to know if they were injured. He turned away for a moment, but quickly peered again through the bulkhead's small window. As before, there was nothing to see: the shuttle's windows were covered by its emergency shielding. Finally, he heard the welcome hum of motors closing the outer doors, followed by a deep, resonating bang as the locks and seals engaged. There was a muted hiss of atmosphere flowing back into the chamber; their eyes, though, were fixed on the door's red hazard indicator.

The hissing softened, then ceased altogether, and the hazard light changed to green with an anticlimactic beep. Jack stepped back as Kurt and Helena pressed through the airlock door. By the time he finally entered, Kurt was already attaching an emergency hand-crank to the shuttle's outer door. Helena, hovered near the cockpit window, repeatedly tapping on the shielding. She paused periodically to bring her ear close to its surface to listen for a response. After her third iteration, she looked up excitedly. "Someone's tapping back!"

Jack felt some tension ease with the statement, and asked, "Kurt, how much longer?"

Kurt answered as he turned the hand-crank, "I should have it open in a minute or so."

The door creaked with each turn, and slowly slid aside, revealing the small airlock within. The inner door was still sealed, but to their relief, they saw Masako's face peering back at them. She gave them a quick wave and then disappeared from view. Barely a second later, the inner door swung open. Palmer exited first, squinting in the brightly lit bay. He didn't have a chance to say a word before Helena took him by the elbow and pulled him aside for a quick examination. Masako then stepped out of the darkened shuttle, and Helena quickly said, "You too, over here."

Jack went to his rescued crewmen. On the surface, at least, they both looked fine. Before he could get a word out though, Masako said, "So guys, what took you so long? We were beginning to wonder if you even missed us."

As they laughed, Jack noted that both were shivering. "So, how're you two holding up?"

Palmer made a deliberate effort to free himself from the doctor's prodding, and answered, "OK, I think. But we were without power for a while – I don't even know how long. Even our emergency battery was off-line. Plus, I think we may have been unconscious."

"I know," Jack answered, "We were too."

Palmer gave him a questioning look, to which Jack replied, "I'll explain in a bit."

"How long were we out of contact?" Masako asked. "From how cold it got, I'd guess at least a few hours."

"More like nine," Jack answered.

"Damn!" Palmer said loudly. "All I remember is some sort of flash of light, then everything went black. What the hell happened?"

"We're not sure yet, but once the Doc here is done checking you out, I'll bring you two up to speed on what we do know."

Jack stood back patiently while Helena finished her cursory examination of Palmer and moved on to Masako. She methodically checked her temperature, blood pressure, and tended to a few scrapes on her forehead.

"So how are the patients?" Jack finally asked.

"Overall, they're in good shape. They're cold, but have no signs of hypothermia. Had they been out there for another few hours, though, we would've had some problems. Aside from that and Masako's scrapes, they're in good health."

"Good, then we're done here," he declared. "Kurt, go over the shuttle with a fine-toothed comb – especially the outer hull since you have easy access to it in here. See if you can piece together what might have happened to it."

"I'll start right away."

"Palmer, Masako, come with me."

The two followed Jack into the hall, where Jack quickly stopped and tapped his comm. unit. "Don, respond please."

"Here Jack."

"Have you made any progress?"

"Still none. How're Palmer and Masako?"

"They're right here beside me: both are fine. I'm going to send Masako straight up to work with you. Bring her up to speed."

"Good. I can use the help."

Jack led the way down the narrow main passage until he reached the conference room near the bridge. "Palmer, we can go over everything in here. Masako, let Don know where he can reach me. Also, tell Devon to hold this position until we get some sort of reliable navigation data."

"What do you mean?"

"Don't worry. Devon'll know what I'm talking about. They'll fill you in on everything up there."

As Masako headed away Jack turned to see Palmer's confused expression. He reached around his first officer to turn on the room's lights and said, "Sit down and I'll tell you what little we know. Who knows, when I'm done, you may wish you were still in that pitch black shuttle."

"That doesn't sound too promising."

Palmer sat motionless for the next hour as Jack explained their situation, describing everything in detail, from the dome on Epsilon Eri-D to the point at which they brought the shuttle into the bay. Palmer probed him politely about the bodies found in the dome, but otherwise didn't interrupt his briefing. His first officer's face said he was taking it all in, but gave no clue as to how he felt. Jack took a breath and was considering whether to ask Palmer directly for his opinion when the computer interrupted.

"Captain?"

"Yes, what is it?"

"We have some very disturbing news. At Don's request, I've asked Kate, Maurice and Masako to join you in the conference room."

"Explain."

"It's based on the data that Maurice and I reviewed with Devon. At my suggestion, Maurice asked Kate to check a problem we encountered. She used an innovative approach that uncovered an unexpected answer. Don and Masako were already coming to the same conclusion when I consulted with..."

"Can please just summarize what you found for me?" Jack pressed.

"Don will be with you in a minute. He asked that he explain it to you. I concur that it would be more appropriate. Also, I think that Kurt and Nadya should join you."

"Fine. Let them know."

When he was sure that the computer was done, Palmer said, "Time for another of Don's presentations."

Jack smiled. It was a rare moment indeed when Palmer made a comment that was even close to humorous. "It would've been nice if he allowed the computer to give us at least a hint of what was coming."

The others filed into the room in silence and filled the remaining seats around the table. Once Don was sure everyone was there, he said, "We're not in the Epsilon Eri system anymore."

As was his custom with important statements, Don paused for dramatic effect. Jack held back his urge to comment on the impossibility of the statement, and Don continued, "I'll start with the most convincing data which comes from the computer's analysis." Don stared off into space for a split second before saying, "Oh and from Maurice too, sorry. They've been working on correlating our stellar observations with data from the astronomical database as opposed to the navigational files. The problem as we all know is that the observed stars didn't match the navigational charts. However, after they converted the astronomical data into nav-format, they didn't match the observations either. That pretty much ruled out file corruption. The computer suggested expanding the comparisons beyond just visual data. That was when Kate was brought in and made a hell of a leap. She suggested looking purely at the radio-spectrum and looking only at pulsars."

Seeing a perplexed look on Kurt's face, Don took a moment to explain. "Pulsars are rapidly rotating neutron stars: the burnt out cores of massive, ancient stars that went super nova eons ago. What remains are ultra-dense, stellar remnants with extremely powerful magnetic fields. As a result, they emit powerful beams of radio waves. When rotating, these beams sweep through space like the light from a lighthouse, we then see them as pulsed radio wave sources.

"What's useful is that the rotational rate for each pulsar is unique. Thus by measuring the amount of time between pulses, we know exactly which one we're looking at. So, Kate's idea was to reconfigure the communications antenna array to look at the thirty strongest ones that we know of. She was still betting on the fact that somehow the visual data in both the astronomical and navigational databases was bad, and that the radio data, being stored in an off-line library would have been unaffected. Though her assumption proved wrong, this method gave us the answer."

Don paused again, prompting Jack to say, "Just tell us what you found!"

Don took a breath and said, "The computer was able to identify all of the targeted pulsars, however, they were in the wrong locations. A few quick simulations showed that you would see these pulsars in their observed locations if we were about three hundred thirty light years away from Epsilon Eri, in the direction of the galactic core."

"What the hell are you talking about?" Jack shouted.

"This is total nonsense," Palmer added.

Don ignored them and typed a few commands into one of the table's embedded terminals. The room went dark, and the holographic display came on line. Evenly spread throughout the room were thirty bright red dots. Don continued, "Since the pulsars are visible primarily in the radio region, I have highlighted them here in red." He entered a few more keys and thirty open green circles appeared. Each circle was near a corresponding pulsar, but ranged from a couple of centimeters to nearly half a meter away. "The green circles represent the expected positions of the pulsars if we were still in the Epsilon Eri system. Now watch."

The room felt as if it was slowly moving as each pulsar moved toward its respective circle. The holographic animation stopped when each was in, or nearly in, one of the circles: the furthest being only a couple centimeters away. "This is our best match. At a little over three hundred thirty light years from our original location, the calculated positions match up pretty nicely with what's observed. We're not quite sure why we don't have a one hundred percent match, but I'm hopeful that we'll have an answer soon."

Palmer jumped in with the first question, "Why couldn't we determine this from looking at the regular stars?"

"For obvious reasons the nav-system uses the brightest visible stars for its comparisons. The distances of these reference stars should range from tens to hundreds of light-years away from our position – whether that be back home or at Epsilon Eri. So, one might surmise that if we move ten light-years one way or ten the other, some will get somewhat dimmer as we move away from them, while others may grow a bit brighter as we move toward them. We can easily compensate for changing magnitudes as long as you stay within a couple dozen light-years of your original charts. However, a jump of over three hundred light-years would make most of our main guide stars appear significantly dimmer and thus unrecognizable by the matching routines. That's what kept the navigation system from properly initializing.

"The pulsars on the other hand, are very bright radio sources, and are between five hundred and two thousand light-years away. As a result, traveling three hundred light-years wouldn't cause as dramatic a shift in their observed position or brightness. Plus, since we were using their timing to identify each one individually, the shifts that did occur in their brightness didn't cause any confusion. That's why it worked."

Palmer continued his challenge, "How can you be so sure of this explanation? Seriously, it flies in the face of reason. Have you checked this against the expected positions of regular visible stars? I mean since you supposedly know where we are now."

Don shot back defensively, "No. That'll take at least a few days to do. First, identifying main-sequence stars will have to be done by matching their spectra against known references. That's not nearly as easy as timing pulsar flashes. Then we'll need to take parallax measurements, which will involve moving the IPV to a few locations in this star system. On top of that..."

"That's enough for now," Jack said, trying to end the argument before it escalated any further. He allowed them a few seconds before continuing, "Don, you said Kate's data was the most convincing. What else do you have?"

In a more measured tone, Don answered, "Earlier you asked me to find our location by looking for Epsilon Eri-D. This, of course, led us to that unknown planet. However, after unsuccessfully scanning the region further for Eri-D, I began to doubt my original assumptions. Basically, I thought that maybe somehow, we were thrown some great distance within the Epsilon Eri system, and began looking for the asteroid belts and the other inner planets. We couldn't find them either. At that point we took things a step further and pointed our instruments at the star itself. It was more for calibration purposes than anything else. However, it was immediately clear that the star isn't the same color as Epsilon Eri. I mean, Epsilon Eri is a K2 star, which is somewhat cooler and oranger than our sun. This star looks like our sun! I took several spectra and have identified it as a G3 star which is just about the same color as the Sun and only a slight bit warmer. Based on that, I knew for a fact that we weren't in the Epsilon Eri system. My method, however, doesn't tell us where we are, whereas Kate's does."

The room stayed silent after Don finished. There wasn't anything to say. Jack looked to Kurt, who was staring at the table and running his hand through his hair. His engineer finally looked up and said, "You'll have to bear with me on this. I'm just an engineer. I know antimatter drives, life support systems, avionics and the sort, but I'm no astrophysicist. So if I understand you right, you've looked at a couple dozen of these pulsars ..."

Don interrupted, "Thirty."

"OK, thirty. And then based on where you see them in the sky, you figured out where we are."

"That's correct."

"No it's not! What you've said is insane. How the hell can we have traveled three hundred thirty light-years in a couple of hours, when it took us over a decade ship-time to go the 10.8 light-years to Epsilon Eri?"

"I didn't say it took a couple of hours."

"So, what's that supposed to mean? Our clocks say only eight or nine hours passed since we flew by those damned rings."

"It's supposed to mean that we experienced only a few hours. Think about it. When we were on the Magellan, due to time dilation, we experienced only ten years pass. Back on Earth, however, over fifteen years passed. I'm just saying that it's not inconceivable that if you could accelerate to hyper-relativistic speeds, you could do such a trip in a few hours of ship-time. Back on Earth, though," Don took a breath and then continued in a much more subdued tone, "three hundred thirty years would still have passed."

Nadya jumped in saying, "The acceleration necessary to do that would be unimaginable. Saying that it would've ripped the ship apart would be a gross understatement."

"Yet we find ourselves looking down on an alien world with a globe-encompassing city," Don replied.

Kurt slapped the table and pushed himself deep into his seat.

"What about a wormhole?"

Jack turned quickly to his left to see that Masako had posed the question. Before Don could answer, Jack intervened. "Let's hold off on any wild guesses for now. Don, you said it would take a few days to confirm our position using normal main-sequence stars."

"Actually, more like two or three days."

"Let's skip doing a full navigational analysis, and assume that the pulsar data is correct. What if we just want to confirm our distance, not validate our complete position and orientation?"

Don stared off into space as he thought it over. Nadya then interjected, "Couldn't we do it basically by just looking for our sun and simply measuring how bright we see it?"

As all eyes in the room shifted to her, she continued, "If we do assume the pulsar data is correct, then we know roughly where we are, and our orientation. That means we would know where to look with the ship's telescopes to see our sun. All we'd need to do then is take its spectra to confirm that whatever we're looking at is the sun, and measure its magnitude. You know, the further you are away from a bright object, the dimmer it appears."

"That would give us independent confirmation," Kurt added.

Don sat silently, staring at his terminal, prompting Jack to ask, "Don, how long would it take to do this?"

"I don't know – maybe a day."

"Good, use whoever you need and get this done asap."

As they started to get up, Palmer called out, "Captain."

Turning to the somber-faced man, Jack replied, "Yes?"

"We do have one fundamental and critical issue to deal with."

Jack nodded his head for him to continue as he sat back down.

"If we're truly three hundred thirty light-years from Epsilon Eri-D and the Magellan, then we've got a critical supply problem."

Jack's stomach dropped as the room fell deathly quiet. Palmer continued, "We only have seven days' worth of rations left on board. The expectation was that we'd routinely restock our supplies from the Magellan until we were self-sufficient on the planet. We need to immediately implement survival protocols. At one-half rations we should be able to stay healthy and extend our supplies to fourteen days."

"Two weeks? What the hell are we supposed to do?" Don shouted.

Palmer stared grimly at Jack. As the cross-conversations in the room grew louder, Jack said, "Quiet down, everyone." Turning back to Palmer, he continued, "What else?"

"We should start trying to put together a plan...hopefully either to make contact with someone on this planet, or at very least go down and scavenge supplies of some sort."

"We'll do both immediately," Jack replied. "Have Kate broadcast messages in all frequencies explaining our situation. If someone's down there, I want them to know we're here and need help. In the meantime, I want a complete inventory of everything on this ship – water, food, fuel, spare parts – everything. Send me the results asap."

"Understood," Palmer replied.

Chapter 17 – July 19, 2124

Kurt allowed himself to relax as he floated by the window in the IPV's observatory. The small room was dark; the only light came from the cloud-enshrouded planet looming outside. Nadya and Claire had just left to prepare their data for the meeting and he welcomed the chance for a bit of solitude. He drifted closer to the floor-to-ceiling window until his face was barely a few centimeters from the glass, making it easy to forget the IPV's cramped quarters. With only the planet and open space in front of him, he felt a sense of freedom that he missed dearly. "Computer," he said softly.

"Yes Lieutenant Commander."

"Can you pipe some music in here?"

"What would you like?"

"Mozart...something not too loud."

The opening strains of a violin concerto drifted through the air, tempting Kurt to close his eyes. Exhaustion weighed him down. He couldn't remember when he last slept – not counting the time they were unconscious, it had to be at least two days. The image outside though forced his eyes to remain open. They had entered orbit uneventfully earlier in the day, and the mysterious planet now filled his entire field of view. Its alternating bands of muted red, grey and brown clouds formed a hypnotic pattern. Scattered along each band's edges were large cyclones that seemed to be gently blending the bands into a bland, neutral gray mass. He imagined that over time, the entire atmosphere would be converted into that same, drab hue.

Their orbit carried them over one of the few breaks in the cloud-cover. The dark, metal surface made it look as if he were gazing down upon some intricate piece of machinery. In the fading light of sunset, Kurt strained hard to take in all of the details of the enigmatic city. He imagined the parallel lines to be roadways or transport tracks. They were bordered by countless rectangular and oval structures, each with progressively more complex patterns engraved within them. The structures must surely have soared above the planet's surface, but from his orbital vantage point, he was unable to venture even a guess as to their true dimensions.

The music reached a crescendo, driving his imagination to explore what the planet must have been like before it succumbed to whatever forces ravaged it. He could see a world populated by tens of billions, and assumed it to be a utopia. Any civilization that reached this pinnacle of development must have solved the more mundane woes of social inequities and basic survival. It would be a race who's only remaining mission was to explore the sciences and arts, expanding their own minds and understanding without even a hint of violence. It was something he would never have dreamt of without having seen it. But it was this same sight of an abandoned, ruined world that spoke against this. All of the IPV's observations and their failed attempts at communications confirmed that it was indeed a dead planet. Something did this, and it wasn't a natural event.

They crossed into the night-side, and Kurt lost his view of the city to darkness. On Earth, any metropolis seen just after sunset would have been ablaze with lights. He remembered looking down on the east coast of the United States, and marveling at how the lights of that urban expanse clearly outlined every intricate detail of the Atlantic coast. The receding city below, was pitch black.

They traveled deeper into the night and all that remained of his view was a ghostly, jet black disk that blotted out the surrounding stars. The darkness was interrupted only by the sporadic flashes of lightening deep within the clouds below. The fleeting blue-white bolts gave off barely enough light to make their presence known, and provided only the briefest of glimpses of the surrounding clouds.

His attention drifted away from the darkened globe as his mind focused on the stars. At three hundred thirty light-years distant, the Sun was far too dim to make out. That thought alone made their isolation disturbingly apparent and shook him free from his trance. He was aware again of the music and listened as a violin sang its melody against the chorus of a subdued orchestra. The piece was already in its final movement: nearly half an hour had passed.

"Computer," he called out quickly, "time please?"

"Ten-forty-two."

"Damn it, the meeting! End music please." He opened the door and pushed his way into the corridor. His mind raced ahead as he tried to collect his thoughts and focus on the status reports he needed to present. But he couldn't. He knew something big was going to happen. Nadya had hinted that she'd found something but wasn't letting him in on it. All he knew was that she was pissed as hell when Don assigned the most mundane tasks he could find, to her and Claire: they had to double-check the unexplained errors in the pulsar data and see if there was any correlation between them. As far as she saw it, it was just grunt work. Kurt wasn't sure if it was payback for something or a typical Don-oversight. The man was a bit egotistical, but he was also more oblivious to conflicts than vengeful. By morning, however, Nadya's anger was gone and all she and Claire would say was, "Wait and you'll see at the meeting." He had even tried pressing Nadya into giving up her secret, but she ended the conversation quickly by giving him a disarming kiss and telling him with a mischievous smile, "You'll have to wait like everyone else."

Kurt turned the final corner and entered the crowded room; it seemed that most of the crew was already there. The eight seats around the table were long since taken, so he made his way over to an empty corner near the back. He looked to Nadya, but she and Claire were completely engrossed in their work at a terminal and didn't notice him.

At exactly ten-forty-five Jack rose from his seat and said, "OK everyone, let's quiet down and get started." The conversations quickly ceased, and Jack continued, "Don, do you want to start?"

Kurt watched Don nod in acknowledgement and begin, "We completed a map of the immediate vicinity, and confirmed what Devon's nav-data first suggested. There are two gravitational anomalies in relatively close proximity to this planet. Telescopic views show each to be composed of a group of three rings, identical in size and mass to the objects we encountered back around Epsilon Eri-D." He quickly tapped a button on his console, and a small, gray-banded, softball-sized globe appeared above the table. Two tiny, bright red circles hovered at opposite ends of the table, equidistant from the globe. "As you can see, the objects are located roughly a million kilometers from the planet, in opposing, balancing positions. We still don't know what these things are, but it's not a big leap to assume that they're associated with how we got here."

The room grew loud with discussions before Kurt called out loudly, "You say that like you've confirmed where we are?"

The conversations quieted down as Don turned thoughtfully toward him and answered, "Yes, maybe I should've started with that info. Anyway as we discussed yesterday, we needed independent verification of our distance from Earth. We located the sun, verified it with its recorded spectrum in our database, and then calculated our distance based on its brightness. We are currently about three hundred and thirty-five light-years from Earth."

Don paused a moment, but this time no one questioned him. He entered another command at his console; the holographic map disappeared and the three large monitors around the room displayed a set of numbers. "The sun is located at these coordinates. We then took the following spectra and compared it against the reference data." The monitors obediently showed two side-by-side graphs of jagged, peaked lines. As expected, they were identical. "They are from the same star – our sun. I would put the chance of error in our conclusion at less than one in a hundred thousand."

"Three hundred and thirty-five light-years," Jack repeated. "And we still have no idea how we got here."

"No. Just that we encountered these...these objects around both Epsilon Eri-D and here. There's no evidence, no scientific basis to believe that they're connected with this, but I just think that they are; it's too coincidental. We need to put some real effort into studying them."

Jack continued, "We'll get to that. Now, what about the errors with the pulsar data?"

"We haven't made any headway on that front."

Nadya quickly cut in, "Actually, we have."

Jack and Don turned to face her. Kurt wasn't sure who moved more quickly.

"What do you mean, *we have?*" Don asked with an edge.

"Early this morning Claire and I made a breakthrough with the data."

"I haven't seen this..."

Jack cut him off, saying, "Let's hear what you've found,"

"But I haven't reviewed it yet," Don protested.

"I want to see it now. We can review it here together."

With Jack's nod to her, Nadya stood up with a slight smile on her face. "First, let me be clear, we've reviewed and re-run these results a half-dozen times already, so I'm quite sure we've ruled out any obvious errors with what we're about to see. But, I think that everyone has to scrutinize this further because we're still having trouble accepting it ourselves. We'll start by displaying a holographic animation that shows how we arrived at our initial results with the pulsar data. The second part will illustrate our new interpretation."

The room went dark. Scattered around them were the red points they had used before to identify the pulsars' positions, as well as the green rings representing their predicted positions. Nadya began, "As you can see, this is the same data Don showed last time. The pulsars are pretty close to their predicted positions, but it's obviously not an exact match. We then thought a bit about Don's suggestion of hyper-relativistic travel – travel so close to the speed of light that our internal clocks would be nearly stopped. As we all know, however, the stars outside would still have continued moving and interacting according to time in their own reference frame. Basically, three hundred thirty-five years would pass out there. If this was the case, then over the course of those centuries, the stars themselves will have moved with respect to each other."

"Of course," Don said loudly, "I should've seen that."

"Don't worry Don," Nadya answered in a conciliatory tone, "we were sure that that was the case too, but it turned out not to be the exact answer. Let me show you." She pressed a key on her console, and the stars around them began to drift. "Right now we are looking at how the pulsars would have moved if we progressed from the year 2100 to 2400." It quickly became apparent that they were going the wrong way. Without exception, every red pulsar moved away from its corresponding green ring. As the animation finished, Nadya continued, "To say the least, this was disappointing. We were positive that we were on the right track, so we worked through the night refining and re-running the simulation until there were no more adjustments that could be done.

"Then, as we stared at it, we noticed an odd coincidence: When we ran the simulation, every pulsar exactly doubled its distance from its predicted position. I don't believe in coincidences. So we ran the simulation in reverse."

The stars began to drift again. This time, however, each moved towards its respective green ring. The displays lining the walls around the room showed the years marching backwards: 2050, 2000, 1950, 1900...until they finally stopped at 1790. Every pulsar was perfectly centered in its corresponding ring. The room dissolved into pandemonium as nearly every voice shouted for Nadya's attention. The voices ebbed slightly so that Kurt could just make out her shouts over the din.

"Quiet! Please quiet down! I think we can answer some of your questions if you let us outline some of the details for you."

The noise began to subside, but not enough to satisfy her. "Come on! Give me a few minutes here. We'll get to your questions one at a time." When the voices calmed to a hushed murmur, she continued, "First, let me assure you that the results in this simulation are real. The speed that each of the pulsars is moving through the interstellar medium is well documented. We simply pulled that information from the ship's library files and calculated their locations backwards from there. And yes, we triple-checked for the obvious possibility of a sign error – there is no chance that we got our equations backwards."

Nadya continued with her technical review of their findings, but Kurt's mind drifted. He knew the whole thing was impossible, but deep down inside, part of him couldn't help but dwell on the possibility that this was for real: they had actually traveled back some three-plus centuries in time. He couldn't resist the temptation to go a step further and dream about what it meant. The American Revolution would have ended just a few years ago, and the French Revolution would be just getting underway. At this very moment Louis XVI could be marching to the guillotine. What he wouldn't give to actually see these events himself – could he? Reason tried to creep back into his mind as he thought, "Can this be for real?" He ignored that small voice, and thought about the violin concerto he'd just heard: had it even been written yet? A moment's calculation in his head told him it had, though it would only be about twenty years old. Just the possibility of listening to something that hadn't yet been written shattered his day dream. The paradox unnerved him at a most basic level. Morbid curiosity though drove his subconscious further: People who had been dead for centuries were now alive. Others who had dramatically affected his own history hadn't even been born yet. It was insane!

Kurt tried to rescue himself from this vicious circle of speculation by focusing on the meeting. Don was questioning Nadya on possible errors. The conversation was too dry though, considering the meaning of it all and he gave up on it. A quick look around the room showed that most of the crew appeared as distracted and oblivious to the continuing dialogue as he. The urge to continue speculating about the possibilities of time travel returned, but he resisted. In the end there would have to be some reasonable explanation for all of this. Instead he glanced at a clock on the wall: Nearly twenty minutes had passed. To his relief Jack stood up and brought the discussion to an end. "OK, let's take a break from this right here," Jack said calmly. "Nadya, I trust your work, but I honestly don't know what to make of it right now. To say the least, we have a lot to do to understand your results. But despite the temptation – and believe me, I'm tempted – we will save any further detailed review and analysis for later on. The only thing I can say for sure is that it doesn't change our current situation with regard to our survival. Since that is paramount, we're going to continue at this point with reports on our current status. Once this is done, we'll look at assigning tasks related to our survival. After that, and only after that, will we be able to take the time to try and understand where we are and what's happened. Is that understood?"

The hushed murmur of cross-conversations ceased completely as Jack waited for his statement to sink in. The ensuing silence was the response he wanted. "Good. Palmer, please proceed."

"Thank you, sir," the first officer said, his voice showing no emotion. "The doctor and I completed a full review of our current food reserves and our nutritional needs. As of this point we will be reducing daily rations to thirty-five percent." The noise of hushed conversations picked up again, but Palmer continued loudly over it, "We will be preparing a nutritional supplement to accompany this. It will be in pill form, but it should make up the difference in terms of necessary vitamins, minerals and other nutrients. I expect that all of us will feel some discomfort from this during the first few days until our bodies adjust. Keep in mind that we have very few options and this is necessary. Also, we will be suspending the standard exercise regimen. That means that I don't want people wasting energy on unnecessary physical activity. Following these protocols should extend our supplies to about twenty days. We will review this again in a week.

"Next is fuel. Nadya, you told me earlier that fuel reserves for the ion engines are at seventy-five percent, right?"

"Yes. Pierre checked the xenon propellant levels and they're at seventy-five percent of capacity. The reactor, of course, is not an issue. We'll have enough power for all ship-board systems and engines for the next several months."

"What does this mean in terms of the distances we can travel?" Palmer asked.

"We can make a couple of trips between the inner planets of the star-system before we run out."

"So you're saying, we're stuck unless we can use whatever sent us here to send us back," Don declared.

"You know that'd be the case even if our propellant was at a full hundred percent," Nadya shot back. "The ion engines simply aren't capable of getting us to the speeds we need for interstellar travel. The IPV's top speed is only one percent of the speed of light – that means it'd take us better than thirty thousand years to get back. What I'm saying is that to conserve what propellant we have, we should pick our trips within the star system carefully. It'd be real easy to run out within a week or two's time."

Palmer nodded in acknowledgement, and then turned to stare straight at Kurt. "Hoffman, what's the status of our other expendables?"

Though caught off guard by the question, Kurt recovered quickly. "Normally I'd be concerned about the chemicals we use for carbon dioxide scrubbing, and water and biomass recycling. However, our stores of all of these will easily outlast our twenty-day food supply. So, in short, we've got adequate stocks of these."

"Good," Palmer replied tersely.

Kurt watched as Palmer leaned over to Jack to say something. Jack then stood up and said, "OK, since there're no surprises with our supply situation, then I'm going to lay out how we're going to proceed from here. As I mentioned, right now I want all efforts focused on our survival. To this end, I'm going to divide you up into three groups. You will receive your assignments from your group leader. I expect them to be carried out with the greatest possible expediency.

"The first group will focus on analyzing the damage we sustained. In short, we're going to go under the assumption that the rings are what sent us here. As a result, we will need to develop a way to better protect ourselves should we have to go through one of those again. Kurt, you'll head up that group."

Kurt did his best to hide his surprise at the sudden assignment as he said, "I'll do my best."

Jack shot him a quick smile that said he saw through his guise of preparedness, before continuing, "The second group will be focusing on reconnaissance and possible salvage missions. After a day and a half of scans and unanswered attempts at communications, we will proceed under the assumption that there is no one alive down there. So to be clear, we will be looking at possible salvage sites. Unlike Epsilon Eri-D, though, my guess is that this place was inhabited until recently, so I am holding out hope that we will be able to find something. I will be leading this group. I know many of you will, by nature, be interested in doing a lot more than just scavenging for supplies. But, let me be clear, anything we learn will be useless if we die out here. So, this is first and fore-most a salvage mission.

"The third group will study the devices themselves. As Don stated, initial observations show them to be identical in size, shape and mass to the one observed around E Eri-D. We're going to need to find out very quickly how these things work. Our only hope at this point is that they are linked with how we got here, and that somehow we can use one to get back to E Eri-D. Commander Palmer will be leading this group.

"You will all be getting your group assignments within the next couple of hours. In the meantime, I want you to wrap up whatever projects you're currently working on. Obviously, what I've just outlined will supersede all other duty assignments."

Before anyone had time to react, Jack continued, "One last thing: I want you all to know that I have complete confidence that we will get through this. You know me well, so you know that I wouldn't say this unless I believed it. Let's stay focused."

Kurt surveyed the faces in the room as Jack paused to scan the room himself. All eyes were focused on the captain, all but Don who was fidgeting with a hand-held computer. Jack's voiced carried over the growing murmur as he said, "OK everyone, let's get to work."

The room slowly emptied in a stunned, almost orderly manner. Kurt stayed back, looked for Nadya, and spotted her just as she caught sight of him. He glided over to her and asked sarcastically, "So that was your little surprise?"

She only smiled in response.

"And you couldn't tell me in advance?" he pressed with mock indignation.

"I knew if I told you, then within an hour you and your buddy Jack there would be discussing it. It would only be a matter of time after that before Don got wind of it and spoiled everything. Call me selfish, but it was our discovery, and we wanted to take it through to the end ourselves."

"Well, you could've told me and asked me to keep it secret."

"Would you have?"

Kurt's hesitation in answering was enough of a response for her. She continued, "Anyway, I need to get down to propulsion. Meet you back in the cabin in an hour."

"Sounds good," Kurt replied. "See you then."

Chapter 18 – July 22, 2124

Jack settled into the shuttle's co-pilot seat and felt a dose of adrenalin rush through his veins. The anticipation was undeniable: They were about to land in a city that spanned an entire globe. He labored to suppress his feelings, though, and concentrated on the tasks at hand. This was nothing more than a desperate salvage mission – there was no place for excitement. Turning to Devon, he said coolly, "Let's get started." His pilot answered with a nod, and powered up the engines.

It had taken three, long days to find a location hospitable enough for a landing attempt. Most of the planet appeared to be little more than a furnace lashed by winds exceeding the strongest of hurricanes. Mammoth blazes burned at the dozens of impact points evenly spaced around the globe. They would likely smolder for years to come, further heating the blistering gasses that passed for its atmosphere. Don's analysis suggested that the attack occurred within the last two or three months, likely with antimatter bombs having yields in the millions of megatons. There was no way to tell who did this. However, their goal was painfully obvious: total annihilation.

Their landing area was in the North Polar zone – a region that showed little obvious damage. Considering the thoroughness of the devastation, Jack was unsettled by the fact that this convenient little area was left intact. His gut told him not to trust it, but they'd already consumed over fifteen percent of their supplies and hadn't made any progress on understanding how to get home. There was no choice. At least the knowable risks were minimal. The landing zone's temperature was a tolerable forty degrees Celsius – the temperature of a hot summer day back at the old Johnson Space Center. The winds were much calmer too, but still blew at gale force.

The shuttle bay door slowly slid aside, revealing the expansive cloud covered globe. Directly below lay a large cyclone ripping at the surrounding cloud bands. Even from orbit he could see movement as streams of clouds slowly spiraled into the vortex. Devon touched the controls and they glided toward the storm. A moment later he banked the craft left, and the polar gap in the clouds shifted into view. Though partially obscured by a persistent haze, Jack could already make out the features he'd studied in earlier reconnaissance images; far below lay row after row of identical, dull metallic domes. At this altitude they looked like inverted dimples, belying the fact that each dimple rose nearly two kilometers above the surface. The artificial landscape was the same pewter hue he'd seen in other photos.

As the shuttle descended toward their target, Jack focused on the individual domes. Their surfaces were smooth, and lacked the finely etched details seen elsewhere. Each one's downward slope butted up against the rise of its neighbor, yielding a surreal, grid-like panorama of uniform hills and cusped valleys. The low angle of the sun, reflected gently off the top of each row, and cast long, arcing shadows across each adjoining row. Devon banked right to follow a trench formed by adjacent lines of domes. The shuttle was low enough now that the domes were large, dominant structures that passed quickly beneath them. The repetitive rise and fall of their smooth, metal surfaces was hypnotic, and fooled his mind into thinking that he was skimming just above waves of some steely sea. There was no frame of reference, no way to objectively tell how high they really were. Jack was surprised when a quick glance at the altimeter told him they were still more than five kilometers above the peaks.

He gazed ahead past the monotone progression, toward the horizon. There, the drab, metallic surface arced gently against the pale, orange sky. Its innocuous color and clear air hid the menacing nature of the gasses that surrounded them: The poisonous mixture would kill as quickly as the vacuum of space. Don couldn't say for sure whether the air had been breathable before the attack, however the planet-wide fires now filled it with an endless collection of toxins.

"What's our ETA to the landing site?" Jack asked, more as an attempt to pull his attention away from the mesmerizing view, than to actually obtain an answer.

"Two minutes," Devon answered curtly, focusing his attention instead on the shuttle's instruments.

Jack strained his eyes as he stared at the horizon, and was just able to pick out a distant, vertical line rising above the endless sea of domes. This was their destination. As they closed on it, it transformed from a near dimensionless line, to a majestic spire, towering some thirty kilometers above the surface. Its square base was more than twice the size of the adjacent domes, but tapered quickly to a thin, sharp spear that stood centered above the planet's North Pole. The graceful form brought to mind images of the Eiffel tower. The alien spire, however, was solid and devoid of any decoration or feature. The crew had debated its purpose, but came up with little more than fanciful speculation. His favorite was Don's idea that the spire worked in conjunction with the planet's magnetic field to harvest energy from the central star's solar wind. It would yield vast amounts of energy, but this was all little more than guess-work.

Devon slowed their approach at a kilometer's distance, and circled the dominating structure. As they glided around to the far side, Jack caught sight of their landing zone: a large, oval platform about a quarter of the way up the tower. It was a few hundred meters long and extended nearly a hundred meters out from the sloping wall. Centered against the spire was a tall, recessed, arched entry way. The shuttle descended slowly and shuddered as it was buttressed by the gale outside. Jack looked past the blowing clouds of dust, and estimated that they were about fifty meters from the entrance when he finally felt the firm bump of the landing pads making contact with the ground.

"We're down. I'm shutting off main engines," Devon announced.

The hum of the thrusters died out, allowing the whine of the winds outside to fill the cabin. Jack drew a breath and opened his mouth to say something, but nothing worthwhile came to mind. Instead, they sat in silence, listening to the ebb and flow of the powerful gusts. Devon typed a few commands into his console and read off the results, "Winds are blowing at ninety k-p-h, with gusts up to...about a hundred and twenty. External temperature is forty-three degrees Celsius."

Jack turned around to look at the other two members of his expedition team. Kate, the communications engineer who doubled as a linguist, sat expressionless. Alex, on the other hand was glued to the port window. They were friends long enough for Jack to know there was no taming his raw enthusiasm. The man was brilliant, but didn't seem to have a grasp on how desperate their situation really was. Catching sight of Jack's gaze, Alex quipped, "Well, are we going to sit here all day or what?"

There was no proper answer. If it wasn't for the fact that he needed Alex's skills as an exobiologist, he would have left him back aboard the IPV. "OK, listen up. I know we've gone over this before, but it bears repeating.

This environment is as hostile as open space. You must at all costs protect the integrity of your suits. If your suit is compromised, the toxins out there will kill you. So once we get into the building, assuming that we do, be very careful about jagged edges and other sharp objects. Is that understood?"

He waited until he was answered with a series of muted OK's, and then continued, "Alright then. Let's suit up."

The cramped environs of the shuttle became even more crowded as they struggled with their suits. Devon's elbow glanced off of Jack's jaw, prompting him to think that maybe jamming four people into a three-person shuttle wasn't such a good idea. However, time wasn't on their side, and he needed every one of them on this landing in order to accomplish what he wanted. As he snapped the seal on his helmet shut, Devon's voice came in over his suit radio, "My air supply and comm. equipment check. Jack, turn around, and I'll check the hoses on your environmental pack."

He obliged, and after getting confirmation that it was ok, double checked Devon's. It took a moment longer until Alex and Kate confirmed they were ready. "I'll exit first," Jack said. Squeezing past the others, he slid into the small airlock, drew a deep breath, and closed the inner door behind him. A soft warning tone buzzed when he pressed the "Open" button on the outer hatch. The door quickly slid aside, and he was instantly stunned by the din. The roar of the wind shook his body, and was accompanied by a steady shriek as the gale whipped past the ship. He stepped down onto the landing platform, and barely kept his footing as a gust shoved him up against the side of the shuttle. There was a crackling sound that he quickly realized was sand and dust lashing his suit. The immense tower stood in front of him; its broad, sloping walls curved upward and converged into a spire that faded away into the dusty, orange sky. He stared in awe until a voice in his helmet caught his attention, "...outside. Are conditions safe for..."

It was Devon, but the waves of wind and sand drowned out the message. Jack shouted in response, "You're going to have to speak up. I can barely hear you."

"Is it safe for us to proceed?"

"Yes, but be careful." He leaned into the wind to keep his balance as he took a few steps and surveyed the surrounding terrain. The dark-gray, metal platform was devoid of any markings. The fact that it sat above the surrounding structures, though, afforded him an uninterrupted view of the endless rows of domes stretching toward the orange horizon. Despite the violent weather and attacks, the pad's surface was smooth. Surreal ripples of dust and sand danced across it, their reflections following in the lightly polished finish. His eye, though, was drawn back to the mammoth, tapered structure before him. Broader than the platform, the tower stretched for a kilometer to either side. In front of him was a peaked arch of polished metal standing nearly three stories high, and framing two, heavy black doors. It had the feel of a medieval cathedral's entrance, or at least a modern variant on one.

"Damn it's loud out here!" Alex shouted with a voice loud enough to make Jack cringe. He turned to see the scientist walking toward him. Behind him, Devon was helping Kate out of the airlock. "What've you found so far?" Alex asked as he reached Jack.

"Nothing that I can make any sense of. Let's just proceed slowly." He fought against the wind with each step, stopping a couple meters short of the entryway's threshold. There were no handles or obvious buttons. "Fan out and see if you can find any controls."

Jack stepped forward and ran his hand along the metal frame. Its burnished surface was perfectly smooth and devoid of even the smallest scratch or imperfection. He brought his face close to scrutinize it, but instead found himself staring at his helmeted reflection. As with the rest of the structure, there were no markings. He stepped back to examine the doors, but the featureless, black forms told him nothing. Their sheen made it difficult to focus on them, and instead he caught himself gazing more at the reflection of his beige, environmental suit, than at anything else. "Alex," he called out.

"I haven't found anything yet," was the response.

"I didn't expect you or anyone to. Go back to the shuttle and get some equipment: hand-held radar, ultra-sound, anything you think'll let us get a glimpse of what's behind this."

"OK. Be back in a minute."

"Devon, go with him. Get the torch and some explosives."

"Explosives?" Alex protested.

"Yes. We don't have time to fool around here. We need to get in, one way or another."

"I still think that's a little extreme," Alex pressed.

There was no time for debate. Jack opened his mouth to chastise the man, but thought better of it. "Please, just do what I asked."

There was no further deliberation as the two men made their way back to the craft. Jack looked to Kate, who was examining the area around the entrance through a hand-held, wide-spectrum viewer, and asked, "Find anything?"

"I've scanned across the UV and near-infrared but don't..."

A powerful gust and its accompanying a spray of sand drowned her response. He waited for the din to subside before calling back, "Say again. I can't hear you."

Kate's shouts were barely audible over the tempest. "As far as I can tell, there are no external markings."

Frustrated, Jack walked back to within arm's reach of the doors. Reaching out hesitantly, he ran his fore-finger along the seam where the doors met, but didn't feel anything. They were sealed so perfectly that it might as well have been a line painted on a single, solid surface.

Alex tapped him on the shoulder. "Want me to start there?" he asked, gesturing toward the seam with the ultra-sound sensor.

Jack just nodded and stepped out of the way. "Devon, besides the torch, what were you able to get?"

"Half a dozen shape-charges with RF triggers – each has got a two-hundred-pound yield, so I don't think we'll need more than one or two."

"I wouldn't bet on that. If it's anything..."

"Jack, I've got something!" Alex called.

"What?"

"The readings are noisy, but I'd say the doors are only ten centimeters thick. After that, there's a void. I'm not getting anything else on what's inside. But at very least it means there's a hallway or room in there."

"That's about what I expected." He didn't need to say anything else. Devon quickly moved into position with a torch and set to work. He watched intently, but couldn't tell if any progress was being made. After about a minute, the blue glow from the torch faded, and his pilot took a moment to examine his work before standing up. When nothing was said, Jack asked, "Any luck?"

"It didn't even mar the surface..."

Jack quickly cut in, "Don't worry, this wasn't unexpected. That's why we've got the explosives. I'm going to use them all on the seam."

"All of them?" Alex's interjected.

"Yes, all of them. I think it's relatively safe to assume that this is the same stuff we encountered on the asteroid. I'm not even sure the twelve-hundred-pound yield of the charges will crack this thing. But it's all we've got. How about those readings you were taking – did you find any weak spots, besides the void behind the door?"

"No, it all looks the same – at least as best as I can tell. It's so dense that I'm not getting a very clear signal. I guess it makes the most sense just to go with the seam."

Jack took a black, metal, storage case from Devon, knelt down by the base of the door and opened it. Inside, six, grey, hemispherical charges the size of softballs were set in protective white foam. Though unarmed, he exercised care as he pulled them out and affixed them one by one, in a straight line along the bottom portion of the seam. "I want you all to take up positions along the wall, outside of the arch. The charges will detonate inward, but I don't want any injuries from flying debris. In fact, make sure you're at least twenty or thirty meters away from the arch itself."

Jack tapped a button at the top of each charge, activating their small green ready lights. His doubts about their possible success were growing, but he had to try. Taking a deep breath, he stepped back and surveyed the area one more time: Devon and Alex were standing off to the left of the archway, Kate was waiting for him several meters away on the opposite side. He strode at a measured pace against the wind toward her, and pressed a button on his small handheld controller. A synthesized voice in his helmet announced, "Explosives armed."

"Devon, Alex, move a little further away, and face the wall," he called as he took his own position against the structure. Once he was sure the others were clear, he called out, "Detonation in five...four...three...two...one..." He pressed the "detonate" button, and the landscape was instantly bathed in a flash of brilliant, blue-white light. The sharp, crack of the explosion overwhelmed the roar of the wind, and forced him to turn away. The echoes of the blast dissipated quickly, allowing the omnipresent sound of the wind to return. He looked to Kate and opened his mouth to speak, but his helmet was suddenly filled with an ear-splitting shriek. He couldn't tell who it was, but Kate's look of dismay told him it wasn't her. The scream was replaced by two distinct voices: one grunting under duress, and the other making the unmistakable sounds of gasping for breath.

Jack spun away from the wall too quickly, and was knocked to the ground by the wind. "Devon, Alex, report!" There was no verbal response. He scanned the platform for them as he got back to his feet, but his view was obscured by clouds of mustard yellow smoke pouring from a break in the doors. The high winds caught the plume and blew it away from him, forming a steady stream of yellow gas that rushed past Devon's and Alex's position. He steered clear of the smoke, and finally spotted two figures — one dragging the other out onto the platform.

"Devon?"

"Here, sir! Alex is hurt bad."

As Jack ran toward them, the gasping ceased. Devon was crouching over the other man, turned to look Jack in the eye, but said nothing.

Jack pushed him aside in disbelief. Alex's motionless form lay there, his lifeless eyes staring straight back at him through his helmet. The numbness of shock washed over him, as he looked upon the frozen expression of pain on his friend's face. His stomach churned and he tried to turn away, but the effort was futile. He only managed to divert his attention slightly and saw that something had burnt away whole sections of Alex's suit. His singed right shoulder was fully exposed to the noxious fumes outside. There were similar burns and breaches all along his right side. The numbness gave way to a burning rage. He swung around to face the structure and its continuing stream of smoke. His fists were clenched to the point of pain. He wanted to do something, throw something, anything to release his wrath, but there was nothing he could do.

Kate stared blankly at him from a few meters away – it was as close as she dare come. Devon walked over to face him and said something that was rendered unintelligible by a gust of wind and sand. Jack didn't care and just stared back at the billowing yellow smoke. As he took a single step toward it, Devon repeated himself more loudly, "Sir! I think that gas did this."

Devon pointed to charring on his own suit. "When the charges blew, I immediately looked back at the doors and saw the cloud coming toward us. It was reflex, but I just dove out of the way. It barely clipped me, but hit Alex head-on. If I'd..."

"Stop!" Jack said with all of the force he could muster. "Get back to the shuttle and out of that suit now! If it's been compromised, then it could breach any minute. I'm not losing anyone else."

Devon took a couple hesitant steps away, prompting Jack to shout, "Move it!" His pilot's attempt at self-blame only amplified his own feelings of guilt. He himself had set the charges and detonated them.

"Jack," Kate called.

He took a deep breath before turning and nodding for her to continue.

"I don't think we want that suit in the shuttle. If that stuff can burn through composite-reinforced Kevlar, then we don't want even a trace of it in our breathable air."

She was right. "Devon, do as Kate said. Follow full decontamination procedures when you're-board. Stow it in a hazard container."

"Understood."

He looked back at the Arch. The charges had ripped open a jagged, two-meter wide hole, though there was no way to tell where it led. The yellow gas continued pouring out and showed no signs of letting up; it just streamed off into the distance, guided by the howling winds around them. Turning to face Alex's body again shined a spotlight on his error: they should have been upwind of the blast like he was. He should've ordered them there, instead of just telling them to move further away. Replaying it again and again in his mind, he vainly looked for some way to change what had happened. Part of him was honest enough, though, to realize there was no way to foresee this; and no matter how many times he walked through it, he would have made the same decisions. Right now, he loathed that part of himself.

"Sir?"

It was Kate. "Continue."

"It might be prudent to head back."

"I know."

"Captain?" This time it was Devon's voice on the comm. link.

"Go ahead."

"I suggest you take the same precautions with Alex's body as with the suits."

"I know!" He didn't need to be reminded of what he had to do. "We're on our way."

Chapter 19 – July 23, 2124

Kurt sat alone at his table in the small mess hall, staring at his breakfast. It was tough enough under normal circumstances to enjoy reconstituted scrambled eggs; but now, despite his persistent hunger, he actually had to force himself to eat. His first bite of the bland meal brought on an urge to throw the rest out. Their current rationing, however, prohibited that.

He drew a deep breath and poked at his meal before taking another bite. He knew his disgust had nothing to do with the eggs; he just had no desire to eat. An all-encompassing fatigue weighed on him. His head and eyes ached from exhaustion. All he wanted was a good, long night's sleep – a chance for his mind to let go of everything and relax. There was no time for that, though. He didn't even have time to collect his thoughts and approach his work methodically – time that he desperately needed. Jack had made it clear that the damage report needed to be finished within the day. After that he still had to come up with a way to protect the ship, should they have to go through another one of those devices. The problem was, he hated being pressured. It made him feel like he was being manipulated. He was well aware of their situation and didn't need anyone, especially Jack, spelling it out for him. Anger grew easily from his exhaustion, and his thoughts of Alex's death only fueled it further. The fact that their friend died so pointlessly was too much. He pushed himself back from the table and tried to regain control of his thoughts. The work he had just been dreading offered him his only escape. Immersing himself in damage and structural analyses would force everything else from his mind. The tension started to ebb as he glanced at his watch: He had to be back in engineering in fifteen minutes. "I guess Nadya'll eat alone later," he said softly to himself. As he took another bite, he felt a tap on his shoulder and found his wife standing behind him. "So, you did make it," he said.

Nadya gently rubbed his shoulders and asked, "You OK?"

"I don't know. I mean it just doesn't feel like any of this is real. Now

Alex on top of this…"

"I know," she answered softly.

"I just can't believe he's dead. Who would do that…fill an entire building with that stuff?"

"I don't know," Nadya said as she kissed the top of his head. "I don't know."

"It doesn't make any sense."

"Jack seems to think whoever attacked this planet used it to kill off any survivors from the initial attack."

"Why?" he asked, knowing she didn't have any answers.

Nadya just rubbed his shoulders again as the paradox ate at him: he needed to know what was going on, but didn't want to think about any of it anymore. His mind struggled to find anything else on which to focus. Finally, latching on the mundane, he asked, "Anyway, what happened? I thought you'd get back here before me?"

"Don and I got tied up reviewing some of the data. It looks like we came up with an idea."

Kurt looked up, pushed out a chair for her to sit down and said, "Tell me about it."

"Actually, there's no time to eat right now. We need your help."

Kurt had no objection to putting the rest of his breakfast away for later. "What do you need?"

She led the way out the door. "Well, let's just say it's a little unconventional. Anyway, I'll let Don explain it since it's mostly his idea."

Don was waiting for them in one of the IPV's small labs. Kurt gave him a quick "Hi." Don responded with a polite nod, and asked, "Has Nadya explained what we're trying to do?"

"Not yet."

"OK, well we've finished our analysis and have confirmed that we are indeed three hundred thirty-five light-years from Earth. With respect to a time measurement, we can't be quite so precise. Basically, our knowledge of interstellar drift velocities isn't that accurate. We have, however, been able to refine the previous estimates a bit and now believe that we moved back between three hundred ten and three hundred sixty years."

Kurt was still having trouble accepting the concept and just repeated what Don had said, "Three hundred ten to three hundred sixty years?"

"Yes."

"So what does that really mean to us?" Kurt asked.

"The ramifications of course are immense. But leaving philosophy and science aside, it does have one important consequence for us right now."

"Consequence?"

"Well, maybe I should say that it offers us an intriguing opportunity. If the actual amount of time we traveled back was more than 346 years —within the range we've determined – and we're roughly only 335 light-years from Earth, then any message we transmit back home would arrive early enough for them to relay it to us at Epsilon-Eri – *before* we entered the alien device."

Kurt realized that his confusion must have been obvious as Don continued, "Since we're 335 light-years from Earth, then it'll take any message we send 335 years to get there. If we traveled back let's say 346 years, then the message will arrive at Earth just over a decade before we arrive at Epsilon-Eri."

Nadya jumped in, "Don't you see Kurt? Earth could then relay a message warning us not to go near the rings!"

"But we already did," Kurt protested, "we're here now!"

"You're missing the point," Don said. "Don't think of time as a linear flow of events written in stone."

"Come on Don, time is time. Events have happened. What you're talking about is a paradox. I mean how can you just re-write what's going on? It's not possible."

"I don't pretend to understand how or what is possible anymore," Don continued. "How we got here is completely irrelevant. Put it out of your mind. All that matters is that we are sitting 335 light-years from Earth, and our date is quite possibly 346 or more years before we left. The laws of Physics, at least the ones that we understand, still apply. If we send a message from here to Earth, it will take that message 335 years to get there. There's definitely no doubt about that. That means it may well arrive eleven or more years before we enter that ... that thing. If so, Earth could relay the message to us. Taking into account the fact that it would take ten-and-a-half years for their messages to reach us at Epsilon Eri, we could receive it before we go in. Don't you see? We'd simply know not to go near the device. None of this will happen."

Thinking he saw a simple error in their logic, he asked, "Why would you send it to Earth anyway, and not just to us at Epsilon Eri?" As the statement left his mouth, he became frustrated by the ridiculousness of the concept of 'sending a message to themselves.' Don started answering though before he could react.

"It wouldn't work – any signal sent from here would be far too weak for anything we have on the Magellan to detect. Earth on the other hand does have..."

"Just stop!" Kurt demanded. "I don't want to get pulled into this hypothetical crap. It doesn't matter anyway. We can't just stop ourselves from doing something that gets us here if we're already here. I mean if the warning were to work, then wouldn't we be back at Epsilon Eri right now? Talking about setting up base camp or something much less insane?"

Nadya replied, "Maybe we need to complete the action of sending the message in our time-frame before we see the results."

Don grew impatient and said, "Kurt, we can spin our wheels all day on the meaning of paradoxes and timelines. But, what we really do need to do is to figure out how to send this message. I mean it's worth a shot and is certainly better than just sitting here."

Sending a message was a real enough issue on which he could focus. He also immediately saw a problem. "At three hundred thirty-five light-years, even with a mega-watt radio transmission, it'd still be too weak for Earth's communications networks. If we had the Magellan maybe, but we don't..."

"Don was asking me before about the IPV's laser system," Nadya interjected.

"Maybe," Kurt answered. "But the lasers are in the visible range. Earth wouldn't be looking for communications at those wavelengths..."

"What wavelengths did the Magellan use?" Don asked.

"We used frequency modulated X-ray laser bursts," Kurt replied. "It gave us the bandwidth necessary to send any amount of information we needed. There are orbital receivers around Earth for that, but we don't have that type of equipment on the IPV."

"You said we have a visible light laser system, right?" Don asked.

"Yes. But like I said, nobody would be looking in that range for communications. Plus, the signal would be so weak when it got there, I don't think anyone would see it."

"Telescopes might be able to see it," Don offered.

"What do you mean?" Kurt asked.

Don ignored Kurt's question, and instead asked, "How powerful a laser pulse could you generate using the IPV's equipment?"

"We might be able to achieve powers on the order of a Gigawatt per pulse," Kurt answered.

"That sound promising," Nadya added.

"I'm not sure yet," Don replied. "Laser beams diverge. I mean not a whole lot, but over this sort of distance, that could be a real problem. Kurt, any idea of the laser's divergence?"

"Give me a second," Kurt replied. He worked his way through a series of specifications on his hand-held console before answering, "On the order of ten micro-radians."

"Ok, that might be promising. I just need to do the math for a second,"

Don said softly as he set to work on his own terminal. Then speaking mostly to himself he continued, "We're roughly three hundred thirty-five light-years from home; there're nine-point-five trillion kilometers per light year…"

Kurt watched the man's fingers dance across the terminal. Suddenly, Don paused and just stared silently at his screen.

"Well, what did you find?" Kurt asked.

"The laser beam will be thirty-billion kilometers wide when it reaches home; we're talking about three times the size of Pluto's orbit."

"How weak will the light be?" Nadya asked cautiously.

"Very weak…about as bright as a twenty-seventh magnitude star. It's something any moderate-level observatory can see. But the problem is they use long exposures to see things that dim – they'd never see the modulation containing our signal."

"Wait," Kurt said. "What about the lunar telescope array?"

"What about it?" Don asked.

"It's only the most powerful astronomical facility ever built. Heck, Jack was on the design team and on-site for its construction."

Don just glared back at him. Kurt knew the two had barely spoken since Alex's death, but Don's look said this ran deep.

Nadya hit the intercom before Don could react and said, "Jack, respond please."

There was a barely perceptible pause before Jack replied, "Yes, Nadya. What do you need?"

"Can you come over to lab suite one?"

"OK, give me a minute."

An awkward silence followed. After a few seconds Kurt felt the odd need to break it by saying something. "One of my early assignments was on the portion of the array near the lunar north pole. It's where I met Jack."

Neither said a word in reply. Nadya, of course knew the story, but it felt like Don outright resented the comment. Rather than pursue the issue, Kurt just looked down at his terminal.

Jack entered a few moments later and immediately looked to Nadya.

"We've got a question for you," she said.

"I figured that," Jack replied.

Before she could continue, Kurt said, "They want to send a message to Earth."

They room stayed silent. Kurt watched Jack, looking for some sort of reaction, but he just stared ahead, not looking at anyone in particular. His face was expressionless as he no doubt was starting to see what it might mean. A few more seconds passed before Jack softly said, "Shit, why the hell didn't

I see this before."

"Because I'm the scientist and you're the captain," Don shot back. Kurt hoped it was an attempt at humor, rather than a swipe at Jack. The grin that formed on Jack's face, though said he either took it to be the former, or just didn't care.

"Hey, I was and am still one of those *scientists* too you know." Don didn't answer and Jack continued, "Don, give me the details."

There was only a brief pause, before Don relented and spoke. "We're about three hundred thirty-five light-years from Earth and our time displacement is somewhere between three hundred ten and three hundred sixty years in the past."

"So what's the plan?"

"Kurt's calculated he can push the IPV's laser to about a Gigawatt per pulse. The problem is the intensity when it reaches Earth."

"What're we talking?" Jack asked quickly.

"About zero-point four attowatts-per-square-meter."

Kurt watched Jack pause, then look directly at him as he said, "And I assume Kurt suggested the lunar array might be able to see it."

"Yes," Don replied, then ignoring the comment continued, "It's about the same as a twenty-seventh magnitude star."

"I see," Jack answered. "The array's limit is far dimmer – about forty-fifth magnitude. So it can see objects about six-million times weaker than our beam. The problem is, it uses a twenty-hour integration time to achieve that limit.

"That means even at six million times brighter, we still won't be able to modulate the amplitude very fast," Kurt said.

"Right," Jack replied. "Under ideal conditions, it wouldn't be able to see any modulations faster than a hundred hertz. From a practical point of view though, I'm thinking more like ten hertz."

"Ten bits per second," Don muttered. "That's practically Morse code. We're going to have keep the message simple."

"That shouldn't be too hard," Kurt said. "We'll just give them enough information to know the message is from us, and what we need them to do."

"Then there's the next problem," Don said. "How do we get them to pay attention and look for an embedded message?"

"I assume you already have an answer to that," Jack said.

"In principle," Don replied with a hint of condescension. "Kurt, what's the laser's wavelength?"

"I think it's around 650 nanometers…I'd have to check."

"Before you do that, can you tune it? I mean to a very specific wavelength?"

"Yes, it's a solid state system, so it wouldn't be that hard. Just as long as your target wavelength is relatively close to 650."

"I need it to be 656.3 nanometers," Don said.

"That's the Hydrogen-Alpha line...clever," Jack added. "They would definitely be monitoring that."

Kurt thought about it for a moment and said, "We can do that."

"That's good," Don said thoughtfully. "Now the remaining problem is: if the signal just appears, the observing programs will assume it's any one of a variety of natural phenomena and start a long-term observation schedule."

"That's good, right?" Nadya asked.

"No, they might overlook the rapid modulations of a message."

"So we need to convince them it's artificial," Nadya added.

"Right," Don answered. "But how?"

"Prime Numbers," Jack said.

"What do mean?" Nadya asked.

"I read an article about the old SETI programs years ago. One of the premises during the early attempts to detect signals from extra-terrestrial civilizations was that they would want to be found, and thus transmit an obviously non-natural signal.

"So we should send a pulsed message immediately preceding our real message: Something easy to recognize that couldn't occur in nature," Kurt said.

"Yes," Jack replied. "We could pulse the laser through the first ten prime numbers. You know, 1, 2, 3, 5, 7, 11, 13, 17, 19 and 23."

"That makes sense," Don said softly.

"Wait, why ten?" Kurt asked.

"To show them that we're thinking in a common language," Don answered. "You know, base ten, our basis of arithmetic. Plus, we'd need to modulate this part even slower, just to be sure it catches their attention. Remember, they won't be expecting this message to be from us."

"How long do you think it'd take to adapt the ship's laser system for this?" Nadya asked.

"I could do the whole thing from within the laser assembly itself. All I'd have to do is modulate the power going into the laser to create the signal. To tune it, I'd just need to run some extra current through and adjust an etalon...," Kurt paused and did a quick calculation. "It'd take about twenty minutes to get it ready."

Don didn't try to hide his excitement as he said, "Excellent."

There was a brief silence as Nadya looked at the three of them and added,

"Now all we need to do is figure out what to say."

"I'll leave that to the three of you," Kurt answered. "I'll just focus on my engineering." As he turned to leave, Kurt couldn't help but continue his earlier argument, "I still don't think any of this will work. I mean seriously, you can't change what's already been done." An awkward silence followed, forcing Kurt to add, "But, I'll do what I can to help you give it a try."

"Kurt," Don called out. "Let us know as soon as you're ready."

"OK." He replied.

When he reached engineering he said, "Computer."

The machine answered promptly, "Yes, Lieutenant Commander."

"I've got an interesting problem for us to work on. First I'm going to need some help locating the power controller for the IPV's primary laser system."

The machine answered quickly, and Kurt immediately set to work. The main power supply for the laser system was easily accessible near propulsion. It took only a couple of minutes to adjust a voltage limit on the power supply and connect an external trigger. As he closed the supply's case, he called out, "Computer, turn on the laser and run a ten Hertz square wave modulation in the injection current, then monitor the laser output."

After a moment, the machine replied, "System is functioning properly."

"Good. Turn it off now."

"Power-down complete."

He worked his way over to the main laser housing, and turned a few thumbscrews to remove the top panel. After putting on a set of goggles he said, "Computer, set power to thirty-percent. Report the output wavelength after each adjustment I make." Even though a high-power beam of light worked its way through the optics that lay before him, his goggles cut it down to a dim glow. He carefully reached in and made a small adjustment to the etalon. After each turn the computer analyzed the output and relayed his progress. The work was tedious and couldn't be rushed. However, in some ways Kurt found it mesmerizing, almost relaxing. It allowed him to clear his mind. The pattern of adjustment followed by computer update continued, until the machine announced, "Pump and primary lasers are now optimized on H-alpha."

He replaced the cover panel and made his way back to the bridge. As he entered, Jack saw him first and said with mock impatience, "So what happened? You said it'd be done over ten minutes ago."

"Hey, if this actually works it won't matter anyway, right? We probably won't even remember any of this."

Jack ignored his doubt and asked more seriously, "OK, so how do we do this?"

"It's actually quite easy," Kurt said. Turning to Kate, who was sitting at the communications station, he continued, "I've set the interface so that all you need to do is enter the message as you would with any normal transmission. The only difference is that when you're ready to press 'send', you'll go to a command line and enter 'LSEND.' That'll tell the system to use the modified laser."

"That's it?" Jack said abruptly.

"Yes. Why did you want something more complex?"

Jack just smiled in response and said. "Don, are we ready with the message?"

"Yes, I've already sent the text to Kate's terminal. We're ready for transmission."

"We're all set here," Devon interjected. "The ship is aligned properly."

"Wait," Kurt said with some urgency. "What's actually going to happen to us once we send it?"

There was a short pause before Don offered an answer, "We're not really sure."

Kurt couldn't hide his lingering disbelief any longer and continued, "I mean will we be suddenly back at E-Eri? What about Alex?"

"I don't know!" Don shouted.

The ensuing silence told him that his last question struck a nerve. If they didn't remember any of the last couple of weeks, and had no record of the trip through the device or the planet-wide city on G3-Alpha, did it really happen? The idea scared him more than he thought it should.

The silence was broken by Jack saying, "Transmit the message."

Every muscle in Kurt's body tensed as he watched Kate enter the command. He had the urge to close his eyes when she hit the last keystroke.

Kate looked up after a moment and said, "The message is transmitting."

"How long will the full transmission take?" Jack quickly asked.

Don answered, "It'll broadcast and repeat the prime number sequence for one minute, and then send and repeat the main message itself for another two minutes. After that it will repeat the pattern for three more hours."

The room remained silent until the computer announced, "Prime number header complete. Commencing with main message."

Kurt glanced from person to person around the room. Each was dealing with the wait differently. Don was staring at his terminal. Jack and Nadya had their gazes fixed on the main view screen. Kate typed something into her console, but said nothing. The silence felt like it would drag on without end. Kurt wanted to do something, but of course, there was nothing to do. The computer's ever calm voice broke the stillness, "Starting iteration number two."

A feeling of disappointment permeated the room as it became apparent nothing had changed. No one said anything. Kurt still wasn't sure whether it was disappointment or relief that he was feeling.

Don spoke up, "We should review the results in three hours after all the iterations have completed."

"Good," Jack said. "In the meantime, I think it would be wise for us to return to our regular tasks. We'll discuss this more later."

Kurt watched Nadya's face for some indication of her thoughts, but was unable to discern anything. As she moved towards him, he asked, "What does this mean? I mean everything being unchanged."

"I'm not sure. There're so many unknowns." She drew a deep breath and continued, "We probably shouldn't expect anything to happen right away. Our main theory had been that we needed to complete the act of transmitting the message. However, we've only sent it once so far. What if they don't see or recognize that it's a message until the twentieth or fiftieth repetition?"

"So you're saying that maybe in an hour or two, reality will suddenly change."

"That's one possibility," she answered, though there was no longer any confidence in her voice.

"And if we didn't move back far enough in time?"

"Then nothing will happen. Earth will just get a very confusing message." Some agitation crept into her voice as she continued, "But listen, we can second guess ourselves all day long. It's not going to do one bit of good. Why don't we just wait for the three-hour cycle to complete before talking about this any further?"

"OK," Kurt answered apologetically. As he followed her off the bridge, he had an insatiable desire to keep looking over his shoulder to see if anything had changed.

Chapter 20 – July 25, 2124; 11:35:00

Jack sat at his desk, paging through the supply report and grimaced: over a third of their expendables were gone and they had nothing to show for it. Even with the harsh rationing, it meant they had less than two weeks left. He pushed the display aside in disgust, but knew well that his frustration wasn't due to the details of a simple report. Alex's death had already cast a pall over the crew. The apparent failure of their message to Earth only darkened things further. Add to that the fatigue and discomfort caused by the rationing, and Jack knew he had to do something. The problem was, there was no obvious solution.

The knock at his office door brought a welcome distraction. "Enter," he called out.

Palmer leaned in and said, "We need to talk, sir."

"Fine," Jack replied. "Take a seat."

Palmer did as instructed and waited until Jack said, "Proceed."

"Sir, we've got a problem with the science crew."

"Explain," Jack said without hiding his impatience; he had no interest in dealing with personnel issues right now.

"They're idle. Half of them are just sitting around doing nothing – just dwelling on our situation and Alex's death."

Jack just sat there and studied the man. It wasn't like him to care that much about people's moods. He took a breath and said, "Don't beat around the bush; what's the real problem?"

"It's Dr. Martinez."

"What's Don done now?"

"He's aggravating the situation."

"Explain," Jack said tersely.

"He's blaming you for Alex's death."

"Palmer, he died under my watch. It's as simple as that. So if he wants to say it was my responsibility, I really can't argue with him."

"That's not the point, sir..."

"But it is," Jack shot back. "Anyway, everyone knows how it happened; so, Don's not going to be able to do much more than whine about it."

"But he is doing more. He's accusing you of recklessness – that you should have foreseen the risk and had everyone stand upwind of the blast. Plus, he's blaming you for taking us through that alien device in the first place – as if it was another risk you should have avoided. If he gets them to start doubting you and the chain of command..."

"Thank you, Palmer," Jack said calmly without breaking eye contact. He had the urge to tell the man to just calm down, but he couldn't outright ignore his first officer's concerns. The last thing he needed was a complete breakdown in discipline. He took a deep breath and then said, "Get him in here."

"Yes, sir," Palmer replied. "If you don't mind my asking, what are you planning to do?"

"You are right about this being a problem. However, our options are limited. We can't take any disciplinary action at this point. And, threats won't work with him, they'll only make things worse. We're going to address the root cause of this."

"Sir?"

"Like you said, they're idle, and idle minds have too much time to speculate and jump to conclusions. I'm going to put more of the responsibility on their shoulders and get them all back to work. It'll be Don's responsibility to manage them and show some results."

Palmer smiled, and Jack continued, "The bio and chem. groups are going to be tasked with finding out how to neutralize that gas."

"I thought it wasn't possible?" Palmer asked.

"It probably isn't, but that's irrelevant. They're going to put all of their time into it as if their survival depends on it. I'm going to let them know just how desperate things really are."

"And the others?" Palmer asked.

"They'll join the rest of Don's group working on understanding exactly what the hell those devices are out there."

"Understood," Palmer said.

As he turned to leave, Jack said, "Better yet, I want you to tell him the new assignments for the science staff. Then bring him back so he can update me."

Palmer nodded as he said, "Yes, sir," and left the room.

Jack leaned back in his chair and let his mind drift through their problems. There were just too many of them and no obvious solutions. The irony was, their long-shot message to Earth had grown to be their only real hope. The problem was, it was two days later and nothing changed. Some had made a vain attempt to deny that the message was a complete loss by suggesting they'd have to wait the complete three hundred thirty-year travel time for the signal to get to Earth before anything would change. Of course that was long enough for them to be dead for centuries. But they reasoned, or more accurately rationalized, that at that point they'd suddenly be alive again in their regular time-line. Kurt's assertion that it was all completely ridiculous now made the most sense. It didn't matter anymore. At this point, their only choice was to try to find a way to survive. His thought of Kurt's argument reminded him that Don wasn't the only one slacking off in his duties; Kurt owed him an update on his shuttle analysis as well. He impatiently tapped his comm. button and said, "Kurt respond please."

To his relief, Kurt responded almost immediately, "Here Jack."

"Report to my office, we need to go over your analysis of shuttle two."

"On my way."

Palmer returned with Don and they took their seats without a word.

Jack looked to Don, who refused to make eye contact, and said, "Don, you were supposed to give me a report earlier today about your research into those alien devices. Let's just review your findings now."

The chief scientist glanced at each of them before finally saying, "There's nothing new to report. We've continued a detailed study of both devices near this planet, now designated G3-alpha. However, we haven't been able to obtain any deeper understanding of what we're dealing with. Our best bet is that the rotating central cylinder could be related to a Kerr black hole, and that it may be key to supporting some sort of wormhole. But this is really just complete speculation: these objects don't have the density to create a singularity. Hell, normally I wouldn't even bring up such an insane idea. However, there is the obvious fact that we are three hundred thirty-five light years from home and have no explanation for how we got here."

Jack gave the man a second to be sure he was done speaking before saying, "Do you have anything else?"

"We've decided to call them Artificial Gravitational Conduits – AGCs for short."

"Something useful?" Jack asked sharply.

Don glared back before answering, "I don't know what to say. We've haven't got a clue. The tough part is the fact that the objects are inactive when nothing's in close proximity to them. So there's obviously something else going on, but we can't see it. From what we've seen with Palmer's shuttle and the IPV, the AGC on the other side became active once we were within a few kilometers of the center of the outer ring. But aside from observing a large energy burst, and our obvious position, we've learned nothing. If we had the facilities here that we had on the Magellan, I'd suggest we build a small probe and send it through to see what happens. But we don't have that here."

A knock on his door broke the momentary silence. "Enter," Jack said.

Kurt came in, and quickly said, "Sorry, I should've sent you my report earlier."

Jack just waved off his comment and said, "We're just covering our status. Don, were you at least able to tell which one got us here?"

Don answered softly, "Unfortunately, we've haven't made any progress on that front."

Jack didn't want to hear the word "unfortunately" one more time. Nor did he need to hear repetitive reports about them not knowing what was going on. "Damn it! It's been over a week since we got here. We need something!"

There was no response. Rather than say anything, he just looked back at his computer screen and mulled the situation over. He was well aware that it wasn't Palmer's fault – or Don's, or Kurt's or anyone else's for that matter. They just didn't have the luxury of sitting around and waiting for answers to present themselves. The urge to apologize for his outburst crept into his mind, but he decided against it. It wouldn't hurt for them to be reminded of the pressure they were under. He finally looked over to Kurt and said, "OK, what's the status of your group?"

Kurt replied hesitantly. "I do have some new material to go over with you. We've completed our review of the damage that shuttle-two sustained, and have a plan on how to keep it from happening again."

"Go on."

"Assuming that this is indeed a wormhole, we believe that a significant amount of electric charge may have collected just outside the surface of its event horizon. So, when a ship passes through this region, some of the charge would then flow onto its hull. The resulting current likely caused the power surge that knocked out the ship's systems.

"If we were to install a set of surge protectors and breakers on all of the IPV's main circuits, thereby isolating their grounding with the ship's hull, and cut all power just before entry, we may be able to completely protect most systems from damage."

"But we'd still have to do a cold restart once we reached the other side, right?" Jack asked.

"True, but restarting after a controlled shut-down takes a quarter of the time. Plus, I can program a trigger into an isolated computer. That way it will automatically initiate the restart sequence as soon as we're through. So even if we're...unconscious again, and assuming that computer doesn't shut down during the transit, everything should be up and running by the time we come to."

"Not bad. What about protecting us?"

"That's a different story," Kurt replied. "Helena's been working on that one. The problem is that she doesn't know what knocked us out in the first place."

"So it's not the buildup in charge?" Palmer asked.

"No. She said that it would have left some detectable injuries. There were no burns, abnormal body chemistry, arrhythmias, nothing. She looked for internal and external bruising indicative of physical trauma as being the cause, but found nothing significant. We're running out of conventional ideas."

Asking the obvious, Jack said, "OK, what about the unconventional?"

"That's where we're starting to get a little creative," Don said, finally looking Jack in the eye. "Assuming that the AGC is a wormhole, then the question we all considered was, 'how would the body react when exposed to significant distortions in space-time?' I mean, distortions in the actual physical dimensions in which we exist. What would happen if you stretch say in length, but contract in width, and change the rate or even direction in which time flows? Would we even notice?"

"What do you mean, *would we even notice*?" Palmer asked with an edge.

"I mean, if you stretch or shrink a region of space and all of the properties associated with it, then is it possible that we might just flow with it?" Seeing their puzzled looks, Don continued, "Think of it this way: If you and all of your immediate surroundings shrunk by a factor of two, how would you know? In this case, I mean the definition of a meter's space between you and the wall would've shrunk so within your own perception, there would still be a meter between you and the wall next to you."

No one answered. "That's the problem here. A wormhole would asymmetrically twist space-time itself. So we're dealing with the completely hypothetical question of whether there would be any stresses involved. I would think that there has to be, but of course, we just don't know. In any event, the bottom line is we've got no idea how to protect ourselves from being knocked out again."

They sat in silence. Jack knew that Don was waiting for comments, but there was nothing to say. He allowed a few more moments to pass before finally responding, "So, in short, we think we may be able to take the ship through one of these things safely. And, assuming that the effect on us is the same as before, we'll only be dealing with a few hours of unconsciousness."

"However," Palmer added, "those are large assumptions. Let's ask the very relevant question: What if we got lucky the last time through?"

"I know," Jack said somberly. "Kurt, how long do you need to prep the ship?"

"Captain," Palmer interrupted, "I think it's essential to consider what I just asked. The only data we have is a near-disastrous transit through one of these alien devices a single time. It would be prudent to assume that any future trip would be worse."

"I understand," Jack replied. "For now, we're just setting up contingency plans. Kurt, how long?"

"Two days should be enough."

Palmer cut in again, "Don't you think we need to discuss this with the rest of the crew?"

"We will," Jack said firmly. "As I said, I'm not committing us to anything yet. I just want to make all necessary preparations so that we can act without delay should we need to. Palmer, keep in mind our supply status. We can't stay around here forever – especially if this planet is nothing more than a death-trap." He watched his first officer for a reaction, but he showed no emotion at all. Jack continued, "Is there anything else?"

Each replied with a simple, "No."

"OK, then we'll meet at thirteen hundred hours sharp tomorrow. And Palmer, prepare an updated inventory of our supplies."

Palmer gave an unenthusiastic, "Yes, sir," as he headed out the door; Don followed close behind.

Kurt stayed, waiting for Jack to meet his gaze, before saying, "You're a mess. When was the last time you slept?"

Jack was amazed at his friend's ability to focus on the trivial. "Last night."

"No, I mean really slept. An hour or two doesn't count."

"That's all I've had time for."

"You're not going to be any use to us if you pass out from exhaustion."

"I know my limits. I'll take a break when I need to."

Kurt gave a disbelieving sigh before continuing, "You know, working yourself into the ground isn't going to bring Alex back."

He glared back in response, but it didn't stop Kurt from continuing, "Who gives a damn what Don thinks?"

Jack didn't feel like answering, but knew Kurt would keep it up if he stayed quiet. He drew a deep breath before replying, "I don't particularly care what he thinks. But that doesn't change the fact that my actions resulted in his death; nothing's going to change that."

"Well, you're wrong. You did everything by the book – everything you were supposed to do. Poison gas left by some goddamned alien race killed him!" Jack turned away, prompting Kurt to press on, "Look at the facts. First, there was no way anyone with any of our equipment could've known it was there. Second, who the hell could've dreamt they could create a mix like that that would eat right through a suit?"

It was becoming hard to contain the burning anger within him. Part of him didn't want to maintain his composure anymore. On top of that, he didn't need anyone making excuses for him. He finally replied, "You're missing the point. I should've taken more time to think of things like that. Look at where we are. Think of it! We were standing on a planet completely covered by a city that had been totally wiped out by weaponry we can barely even imagine! It was idiotic to think of things in terms of what we know. Who could've dreamt that lay ahead? I should have. Maybe Alex would be alive today if I had."

"You can't second-guess..."

"I can because it was reckless!" He grew tired of the debate. "The only thing I can say for sure is that I'm not going to make our next decision while blinded by ignorance!" He pushed his way past Kurt into the hallway, but his friend followed him.

"Jack – I'm not done."

"I am."

"You're missing the point."

"No!" He shouted as he backed Kurt against the wall. "You just don't understand do you? This has nothing to do with Don!" Jack slammed his fist on the door-jam; the sharp pain that shot through his hand was an almost welcome feeling. He hit it again, letting the pain ease some of his guilt. Taking a deliberate, deep breath, he continued in a measured tone, "Kurt, there's no time for rest. We're running out of food which means we've got to do something soon. But we still don't know what the hell we're dealing with. If I give the order to go through an AGC without knowing what's on the other side of that damned thing, it'd be the same thing as with Alex."

"Then we take some more time here and see what we can learn."

"But we can't! Think ahead Kurt. What if the AGC we choose doesn't take us back to Epsilon Eri-D? What if we end up in another completely different star system? We're going to need to have some supplies left if we want a chance to survive and try again.

"It means I've got to decide without knowing for sure..." As he drew in a deep breath, he muttered, "It won't be a hell of a lot more than a guess. But I swear I'll do everything in my power to get as many answers as I can first. I owe it to the crew. I owe it to Alex."

"Jack..."

"You didn't have to hear him die! And you didn't have to pack him in a god-damned external cargo-hold like a piece of scrap!" Jack didn't realize he was shouting until he was done. "Damn it all! I've got to clear my head." He needed quiet: someplace to be alone, and was halfway down the hall before realizing he left Kurt standing alone. Forcing himself to turn around, he called back, "I'll talk to you later," but didn't wait for a reply. The IPV had never felt so small before. He made a quick left toward the observatory: it would be empty.

He left the lights off as he entered the small room and found the darkness calming. Rows of inactive equipment lined the back wall; the window in front drew him closer. He moved forward until his forehead touched the glass - all aspects of the IPV were gone from view. The expansive, pitch-black disk of the planet's night side floating against a myriad of stars lay in front of him. He could have been drifting on his own in open space. The ravaged world's cloud-cover was so thick that it completely hid the blazes that raged below. The blackness was interrupted only occasionally by distant, fleeting flashes of lightning. Rather than bringing to mind the violence that raked the planet's surface, the silent, random sparks were almost peaceful and hypnotic.

Time passed quickly, and his mind released its grip on the conflicts of the past few days. The built-up tension finally ebbed. He could see their choices more clearly. The math was simple: by the time they were properly prepped and ready to enter an AGC, ten days will have passed. That translated to expending one-half of their supplies. If the device took them somewhere other than Epsilon Eri, then they would need at least a couple days to determine where they were, and if the new location held any promise for them. If it did, they would still need the better part of a week beyond that to gather any supplies they might find, as well as analyze and process them so that they would be safe for consumption. The bottom line was, if they pushed themselves to the limit, then they might have enough provisions for at most two tries through AGCs: but only if they left soon.

His real problem lay with the crew. They would be apprehensive about the prospect of deliberately going through an AGC. He expected some, Don in particular, to outright resist the decision. He wasn't sure how far Don might take it; it probably depended on how many in the crew followed his lead. To be sure, Don wasn't a coward. It had more to do with his being in control of a situation. He was prone to over-analysis and tunnel vision. Jack understood his motivation – he was painfully aware himself about the need to minimize risks. The problem was that Don needed to reach an absolute answer; the consequences of inaction never factored into the equation.

Palmer on the other hand was still a question mark. He understood the need for action; however, he too was too dependent on certainty. Devon's voice over the intercom brought him back to the present. "Captain, respond please."

Jack turned away from the glass and responded, "Yes, I'm here...what is it?"

"We've got some new readings that you'll want to see."

"Go on."

"The feed from a satellite we have over the day-side shows that the gas has stopped flowing."

"Stopped completely?"

"Yes, sir. As soon as it showed signs of dissipating, I started taking detailed readings. As of now even the residual traces are nearly down to zero."

"I'm on my way. Tell Kurt to meet me on the bridge." He had already given up hope that they'd ever be able to get into the tower – three straight days of watching the corrosive yellow gas pour out of the opening had convinced him of that. The powerful winds carried it for tens of kilometers before it disappeared in the distance. Their best guess was that the interior of the structure had been filled with it.

He arrived at the bridge to find Kurt already there. Devon immediately looked to him and said, "Captain, let me show you what we've got."

The main display came to life showing a magnified view of the tower doors. The large, pewter arch stood peacefully – the only hint of the last two days' events was a dark, jagged, two-meter wide hole in the entry-way's seam.

"How long since it stopped?"

"Twenty minutes," Devon answered.

"You said the residuals are nearly zero. How close are we talking?"

"I can only give you an upper limit. From orbit, we can read down to the part-per-billion level, and I'm reading zero. So if there's any left, it's below that threshold."

"Kurt, you got some reasonable data on the properties of that stuff from before right?"

"Yes and no. I mean, we still don't know what it is. But, we were able to figure out how quickly it eats through various materials."

"That's all I need right now. I want you to calculate the safe exposure time for an EVA suit using Devon's upper limit."

"It'll take a few minutes."

"Good, get on it right away." Turning back to his pilot, he said, "How long until we're in position to launch another shuttle to the surface."

"One hour."

"OK." Jack took a minute to slow himself down. He didn't want things moving too quickly. "How long after that?"

"If we stay in this orbit, it'll be another seven hours."

It was about what he expected. Though he wanted more time to prepare, the additional seven hours was too long a wait. He took a second to consider moving the ship to a different orbit, but their limited propellant ruled that out. "Devon, you're with me. Where's Kate."

"I'm not sure, sir."

Jack quickly activated the ship-wide comm. "Kate Stewart and George Palmer, please report to the shuttle bay. I repeat, Kate Stewart and George Palmer please report to the shuttle bay." He looked up and met Devon's waiting gaze. "Let's go."

Jack wasn't surprised to find Palmer was waiting for them in front of the bay's door. If nothing else, the man was prompt. Not waiting for him to ask anything, Jack simply said, "The corrosive agent at the tower has dissipated. I'm going to need you to take command up here while I take a small team down."

"Now?" Palmer asked politely.

"It's either now or wait another seven hours until our next orbit."

"I understand. May I ask what precautions you will be taking?"

"With this little time to prep, it'll be purely a survey mission. We'll leave recovery issues for a later expedition. We'll stay in continuous contact. I expect the structure to block our signal, so we'll be placing repeaters along our path."

"That sounds wise. I'm just not too optimistic about finding anything useful."

"Neither am I, but it would be foolish not to go. Maybe we'll find some sealed compartments or something. We've got to try."

"I agree. What about residue from the gas?"

"Kurt's working on exposure limits right now..." They both turned as Kate came down the corridor with Don trailing close behind. Jack had hoped to avoid dealing with Don until their return. Don, however, didn't waste a second. "Just what are you planning?" he asked without hiding the edge in his voice.

Jack fought off the urge to ignore his science officer's demand. Even with their loose command structure, he wasn't obligated to explain himself. But, there was already more than enough friction between them. "The corrosive agent exiting the tower doors has dissipated. I'm taking a small team down for a preliminary reconnaissance mission. Kate will take care of communications for us. Plus, if we're lucky enough to find any artifacts or written material, we'll need her to start building a basis for a translation matrix. Devon'll be piloting the shuttle."

"When were you going to inform me?"

"The launch window we've got is short. If time didn't permit, Palmer would have updated you."

"But you're taking a member of my staff. Kate's a linguist first, and thus is a member of the science staff."

"Don, this discussion can wait." Jack didn't give him a chance to respond as he continued, "Palmer, Kurt will update you on the details of the gas mixture..."

"Jack, respond please."

It was Kurt's voice on the comm. "I'm here, go ahead."

"I calculate a safe exposure limit of thirty minutes."

"Thirty minutes?" Don protested?

Kurt answered before Jack could intervene. "They'll still be safe for another half-hour after that, but at that point, the suit fabric might start to degrade. Jack, this is all based on an upper limit of one part-per-billion. If the concentrations are lower, then you'll have a good deal more time."

"We'll err on the side of caution and stick with thirty minutes. Thanks."

"No problem. Kurt out."

Realizing the best way to diffuse Don's resistance would be to keep him fully involved, Jack said, "Don, I'm going to want you to continuously monitor our communications and video feeds. We're going to need all the help we can get from your team up here."

Don replied with a confused, "Uh huh."

He glanced around and was just becoming aware of Devon's absence, when his pilot poked his head out of the shuttle bay bulk-head.

"Captain, the shuttle's all prepped."

Jack welcomed the chance to escape and said, "Kate, let's get moving."

Chapter 21 – July 25, 2124; 13:30:00

The trip to the surface was uneventful if not somber. Barely any words were spoken as they all fully recognized the gravity of their situation. Jack realized that it was likely weighing too heavily on him, as he neglected to portray even a superficial feeling of optimism. On landing, he simply said, "OK, let's get this done," and climbed into the shuttle's small airlock. He stood there now, listening to the muted howl of the winds on the other side. The eerie sound only brought back lingering doubts about moving forward so quickly, but he pressed the "open" button anyway. His ears were once again assaulted by the unshielded roar of the gale. Bracing himself, he stepped out and was buffeted by a blast of sand. It made him flinch, despite knowing he was well-protected by his EVA suit. The tower's long shadow fell across them, darkening the platform. The wall in front, with its embedded arch, looked more like it was made of onyx than the lighter, pewter hue they had seen in bright daylight. Looking up, he gazed at the immensity of the spire as it pierced the alien world's deep-red evening sky. It was still awe inspiring, and he had to make a deliberate effort to bring his attention back to their mission. Turning on his flashlight, he made his way to the arch. The stark shadows accentuated the hole's jagged edges, but it was large enough for them to fit through.

Devon and Kate joined him as he peered inside the gap. "OK, we don't have much time, so let's get started. Watch the edges as you enter. Kate, place the first comm. relay just inside."

Jack stepped gingerly through the opening and scanned the immediate area with his light. They were in a short corridor that led to a large arch at its far end. The smooth black walls were lined with metal brackets that he imagined once held equipment or ornamentation which had long since been eaten away by the gas. With each step, the roar from the winds subsided. By the time they reached the end, it was quiet enough to hear their feet shuffling along the dust covered floor.

The inner arch served as an entryway into a mammoth hall; their flashlights were too feeble to reach the ceiling, or the walls on the other side. Jack turned to look behind him and let his light trace a path up the slowly arcing wall until it disappeared into a dark haze above. They stood, transfixed by the size of the structure until Don's voice crackled over the radio.

"Jack, do you read me?"

"We're here," he replied still distracted by his surroundings.

"It's been over five minutes since you exited the shuttle and we hadn't heard from you. You need to..."

"Sorry, you're right," he said quickly. "We're inside the structure. There was a short corridor that seems to have been gutted by the gas."

"Yes, we saw it from your helmet cam. It makes me think that there's not going to be much prospect of finding any sort of supplies."

"I know, but we're still going to continue." Looking ahead, he spotted several scattered piles of debris. Devon led the way to the nearest one. They stood for a moment and stared at a lump of twisted metal.

Don's voice broke the silence, "I can't get a good view of what that is. Your video is breaking up a bit."

"OK, I'll leave the comm. link open and try to describe what we see. We're standing by the nearest pile. It's a mass of twisted metal maybe thirty meters across and ten or so meters high. It looks like it fell from above, but I can only guess as to what it once was. The metal looks sturdy, maybe it used to support some structure that was suspended overhead."

They slowly worked their way deeper into the room, past several similar, equally spaced mounds. Jack provided Don with any details he thought were useful. To assist with their analysis later, Kate took out a small video recorder and documented their findings.

"Captain, over here," Devon called out.

Jack looked up to see his pilot's flashlight cutting through the dusty haze about twenty meters ahead. "What is it?"

"I don't know, just come here."

Another collection of twisted rods and beams lay in front of him. It took a moment longer to see what had caught Devon's attention: their flashlights revealed the blue-grey sheen of a polished metal wall behind the pile. He pointed his light upward and saw that the wall was actually part of a massive, gently sloping column that rose above them. It was at least fifty meters in diameter at its base. The seamless curve of the structure gave it an almost fluid-like quality. Embedded in it was a ramp that spiraled upward, ending at a platform a few stories above them. Jack strained his eyes in the dim light to see beyond the platform. But the column simply continued its climb upward, and vanished into the darkness.

"It's beautiful, Kate said softly. "It looks like this could have been some sort of grand hall."

Jack stood next to her, admiring the gently tapering structure when Devon's voice broke the silence.

"I found an entrance to the ramp."

Without answering, they joined him and began their ascent. As they reached the base of the platform, Don's voice came in over the comm., "You're at eighteen minutes. That means you have twelve minutes of safe exposure left."

"Thank you," Jack replied.

Don continued, "I suggest you start heading back in five."

Jack suppressed any annoyance at their limited amount of time and simply said, "Agreed."

They walked to the platform's edge and gazed out into the vast open chamber. The all-encompassing blackness however kept them from truly appreciating their view. For Don's benefit, Jack said, "It appears that the entire interior of the tower may be open. This has the feel of some sort of raised podium or reviewing stand."

"I agree," Kate said. "I'd love to spend some time in here with an archaeological team. We might be able to learn about their culture, their architecture, and find out who these...these beings really were."

"I would too," Jack replied gently, trying not to the quash the first hint of passion he'd heard from anyone in days. "Right now, though, let's focus on surveying the area for anything worth salvaging."

Their lights allowed them a view of only the nearest portion of the chamber's gently curving outer wall. Aside from the piles of debris, the room seemed grand, but featureless. "Kate, does the camera have an infra-red setting?"

"Yes, I've already tried it. It doesn't show me much more than what we've already seen. All that I can tell you is that it looks like you're right, the entire interior of the structure is open. There are some more debris piles, and another column like this one much further in – a good three or four hundred meters away."

Jack looked back at Devon and found him staring straight up. "What do you see?"

"Nothing really, just that our ramp stops at this level." Devon pointed to his left and continued, "There's a set of doors over there. Maybe it leads to an elevator or stairs."

Jack glanced at his watch, "It doesn't matter much now. We only have another minute or so before we have to leave." They aimed their lights back out into the dark chamber, but saw nothing more. "I want each of us to take a different route back to the corridor. Let's cover as much ground as possible during this visit. Maybe we can find something. Just remember – don't linger. We'll meet at the arch in five minutes."

"Understood," Devon answered.

At the bottom, Jack headed right and made his way toward the wall. He passed more piles of debris in silence. There was nothing that seemed even remotely useful. Growing impatient, he called out, "Has anyone found anything?"

"Nothing yet," was Devon's reply.

Jack waited for Kate's response, but heard nothing. After a few more seconds, he called out, "Kate, respond please."

"Here Jack. Yes, I think I've found something."

"What is it?"

"There's a wide section of the floor over here that slopes downwards – almost like a broad path or walkway. It ends in front of several sets of doors."

"Are they open?"

"No."

"Don't touch anything!"

"Uh…Ok," was Kate's surprised response.

Realizing that his reply must have sounded too urgent, he added, "I'm just worried about what might be behind them. I'm heading over to you. Tell me what you see."

"Well, the doors are set about 5 to 7 meters below the main floor. They're windowless and made of the same, blue-grey metal we've seen throughout the structure. It looks like they should slide open, but I don't see any obvious control panel or handle. The walls are similar to the corridor we saw on the way in. They're covered with brackets and must have held some sort of less durable surface. My guess is that this is an entrance or exit for a large number of people…or aliens, I guess."

"I see it now," Devon said. "I've doubled back and found the ramp. It'd be great to see what's behind those doors."

"It's too dangerous right now," Jack answered.

"What if …"

"No 'what ifs'. We need to be outside in three minutes," Jack said sternly.

"Wait, hear me out first. I've got two shape-charges in my tool kit. I could attach them to one of the doors and detonate them remotely."

"Where would that get us?"

"I assume that you're worried that there's more of that gas in there. We'll set the camera here to watch what happens, and detonate the charges when we're safe in the shuttle. This way we'll at least get an idea of the risks now, instead of wasting another half-day before we can come back.

It only took a second for Jack to admit to himself that it was a good idea. He waited, though, until he finally caught up to them at the top of the ramp before answering, "Ok, do it. But, move quickly."

He turned to Kate, "Download the images on the camera to the computer now in case it gets destroyed when we blow the doors."

"Got it."

Jack stood back for a moment as Devon set to work. He was a little frustrated that he hadn't thought of the idea – maybe he was playing things too safe now. Turning away from them, he looked at their surroundings again and fell back on a single recurring thought: 'What happened here?'

Devon came up from behind and said, "We're all set. How do you want to proceed?"

"Like you said, we'll detonate them once we're in the shuttle. We can watch the feed from Kate's camera." Drawing a deep a breath, he turned to Kate who had carefully balanced the small device on a ledge at the start of the ramp. "Is it ready?"

"Yes. Since it's not made for remote operation, I'm just going to start recording now and let the feed go directly to the shuttle's computer. We can watch everything on the screen from there."

"Good, let's go. We're already a couple of minutes over our limit." He started back at a light jog and the others kept pace with him. As they approached the break in the tower's outer door, the roar of the planet's winds grew again to the point where he had to shout his instructions. "Take your time climbing through here," he called out.

It took only another minute to reach the shuttle. The relief that swept over him once the airlock door sealed behind him was unexpected, though he knew its source: there were no surprises or mistakes this time. His peace was broken by Don's voice over the comm. "You were in there three minutes beyond the limit."

"I know, but we couldn't pass up this chance to find out what else may be in there."

"I'm just saying, we need to be careful."

Jack ended the discussion with a polite, "Agreed."

They gathered by one of the shuttle's monitors where Kate typed in a few commands to display the video feed. A clear, wide-angle view of the alien ramp and its row of doors appeared. "Don, are you getting this too?"

"Yes."

"Devon, are we ready?"

"Affirmative," was his pilot's quick answer.

"OK, blow the charges."

He fixed his gaze on the plain, pewter doors. They were instantly obscure by a bright flash. Small chunks of debris streaked past the camera. Thick clouds of grey smoke filled the screen, but soon pulled away, revealing a one-meter wide, jagged opening. Hope began to take hold as the view remained clear. His stomach dropped, though, before he could fully form any thoughts; a cloud of yellow-grey gas suddenly billowed out from the opening. They watched quietly as it gently flowed toward the camera. Two quick bursts of static swept across the screen before it went blank.

"Shit!" was all that Jack could say.

"What do we do now?" Kate asked quietly.

"We go back to the IPV."

Chapter 22 – July 26, 2124; 13:00:00

Kurt pushed himself back from the tangle of wires with which he was working, and wiped the sweat from his forehead. His creation resembled a rat's nest more than a carefully constructed series of relays and circuit breakers. With the schedule Jack had set for them, however, there wasn't time to consider appearance.

He turned to Claire, who was looking over his work, and said, "I assume if one of your students back on Earth tried to pass this off as an assignment, you'd have failed them in a minute."

She laughed and said, "I don't think it would have taken that long."

Kurt smiled, "Can you pass me that cover plate? I don't want to leave the high-voltage lines exposed."

She handed him the plastic plate and he began re-attaching it to the wall. He felt that it was almost demeaning to have her assist him with such a mundane task. True, she was technically his assistant, but she held a doctorate in electrical engineering and had given up a faculty position at MIT to join the mission. It made him wonder how crew members like her dealt with their place on the ship. To be selected, of course, you had to be the very best in your field. But once they were underway, Claire and Pierre, among others were relegated to 'assistant' positions for the next thirty years. Barring someone's death, there would be no advancement to a higher position or rank. He began tightening the last of the screws, but his mind wouldn't let go of the thought. Of course, being an 'assistant' on humanity's first foray to another star-system was more rewarding than any title he could imagine. But to have made it this far in their careers, they had to have had a strong desire to be the very best, to be the top person around. At some point being second wouldn't be good enough.

Claire handed him a few more screws and he finished tightening the cover. Looking up, he said, "That's the last one, right?"

"Yes. We've installed twenty of these relay and breaker units over the last ten hours. This better be the last." Her tone stated very clearly that there was no doubt.

"I hope so," he said with a smile. Then more seriously, "I'm still just worried about how much charge will actually build up when we pass through...the AGC. I mean, we're just guessing what's going to happen. What if each transit isn't exactly the same? If it's more severe, we could be in some serious trouble. Then there's still the problem of what happens to us."

"You're not going to start that again, are you?"

"What do you mean?" he asked incredulously.

"Aside from blacking out, we came through fine last time. There were no serious injuries."

"You sound as confident as Jack. I just wish I could be."

"Well, think of it this way, it's not like we have any choice."

After they packed away the last of their tools, Kurt asked reluctantly, "Well, are you ready to actually go through with this?"

"Like I said, what choice do we have?"

Claire led the way down the corridor and asked, "Any word on what's up with Don?"

"What do you mean?"

"You know, he seemed to accept the decision to go through the AGC without too much of a problem."

"Well, if you mean he didn't yell at anyone...I could see someone thinking he's OK with it. But, I doubt it."

"What do you mean? I didn't hear him say much of anything."

"No, but he didn't take it well," Kurt said shaking his head. "Nadya was on the bridge earlier when Jack told him. She said that all he did was turn his back on Jack and storm off the bridge."

They took a moment to move to the side of the corridor as Maurice pushed his way past. "Maurice, what's the hurry?" Kurt asked loudly. There was no response as the computer engineer simply continued down the hall and ducked into one of the labs.

"Did you really expect an answer?" Claire asked.

"I swear he's getting stranger each day."

"You say that every time you pass him."

Kurt laughed, then replied thoughtfully, "If you ask me, he's the one to be worried about, not Don."

"I guess. I've barely seen him since we went through the first AGC."

"Why, have you been looking for him?"

"No," she answered defensively. "But think of it. I mean on the Magellan it was no big deal if you didn't see someone for a few days. It was big enough that it simply meant that your paths hadn't crossed. Here, though, you can't help but bump into each other a few times a day."

They came to the end of the hall and pushed their way up to the next level. He was about to ask Claire what she thought Maurice's absence really meant when he heard raised voices coming from just outside the bridge. Heading quickly toward it, he found Don shouting at Jack, "...no damned way you're going to make this decision yourself! You've got no right!"

Jack cut him off, "Right? What the hell do you mean? We went over this yesterday. I told you if you could give me a reason, a real reason to delay, then I would."

Don pushed his finger toward Jack and continued, "You can't just give some bullshit deadline. You need me and my staff to check everything and give you an OK. There's no..."

"This is not a goddamned science mission anymore!" Jack shot back. His voice was laced with exasperation as he continued, "We're trying to survive. Saying 'you're concerned' or 'need more data' isn't good enough."

Kurt kept his distance as Don's voice turned decidedly sarcastic. "So, you alone are right until you're proven wrong. Let me tell you, if you're wrong, we're all dead."

"What would you have me do? Wait here another three or four days?"

"Until we're sure our choice is safe."

"Would you even know in that time?"

"I'd have to be given a chance to try first!" Don shouted as he leaned in toward Jack.

Kurt's only worry now was that Don would actually take a swing at Jack. Instead Don paused, thinking he'd made his point. Jack, however, continued, "The problem is that you don't know if you'll ever be sure any choice is safe. To me it's simple. That planet down there is dead. There is no hope at all for us here. That means every day longer we sit here serves no purpose – it just means we've wasted another day's supplies."

"What good are supplies if we just recklessly push ahead and kill ourselves?"

"If you can tell me that you can significantly reduce our risk given a day or two more time, the I'll wait."

"I can't guarantee anything. All I can do is try."

"Don," Jack said calmly, "we've wasted nine days here. That's about half of our food. Once it's gone, that's it – we're done. There will be no survival or other chances, we'll just sit there and starve to death. I won't take that risk unless you can give me another option."

Don paused barely long enough to take a breath before challenging him again, "You don't even know which AGC is the right one to take."

"If I remember right, you were the one who said that there's no way to tell. As far as I see it, the issue's irrelevant. A fifty-fifty chance of getting back is better than no chance here."

Don just glared at Jack.

It took a moment for Kurt to realize that Jack was now staring right at him. "Are we ready?" Jack barked.

He tried to answer but instead was aware only of his hands trembling. It wasn't from the argument. Rather, it was from the rush of adrenaline that accompanied the fear that he might have to step in between the two of them. Jack's continued stare forced him to answer, "Yes, everything's in place."

"Good." Then looking back at his still fuming science officer, "Don, I'll need you at your station on the bridge."

Don didn't answer, but just stood in place with his arms folded.

Jack turned and entered the bridge. Kurt and Claire obediently followed.

As he made his way to his station, Kurt noted that the two AGC's were displayed prominently on the main screen. Their perfect silver surfaces glimmered in the sunlight.

"Kurt, I want you and Don to keep a close eye on all status indicators. Let me know the second anything looks wrong."

Kurt answered with a simple, "Yes," and made his way to the science station.

"Devon," Jack called, "display the course we plotted."

The main screen switched to a graphical representation of the space around them. Kurt focused on the gently arcing red line that led into the AGC on the left. He then glanced at Don who was now standing next to him and said, "I think it makes sense to shut all systems, including the engines, down when we're still about five hundred kilometers out. Our momentum will simply carry us through."

"That sounds right," Don answered grudgingly.

Devon called out, "I'll need power at least through the last course correction. It's about four hundred kilometers out. From there we'll just coast into position."

"That'll work," Kurt answered.

"OK, proceed with that," Jack said. "I just don't like flying in completely blind."

"Don't worry, I've wired a single external camera to a separate circuit. That way, we'll be able to see what's going on. And, if it burns out, that's all we'll lose – just one camera."

"That's a bit better." Jack hit the comm. button on his console and said, "Nadya, are the engines ready?"

"Everything's primed."

Kurt watched Jack take a deep breath and activate the ship-wide intercom. "This is the captain. All preparations have been completed for our transit through the AGC. In about thirty seconds we'll commence our run. At this point, I want everyone strapped into their flight seats with full crash restraint harnesses. Department heads, check in with the bridge once you're secure.

Nadya's voice was first, saying, "Propulsion is ready." The others followed quickly enough that Kurt lost track. After a brief moment of silence Palmer leaned over and whispered something to Jack. An expression of annoyance flashed across his face as he slapped the intercom button and said, "Computer engineering, respond." No more than five seconds passed before he hit the button again, "Maurice Traynor, respond."

The few seconds of silence that followed felt like half an hour. Jack called out, "Computer, locate..."

"Computer engineering here."

Without trying to hide his frustration, Jack answered, "Are you ready and is your equipment secured?"

"Yes, everything's ready." Kurt was sure Maurice's voice had an edge of annoyance to it. His thought was cut off though as Jack said in a measured tone, "Devon, take us in."

The hum of the engines passed through his seat as they began accelerating. They were approaching the closer of the two AGC's from the side. In a few moments, though, they would swing around and come in at a forty-five-degree angle towards the device. The thought was that if they had a forward component to their velocity, it might get them through any hazardous region more quickly. That thought, however, was not much more than a guess.

Devon called out, "T-minus five minutes. Velocity twenty thousand k-p-h, parallel to the ring-plane."

The engines were at full power – their whine filling the ship. All eyes were fixated on the main screen as the silver device grew. "Adjusting course now," Devon said loudly over the din. The object appeared to pivot toward them in response.

Kurt kept an eye on his own computer display: a single line read, 'Shut-down trigger' and was followed by a chronometer indicating they only had thirty seconds left. A wave of tension swept across him. He dug his fingers into the armrest and looked around, but everyone was completely absorbed by the view in front of them.

"Shut down in ten seconds," Devon called out. "Five…four…three… two…one…"

Instantly everything went black. The ship was silent. A moment later, the battery-powered emergency lighting bathed them in an eerie red glow. The main display, however, stayed blank.

"Kurt, I thought you said we'd be able to see?" Jack said impatiently.

"Give it a second," he answered. "The relays need to switch it over to the isolated circuit." He hoped Jack couldn't tell that he wasn't one hundred percent confident it would work. There was enough time for his doubts to take an even greater hold before he heard the click of a jury rigged switch, and the screen came back to life.

"Distance three hundred kilometers. Contact in two minutes," Devon said almost mechanically.

They were close enough now that the nearest ring completely filled their field of view. Kurt's attention, however was drawn to the massive middle ring with its unnatural black center. None of their analyses were able to determine what it was. They had toyed with thoughts that it was the actual event horizon of a wormhole, or that it was some other exotic alien material. No one really had any idea. He just continued staring at it, pondering the possibilities.

"Distance two hundred kilometers," Devon announced. "thirty seconds until contact."

They sat in dead silence as the image grew in front of them. Time passed agonizingly slowly. Kurt checked his watch to gauge how much longer they had, but was frustrated to find that only a few seconds had passed.

Devon's calm voice broke the silence, "Twenty seconds."

They were close enough now that that he could no longer see the outer ring itself. It felt as if they were already inside it. The pitch black center of the thick, middle ring continued to grow until it dominated their field of view. Kurt focused on its center to see if they were rushing towards some solid wall. The blackness though was perfect and unchanging. It gave no hint as to what it really was.

"Ten seconds until contact."

Kurt reflexively grabbed his armrests with all his strength. Every muscle in his body tensed as if he was about to be punched. "Something's wrong," he whispered aloud. Out of the corner of his eye he caught a glimpse of the blue-green light. It was all around him, not just on the view screen. Dizziness swept across him as the room seemed to bend. There was a flash of agonizingly bright, white light.

PART 4: CONTACT

Chapter 23 – July 26, 2124; 15:25:00

Jack opened his eyes and was forced to squint in the brightly lit bridge. A field of stars slowly panned across the main view screen, followed by the near blinding disk of a sun. After a moment it was joined by a thin crescent bordering a large, pitch black disk. Frustration grew with the realization that he'd been unconscious again and that the IPV was spinning out of control. It was expected – but that didn't matter. He just wanted some hint of normalcy and hope.

His thoughts were interrupted by Devon's voice calling his name. He noted his pilot's disoriented look and asked, "Are you OK?"

"I think so. I just feel...hungover."

Jack shook off the effects of the transit and glanced around the bridge: Kurt and Don were still slumped over in their chairs. Claire, however, looked like she might be stirring. "Has anyone checked in over the comm.?" he asked.

"Helena did a moment ago," Devon replied. "Before that, I don't know. I only came to when she called."

"What's her status?"

"She said she's OK, and was going to work her way through the ship to check on the others."

"Good. Any idea how long were we out?"

"If the chronometer can be trusted, only an hour this time."

Jack didn't say anything: even an hour was too long. Devon must have sensed his aggravation, and said, "It's not as bad as last time."

"True," Jack answered without sincerity. He just stared at the screen and said, "Is this the main system, or Kurt's separate camera?"

"The main one. It looks like all systems are up and running. His circuits and reboot routine worked."

"Good. Get us stabilized first, then see if you can determine if this is the E-Eri system."

"I'm already working on that."

Jack looked more carefully around the bridge as he unlatched his harness. A few items drifted weightlessly, and he pushed himself toward a loose flashlight that was just out of reach. Seeing Palmer stir, he said, "George, can you hear me?"

His first officer opened his eyes and stared straight at him, but appeared not to see him.

"Palmer, I need you to wake up. Do you understand me?"

"Yeah...yes, what...," he cut himself off as he recognized what had happened. "Damn...how long was I out?"

"About an hour. I only came to a minute ago."

"Where are we? Did we make it back?"

"I don't know yet. Devon's just started working on it. I need you to get things stabilized here on the bridge while I check on the rest of the crew. Work on getting our navigational references first."

Palmer looked around and said, "It'd make more sense if I went. It's an emergency situation; you should be up here."

Palmer was right of course, but Jack couldn't stomach the idea of sitting still when there was work to be done. His vain attempt at formulating a response made him realize that running around the ship wasn't going to accomplish anything either. True, checking on things in-person might feel better, but that was irrelevant. He took a deep breath and finally relented. "Go, but let me know immediately if there are any problems."

"Yes, sir."

As Palmer exited the bridge, Jack saw the main screen start flashing through different views of stars, and asked, "Are all of the external cameras back on line?"

"Yes, I just did a full system test on them," Devon replied.

Before he could continue, Kurt spoke up from behind him, "What about E Eri-D? Did we make it back?"

Without looking up from the control panel Devin said, "It's too soon to tell."

The display changed again to show the black disk with its thin, white crescent edge. This time, though, the planet and its surrounding stars were still. Anticipating the questions, Devon said, "There's not enough to go on yet. Once we come around to dayside we'll know more."

"Have you located the AGCs?" Jack asked.

"Almost there," Devon said softly. Barely a second later his pilot whispered, "Damn it," but didn't say anything further.

A part of him didn't want to ask, but Jack asked anyway, "What's wrong?"

"I've located three gravitational anomalies...give me a minute..."

It took a deliberate effort to sit silently as Devon typed furiously at his workstation. The few seconds that passed felt unbearably long. Even the image of the planet on the main screen seemed frozen in time.

"They're close to the planet. Just another second."

The main screen's image disappeared and was replaced by a schematic showing a plain blue disk he assumed represented the planet, surrounded by three smaller green circles. "I don't have enough data yet to display their orbits, but this is the current layout of the system." Devon explained. "The blue disk in the center is the planet. The other objects are the right mass to be AGCs. Once the telescopes are back online, I'll be able to confirm all of this."

"So we're not back at E-Eri?" Don practically shouted from behind him.

There was no need to answer the man. Jack knew the Don's outburst was more of an accusation than a question.

"Goddammit," Don continued, "I told you we shouldn't have gone through!"

Ignoring him, Jack just stared at the diagram and said, "They look like they're symmetrically spaced around the planet."

"Yes," Devon answered. "And, that could be a problem for us. Since the systems were down for an hour, and since the AGC's seem identical in all other aspects, it may be difficult to determine which one we came though."

"What do you mean?" Jack asked impatiently. "Just look at our current velocity and trace a path back."

"The problem is that we're equidistant from the two nearest AGCs and we're not moving with respect to either one," Devon answered. "It's really strange..."

Before Devon's voice finished trailing off, Don cut in, "What in the world are you talking about?"

"Like I said, we're not moving with respect to the AGCs – it's like we're exactly at the cusp of some sort of unstable equilibrium position. We're safe for the moment, but it is precarious. All we'd need is a small push from our thrusters and we'd literally be pulled straight into an AGC or the planet. The problem is, since we're stable and didn't use our engines to get here, I can't determine our point of origin."

"But how?" Kurt asked.

"I don't know. It's like we were spat of the AGC with just the right amount of energy and in the right direction to stop us here. My only guess is that this is like some sort of landing pad."

"Are you saying they designed entire planetary system like this?" Kurt asked with obvious awe.

Again, there was no need to answer. The magnitude of their engineering was unimaginable.

"Look for a faint ion trail." Don said impatiently.

"Don, the engines were off," Devon answered.

"Think about it," Don shot back with an edge. "Even though we shut the engines down, there would still have been some residual xenon in the feed tubes, as well as a small but significant charge on the discharge grates. That'd give us enough of a trail to follow."

"OK, give me a minute and I should have an answer."

"Jack," Kurt called from behind him.

"Yes?"

"I'm going to get down to engineering. I want to get a good look at the circuit breakers to be sure eveything's..."

"No need to explain," Jack answered. "Let me know what you find."

Kurt headed off the bridge as Devon announced, "I've found the trail. It leads back to the AGC on the left. We'll call it AGC alpha. What do you want to do?"

"You're not taking us back through that damn thing," Don sneered.

The answer was of course, no. But Jack felt the urge not to completely agree with his science officer and said, "We're not making any decisions right now. Devon, can you plot a course that'll take us into an orbit clear of the AGCs?"

Devon stared at the screen for a moment before answering, "Not an orbit – the system's too complex. The best I can do is just keep transferring us between different trajectories. The problem is, I'm going to have to fire the engines every few hours and that'll use up propellant."

Jack stared at the schematic – the last thing they needed to do was unnecessarily waste their xenon.

"Keep in mind, we are stable here right now," Devon quickly added.

Jack nodded and said, "Fine keep us here for the moment, but plot a course out to a more distant stable position. We may move out there later."

"Yes, sir," Devon replied.

"Don," Jack said. "We'll need to get a good look at where we really are…"

"I'm already on that," Don answered brusquely. "I just pulled up a spectrum of the central star and it's a K-0 – definitely different from Epsilon Eri." The edge left Don's voice as he continued, "If you give me a minute, I'll even be able to tell you where we are. The pulsar program I wrote is completely automated. I should have those results in a moment."

Jack stared back at the main screen as his science officer worked at the terminal. It seemed that they, along with the AGCs, were locked in a synchronized orbit over the planet. What was once a thin, white crescent bordering a jet-black disk had broadened and now showed hints of blue – possibly an ocean. Their continued slow progression toward day-side would soon give them a better view of the planet's surface. The prospect of finding a habitable world, though, quickly consumed him. They would need to move quickly to set up landing missions and hopefully resupply.

"I've got it," Don announced.

"That fast?" Devon blurted out reflexively.

"Yes, that fast," Don answered flatly. "All we needed to do was identify the positions of the thirty pulsars we've been using as our reference. It was easy work for the computer. This star is two hundred twenty-five light-years from Earth. But what's more interesting is that the we've also shifted again in time: we're two hundred twenty-five years into our past based on the earth date – not our ship's calendar. That means it's the year 1904. The time shift and distance match again, like with G3-alpha…" Don's voice drifted off for a second before he continued, "This one's plus or minus five years; we got better measurements this time."

"That's starting to get close enough to be on our charts," Devon said.

"Does Earth know of this planet's existence?" Jack asked.

"I'm not one hundred percent sure," Don answered. "The last stellar cartography update we received was dated Earth year 2114. Based on our readings and that data, this star could be BD-10-3166. It's a K-0 star at the right distance.

"What about its planetary system?" Jack pressed.

"It's listed as having only one hot, Jupiter-sized inner planet and nothing else. However, that doesn't really mean this isn't BD-10-3166 since the planet below us may well be in a highly inclined orbit around the star. That would be typical of a system with a closely bound Jovian. They tend to wreak havoc on the other planets' orbits. Anyway, if that's the case most planet hunting techniques would have missed this one."

Jack just stared at the growing blue crescent; the fact that the planet might be Earth-like eased his frustration – but only slightly. The problem was, they were again in a completely unknown system with limited supplies, and no obvious way to get back. His irritation grew again, amplified by the fact that he had to hide it. He needed to play the part of stoic captain – someone who was sure he'd find all the answers. Instead, all he managed was to state the obvious, "So the bottom line is that we're orbiting the second planet of star BD-10-1366, we're two hundred twenty-five light-years from Earth, and the Earth date is 1904."

"Yes, if you trust our data," Don answered.

Jack just stared at Don after that last comment. The man was confusing, but at least he wasn't arguing anymore. Fatigue tugged at him and his mind relented, wandering back to Don's statement about the date: 1904. He remembered a small coin collection back on Earth with a silver dollar from that year. It was a heavy palm-sized coin with a profile of lady liberty on the front and a stylized spread eagle on the back. It was in good enough condition to still show its details, though years of tarnish left it dull grey. Its edges were nearly black with two centuries worth of grim. His great-grandfather gave it to him when he was just a boy, and told him that his own grandfather had given him the same coin collection when he was a child. If Don's measurements were right, that same silver dollar was now a perfect gleaming medallion having just left the U.S. mint. Sometime in the next few years, it would find its way into his ancestor's hands and work its way through the centuries back to him.

Jack was jolted back to the present by several loud cracks; they had the sound of small caliber gun shots. He spun around, looking for the source of the noise, when his ears began to pop. Instantly his stomach dropped: they were depressurizing. The loud buzz of the IPV's alarm system filled the air as he jumped from his seat.

"Devon, status," he called out.

"We have four impacts across the bow, sir. They appear to be small, but we are losing atmosphere. Auto-sealants have been deployed – we'll know in a moment if they're going to hold."

"Life support status?"

"We've lost point-zero-one atmospheres. Not enough to trigger automatic bulkheads yet. All other systems are functioning nominally."

He waited for Devon's follow up; the only sound was the continued buzz of the alarm. "Auto-sealants are holding, sir," Devon finally said.

"Very good." Jack skimmed the ship's sensor log before continuing, "Why didn't we see the objects on radar before they hit?"

"Don't know, sir," Devon answered. "Maybe it was compromised from the transit."

"Run a full diagnostic on it. We can't afford to miss anything else like this." Jack ran the scenarios through his mind for a moment before continuing, "Can you tell if there are any exit points? Did anything pass through the ship?"

"Actually I was thinking about that too. I've identified two sets of breaches on opposing sides – probably entry and exit points for two objects. We could estimate a trajectory from that."

"Exactly," Jack answered. Even though he was sure Devon had already thought of it, Jack said, "Compensate for our own velocity relative to this system."

"Got it," Devon said as he started working through the calculation. "Based on the entry and exit points, it came from bearing one-four-zero degrees, relative elevation of fifteen degrees. I'm using the line joining the star and this planet as a coordinate reference…"

"Repeat that," Don said suddenly.

"Bearing one-four-zero degrees, relative elevation of fifteen degrees."

Don just stared intently at his terminal and didn't reply. Jack allowed barely a second to pass before saying, "Don, what is it?"

"I've had the computer running a full optical scan of the surrounding region. It flagged that location as potentially having a planet. I just haven't followed up on it yet."

Impatient with having to ask for details, Jack said, "Just tell me what you've got so far."

"Just a sec…Ok, I've got one of the scopes on it now. It looks like a roughly Earth-sized planet at a distance of one hundred seventy million kilometers."

"Put it on screen," Jack ordered. The view was unimpressive; a small blue–white disk, no bigger than a pea held at arm's length, sat amid a background of stars. Jack stared at it intensely, trying to glean even a little information from the near-featureless world. "Are we at maximum magnification?"

"Not yet," Don answered, "I'll switch magnification in a moment."

The screen went black before displaying a distant, Earth-like globe. The image wasn't much of an improvement; the planet was roughly baseball-sized now. It seemed similar but not identical to Earth. Landmasses covered over half the planet, and its polar caps extended a significant distance towards its equator. There wasn't any obvious trace of vegetation, giving it a cold, inhospitable feel. A short burst of orange flashed above the northern continent, catching his attention. "Devon," Jack called.

"Yes, I saw it too," his pilot quickly answered.

"Increase magnification."

"We're already at max."

"Ok, replay that last segment. Freeze on the flashes."

Seven orange pinpoints hung just above the large, icy north pole. A larger yellow-white flash seemed to hover a short distance away. Aside from their color, Jack couldn't make out any details.

"Jack," Don said, "We should call down to Masako – she's got some programs that might be able to pull out some extra detail."

"Good, do it," Jack replied.

Don activated his comm. channel and said, "Masako, we've got some images we just recorded – I'm sending you the details right now. I need you to do a spectral analysis of the flashes in the upper right quadrant."

"Understood," was the quick reply.

Barely a minute passed before Masako's voice came back online, "They're broad band emissions centered at five hundred thirty nanometers. There's also a strong gamma ray peak associated with each one. The sensors recorded spikes in that region just before each visual burst."

"Gamma?" Don said aloud. "There's nothing in this system that should be capable of producing that, at least focused bursts like that."

"What do you mean?" Devon asked.

"Gamma ray sources are things like supernovas, or cosmic rays interacting with interplanetary or interstellar gas. They wouldn't look anything like these images."

"What about matter-antimatter annihilation?" Masako asked over the comm. "I mean, we used it in the Magellan's drive system."

"Well, yes, it emits gamma rays, but it's not a natural event. It'd be impossible to have a natural source here with a large enough concentration to create these flashes."

"I wouldn't limit ourselves to natural sources, considering what we've seen so far," Masako replied. "Think of it. Cities and planets completely wiped out…"

"Captain!" Devon called out urgently.

"What is it, Devon?" Jack said as he stood up.

"I've got radar working and we have contacts."

"How and what?"

"I thought about the impacts, sir. They were high energy strikes. It seemed highly likely to me that they were moving fast – I mean extremely fast. It gave me an idea. I checked the system and if the particles that hit us were moving above fifty percent of the speed of light, then the reflection of our radar pulses would be blue shifted out of the range of our receiving filters.

We wouldn't be able to see our own pulses coming back at us."

"You sure?"

"Yes. I just deactivated the filters and I've got eight contacts heading towards us. All are much larger than the objects that hit us. Seven are a bit smaller than the IPV, the eighth is huge; it's maybe ten kilometers across. They're moving at zero-point-six-c – sixty percent the speed of light."

"How the hell is that possible?" Jack asked reflexively.

"I don't know, sir. But those are the contacts that I have. Their bearing is 140 degrees, relative elevation of 15 degrees. They may have come from that planet, but they're already most of the way here."

Jack stared at the screen but could only see a field of stars. "Where are they?"

"Still too far to see. I put them at ten million kilometers out. ETA sixty seconds."

A small white pinpoint was visible now on the display. In the few seconds it took Jack to realize it was a large ship, it brightened considerably and now dominated the surrounding stars. There were two quick flashes of orange near the object, followed by a yellow glow that persisted for a few seconds.

A second later, the comm. line came to life. "Captain, this is Masako, respond please."

"What is it?"

"We just observed a major burst of gamma rays. Same point of origin as before."

"Damn it. How bad?"

"Not life threatening yet, but a few more like that could be a problem."

"Our thickest shielding is the aft engine section, right?"

Devon answered this time, "Yes, sir."

"Use maneuvering thrusters and point us tail-first towards it. That should help a bit."

The screen now showed a small, silver globe, with a blinding white light emanating from its rear. Several small blue lights that Jack assumed were smaller ships, were clustered near it.

"Fifteen seconds until contact. Distance, two point five million kilometers," Devon announced.

A barrage of orange bolts leapt from the small ships and struck the rear of the globe. The resulting explosion overwhelmed the cameras, bathing the bridge in bright, yellow-white light. An automated computer warning blared through the ship, "Gamma radiation warning. Exposure at three hundred percent of safe limit."

The glare of the explosion faded, showing that the larger ship had somehow survived. The pursuit continued.

"Devon, cut all main power now! Keep only camera circuits active."

"Sir?"

"Do it now! I don't want us to be seen."

Jack quickly hit the ship-wide comm., "Attention, we're cutting all power. There is to be no use of internal radios. All communication is to be done by voice. This is until further notice."

The bridge went dark, except for the image on the main screen. "Five seconds," Devon announced. "Their closest approach will be within one hundred thousand kilometers."

"Captain, what's..."

Jack turned to see Palmer just entering the bridge, his mouth still open as he paused mid-sentence. Jack ignored him and turned back to the main screen. The large vessel dominated their view. It was a featureless, 10-kilometer-wide, silver-blue sphere. The blinding white glow of its engines was diminished, but still powerful enough that Jack couldn't look directly at it. They were heading straight for AGC-alpha. The pursuers, however, caught up and swarmed their prey. Though Jack could only make them out as bright, blue pinpoints, there was no doubting their power. They darted around the mammoth ship, repeatedly striking it with bursts of orange light. Each tore a fresh gash into the pewter globe. Though it was only seconds from the AGC, Jack knew it wouldn't make it. One final orange bolt cut through the large ship's underbelly. A second later it was swallowed in a brilliant white explosion. As the shockwave traveled outwards, the pursuers turned to flee. The energy pulse was too fast though, and within seconds each of them was consumed by the advancing wall of fire.

"Devon, activate radar and sensors, we need to see what's going on." Instantly, an automated warning cut through the stunned silence on the bridge, "Radiation alert. Exposure monitored at five hundred percent above safe levels."

Almost immediately, Devon shouted, "Captain, I've got radar contacts. Hundreds. Maybe thousands."

"Position?"

"It looks like debris from the large ship. Lots of it."

"Range?"

"One hundred fifty thousand kilometers. Impact in ... forty-five seconds."

Jack flipped open a protective cover on his chair labeled 'safe mode,' and pressed the underlying red button. A series of loud thuds shot through the ship as the emergency bulkheads sealed each section.

"Devon, give me more information."

"Radar's overwhelmed, sir. There's too many ... It reads almost like a solid object coming right at us."

"Understood. Just keep your eyes on those instruments. You have permission to take any evasive action you deem necessary."

Kurt's voice cut through the momentary silence on the bridge. "Jack, respond please." Jack pounded the comm. button and said, "What is it?"

"What's going on?"

"Just brace for impact. We've got incoming debris." Turning his attention to Devon, he continued, "Proceed with maximum acceleration. Take us towards AGC-beta, we can use its gravity to help gain some additional speed."

"Beta, sir?"

"That debris field's between us and alpha. We've got no choice; just do it."

"Yes, sir."

Jack welcomed the heavy pressure of two g's forcing him into his chair. Maybe they could buy themselves some time, or at least reduce the relative velocity between them and the oncoming shrapnel. Anything that could minimize damage would help.

"Engines are at one hundred ten percent. But it's not going to be enough, sir. Impact in fifteen seconds. It's just coming at us too fast – up to zero-point-three c."

"Damn. Anything that hits us will tear right through the length of the ship," Jack said.

"Sir?" Devon asked, unsure what he meant.

Jack mulled it over for a split second and realized what his gut was telling him: with their tail facing the oncoming debris, a single piece could go through every single compartment and kill everyone.

"Engines off. Turn us transversely. Ninety degrees with respect to the field."

"Sir, we'll present more surface area ..." Palmer protested.

"Yes, but we won't risk a single impact tearing through us axially. That'd kill us all," Jack replied. "Devon, Do it now!"

"Understood."

The pressure of acceleration immediately ceased, making him feel as if he'd been launched forward. There was a sudden tug to his left as Devon pivoted the ship into position. "Five seconds," Devon announced.

Jack activated the ship-wide intercom and said, "Brace for impact."

The final seconds ticked by so slowly that he started to feel a false sense of relief. It was quickly eradicated as a series of cracks and metallic bangs echoed through the ship. He counted at least a dozen impacts before he lost track. There was a sudden loud hiss all around him, accompanied by a sharp pain in his ears.

"Hull breaches, sir. Throughout the ship!" Devon called out above the blaring alarms.

Jack's attention, though, was fixated by the next automated warning message, "Warning, bridge atmospheric pressure dropping. Pressure at ninety percent and dropping." He dove across the room to the emergency repair kit on the far wall. Retrieving pieces of sheet metal and sealant guns he tossed a set to Palmer and took the other as he searched for leaks.

"Pressure at eighty-five percent," the computer's emotionless voice announced. His head was splitting, but he easily pushed the sensation from his mind. Looking up, he saw a wisp of smoke flowing from a control panel directly toward a small crack in the ceiling. Years of training made the repair a nearly reflexive action. With one hand he quickly squeezed a bead of sealant around perimeter of the crack. A second later he tossed the gun aside, grabbed a handhold for leverage and forced the square of sheet metal up against the hole. The adhesive was strong and immediately held it in place.

"Warning, pressure at seventy-five percent and falling."

Jack's lungs labored in the thinning atmosphere. Ignoring the piercing pain in his ears, he pushed his way toward Palmer who was laying a bead of sealant along the floorboards. Seeing him approach, Palmer said, "Almost there." He forced a metal patch in over the hole and held it in place, at which point Jack said, "Computer, give the atmospheric status of the bridge compartment."

There was the briefest of pauses before the machine answered, "Pressure is at sixty-five percent and stable. Manual repairs are holding. Auto-sealants have also been deployed and are holding."

"What about the other compartments? List the worst sites first."

The computer proceeded, "Complete loss of atmosphere in cargo hold B. Complete loss of atmosphere in shuttle bay. Complete loss of atmosphere in secondary engineering compartment. Thirty-five percent loss ..."

"Stop," Jack demanded. "Repeat status of secondary engineering compartment."

"Complete loss of atmosphere. There are three major hull breaches that are too large for auto-sealants."

"Was anyone in there?"

"Affirmative. Assistant Engineer Claire Hughes, Lieutenant Commander Kurt Hoffman. Structural integ..."

"Enough," Jack said softly. He drifted to the floor and fought off a wave of nausea. 'Not Kurt,' was the only thought in his mind. It took him a moment to realize the bridge was silent; no one wanted to say anything. Forcing his own feelings aside, Jack continued, "Computer, are there any other casualties?"

"None in depressurized compartments. None reported by other crew members."

Without looking at anyone, he got up and went to leave the bridge. "Computer, open the bridge bulkhead."

"I am unable to do so due to the pressure difference. The bridge is at zero-point-six-five atmospheres; the hallway is at zero point nine five atmospheres."

"Damn it! Re-pressurize the damned bridge!"

"Complying," was the near monotone response.

He listened impatiently to the hiss of air entering the bridge, and avoided looking back at anyone. It was taking too long. Trying to keep the edge out of his voice, he said, "Devon?"

"Yes, sir?"

"Are there any other radar contacts?"

"No. Just the one wave of debris."

"What about long range?"

"Nothing, sir. However, sensors did record some more orange flashes in the direction of that planet just before the debris hit."

"We can't stay here," he whispered to himself.

"Sorry, sir. Say again?"

"Nothing. Are engines available?"

"Yes, sir."

"Good. Plot a courses to AGC alpha and beta. Give me ETAs to each. We'll activate engines on my command."

"Beta too, sir?" Palmer said

"Yes," Jack replied. "I want all options available.

"Understood."

The computer interrupted, "Re-pressurization complete." The door in front of Jack slid aside and he quickly exited the bridge with Palmer close behind. By the time he reached engineering, he found Nadya pulling furiously at the door to secondary engineering. Seeing him, she turned and shouted, "Jack, open the goddamned door and get Kurt out!"

The desperation on her face told Jack there was nothing he could say that would be satisfactory. Palmer offered in a subdued voice, "Nadya, there's zero atmosphere in there."

"Jack, please!" Nadya pleaded.

Before he could answer, Devon's voice came in over the intercom, "Captain, respond please."

Keeping his eyes on Nadya, he tapped his comm. unit and said, "Go ahead."

"I've got long range contacts like you suspected. They're coming from the same direction as those other ships - still too far out to count how many. Velocity is about zero point one c but they're accelerating hard."

"Jack?" Nadya said weakly, "I need ..." He put his hands on her shoulders and stopped her as he said softly, "I know." Looking away from her, he continued, "Devon, time to intercept?"

"Assuming they reach a max velocity of point six c like the others, about twenty-nine minutes."

"Damn it. What are the ETAs to the AGCs at full acceleration?"

"Thirty-five minutes to Alpha, twenty-two minutes to Beta."

"Understood. Set course to Beta, start engines as soon as you're ready."

"Beta?" Palmer protested.

Ignoring him, Nadya said, "Jack, we need to get to Kurt!"

Looking her carefully in the eye, he said, "Nadya, I've seen the damage report. We can't go in there."

"No!" She shook her head and started to turn away, but quickly turned back. "We can't just leave him."

"I'm sorry, but there's ..."

"Don't give me the 'there's nothing we can do' speech. You can do something. Do something!"

It tore at him; he wanted to help, to comfort her, anything. But the truth was, he hated himself too for not being able to do anything.

Devon's voice came in over the intercom, "Prepare for acceleration in one minute."

"Jack, we can't leave him there like this," she pleaded. She started sobbing but quickly choked back the tears and just stared at him.

"We can't stay here. We're in danger and have to move the ship. I promise, once we're through this, we'll get him. Right now, let's get prepped for acceleration."

"No," she replied.

"You don't understand." Forcing a measured but firm tone to his voice, he said, "We just witnessed a battle between two groups of aliens that are God knows how much more advanced than us. We were struck by debris from one of their ships. Now there are more of them heading towards us."

Devon's voice announced, "Acceleration in thirty seconds."

Jack continued, "We don't know who's the aggressor, or even if they're both aggressive and just battling over this piece of turf. All I know is that we're defenseless and cannot risk an encounter with them."

Nadya just stared back silently, obviously overwhelmed.

Palmer took advantage of the silence and said, "Captain, we can't go through Beta - we don't know where it goes."

"Palmer, you heard the ETAs. It's simple math; we have no choice."

"So you just want to jump off a goddamned cliff and look for the ground later? You're insane!"

Jack spun around to see it was Don who had questioned him.

He tapped his comm. unit and called to Devon, "Delay acceleration until my command."

"Understood."

Turning back to Don, he said, "You heard what I just said. We don't know who these ... these aliens are. They'll be here in twenty-five minutes now. It's too big a risk to stay here and we won't make it to Alpha in time. It's that simple."

"But we don't know what's on the other side of that thing. You can't just make decisions like this!"

"You just don't get it do you?" Jack shouted, not even trying to hide his anger. Releasing it almost felt good. "You never did! There is no choice. We've got a chance to survive through Beta, and nothing here. End of discussion!"

He hit his comm. button and said, "Devon, engage engines in two minutes."

Looking back at Palmer and Don, he continued, "Get to your seats and get strapped in. Or hell, just stand here, I really don't care."

He turned to Nadya, who was sitting on the floor, and put his hand out. "Come with me." She followed him passively as he led her to her quarters. "Get strapped in. After we're through this, I want you to see Helena."

"I'm not injured. There's no need to see a doctor," she said calmly.

Jack could see that she was using every ounce of her strength to retain her composure. He said, "Still, I think ..."

"I'm OK Jack. I just need to be alone right now."

"I understand. I'm still going to ask her to check in on you, OK?"

"Whatever you want. I'll either be here or down by propulsion," she answered and quickly closed her door.

Chapter 24 – July 26, 2124; 16:30:00

Jack stared at the engineering console as the ship's acceleration pressed him firmly into his seat. However, he couldn't focus on its readouts. A brief text message from Devon flashed across his screen: they were still on track to reach the AGC before the alien ships caught up with them. That too, was little consolation – his mind simply kept focusing on Kurt. The image of Nadya pleading with him was inescapable. What if he hadn't turned the ship broadside? The question tore at him. Intellectually he knew there were no 'what ifs.' Events couldn't be undone. And besides, his strategy was textbook. But, none of that mattered; his feelings dominated his mind and he didn't have the strength to resist. It just hurt.

He tried again to force his eyes back to the screen, but the graph staring back at him held no more meaning than some random jagged line. All he could think about was the fact that he was sitting in Kurt's seat. There was no choice about that either: without Nadya, Kurt and Claire, there was no one else qualified to run engineering. Palmer, of course was more than capable of running the bridge in his absence; Jack just felt a need to oversee everything. He strained against his emotions to keep his eyes on the console, and after a few more moments, a pattern finally emerged. The engine output seemed to level off, but there was still a strange series of small spikes and dips in the thrust. It had been ten minutes since Devon engaged the engines and the readings should have stabilized by now. He tried running through the possible causes, but there was too much going on. The potential threat of the approaching alien contacts demanded his attention. Instinct told him to head to the bridge and work directly with Devon. At least Devon had been dutifully updating him on their status. He worked again to focus his attention back on the screen: the power levels did finally seem to be stabilizing.

His relief was short-lived, though as a small vibration ran through the ship. The display showed two new spikes, but the output levels quickly drifted back to normal.

"Computer," he called.

"Yes, Captain?"

Can you correlate this data with any other anomalies in the IPV's systems?"

"There are two possible correlations. One is a zero-point-seven percent drop in engine output. The other is a two-degree rise in the main power line temperature. The temperature is still well within limits."

"Is it dropping back down?"

"No, but it is stable at the new temperature."

It didn't make sense. "What about the spikes from two minutes ago?"

"There was similar behavior. A short drop in engine output followed by a corresponding rise in power line temperature."

There was a connection, but he couldn't see it. He had the urge to call Nadya, but resisted. She needed time. Another, smaller vibration briefly shook the ship. It was accompanied by a similar spike on his screen. He had no choice now and activated to comm. channel to her quarters. "Nadya," he called politely.

There was no response. Despite his need to act, he waited a few seconds before activating the channel again, "Nadya, I don't want to bother you, but…"

"I'm here Jack."

He turned quickly to see her entering the room and climbing an embedded access ladder.

"Sorry, I didn't mean to startle you," she said politely.

"No…no, it's OK. What are you doing here?"

"I came as soon as I felt those vibrations. I couldn't just sit there."

"I know. Take a look at this," he said as he transferred the readouts to the console next to him. She quickly took a seat and studied the data; her hands raced across the keyboard, activating a series of diagnostic screens. "Power spikes, drops in thrust…," she said to herself.

"I had the computer look for correlations with other anomalies. There appear to be corresponding increases in power feed temperature," Jack offered.

She stared at the screen for barely a second longer before saying, "Shit, this is bad."

"What're you talking about?"

"Here, look at this." She displayed two graphs, one above the other. The top line was relatively flat, except for a few prominent downward spikes. The lower one was looked perfectly constant and stable.

"What am I looking at?"

"The top trace is the power flow form the reactor to the engines. The bottom one is the temperature of the superconductive cable. You'll see that the temperature scale shows a max of 40 degrees C. That's the upper safety limit for operation."

"Yes, I understand. It looks like we're well within that."

"Yes, but watch now when I magnify the trace. We'll look at it on a scale of tenths of a degree."

Jack saw it immediately. What had appeared to be a flat, stable line, was actually slowly increasing.

Nadya continued, "It's so small and within safety limits that the computer didn't flag it for us. The problem is, I don't think it's increasing linearly."

"Computer," she said, "fit the temperature records using an exponential curve." A red curve perfectly overlaid the temperature history, and then continued rising more quickly as it moved forward in time. "Change scale and show time of cable failure." The graph zoomed out and showed the red curve rising sharply upward, reaching the forty-degree level at the seven-minute mark.

"Seven minutes to failure," Nadya said calmly.

"But what's causing this?" Jack asked.

"I'm not sure, but the most obvious thing would be damage to the main power feed – they're made of room-temp superconductors. Their crystalline structure is what lets them carry all of that power. A single crack from the one of those impacts before would disrupt that structure and give it some resistance. Once you send a few hundred thousand volts across it, it'd heat up real fast. That heat would instantly bring the rest of the cable above the critical temperature, causing a complete loss of superconductivity. At that point it'd short out across any of the near-by metal components and burn the whole thing up."

"Can we buy any time?"

"I don't know how. It's simple physics. We need to carry that high current load to run the ion engines. The only things that can do it are the superconducting cables. When they go, the whole thing'll go."

Jack quickly activated the comm., "Devon, how long until transit through Beta?"

His pilot replied immediately, "Twelve minutes."

They needed five more minutes than the cable could give them. He looked up at Nadya and said, "What if we cut power through this cable by some fraction, say twenty-five percent?"

"That would reduce the stress on it ..." She typed at her console for a moment and continued, "It should hold for fifteen minutes."

He called back to the bridge, "Devon, recalculate our ETA if the port engine bank is reduced by twenty-five percent."

There was a pause before Devon answered, "I'd have to cut back on the starboard bank as well to maintain balanced thrust ... it'll be close. That'll push us out to fifteen minutes. We'll be only three minutes ahead of them."

He didn't like the answer, but there was no choice. "Throttle both back now."

"Understood."

The hum of the engines dropped noticeably as he felt the pressure holding him in his seat ebb as well.

"Where's the cable?" Jack asked. "Maybe we can inspect the damage ourselves and do something."

"It's in...secondary engineering." She started typing but suddenly stopped and just stared straight ahead. Jack didn't know what to say, and could only watch as she forced herself to take a deep breath, visibly shake her head and say, "That's the only access point. It was probably damaged when we were hit before."

Jack found himself grasping at straws as he asked, "Can we re-route the power through another cable?"

Nadya didn't reply and continued staring at her screen. He gave her a few seconds before calmly saying, "Nadya, I know it's hard, but I need you here right now. Can we..."

"Jack, I'm paying attention," she said with an edge. She pointed to her screen and continued, "But we've got a problem. Look over here – the temperature increase is accelerating – the reduced current isn't helping enough. We're going to lose engines sooner."

"How much time do we have now?"

"Maybe five or six minutes at most. The problem is we can't just let the cable burn out. It'll wreck the whole system. I'll have to shut them down at the last second and hope we don't do too much damage."

"What about re-routing..."

"We can't do that," Nadya quickly shot back. "We don't have the time or the cabling."

"That's not what I was thinking," Jack replied. "The damage is affecting the port side of the three engine banks, right"

"Yes."

"What if we disable the safeties, drop power to the port and starboard banks further to keep them going and make it up by running the central bank well above max. – maybe at one hundred fifty percent. It should be able to withstand that for a few minutes."

"Maybe..." Nadya said thoughtfully. She turned quickly and pointed at a mass of circuitry in the far side of the engineering room. "You'd have to manually lock the breaker into place so that the increased current doesn't trip it."

"I'm on it," he said as he got up from his seat and started climbing an access ladder. "Tell me what to do."

"OK, it's pretty simple. But you're going to need to move fast – I'm showing that we only have a couple minutes left on this cable."

As he climbed, he tapped his comm. unit and said, "Devon, what's our status?"

"We're five minutes out from the AGC."

He reached the circuits and Nadya called out, "Open the gray box to your right. There'll be three large switches inside. Tell me when you're ready and I'll cut power for a few seconds so that you can throw the middle one. Use the hook by the side to lock it into place."

"Devon," Jack called, "did you catch that?"

"Yes. You're going to shut down power for a few seconds."

The box cover opened quickly and he found himself staring at three large, rubber-handled levers. "I'm ready," he called out.

"Thread the hook through the holes at the base of the switch. Ready…cutting power now," Nadya said.

Instantly, jack found himself floating away from the box. He grabbed the center lever, looped his feet around a ladder-rung for leverage and pushed it forward, lining up the holes. It took two tries to keep it in place and insert the hook. "It's done," he called to Nadya.

"Jack grab on firmly, I'm restarting the engines."

Jack did as told, but instead of the smooth hum of power flowing through the engines, there was a sharp, deafening crack. The acrid smell of ozone followed, confirming what his gut instantly told him – something blew out.

"Goddammit!" Nadya shouted. "The center grid power cable blew anyway."

"Do we have anything?" Jack called out.

"Give me a sec…"

"Captain." It was Palmer's voice over the comm.

Not waiting for the obvious question, Jack replied, "We've lost engine power. Stand by."

"Understood."

Jack pushed his way back over to Nadya who was typing furiously at her terminal. He needed an update, but dare not interrupt her. Barely thirty more seconds passed before Devon called,

"Captain, I'd really like to have engines back."

Jack turned to Nadya who just looked back and shook her head.

"It doesn't look like it's going to happen. What's our status?"

"I'm unsure, sir. We needed engine thrust to ensure entry into the center of AGC-Beta. Without it I can't complete the course correction."

"And?"

"It's going to be close, we may impact the left edge of the outer ring."

"Give me specifics," Jack said with obvious frustration.

"There's no time, sir. Contact with the AGC is in two minutes and four seconds."

"Shit!" Jack looked at Nadya who just stared back silently. "Palmer," he called out.

"Here, sir," was the prompt reply.

"Prep for collision. Seal all bulkheads now. Have all departments do what they can to prepare. I'll get back to the bridge as soon as I can after transit."

"Understood."

The engineering compartment bulkhead started to close. He looked to Nadya as he said, "I know the main power feed is gone, but can we use one of the secondary ones to pulse just the port side of the ion grid. It might give us enough of a push to avoid a collision"

She didn't answer immediately, and Jack said, "Nadya, I need you with me here, right now."

"Uh…maybe," was her sluggish reply.

"We've got maybe a minute and a half, can you do what I asked?"

"There's a chance, but it'll burn that cable out too in the process" she answered. "I'll need you back by the breakers you threw before. You're going to have to lock the left one in place."

"Got it," Jack said as he pushed back across the room. With the cover still open, it only took a few seconds to throw the switch into position and insert its hook. "It's ready," he called to Nadya

Devon's voice came in over the intercom. "Fifteen seconds."

"Devon," Nadya called into the comm, "I'm going to give you a five second engine pulse now. Will that get us clear?"

She didn't wait for his reply, and Jack felt a sharp quick force pull him to the side. He reflexively grabbed on to a nearby railing to keep from falling as Devon responded, "It looks like that'll be enough. We'll just miss the rim of the ring, but we will be going through off-center."

The engine pulse stopped and Jack briefly thought about getting back to his seat, but there wasn't time.

"Five seconds," Devin announced.

Taking a deep breath, he wrapped his fingers tightly around the railing. The ship shook violently, pulling hard to his left. He found himself hanging sideways. Using all his strength, he locked his fingers around the metal bar, but they lost their grip. He was falling and tensed his body in expectation of the sharp pain that would come when he landed.

Chapter 25 – July 27, 2124; 01:15:00

There were voices, but Jack couldn't tell who was speaking. A sharp stab of pain ran across his right arm and he flinched.

"Hold still," a voice yelled.

The words were clear, but he still couldn't tell what was going on. Opening his eyes only brought more pain; the lights were too bright. Someone was leaning over him. The pain shot through his arm again and he moved.

"Devon, hold his arm still! I've got to stop the bleeding. Just another minute," the voice said.

It was a woman's voice. "Helena?" he managed.

"Doc, he's coming too."

That was definitely Devon's voice. "What's going on? Where..."

"Jack, give me one more second here and I'll explain," Helena said. He felt another jolt of pain, but resisted the impulse to move. "There, done for now."

Jack opened his eyes and tried focusing on Devon. His vision was blurry and he was dizzy, but at least the pain was receding. "You got banged up pretty good, sir," Devon said.

"Actually Jack, that's putting it mildly," Helena added. "You nearly bled out. The gash in your arm wasn't necessarily that bad, but between the time we were incapacitated and..."

"Time? How long were we out?" he said and tried to sit up. A jolt of pain ran through his side, convincing him to stay down.

"Most of us were out for three hours."

"What do you mean most?"

"You and a couple of the others were unconscious a while longer."

"What's our status?"

"That's enough for the moment Jack," Helena said calmly. "I need to get you moved back to sick bay and do some more work on you."

"What're you talking about?" Jack asked as he again tried to sit up. The room began to spin and a wave of numbness swept through his body. He could see that Helena was talking, but couldn't hear her. He laid back down and her voice made it through the fog that was encompassing him, "...before we continue. Plus, you're going to need a transfusion of at least two more units of synthetic blood."

Jack's mind raced back across the events that led up to the transit. "What about Nadya and Palmer?" he asked. In a near panic, he tried to push them away and get up, but this time blackness engulfed him.

Chapter 26 – July 27, 2124; 11:35:00

The room was quiet; the only sounds Jack could make out were the various tones from some sort of electronic equipment, and the soft clicking of a nearby keyboard. He opened his eyes and worked at focusing on his surroundings. It took only a second to confirm that he was in sick bay. He tried to move, but his arms were restrained. "Helena?" he called.

There was no answer. He looked to his right, but the privacy curtain was drawn around his bed. An IV tube led from his arm to a nearby pump, and several wires ran from his chest to a small computer. Probably for an EKG, he thought. Craning his head back, he saw someone pull the curtain aside: it was Helena.

"Ah, you're awake. Good," she said softly. "You were out for a few more hours there. The extra rest probably did you some good."

Jack watched as she unfastened the straps that ran across him. "Sorry about the restraints, but you know we're in zero-g so I couldn't have you drifting about the room. Now sit up slowly."

Jack obeyed without making any comments.

"Any dizziness?"

"None. What about all of this?" he asked, gesturing at the wires and IV.

"You don't need that anymore. I finished the transfusion three hours ago, so we can take them off now if you want."

"If I want?" he asked with a smile. "What I do want is to get back to the bridge and..."

"Slow down, you're not going anywhere. I said I'd unhook you from the equipment, but considering what you've been through, I want you here a little longer for observation."

"Helena, there's no time for that."

She pulled out his IV and said, "Jack, you lost over twenty-five percent of your blood volume. Even though I replaced most of it via transfusion, I've only just stabilized your blood chemistry. There's too big a risk if you jump right back into things this second."

"Listen," he said, "We've just gone through another of these alien AGCs, and traveled to god knows where. The ship's taken damage, and we're running low on supplies. There's too big a risk if I stay down here any longer."

"What if you pass out, or go into delayed shock? Or, worse yet, what if there were some internal injuries that I didn't catch?" she asked and stared straight at him.

"I've been here, what, a few hours? If there were any internal injuries, you would've found them by now."

She didn't answer. Jack gave her a few additional seconds before continuing, "I promise, if I feel anything wrong, I'll check in with you immediately."

Helena completely ignored his response. Instead, she picked up a penlight, gestured to her left and said, "Look this way." After shining the light in each eye, she opened the dressing on his arm and looked over the wound. It was obvious she didn't want to give in. It was equally obvious she knew she had no leverage over him. She cleaned around the sutures, covered them with a new piece of gauze, and removed the last of the monitoring tabs. "I'm going to enter into the log as an official order from me, that you are to report directly to sick bay should you experience anything unusual."

"That's your prerogative."

"For the next few hours, you should not exert yourself physically in any way. Do you understand? You could do some real damage."

"Understood."

She let him get up, and as he made his way to the door, he said, "Thank you."

Unhappy with his decision, she just nodded in acknowledgement.

Jack took his time going down the corridor, and headed toward his quarters. His mind, however, raced ahead trying to take inventory of what needed to be done. The problem was, he didn't know where to begin. He had no idea of their status, and more importantly, if there was any imminent threat. He quickly entered the small room and shut the door behind him. A wave of frustration swept across him as Kurt's and Claire's deaths ate at him again. He was trapped in an inescapable loop. Their deaths made him doubt his decision to turn the IPV. Logic told him it was the right move – he couldn't risk losing the ship from a single impact. But had he sacrificed them just based on some off-the-cuff calculation of the odds? What if the risk wasn't as great as he thought? Jack pushed the thoughts from his mind and dug out a new shirt. Reflex kicked in and he tried to put it on quickly, but stopped as pain shot through his arm and shoulder. He finished dressing more cautiously and thought about Don's resistance to his decisions and

Palmer's open questioning of his orders. He needed to control them better.

That last thought made him acutely aware of the paranoia invading his consciousness. Again, he struggled to purge it all from his mind; he couldn't afford to be randomly suspicious of everyone around him. They all needed to be focused on the tasks at hand. Taking a slow pace back to the bridge, Jack was thankful the corridors were empty. Especially since the pain had forced him to pause several times and he didn't need anyone's pity or concern.

Devon was the first to notice as he entered and said, "Sir, glad to see you're back."

"Thanks," he replied with a small grin.

The others turned to acknowledge his return. "Palmer, Don," Jack said, nodding to each. "Where is everyone else?"

Palmer replied, "I've assigned all available hands to Nadya for repair duty. The engines are a mess, and we just barely grazed the outer ring of AGC-Beta during transit. There's significant outer hull damage on the starboard side."

"Casualties?"

"None worse than you, sir," Palmer replied.

Jack nodded and looked at the main view screen. It held an unfamiliar pattern of stars: no main star, no planets. "What's our status?"

"Undetermined so far," Palmer said. "Engines are off line and will remain so for at least another day. Nadya's got no choice but to do a full repair. Our velocity and position are unknown."

"Unknown?"

"Correct," Palmer answered. "We can't tell yet if we're even in a star system. Main cameras and telescopes only just came on line, so we haven't been able to complete a full four-pi, visible-light scan to locate a nearby star. The one navigational camera we have been using hasn't shown us anything. So, without a reference point, we can't even determine our velocity."

Don interrupted, "The only thing I can tell you is our interstellar position relative to Earth. I was able to get the radio telescope on-line an hour ago and locate our reference pulsars. It appears that this transit moved us closer to Earth. That is, we're at a distance of one hundred sixty-four light-years. As before, there appears to be an equivalent time shift. We've moved about sixty years closer to our present: Nineteen-sixty-five.

"A hundred sixty-four years in our past and a hundred sixty-four light-years from home," Jack repeated more to himself than to the others. The numbers no longer held any meaning to him as he stared at the star field in silence. Even his subconscious urge to imagine what Earth was like during that time period was gone. He continued staring at the stars, but they told him nothing. The urge to shout in frustration was strong, but that was clearly not an option. Even his persistent optimism and faith in his crew was fading. None of this made any sense.

"Sir?"

Palmer's voice brought him back to the present. Jack looked at him and said, "There's no near-by star, right?"

"None that we've found yet. I mean the nav-cam should have seen anything sun-like. Like I said, now that the other systems are online, we just started a proper search."

"What about the AGC? It's got to be in orbit around something."

"The problem is – we can't find it."

Jack only managed a look of disbelief in response.

Palmer continued, "It's been nearly twelve hours since our transit. Like I said, we only regained access to telescopes and main sensors an hour ago. At these distances it'll be very difficult to locate a twenty-kilometer-wide object. Especially if there's no light from a local sun to illuminate it."

Before Jack could formulate an answer, Don said, "Think of it Jack, if we carried the velocity with which we entered the AGC to this location, then we should be moving at about fifty thousand kph. That would put us over half a million kilometers from the AGC. It would have an angular diameter of less than one-thousandth of a degree: a bit larger than a thread held at arm's length. With no light on it, it'll appear dark against the backdrop of open space."

Jack shot back quickly, "If we carried that velocity with us through the transit, then we should be moving in the same direction."

Palmer cut him off, "But sir, we struck the AGC going through. That's what threw you and several other crewmembers around. It also made us start tumbling. When we came too, it took Devon nearly twenty minutes to stop our uncontrolled rotation. So we have no idea what our original orientation was."

"And, since there're no near-by bodies to use as a reference, we have no idea in which direction we're moving," Don said, completing their collective thought.

They sat in silence. Anger coursed through him; they sounded defeated. There was no room for that. "What about looking for a residual ion trail like before?"

"It's been too long – twelve hours since transit. There's nothing left to see," Don answered.

"Then what about a Doppler-shift measurement of the surrounding stars?" he offered in vain.

"That's no good either," Don replied. "We were going at a bit under point-zero-one percent the speed of light before transit. That's roughly the same order of magnitude as some stellar drift velocities, so it won't give us any real info.

"What about the gyros?" Jack pressed. "They should..."

"They were knocked off of their pre-transit calibration by the impact," Don answered.

"Let me finish," he shot back with an edge. "I would assume the calibration was lost. But, we can still use them to detect any dark masses in our vicinity. If we were in an inertial frame, you know, simply coasting without engines and nothing around, then the gyros should show no external torques after Devon stopped our rotation. However, if there were any moderate sized bodies out there, their gravity could be seen via a small precession in the gyros. That precession will tell us the magnitude and direction of the gravitational force on us, and thus where the object is. Then we'd have a reference with which we could find our velocity and the direction in which we've been drifting. We could trace our way back to the AGC."

"But Jack, there isn't even a star around here. What do you expect to find?" Don protested.

"What about sub-stars like brown dwarves, or maybe even a cold stellar remnant?"

"Why the hell would they put an AGC around one of those?"

Jack didn't even try to control his anger. "What? Are you going to pretend to understand what motivates an alien race capable of moving planetary masses? We're not going to just sit here until we starve."

Jack turned his back on Don and said, "Devon, can you configure the nav-system to monitor the gyros like I said?"

"Definitely. It shouldn't take much work at all."

"Good." Turning to Palmer, Jack said, "Tell me more about the damage we took from striking the AGC. Was there any loss of atmosphere?"

"None. We got lucky. We grazed it and just did some damage to the outer hull. The aerodynamic surfaces will need repair, and the heat shielding was compromised in several locations. As far as space-worthiness, we're in relatively good shape. Maneuvering thrusters and nav-systems are operational."

"We just don't have main engines," Jack said.

Turning to Don, Jack continued, "I'm going to need you to help Nadya with the repairs."

"Help Nadya?" Don responded incredulously. "In case you've forgotten, I'm the chief science officer of this crew. She's just..."

"There's no time for this, Don. We're short-handed..."

"Because your actions killed…"

"Don," Palmer said calmly as he stepped in front of the scientist, "there's nothing…"

"I don't want to hear a word out of you," Don sneered. Stabbing his finger in Jack's direction, Don continued, "He's responsible for the death of three crew…three of the people we've lived with for the past ten years. All in the last few days."

Palmer tried again to intercede, "Don, this is neither the time nor the place for this."

"When the hell is?" Don pushed by Palmer, pointing his finger directly at Jack's face as he continued, "You even killed someone you called a friend. This recklessness has to stop now."

"Watch your tone," Jack said with complete contempt.

"What the hell do you mean by that?"

Jack looked to Palmer and said, "Get him off my bridge. Have him help Nadya with the repairs."

"That's not my job…" Don stopped as Jack moved to within a few centimeters of his face and said in a level but harsh tone, "In case you're too damned blind to realize it, there is no science mission right now. Either you use whatever skills you've got to help fix this ship, or I'll lock you in some damned closet somewhere. You're of no use to me here."

Palmer pulled Don back. Once he was out of Jack's reach, Don shouted, "You don't have any right!"

Palmer put himself between the two men as he guided Don out and said, "Don…Don, lay off for now. Come, let's talk in the hallway."

Jack watched his first officer carefully usher Don off the bridge. He wanted to hear their conversation, but that wasn't possible. Instead, he glanced at the damage report on his monitor to clear his mind. Its list of ship's systems and statuses confirmed that everything was exactly as Palmer had described: several fractures in the heat shield required repair, and the starboard aerodynamic control surfaces were damaged.

"Captain" Devon said.

"Yes."

"I've got some very preliminary readings from the analysis of the gyros."

"Good, go ahead."

"I think I've found a stellar mass object."

"Explain," Jack said calmly.

"There's a zero-point-seven solar mass object at bearing one-three-zero degrees, at a distance of about nine hundred million kilometers. I also read what seem like two planetary bodies nearby. One is roughly Neptune-size;

the other is in orbit around it and is slightly smaller than the Earth."

"OK, that's a start. Why didn't you call it a star?"

"I'm not really sure what it is. It emits very weakly in the visible spectrum, though I am seeing stronger emission in the infrared. But, it's too large to be a sub-stellar object like a brown dwarf."

"Put its spectrum on the main screen," Jack said. The screen displayed a broad, smoothly rising curve that reached a rounded peak and then tailed back off again. It was broken occasionally by the sharp drops of atomic absorption. "It is thermal radiation, but cool, maybe two or three thousand degrees," he said softly. "Devon, you said it was zero-point-seven solar masses?"

"Yes, sir."

"That's too big for a Type-M dwarf. I wonder if it's a white dwarf?"

"Sir?"

"A burnt-out stellar corpse – it's what our sun will become in a few billion years. The fact that this one's so dim and emits so deep into the IR means it may be ancient and must have died billions of years ago." Jack took a deep breath and said, "How far are the planets?"

"I can't give you an accurate number yet since I used an estimated distance to calculate their masses. I started by assuming that the AGC had to be in orbit around a nearby planet. When I found evidence of the two planet-sized objects I just mentioned through a precession in the gyros, I then estimated the distance to be seven hundred thousand kilometers: the distance we likely traveled since the transit. This gave me what I needed to derive their masses and then the mass of the white dwarf. Now that we know where to look, we can use radar to directly measure the distance to the planets and get a more accurate reading of their masses."

Jack followed most of what Devon was saying, but was much more concerned about their immediate situation. "I take it there're no signs of power emissions, communications or any indications of civilizations or ships in the area?"

"None, sir."

"How about viewing the planets?"

"There's not going to be much to see; the white dwarf isn't putting out much light so everything's dark. There's just no ambient light with which to see them. But...we might be able to look at the planets in reflected IR light. Though, they won't be much above absolute zero."

"Ok," Jack said, "but, I need you to do two things before that. First, concentrate on using radar and IR light to find any AGCs around the main planet. And second, let's get a good gravitational map of the star system. Once we get engines back online, we'll need that data."

"Yes, sir."

Jack looked back at the damage report, but knew their problems were much more serious than the repairs. This star system was almost certainly dead, which meant there was no hope of trying to find supplies here. Add to that the fact that even when they did get engines back online, it would take them a couple of days to get to the AGCs. The bottom line was – they were going to use up nearly a quarter of their remaining food without anything to show for it.

"Jack?" a voice called to him.

He spun around and was surprised to see Nadya standing at the threshold of the bridge.

"Yes?" he replied politely.

"I need a word with you." She glanced around the room and added in a hushed voice, "In private please?"

"Of course," he said as he quickly got up. He exited the bridge with her and gestured to the small meeting room to his left, "Let's go in there."

Nadya followed him in quietly, and without saying anything closed the door. Her drained expression echoed the feeling of the entire crew.

Jack forced a smile and said, "In case I didn't say it before, you've been doing an amazing job holding this ship together."

"Thank you," she whispered while looking at the floor. She drew a deep breath and looked up at him before continuing, "I came because I have a request."

He knew what she wanted, but felt it best to let her ask. "Go ahead."

She spoke softly, "I would like to lead a team on an EVA to seal off the hull breaches to secondary engineering. I want to...to retrieve Kurt and Claire."

"I know Nadya. I've been thinking about that too. But..."

"But?" she said with an unexpected edge.

"But, our atmospheric reserves are at only nineteen percent. There's simply not enough to re-pressurize that compartment after the repairs are done."

"You're wrong Jack. It's not that big a room."

"I know. But remember, we still need to complete the repairs and re-pressurize the shuttle bay. That'll take our reserves down to ten percent, and that's just too low."

"Jack, we can't just leave him out there like that," she pleaded as tears formed at the edge of her eyes.

"We won't leave him there," he said reassuringly. "Once we're able to replenish our supplies, it'll be the first thing we do. They deserve that."

Jack waited for her rebuke, but she just stood there, staring blankly into the room. He chose not to say anything more, giving her the necessary time to think things over.

She turned to look him in the eye and said, "We could still do the EVA and bring them back through the airlock."

Jack didn't need to think very long to realize it wouldn't work. The bodies had been at near absolute zero for a couple of days. They would be rigid, brittle and sprawled in God knows what position. Trying to force them into a closet-sized airlock would damage them: it would be both a physical and emotional disaster. He didn't want to explain the details to her, but had to say something. "I'm sorry Nadya, I just don't think the airlock is big enough to do this."

"Jack, you don't know that for sure."

"Let me give it some more thought, OK? I'll let you know a little later."

"Today?" she asked with forced calmness.

"Yes," he answered. He was willing to say most anything at this point, just to push off the unpleasantness of finally telling her 'no.'

She nodded and said, "OK," before leaving.

He stood alone in the empty room, but wasn't able to focus. There was too much to do, and too much to think about. Only a few seconds passed, though, before the intercom came to life, "Captain, respond please." It was Palmer's voice.

"Yes," he answered.

"We need you on the bridge. Devon has picked up four radar contacts heading towards us."

"On my way!" he nearly shouted as he dashed out of the room. As he pushed his way into the bridge he caught the tail end of something Devon was saying to Palmer, "...at high velocity. Approximately zero-point-five c. Time to contact: thirty seconds."

"What do you have?" he asked.

Palmer answered him, "Four object are on course to intercept us."

"Objects?" he asked.

"They seem too small to be ships…maybe two meters across."

"Missiles or projectiles?"

"Unknown. They've made two course corrections to home in on us…"

"Their velocity's changing again, sir," Devon shouted.

"Details," Jack demanded.

"They're decelerating," Devon said with some doubt. "This can't be right."

"What?" both Jack and Palmer asked simultaneously.

"They're coming to a complete stop. That's too many g's of deceleration. We're talking about millions. It..."

"Devon," Jack said, stopping his pilot's protest. "Give me their locations."

"One second," was the reply. "They've taken up positions surrounding us: above, below, left and right. About a thousand kilometers off in each direction. They've matched our speed."

"Put one on screen."

"This is maximum magnification, sir." The screen showed a small, featureless, silver ball. There were no protruding instruments or obvious engines.

"What the hell is it?" Don asked as he entered the bridge.

Jack ignored him and said to Devon, "Are there any transmissions?"

After a brief pause, Devon answered, "I've just scanned radio and visible spectra. There's nothing; they're just holding position."

Palmer spoke up, "Considering what we've seen so far, I recommend bringing our defenses on line. I know we don't have much, but we were outfitted with a small compliment of missiles just in case. Plus, the high power drilling laser might be able to do some damage."

"I don't think that'd be wise," Jack answered.

"Then, what do you intend on doing?" Don challenged.

"Let me at least track them with the targeting computer," Palmer said. "We can't be caught completely asleep."

Jack gave in and said, "Ok, but do not power up any weapons themselves. I don't want to give them any reason to start shooting."

"Tracking on-line," Palmer said. "Targets acquired..."

A brilliant flash of green light engulfed them. Jack tried to shield his eyes, but it was too bright, forcing him to bury his head in his arms. A second later it was gone. He looked back at the screen, but the view remained unchanged; the silver ball hung motionless in space. "Devon, status," he called out.

Palmer shouted his response instead, "Targeting computer is down. I have no data at all."

"Nav-systems and engines are still online," Devon added.

"What the hell was that?" Palmer asked.

Jack just stared at the screen as he answered, "They must have detected your fix on them with the tracking system."

"Jack, get us the hell out of here," Don said loudly.

Jack looked around the bridge before responding. "All we've got are maneuvering thrusters, and that's not going to do anything meaningful."

"We should try to move off slowly," Palmer suggested. "I mean…they came from that planet. Moving off might be a way to show them that we don't want to provoke them."

They sat in silence before Jack continued, "Devon, try a broadband transmission. Maybe we can make some sort of contact and let them…"

"Sir!" Devon interrupted. "Nav-cameras have picked up several bright objects directly behind us."

"Distance?"

"Unknown. There're dozens of them. They're emitting in the x-ray and gamma ray spectrum as well."

"Is it weapons fire?" Jack asked.

"No," Devon answered. "The intensity's too low."

A second blinding green flash engulfed them. Jack was quicker this time to cover his eyes with his arm. Again, it took only a second for the light to dissipate.

Devon was first to speak, "Engines and nav-systems are off-line."

"Do we have any weapons?" Jack asked, knowing the answer.

"Everything's down," Palmer replied.

"Look!" Don shouted, pointing at the main screen.

The silver sphere quickly closed in on them and disappeared from the camera's field of view. A second later, they heard four, deep, resonating bangs as the spheres made contact. An electric blue haze appeared around them; it was thin enough that he could still make out the stars. A split second later, the star field shifted.

"I'm not doing anything. The engines are still down," Devon said. "But, it looks like we're on course for the planet."

"Devon, bring up a forward view on screen," Jack said.

A small, pitch black disk was silhouetted against a dark grey, Jovian planet. The image grew quickly and within seconds filled nearly half the screen. The bridge was silent as they watched the scene.

"Devon, don't zoom in, just give a static view," Jack said quietly.

"I'm not doing that – our view's been fixed at ten-times magnification. My readings show that we're accelerating towards the planet."

"That's impossible," Don shot back. "I don't feel anything. We're still at zero-g."

"I can't explain it, sir. Velocity is now at one-million k-p-h." The Jovian planet completely filled their view and the dark disk was now large enough to dominate their attention. "One-point-one-million k-p-h," Devon announced.

"Devon, check your instruments," Jack said. "That'd mean we're accelerating at nearly ten thousand g's. We'd be dead."

"I have no way to precisely verify anything. But based on the rate at which we're approaching the planet, it's got to be close to right. I mean the trip should have taken us over a day, and at this rate we'll be there in only another minute."

"Put the screen at actual view, no magnification."

The image shifted to show a near duplicate of what they first saw: an inky black disk set against a charcoal grey world.

"Velocity has leveled off at one-point-six million k-p-h. Contact in forty seconds."

The black, earth-sized moon orbiting the larger grey planet, grew to fill their view. There were no details to be seen. The feeling of helplessness was paralyzing, but there was nothing they could do. Every instinct told Jack they were coming in too fast. He dug his fingers into his armrest and had the urge to shout out some orders for status or to do something, but it made no sense.

"Fifteen seconds," Devon announced. "Wait, we're decelerating. Velocity down to one-point-two million. One-point-one million..." Devon stopped talking as the view abruptly shifted. The black globe seemed to slide smoothly out of the way, and the screen was filled with the deep-grey cloud tops of the gas giant.

"They're taking us into there? We'll be killed!" Don shouted.

Devon ignored him and said, "Velocity is at five hundred thousand k-p-h, and dropping fast. I can't tell if we're going to hit or enter some close orbit."

"How long?" Jack asked urgently.

"Ten or twenty seconds, it's impossible to tell. Altitude is down to one thousand kilometers."

Jack stared at the nearly black screen. Slight wisps of charcoal grey fog on a black background were the only signs of any cloud patterns. The subtle patterns quickly spread out, giving them the only hint of their rapid descent.

"Entering the atmosphere now. Speed is twenty thousand k-p-h."

"Hull temperature?" Jack demanded.

"There's no sign of any heating. They must be doing something, I just don't understand," Devon replied.

The last of the dark grey clouds flew past as they entered the pitch blackness of the planet's upper atmospheric layers. The inky fog unexpectedly pulled away revealing a clear zone. In the distance was an illuminated metal globe. It just hovered in front of them; its deep grey metal sheen was broken by rows of small yellow lights.

Devon broke their collective silence, saying, "Radar shows it to be about a hundred kilometers away."

"My God," Don said. "That means it's got to be twenty or thirty kilometers wide."

They closed on the alien ship fast and slowed only when it completely filled their field of view.

"We're still approaching," Devon announced. "I think they're taking us into it."

"I don't see any docking bays or doors," Palmer said.

The thought had already occurred to Jack as he found himself staring tensely at the still growing, perfectly smooth, curved metal wall. The rows of lights were now out of view, and the only detail they could see was their fast growing reflection.

"Sir, we're not slowing down," Devon said nervously. "Five seconds until contact."

A wave of panic suddenly ran through Jack and he shouted, "Shit, grab on to something!" He turned away at the last moment, but nothing happened. Looking up, the screen seemed completely black.

The bridge was silent. Jack searched his senses for some hint of what was going on.

"I think we're inside," Palmer said.

Jack looked around; everyone's eyes were fixated on the screen. "Devon, Put up a wide angle view."

There was enough light now to make out that they were in some immense, dark cavern. The walls were pitch black. Randomly spaced along them were groups of cylindrical structures, lined with lights reaching in towards the center of the globe. Jack imagined them to be buildings with a myriad of lit-up windows: some reached heights of thousands of meters above the outer wall. They glided through the central void. The buildings seemed to be grouped in clusters, like stalactites. At this scale, his mind immediately thought of them as towns or cities. Their flightpath, though, kept them far from any of the structures.

Don broke the silence with the obvious if inelegant question, "Where the hell are we?"

There was, of course, no answer; instead, Jack continued watching as they progressed deeper into the cavern. The IPV gently changed course and moved toward one of the cities. The towers were enormous, Jack estimated that tops of the largest ones must be at least three or four kilometers from the outer wall. They closed in on the tallest building and Jack could tell that the lights were indeed windows.

The IPV changed course again, gliding alongside the structure before stopping maybe twenty meters from its surface. The gently curving silver wall across from them was windowless. Jack expected to see docking clamps, or doors, or something, but it was perfectly smooth.

"What are they doing?" Devon finally asked.

"I don't know," Jack answered quietly.

"If I was them," Palmer said, "I'd be studying us and our ship to see how we react. To see if we posed any threat."

"Devon, do we have maneuvering thrusters available?" Jack asked.

"No, everything's still off line."

"Damn," was all that Jack could say. There was little that he could think of that was worse than sitting helpless. They were completely at the mercy of these beings. His training and nature taught him to view most everything as a chess game – to look ahead at what your opponent might do, and plan for the various possible scenarios. Here though, there were no moves. Even the silence on the bridge was becoming frustrating. But, there wasn't anything worth saying. Growing tired of sitting still, he started to get out of his chair when small ripples appeared in the seemingly solid surface of the alien wall. A column of silver material flowed toward the side of the IPV.

"What the hell?" Don shouted.

The substance quickly solidified into a cylindrical tube connecting the structure to the IPV.

"They've made a sealed connection to the starboard airlock," Devon announced.

Palmer activated the ship-wide intercom and said, "All hands report to the armory for side arms." He turned to Jack and said, "We're not going to sit by and be boarded."

Jack had misgivings about agreeing, but there were too many unknowns. They'd seen devastated planets, as well as a ship being chased and destroyed. In fact, they themselves had just been captured and pulled into some sort of giant vessel. Palmer was right, sitting still and doing nothing wasn't an option. He answered, "Go below and take up positions by the airlock. But no one, I repeat no one is to fire or take any actions without my order. Is that understood?"

"Yes, sir," Palmer replied.

Jack got up but the bridge was suddenly bathed in the same blinding light as before. A wave of dizziness swept over him. He heard someone shout something – then nothing else.

Chapter 27 – July 28, 2124

Jack opened his eyes and found himself sitting in his command chair. The bridge was silent. A quick look around showed that he was the only one conscious. Devon, Don and Palmer were slumped in in their chairs. He stared at them a moment longer, trying to understand what had just happened, when he realized there was gravity: but from what? They weren't accelerating nor had they landed on some planet's surface.

He stood up clumsily, slightly dizzy from whatever had rendered him unconscious, and made his way over to check on Palmer. His pulse and breathing were stable. "Palmer," he said. There was no reply. He gently shook the man and said more loudly, "George." There was still no response.

"Devon, Don?" he called out, but neither answered.

Everything started to come back to him. He remembered the tube connecting the IPV to the alien structure. Then the bright light, but nothing else. He went back to his seat and activated the ship-wide intercom. "This is the bridge. Anyone who can hear this, please respond."

He waited several seconds in silence; there was no reply. Looking up, he saw that the view screen was unchanged from before; a silver tube still connected them to the structure.

"Computer?" he said.

"Please do not be alarmed," a male voice said.

Jack spun around quickly, but seeing only his unconscious crewmates, asked the obvious, "Who said that?"

"Please, there is no need to be alarmed. We understand your concerns considering all that you have seen. We will not harm you."

He looked around again, but the voice came from all directions. "Who are you," he finally asked.

"Do you want my...designation? Or, who we are?" the voice replied.

The uncertainty in its answer was almost comforting. "Both please," Jack said.

"It is difficult to express how I am designated. I volunteered to make contact with you once we found you. Since I am the first to speak with you, you may refer to me as Alpha."

Jack scanned the room once more, but saw nothing. He could tell that the voice wasn't coming through the comm. system. "Before we go any further, what's happened to my crew?"

"They are unharmed. We felt that it would be most prudent to awaken you first. Our understanding is that you are the leader."

"No ... no. I mean yes, I am the 'captain,' but that doesn't mean that you can choose to speak with just me."

"But we monitored your communications and you were the one who directed the others as where to go and what to do."

Jack thought about his instructions to Palmer for a moment. "That's not how it works. But this isn't going any further until I know that they're alright."

"You can be assured that..."

"No assurances. I want them awakened," Jack said firmly, but politely.

"That will complicate matters. We are concerned that several will panic."

"They are highly disciplined individuals, they will not panic," Jack said, even though he had his doubts. "Whatever you have to say, you can say to all of us."

The voice didn't reply. Jack waited impatiently, but there was only silence. He was about to demand an answer when heard Palmer's voice.

"Captain? What's going on?"

"Are you OK?" Jack asked.

Palmer looked around before answering, "Yes, my head hurts, but I'm fine."

Devon turned around to look at them, as did Don. Jack said, "Good," softly and then activated the comm. link to engineering. "Nadya, respond please."

There was only a brief delay before she answered groggily, "Here, Jack."

"What's your status?"

"I don't know. I just came to when you called."

"What about the others?"

"I don't know. It's like we're all waking up. I guess everyone here seems OK," she replied. "What's going on?"

"Stand by," he answered. He activated the ship wide intercom and said, "This is the bridge. As you've likely surmised, we've all been unconscious for some period of time. However, I need your attention. I've just had initial contact with the alien race that is...for lack of a better word, holding us." Jack saw Palmer ready to interrupt but kept talking, "They will be contacting us again shortly. I will leave the intercom on so that everyone can hear what is being said. Please remain calm."

"Who are they?" Palmer finally asked.

"I don't know yet."

"Do you want me to try and raise them on the radio?" Devon asked.

"That doesn't seem to be necessary," Jack answered. "All I know is that a few moments ago I was talking with one of them. He didn't have a chance to tell me much yet, only that he volunteered to speak with us first, and as a result we can call him Alpha."

"You mean he was in here?" Palmer shot back.

"No, I just heard his voice." Jack looked around the bridge. The others were quiet, waiting for something to happen. Jack called out hesitantly, "Alpha? Can you hear me?"

"I am here," the voice answered.

"Wo," Don said loudly as he spun around. "Where the hell is that coming from?"

"Don, quiet please," Jack said calmly. "Alpha, you may continue."

"Again, I want to restate that you should not be alarmed. We will not harm you."

"I understand what you're saying," Jack said, "but then why are you holding our ship like this?"

There was a short pause before Alpha replied, "There was no choice. You were in danger."

"What danger?" Don challenged.

"Before we brought you here, you detected several ships entering this system."

"No. The only objects we saw were the four...things you used to capture us," Jack said.

Alpha answered calmly, "If I understand correctly, you detected several x-ray and gamma ray sources. What you were viewing were the antimatter drives of a fleet of ships decelerating as they entered this system. This fleet belongs to an aggressive species that has been attacking our colonies. If we left you where you were, they would have killed you."

"What makes you so sure of this?" Palmer asked.

"It appears to be what they do."

"Explain please," Jack said.

"We have only very brief reports from our other colonies about what has happened. Each time a small...swarm of vessels simply entered a star system and did not attempt any form of communication. They just attacked and killed our people. We have no understanding of who they are or why they do this. In each case, they immediately moved on as soon as they were finished."

The destruction they had seen on the other worlds was consistent with Alpha's explanation, however Jack was still suspicious. "Seeing as you're able to communicate with us, why didn't you tell us this first?"

"There wasn't time."

"There was certainly time to say something," Jack shot back.

"There were two problems. First we weren't sure if you were part of their fleet. We..."

"I think it's pretty obvious from our technology that we don't pose a threat to anyone here," Palmer challenged.

"That's not what I meant." Alpha replied emotionlessly. "Our ship is well hidden; we knew we were safe. Your ship, on the other had just appeared through our...AGC as you call it, and drifted helplessly. They have never used the AGCs, so this was very different and unnerving. We weren't sure what or who you were, but there was a high probability that you were some sort of bait to draw us out."

"Bait?" Jack asked.

"Yes, a trick meant to..."

"We understand the term," Jack said with a hint of impatience. "I'm just confused as to how we would serve that purpose."

"Forgive me, but your limited technology makes you helpless out here. We would be obligated to try to assist you, and thus give away our position. But as I said, was a high probability that this was a trap. We needed to study you and the situation. The problem was that the damage to your ship made it very difficult for us to access and interpret your technology."

"Access our ship?" Palmer challenged.

"Yes. As I said, we needed to evaluate you. Once we did see your records, it seemed more likely that you were not associated with...them."

"We would have told you that had you asked," Palmer said.

Ignoring him, Alpha continued, "The problem was that their fleet appeared before we could make a final determination. I convinced the others to take the risk and retrieve you before their ships could start probing the system. I might add that not everyone here is convinced that this was the right move."

"Forgive me for asking," Palmer said with forced politeness, "but how do we know that you're the good guys in this?"

"Good guys?"

"Not the aggressors," Palmer replied impatiently.

"Because you're not dead. It's what they do."

They sat in silence trying to swallow what the alien had just said. Alpha continued, "Their strategy has always been to enter a system with overwhelming force and attack immediately..."

Alpha continued, but Jack's attention was drawn to Don who was desperately waving his arms at him. Don proceeded to make exaggerated motions of covering and uncovering his ears while mouthing the words, "Do this." Confused, Jack followed his lead. It took a few seconds to realize what was happening: the volume of Alpha's voice remained unchanged, regardless of whether his ears were covered.

Jack interrupted Alpha, "Stop for a minute please. I need to ask you a question."

"Yes?"

"How are you communicating with us right now?"

Palmer shot him a confused look, but Jack continued, "Because it's sure enough not by radio. And, if my guess is right, we're not actually hearing you right now. Not via sound and our ears."

Alpha answered without hesitation, "We are using a direct auditory interface. We don't use sound or voice to communicate. We haven't in a very long time. Nor do we use language in the sense that you understand it. An oversimplification would be to say that we are able to transmit our thoughts directly to the auditory cortex of your brains. With a proper translation, you are able to understand this."

"How?" Jack demanded without hiding his anger.

"How?" was the genuinely puzzled reply.

"How do you transmit this?"

"We use electromagnetic waves in the Terahertz region."

Simple ultra-high frequency radio, Jack thought. "Let me be more clear: how am I able to receive and understand your transmissions?"

"We have given each of you a small device..."

"Hold on a minute," Don said loudly. He slowly backed towards the rear of the bridge as he continued, "What devices? Where are they?"

Alpha answered, "They are small receiving and translation interfaces located just beneath the temporal bones of your skulls. They are a small fraction of a millimeter across."

Jack reflexively ran his fingers around his temple while Palmer shouted, "You implanted objects in us?"

"It was the only way in which we could effectively communicate with you."

"I don't care," Palmer shouted. "You can't just implant objects in us."

"Captain," Alpha said calmly, "please help your crew understand that..."

"I want mine out now!" Don shouted.

"Captain, please calm your crew down or we will need to sedate them again in order to continue our conversation."

The bridge went silent with the threat. "Alpha," Jack interrupted, "I am in agreement with my first officer. How are we supposed to know that's all that you did?"

"We did nothing else to your bodies. And, as a gesture of good will, we even effected repairs to much of the damage on your ship. Please trust me..."

"I don't see how we can have any basis for trust here," Jack said. He took a deep breath and suppressed his own feelings of paranoia. "We need time to consider all of this." His instinct was to tell Devon to cut the communications channel, but that wouldn't do any good. Frustrated, he said, "How the hell do we terminate communications for now?"

Before the alien could respond, Don shouted, "How're we supposed to be sure that you're not reading our minds or something with these devices? Hell, I want you to get the goddamned thing out of my head right now."

Alpha's voice remained patient as he answered, "The devices are triggered by your conscious act of speaking. We receive only the information you convey while you are talking. This was done out of respect for your species' concepts of privacy."

"That's bullshit," Don shouted. "If you had any respect for..."

The bridge was suddenly silent. Jack turned to see what had stopped Don's rant, and saw the man slumped in his chair. He barely had enough time to confirm that he was the only one still conscious when Alpha spoke again. "When you want to contact me again, send a signal on your radio at a frequency of 1.43 gigahertz."

"What did you do to them?" Jack demanded.

"They will awaken a soon as I terminate communications. There are others here who believed that the continued arguing was counterproductive. Please explain to them that we have not and will not hurt anyone, but the situation is urgent. We cannot waste time on this type of debate."

"They won't trust me," Jack said.

There was a short pause before the alien said, "We will send you another gesture of good will that may help. Contact me as I instructed when you are ready."

He sat in silence for a few seconds before Don suddenly shouted, "What the hell?"

Palmer followed with the obvious question, "What did they just do?"

"It seems that some of the others with Alpha lost their patience. They sedated everyone and asked me to convince all of you that they mean us no harm."

"Fat chance of that," Don said. "What else did they say?"

"That when we want to contact them again, we should send a signal over the radio."

"How do we know they actually cut communications?" Don asked.

"They're probably listening right now!"

"I certainly would if I were them," Palmer said. "I suggest that we proceed as if they are."

"I agree," Jack answered reluctantly. "We should play it safe for now. But more importantly, we need to show some more self-control. Regardless of how you feel, we are at their mercy."

"Don," Jack continued.

"Yes?"

"I want you to go down to sick bay and work with Helena on understanding exactly what these devices are. Find out what risks there are in removing them."

"I'm on it," Don answered as he turned to leave the bridge.

"Palmer," Jack said.

"Yes, sir?"

"Alpha talked about repairing at least some of our damage as a gesture of good will. Work with Nadya. I want a full top-to-bottom inspection of the entire IPV. Find out what they've done in terms of repairs and otherwise."

"Understood, sir."

"He also said they'd send us another gesture of good will."

"What does that mean?"

"I've got no idea. For now, though, focus on the repairs."

After Palmer left, Jack looked up at the alien structure on the view screen. He was at a complete loss as to what to do. "Computer," he finally said.

"Yes, Captain."

"Good, you're still on-line," he muttered to himself. "The IPV was boarded. I need to know how and when."

"There are no records of the IPV being boarded."

Jack half expected that answer, but thought that there must be some evidence of what they had done.

"Computer, compile a list of all internal sensor readings during the time that we were unconscious."

"I have no record of you being unconscious."

"What do you mean? We just came to."

"My records do not corroborate this."

Jack grew more frustrated and shouted, "Can you at least tell me the current ship date and time?"

"1530 hours, July 27, 2124."

Jack thought back for a moment and said, "That's about the time that we were pulled into this...this ship." He knew something wasn't right. "Devon," he said calmly.

"Yes, sir?"

"What does your navigational console read. It should have its own independent chronometer, right?"

"Yes, it does. It says 1530, July...I'm sorry sir, it agrees with the computer."

"Damn it!" Jack shouted as he slammed his fist into his armrest. His wrist stung for a moment. Looking for the source of the pain, he saw the glint of a metal wristband – it was his grandfather's watch. The antique wasn't linked into the ship's systems or even electrical. He quickly turned his arm and read, '7:45.' The date indicator showed a '28.'

Devon must have seen the look on his face since he asked, "What is it, sir?"

"We were out for at least sixteen hours and possibly as much as twenty-eight. My watch reads seven-forty-five, AM or PM I don't know. The date, though, reads the twenty-eighth. Reset the ship's..."

He was cut off by Don's panicky voice over the intercom.

"Jack, Janet's missing!"

"What're you talking about? Helena's has had her in hibernation ever since her fall," Jack replied.

"Don't you think I know that? I'm in sick bay and her body's missing. They took her. Goddammit, they took her!"

"Shit! I'm coming down now." He looked at Devon and said, "Call me immediately if anything happens – anything at all."

By the time he reached sick bay, he had to push past half a dozen people just to get in. Before he could get a word out, Don looked him straight in the eye and asked, "Why the hell would they do this? Abduct her like this?"

"Calm down, Don," he said, forcing a steady tone to his voice.

"What're you talking about, calm down?" Don shot back. "They've captured us, implanted devices in our heads, knocked us out, and now they've abducted Janet. We've got to do something!"

Jack turned away so he could concentrate. But with six sets of eyes watching, he couldn't focus.

"We need to get our ship's weapons on-line and defend ourselves," Palmer said from the hallway.

A flash of anger overwhelmed him and he turned and shouted, "Don't you get it. Our weapons aren't any use against them!"

"How the hell do you know?" Don said. "You haven't even tried anything."

"Don! All we did was use our targeting computer before and they knocked us right out. Hell, they knocked you out again just for being a jerk! They took our weapons and other systems off-line without us being able to do a damned thing about it. We've got nothing to fight with!"

"So we should just sit here until they grab each one of us or kill us?" Don said, waving his hands wildly.

Palmer spoke up from the back of the crowd, "This doesn't make any sense."

He was grateful for Palmer's interruption; it gave him a second to breath. "I know that," he answered.

"No, I mean I've still got my sidearm." Jack watched as Palmer checked it over. "It's still loaded."

Jack just shook his head. "Even with those, we're not any sort of threat." The room was quiet again. Jack buried his anger at their helplessness and said, "Computer."

"Yes, Captain."

"Do you have any readings of Janet on the ship?"

"Lieutenant Janet Kinkade is not onboard the IPV."

"See? They took her!" Don shouted.

Jack ignored him and turned to Palmer, "They wiped its memory – even the time we were all unconscious. The best I can tell, we were out for either sixteen or twenty-eight hours. The computer has no records of any events during that time." Before Don could speak, Jack continued, "Is everyone else accounted for?"

"Yes," Palmer replied.

"Is there any obvious damage to the ship?"

"No, but I did a quick computerized status check and found signs of the repairs the alien mentioned."

"What do you mean?"

"All hull breaches have been sealed. Preliminary readings even show that secondary engineering has been re-pressurized. It's still sealed, but Nadya wants to go in."

"Not yet," Jack said softly as he thought of Kurt. He looked around and asked Palmer, "Where is she?"

"In engineering still reviewing the ship's systems."

Jack gently pushed his way out of sick bay and walked quickly down the corridor. He heard Palmer following him, but didn't say anything or look back. By the time they reached the engineering section, Jack found what he had expected: the hatch to secondary engineering was open. Nadya was standing in the center of the room. She turned to him, her face flush with desperation. As he walked to her, she said "They took them Jack. They took his body!"

She collapsed in his arms, and for the first time sobbed uncontrollably. Jack held her until she calmed down and said, "I am going to get them back."

She looked at him and just nodded.

As she wiped her face, he asked, "Are you OK?"

"As much as I can be."

"I know it's too much to ask, but I need you to focus. I need you to work with Palmer and finish inspecting our systems. I don't trust them, and want to be ready for whatever comes next. Can you do that?"

"Yes," she answered in a mostly level voice.

Jack turned to Palmer who was waiting politely at the hatch. "Work with Nadya. Do whatever it takes to get engines and some sort of defenses online."

"Do you think they'll even let us get the engines back up?"

"No, but I want what little we've got available."

"Understood."

Chapter 28 – July 28, 2124

Kurt opened his eyes and screamed. He stopped though as the first sounds exited his mouth. His heart was racing and he could feel the adrenaline coursing through his veins, but everything around him was wrong. He was lying on a hard table in a featureless, bright white room. A second earlier he could swear that he'd been staring directly into the cold vacuum of space. He clearly remembered the blinding pain cutting through his head and lungs as the air ripped past him into the void. Reflex had taken over and he remembered curling into a ball. But now all that was gone.

He jumped to his feet and looked around. It was a completely empty, white room, save for the table on which he'd been lying. Light seemed to emanate from all surfaces, and he could barely discern where the walls met the floor. As he took a step, he realized that there was gravity and wondered if he was on a planet or some accelerating ship.

"Hello?" he finally said sheepishly.

There was no response: only a completely smothering silence. Kurt walked cautiously over to a wall and ran his finger along it. It was perfectly flat. There was no reflection or texture of any sort. He pushed gently against it, and was surprised that it gave slightly, like a very tight rubber sheet.

Without warning, a door opened to his left. It didn't slide aside or open on a hinge, but simply appeared. He took a half step back more out of caution than fear. Finally, after staring at it for a moment, he walked to its threshold and looked down a plain, white corridor that led from his room.

"Do you want me to follow this?" he called out.

Again, there was no answer. He waited a few seconds before tentatively starting down the hall. An intersection with another corridor lay about ten meters ahead. A familiar voice suddenly broke the silence as it called out, "Hello?"

It was Claire. "Claire, it's me Kurt. I'm over here," he answered as he ran the last few meters to the intersection. Peering down the hallway, he saw Claire cautiously approaching him from the right.

She was nearly out of breath when she reached him. "What's happened. Where are we?" she asked.

"I've got no idea at all. The last thing I remember was knowing that we weren't going to make it. I remember the pain, and then I was here."

"I thought it was a nightmare," she said. "But this doesn't feel real either."

"But, where's here?"

They stared in silence at the corridors in front of them. The one leading from Kurt's room continued past the intersection for several meters before disappearing from view around a bend. The other continued straight before reaching a dead end.

"What now?" Claire asked.

Without warning, a door appeared at the dead end, and a moment later Janet Kinkade carefully walked through it. She looked at them and then back at the door before asking, "Kurt? Claire? What...where are we?"

"Don't know," Kurt answered. "Are you OK?"

"I think so. I'm just confused. I ... I was on the ladder at the back of the IPV when the Magellan started accelerating. I tried to hold on, but ... I don't know. I remember falling. And then I was on the table in there. But this isn't sick bay."

"I know," Kurt said. "We're not sure what's going on."

Claire walked over, hugged her and said, "It's good to see you're OK."

"But where are..." Janet's voice trailed off as the corridors behind each of them disappeared. "What the hell?" was all that she could manage as they jumped back from the newly formed walls.

Kurt didn't say anything; he just reached behind and touched the new surface. It had the same texture as the wall in his room. Looking past Janet and Claire, down the remaining corridor, he said, "I guess we're supposed to go this way." He led the way at a slow pace; the floor gave a little with each step, like walking on rubber. As with his room, light emanated from all around – floor, ceiling and walls – making it tough to gauge distances.

They rounded a bend and the hallway ended about thirty meters ahead at a vaguely familiar black and grey wall. Realizing it was the outer airlock door of the IPV, Kurt ran the last few meters before stopping and calling out "Hello! Can anyone hear me?" There was no answer. He peered through the door's small, round window, but saw nothing. "I guess we should just go in." Neither Janet nor Claire answered. He flipped open a clear protective cover on the airlock control panel, and pressed the bright green "Open" button. The outer door obediently slid aside and the three of them squeezed into the chamber. Without looking back, Kurt pressed the "Cycle-In" button on the wall. The door slid shut, but there was no hiss of air coming into the chamber: they were already at atmospheric pressure. The excitement quickly built inside him as he pressed the "Open" button on the inner hatch. The door, however, stayed shut.

"What the hell?" he said as he hit the button again. The door remained sealed.

"Kurt? What's going on?" Claire asked.

"I don't know. None of this makes any sense," he said under his breath. "I just want to..." The heavy door slid aside, revealing a dark corridor and two men pointing assault rifles at them. Kurt and his companions pressed themselves against the back of the airlock as he shouted, "Hold on! It's us."

"Stand down!" a familiar voice called out.

The guns in front of him were hesitantly lowered. The man spoke again, "Stay where you are for now." It was Jack. There was a brief pause before the corridor lights came on and the two in front took a step back: it was Palmer and Devon. Kurt could only make out Jack and Don behind them in the cramped hallway, and called out, "Jack, what the hell's going on here?"

"This isn't possible!" Don protested from behind.

"Kurt? Claire? Janet?" Jack said.

Kurt briefly looked at Claire and Janet behind him before answering, "You can see it's us. What's with the guns? And telling us to stay where we are?"

Before anyone could answer, Nadya forced her way past Palmer and Devon. Kurt felt a wave of relief and wanted to take her into his arms, but she stopped about a meter away. She took a hesitating step backward before asking, "Kurt? Is it really you?"

"Of course," was his exasperated answer. "Please tell me what's going on?"

Jack answered him, "Kurt, do you know where you are and how you got here?"

"On the IPV!" he said without trying to hide the frustration in his voice. "But I have no idea about *getting here*," he said waving toward the airlock. "Or, anything else going on."

"You don't remember how you got there? Or what happened?"

"No!" he shouted.

Palmer whispered something too low to hear into Jack's ear before he asked, "Was there any sign of Alex on their ship?"

"No...what the hell are you talking about?" Kurt protested.

"I don't know how to say this," Jack said with forced calmness, "but you and Claire were killed two days ago. We don't know how, but the aliens were able..."

"Jack, you're not making any sense. We're alive."

Nadya moved closer and took his hands in hers. She lightly caressed them but still held back. Kurt looked at the disbelief and suspicion in her eyes and practically shouted, "Can't you see it's me?"

Jack spoke again, "Kurt, what's the last thing that you remember?"

"What do you mean?"

"Onboard the IPV. What's the last thing that you remember?"

He stared back at them and felt his stomach drop. The memories became very real again. "We...we were in secondary engineering checking on the power feed when the ship shook violently. I remember being thrown across the room. Then there was a leak. The air tore by me as a hole opened in front of us. I could see the stars. Everything hurt; it felt like a nightmare..."

"It wasn't a nightmare," Nadya said. "Your compartment depressurized." Kurt watched as she looked at Jack instead of him.

"The ship was in bad shape," Jack continued. "We weren't able to repair the damage and recover your bodies. You and Claire were exposed to open space for days."

"But," Kurt said touching his chest, "how do you explain this?"

"I can't," Jack said. "All I can say is that the aliens must have revived you."

"What aliens?" Kurt shouted in exasperation.

"The ones holding us and our ship."

Kurt looked at Nadya as he practically screamed, "What the hell is he talking about?"

"They captured us, Kurt. They implanted devices into our heads. They knocked us out when we argued with them. I don't know what's real and what's not. I mean you were dead." Tears were running down the side of her face; her voice cracked as she continued, "They took your bodies and didn't even tell us what they did with them."

"Didn't you see the aliens?" Palmer asked.

"We didn't see anyone," Janet answered in a level tone. "We just woke up a few minutes ago and followed a hallway that lead us here."

"They didn't talk to you?" Jack asked.

"No one said anything," Kurt answered. He felt numb; everything was wrong. His mind dwelled again on the pain and the crack in the hull. The obvious thoughts dominated his mind: Could they have died? How could they be here now?

Palmer took a step back from them and said, "I don't trust this whole thing."

Don, who had finally pushed his way to the front of the group added, "I agree with him. How do we know this isn't some sort of trick or set-up?"

Nadya spun around to face him and shouted, "What the hell are you talking about?"

"Nadya, like you just said, he was dead," Don answered calmly. "How do you know that's really him? I know that's in the back of your mind. I see it in your eyes."

Kurt couldn't take it anymore. He wanted to throttle Don, but just pushed toward the man and shouted, "Damn it Don! I'm right here in front of you. I don't know what sort of paranoid shit you've got in your head, but this has all got to stop now."

"Captain," Palmer said calmly, "I think at very least we should give each of them a thorough medical examination."

Kurt looked to Jack, who was mulling over the whole situation. Don started to say something, but Jack finally shouted, "Enough!"

The hallway quieted to a hushed murmur as Jack continued, "I'm putting an end to all of this right now. "Kurt, Claire, Janet...thank God you're back. I don't know how, but I'm not going to question it. I think, however, it would be prudent to have Helena examine each of you thoroughly before anything else. You've been through...well I don't know what. Let's just make sure you're OK."

Kurt nodded and gave a barely audible, "OK."

"Good," Jack said. "I want everyone else back to your stations. I'll update you all as soon as I can."

Kurt felt like the world was spinning around him. He just wanted all of this insanity to end. Jack calmed him, though, as he gave him a pat on the back and said, "I'm glad you're back."

Kurt looked blankly at him and said, "I really don't know what to say."

"Don't worry. Right now, get to sick bay and get checked out."

Nadya said in a low voice, "Jack, the engines are in good enough..."

"I know what you want to ask, and it's OK," Jack said with a smile. "Go with him to sick bay. I'll cover engineering myself for a little while."

"Thanks," she replied softly.

Kurt looked to Nadya who took him by the hand and led him down the hall, behind Janet and Claire. When they neared sick bay, Nadya stopped him and waited until the others went in. The silence was like a weight on his chest. Barely a second past before he had to speak. "Nadya, I don't..."

He stopped as she took him in her arms. "Kurt, you don't know what it's been like," she said nearly sobbing.

He kissed her gently on the cheek and whispered, "It's true then? What Jack was saying?"

"Yes. You were dead. I didn't want to believe it when it happened. Even now I've been avoiding it. And now..."

"And now I'm here."

"Yes," she said and wiped her eyes. "I can't tell what's real. I've had nightmares since you...since it happened. I woke up last night sure you were alive, but the bed was empty. I cried as I tried to crawl back into that dream with you – but, I couldn't. Now you're here. It seems real, but I don't know. I know it's not possible, but I want it to be true."

Kurt kissed her again and just held her in the hallway. Nadya finally pushed back, wiper her eyes and said, "Let's get you in to see the doctor."

Kurt answered with a simple, "OK."

Chapter 29 – July 29, 2124; 11:30:00

Jack walked into engineering and found Nadya briefing Kurt, Palmer and Claire on the ship's status. She looked up at him and said, "We were just finishing up; I didn't know you wanted to join us."

"I wasn't planning on it," Jack replied. "But there're some new developments I wanted to go over with all of you. I assume everything else is in order?"

"Yes, you'll have my full report shortly. But to summarize, the aliens repaired nearly all of the ship's structural damage. Plus, we've managed to get engines on line, and for what it's worth, even have access to weapons."

"That's good news," Jack said. Looking directly at Kurt and Claire, he continued, "I understand Helena's cleared you both for a full return to duty."

"Yes," Kurt replied, "but I don't understand why it took a day's worth of tests and examinations to do it."

"I'm just glad you're back." As Don walked in behind him, Jack said, "I've asked Don to join us. I just finished communicating with Alpha, and they've invited us to send a small group onto their ship for a face to face meeting."

"Did they say anything about Alex?" Don asked.

"Yes," Jack said solemnly. "They found his body where we stored it on the IPV, but it was too damaged to be revived. Alpha said something about that gas on G3 Alpha having a component that ravages the central nervous system while doing the obvious physical damage we saw. He also said that it looked like their enemy designed it to prevent his people from reviving any victims."

His statement was met with stunned silence.

"Do you believe him?" Palmer asked.

"I think so," Jack replied softly. "But it doesn't look like what I believe is relevant right now. They are currently holding us and there is absolutely nothing we can do about it. Since it seems that they aren't overtly threatening us, our only move is to play along with them and see what happens."

The room stayed quiet until Jack continued, "Kurt and Don, you'll join me for this meeting. Palmer, as first officer, I'll need you to remain in command here onboard the IPV."

"I understand," Palmer replied without emotion.

"When is this going to happen?" Kurt asked.

"As soon as we can get to the airlock," Jack said with a smile.

"Don, are you OK with this?" Palmer asked.

Jack was taken aback by the question, but Don answered without hesitation. "Honestly, I don't know. But I think I'd be more suspicious if they didn't offer to meet with us by now."

"What're you going to discuss with them?" Nadya asked.

"A lot of that's going to be up to them," Jack answered. "I have some questions that I want answered, but there's so much else I'd like to know that I wouldn't even know where to start. I'll update everyone when we return. Any questions?"

Jack surveyed the quiet room before saying, "Don, Kurt, let's go."

As they walked into the corridor, Palmer pulled him aside and said, "I need a word with you, sir."

The others turned to wait, but he said, "Go on ahead. I'll meet you at the airlock."

Once they were out of earshot, Palmer continued, "Captain, we need to set up a protocol in case, for whatever reason, you don't return right away."

"Palmer, I really don't think..."

"Captain, I'm just saying as a matter of procedure that we need to agree on this."

Jack took a deep breath and said, "No, you're right. We'll follow a standard non-hostile protocol. The ship will be yours, but you're to take no aggressive action unless you're attacked. I'll check in with you on the hour."

"Understood."

"Good," Jack said, and proceeded down the hall to the airlock.

"Are we going to take any equipment?" Don immediately asked.

"I'm just bringing a recorder. Alpha said that there'll be no need for environmental or biohazard suits."

"You trust them on that?" Don pressed.

"Considering Kurt's and Claire's condition, I think we'll be safe."

Don nodded and said, "I guess. What's next?"

"We go through the airlock." Jack led the way and a moment later, opened the outer hatch. He squinted for a moment as he peered down a bright, white, alien corridor. "Alpha," he called out. "Permission to board your ship?"

"Yes, of course," was the polite reply. "Please follow the hallway in front of you."

"Thank you," Jack said as he stepped forward. He worked to suppress a rush of adrenaline as he slowly led the way. The corridor was straight for the first twenty meters before curving gently to the right. Their path then straightened again for what felt like the length of a football field. Straining his eyes to look ahead, Jack was finally able to make out a dark, blue-grey wall in the distance. The hallway ending in a dead end was puzzling, but he continued toward it. It soon became apparent that darkness at the end was actually the entrance to a much larger room.

Stopping at the threshold, Jack gazed into a large oval chamber. At first guess it seemed to be fifty meters across with a domed ceiling that rose at least twenty meters above them. The alien architecture was plain, but seemed designed to impress. The floor appeared to be cut from a single piece of polished black marble; the walls were comprised of the same blue-grey metal they had encountered on the other alien structures. Here though, there were no scorch marks or other signs of damage – just a smooth, near mirror-like finish. Light emanated from the line where the metallic wall met the ceiling, bathing the base of the dome in bright, blue-white light. The dome's color faded to deep navy at its peak, reminding him of a twilight sky back home. A single glass table with three plain silver chairs sat at the far side of the room.

"Please come in," Alpha's voice announced.

They entered slowly and walked toward the table, admiring the simple, yet elegant surroundings. Don leaned toward Jack and whispered, "Where are they?"

"We will join you in a moment," Alpha replied. "Please, take a seat and make yourselves comfortable."

They reached the table and without hesitation Jack took the center seat. Kurt sat down to his left, but Don paused, standing behind the chair to Jack's right.

"What is it?" Jack asked.

"I don't know. I just don't feel comfortable here."

"Considering where we are, I'd be shocked if you did. Take your seat."

As soon as Don complied, a large door appeared in the wall across from them, and the first of three aliens came through. Jack was surprised at their size: they could be considered humanoid with broad, heavy torsos that were anything but athletic. Their exposed thick, wrinkled grey skin, fit loosely on their bodies. At well over two meters tall, and a meter in breadth, he guessed that each must easily weigh three hundred kilos. Their similarity with humans ended there, as they had oblong heads that were broad near their necks, but tapered to mouths that were little more than slits. The aliens' large, jet black eyes lacked any obvious pupils or irises, making it difficult to tell in which direction they were looking. There were no discernable nostrils, and save for some slightly drooping skin, no other facial features. They didn't walk, but instead sat in silver carts that covered their lower extremities and seemed molded to their bodies. The lead alien glided into place directly across from Jack.

Jack stood up and politely said, "I am Captain Jack Harrison. To my left is Lieutenant Commander Kurt Hoffman, our chief engineer; and to my right is Dr. Don Martinez our chief science officer."

The alien in front of Jack raised its head slightly and Jack heard the words, "I am Alpha. It is our pleasure to meet you in person. On my right is...you may call him Beta. His function is most closely analogous to your chief engineer. You may refer to the individual on my left as Gamma. He and I are scientists."

The alien known as Beta looked to Alpha before turning to face Jack. A new voice, presumably Beta's, said, "May we offer you something to eat and drink?"

"No, but thank you," Jack replied.

A third voice which Jack assumed to be Gamma's spoke, "I assure you that from our understanding of your physiology, it would be completely safe."

The aliens' movements were slow, and had an almost gentle appearance to them. Deciding he didn't want to chance offending them by rejecting their hospitality, Jack said, "If it wouldn't be too much trouble, something simple would be OK."

Don glared at Jack, but their attention was quickly drawn to some motion at the end of the table. A group of silver-grey, spider-like animals appeared, carrying a bowl of fruit and three glasses filled with a clear liquid. Without thinking, Jack pushed back against his seat as they scampered toward them. Don on the other hand, jumped from his chair, exclaiming, "What the hell?" His voice trailed off as the creatures stopped in their tracks.

"I'm sorry to have startled you," Beta said. "They will not harm you."

Jack looked up at Don, who was frozen next to his chair, and said, "Don, sit down please."

As Don took his seat, the creatures approached more cautiously, and left their burden just within arm's reach. Jack didn't take the food immediately, but instead watched the spiders retreat to their alien hosts. They nimbly hopped from the table into small compartments on the side of each alien's cart.

Beta spoke again, "The glasses are filled with purified water. I believe you will enjoy the fruit. It is grown aboard our vessel and has a flavor that you would consider to be a combination of orange and strawberry."

Jack picked up a piece of the round, yellow fruit. It was soft, like a ripe peach, but its skin was smooth and silky, unlike anything he'd ever eaten. He looked to his companions, but neither took one from the bowl. Jack brought it to his mouth, and took a small bite. The flavor was strong, but almost exactly as Beta had described. Its soft, juicy flesh justified his initial comparison to a peach. After finishing what was in his mouth he said, "It is very good, thank you."

"I am glad you like it. It is one of my favorites," Beta answered.

Don elbowed him gently and whispered, "Jack, how do they know so much about us? I mean, our language, the ship's systems, the flavors we taste. Did they read our minds?"

The suspicion had just crept into Jack's mind too. Before he could answer, though, Alpha spoke. "We did not read your minds. However, in order to first determine if you were a threat and to establish some form of communications, we did have to review your computer's data libraries."

"What, you just took a copy of our data?" Don asked incredulously.

"Yes. This was done while your computing system was disabled," Alpha replied unapologetically.

"You can't just take things like that," Don shot back.

"It was necessary for us to understand your nature, and as I said, confirm that you were not a threat. Plus, it was obviously essential for establishing communications," Alpha said calmly. "Otherwise, we wouldn't be able to speak right now. I believe that this is preferable."

Before Don had a chance to continue, Jack said, "I think we understand your point."

"Agreed," Alpha replied.

"Since we haven't had the opportunity to read or review any information about you," Jack continued, "we do have many questions."

"Of course," Alpha replied. "We will answer whatever we can."

"I guess the first are very basic: Who are you and where are you from?"

The aliens turned and looked at each other but Jack heard nothing. It was safe to assume they were discussing how to reply. After a few, seemingly long seconds, Alpha spoke. "Sometimes the simplest of questions are the most difficult to answer. As we do not have an audible language, I am unable to give you a word from our language that represents us. I guess the closest translation that I can provide would be, 'Inhabitants of this region of space.' But, that of course probably isn't very helpful.

"As to where we come from, I assume you are asking about the world on which we originally evolved. The answer is again very difficult. Our species left its home world some one-point-six million years ago. Since then, we have spread across much of this region of the galaxy, and colonized about fifty planets. So the answer is, 'yes' there is a home world on which we originated. However, we are countless generations removed from it and only know of it from deep in our historical records. I would hardly say that I myself come from it. But to satisfy your curiosity and answer your question, it orbits a star listed in your charts as KIC 8462852. It is fourteen hundred and eighty light-years from Earth, further along in the Orion arm of our galaxy. The planet is the fifth of ten, and is a watery world like your own."

"One-point-six million years," Don repeated. "I can't even imagine what that must be like..." Don's voice trailed off for a moment before he quickly added, "Why only fifty systems? We've already found nearly a hundred earth-like planets within five hundred light-years of Earth. I think that it's very likely, if not inevitable that we'll visit all of them within a millennia or so. But you've been out here for..." Don took a breath before continuing, "sixteen hundred millennia."

"We have explored far more than we've colonized, but expand to live on other worlds only when necessary. There is no need to take possession or conquer them," Alpha replied.

"Plus, I imagine that some of them must already be occupied," Kurt said. "I mean...you must have found other civilizations."

Alpha answered with what Jack could only interpret as a trace of sadness in his voice. "Though lower life is abundant throughout the galaxy, intelligent, technological races are exceedingly rare. Not counting you, or the one that is attacking us, in all this time we've found only one other. And they chose not to interact with us. We have found evidence of a few long dead civilizations, the most ancient of which is here in this system. It is the reason that we are here: ours is an archaeological expedition."

"Archaeological?" Don asked, perking up.

"Yes," Gamma answered. "About five hundred years ago an exploratory team of ours found traces of synthetic compounds on one of the planets in this system. We're here to study what they left behind."

"But it's a dead system. The star's a white dwarf," Don said.

"Yes, but it was once alive," Gamma said intensely. "A technological race lived here as recently as three billion years ago. They either died out or abandoned these planets when the parent star died. But imagine if they're still alive and moved on from here – a race billions of years ahead of us. It would be amazing to see what they've become. We've only just begun our studies. So far we've determined that there were once three to four rocky inner planets that were consumed when the parent star went red giant. This erased all evidence of what was likely their original home world. At that time, it seems that they migrated out to these outer planets. Though they were originally frozen, the enlarged, dying star had warmed them for a couple hundred million years, making them habitable. After the star spent what remained of its fuel, it finally shrunk down to its present, cold, white dwarf state; these planets were left to freeze again. However, this frigid environment has helped preserve what they left behind."

"My God," Don said. "But, three billion years? It's hard enough trying to piece together details of ancient Earth civilizations from five or ten thousand years ago."

"Yes," Gamma replied. "The technical issues in studying them have been somewhat challenging. Even the most stable compounds and alloys they were able to engineer experienced significant decay over that time period."

"Were they much more advanced than us?" Don asked.

"That is difficult to say. Because of stellar drift over billions of years, it may not be possible to identify all of the star systems that were near them at that time and determine if this race had visited or colonized any of them. From what we've seen on these outer planets though, it's possible that they didn't expand much further into space than your civilization. So in that sense, they may have been similar to you."

Before Don could continue, Jack said, "This is truly fascinating, and I think we would all love to learn more about this later; but I think we're getting a little off topic. Right now, we are here to get a better understanding of each other, and a better handle on our situation."

"Yes, you're right. Sorry," Don said politely. "Could you tell us more about those other ships out there. Who are they?"

"Don," Kurt said, "what are you trying..."

"It's a major part of our current situation," Don shot back.

"It is a fair question," Alpha said. "The truth is: we don't know who they are. They first appeared about six hundred years ago, when they attacked the colony you visited on the planet you call Epsilon Eri-D. As you correctly surmised, we were in the last stages of terraforming the planet when they came. The approaching ships didn't communicate with the colony – or even slow down. They just entered the system at high speed and within an hour had destroyed a mining facility we had on one of the asteroids and decimated our settlement on the planet. We received only two communications from the colony. The first was a message indicating that unknown ships were arriving and that our people were very excited about the possibility of making contact: it had been over four hundred thousand years since we last contacted an intelligent race. The second transmission was from one of the last survivors before they killed him. She simply said she didn't understand what was happening.

"One of our most densely populated planets sent an expedition to investigate. In fact, you actually visited that planet – I believe you referred to it simply as G3-Alpha. All they found was what you saw: a devastated colony. There were no survivors or any evidence of the attackers. It looked like they left immediately after the attack since the planet was deserted. However, we now think they remotely monitored our expedition, and used them to identify the location of G3-Alpha." Alpha paused as if to take a deep breath before continuing, "They returned last year and destroyed G3-Alpha."

"But there was a six-hundred-year gap. Why?" Don asked.

"We can only assume that it corresponds to the travel time from Epsilon Eri D to their home world, or some other location, and then to G3-Alpha. Plus, they may have taken some time to prepare a larger fleet considering the magnitude of their attack. But, we don't really know."

"And now they're here in this system," Don said softly.

"Yes," Alpha replied.

"And you're just hiding from them," Don added unnecessarily.

"Yes," Alpha replied again. "There isn't anything else we can do."

They sat in silence. Instinct told Jack to consider their options, but there were none. He didn't know enough about any of this. Reflexively he took a mental inventory of the IPVs' capabilities, and realized the futility. Their own technology was pitiful compared to Alpha's or this enemy's. All he could do was sit there and stare impotently at his alien hosts.

"I am sorry to have told you this," Alpha said.

The silence continued until Jack finally swallowed his pride and asked, "Will your government or home world send help?"

"We don't have a government," was Alpha's unemotional response.

"I mean whoever or whatever central authority you have," Jack said, annoyed at being taken so literally. "You must have some organization…some sort of defense."

"We have none," Alpha said.

"What do you mean?" Don asked.

"Think of it. What is the purpose of a government? Alpha asked.

"What the hell has this got to do with anything?" Don shot back.

"Why do you have a government?" Alpha pressed.

Don just stared at the alien without bothering to answer, so Kurt replied, "I don't know…we've always had one."

"A government's purpose is to manage a population's access to limited resources."

"We don't need a lesson in political science," Don said, echoing their frustration.

Alpha continued, unfazed by the comment, "Think of it. All conflict, whether it be between nations or individuals, occurs because of limited resources. Someone has something that someone else wants."

"I think that oversimplifies things a bit," Jack said.

"Not really," Alpha answered. "Whether it's food, shelter, energy, land, raw materials, or finished products, you've always had a limited supply. You have economics and laws to manage how you distribute these things. Governments create and manage these systems. A long time ago, our technology reached the point where every individual could have anything they wanted. With our ability to travel through the galaxy, we even had enough room for individuals to stay together or leave and be alone, depending on their own desires. Any of us can go and do whatever we want. There are no limits and there is no more conflict. And as a result, there is no government."

"Come on, not to sound crude or primitive," Jack said, "but you must have some analogue to human nature. Not all conflict is about things and wealth. I mean there must be times where there is a struggle or rivalry between ideas. What happens when one group insists that another group do or believe things the way they do."

"We don't have that," Alpha said plainly.

"That just doesn't sound natural," Don said with an edge.

"To some degree you are probably correct," Alpha said with a hint of remorse.

"What?" Don shot back with surprise.

"We suspect that it relates to modifications done to our genome very deep in our past. There is no longer any record of exactly what was done and why. But, by analyzing our present genetic structure, we have reconstructed a record of most of what was changed. Some adjustments were easy to identify, such as those that clearly enhanced our physiology and removed our susceptibility to disease. Other, subtler modifications seem likely to have affected our behavior. I can only assume that some more aggressive tendencies and other psychological abnormalities were suppressed."

"That means they changed the essence of who you are!" Don protested.

"What we are now, is who we are; we aren't that ancient species that evolved on a distant world millions of years ago. And, as I've said, we have no conflict. So these changes appear to have served us well."

Jack took a moment to consider Alpha's statement before saying, "I don't know. It sounds like you've suppressed the diversity that comes from natural variations and imperfections. In fact, genius is born from these imperfections. Our most famous and brilliant individuals accomplished what they did because of what some people would call *defects* in their behavior."

"That may be the case, but we see no need for fame. Why sacrifice the chance to live in harmony so that a few individuals may be idolized? Einstein's discoveries on your world would have happened without him. It just might have taken a little longer. Our progress through the galaxy is evidence of this."

A heavy silence settled on them again. Jack's mind was spinning with all of the ramifications. He didn't know what to think first. How could every one of billions of beings actually get along? Had these aliens actually achieved some sort of Utopia? But they changed who they are; the idea seemed repulsive to him. Jack forced it all from his mind and asked, "Does anyone know you're even here?"

"Not really," Alpha answered. "We just decided to explore and learn what was here. Once we learned about the beings who inhabited this system, we would share this knowledge with others. But no one is 'waiting' for us or going to check up on us."

"So you're just going to sit here and hide?" Don asked.

"Yes," Alpha said as if it were the only logical answer. "Those ships will not find us here. At some point they will move on. There is nothing else to do. For now, your ship will remain with us. Once the threat has passed, you can decide what you want to do."

"It seems that we don't have any choice," Jack said with resignation.

"None of us do," Alpha answered.

Again, the aliens gave them a moment to consider what had been said. All it led to though, was another awkward silence. They really had no choice in any of this. Jack was tempted to ask them how long they thought it might take for the enemy ships to leave, but it would just be a waste of time; they had no idea.

Kurt broke the silence, saying, "Since it appears that we do have time, I do have some more questions. If that's not a problem."

"That would not be a problem at all," Alpha said. Turning to Jack, the alien continued, "In fact, Captain, we would like to invite your crewmates to stay aboard our vessel for few hours to learn about the knowledge and technology we have to offer."

The suddenness of the invitation surprised Jack. He didn't answer right away, but instead looked to Kurt and Don. Their expressions were exactly as he would have expected. Kurt had the look of a child about to enter a toy store, and Don was the picture of confusion. He knew Don didn't trust them, but the thought of what they could learn would be irresistible to him.

Before Jack could formulate an answer, Kurt said, "If Jack, I mean Captain Harrison has no objections, I would be honored to stay aboard."

"Captain?" Alpha said.

Though he had his doubts, he couldn't think of any real reason to say no. "I have no objections." He looked to Don who was deep in thought, probably weighing all of the possible pros and cons.

"And Dr. Martinez, would you be willing to join us?" Gamma asked.

Don looked to Jack, who nodded, prompting him to accept with a simple, "Yes."

"Good," Alpha said. "As time goes on, we can create a more regular basis for you and your entire crew to participate."

"Thank you," Jack replied. He stood up and looked at the fruit remaining in the bowl. His expression mustn't have been too difficult to read since Alpha said, "Please, take that with you for your crew to taste. We can also provide you with many other food items to sample. Once you're comfortable with what we have to offer, we will replenish your supplies with anything you find acceptable."

"Thank you again," Jack said as he picked up the bowl. The chance to end their restricted calorie rationing would be more than welcome.

Kurt stood up and with some excitement in his voice, said, "We'll see you in a little while."

Jack wanted to tell him to be careful but realized the uselessness of the statement. Instead he said, "I will want a full report when you return."

"Understood," was Don's reply.

Chapter 30 – July 29, 2124; 13:00:00

Kurt watched Jack disappear down the corridor, then turned back to his hosts.

"If you would follow us, we will take you to our main engineering center," Alpha said as he backed away from the table. A door appeared to their right leading to another hallway. Without hesitating, Kurt obediently followed their hosts; Don trailed close behind. The corridor had a similar appearance to the large chamber they just left – having the same black, marble-like floor and smooth, pewter grey walls. He followed in silence, his eyes darting from side to side, looking for some hint of where they actually were within the ship. A moment later, they came to an intersection at which point Alpha moved to the right and allowed the other two to pass. Don followed Kurt's lead and stopped next to Alpha.

The alien pivoted gracefully in his cart to face them and said. "I'm sorry but I will not be joining you, as there is other business to which I must attend. Please follow Beta and Gamma, and they will take care of you."

"Thank you," Kurt answered, and after a slight hesitation followed Beta and Gamma. The corridor continued without interruption; there were no doors or alcoves, or any decorative features along their path. The two aliens just glided ahead of them at a comfortable walking pace. A moment later they stopped near an unremarkable section of wall; without any physical motion or verbal command, an opening appeared.

"I didn't see a door or anything," Don whispered.

Kurt walked up next to Beta, and peered through the opening. It led into a much larger, adjacent corridor that stretched into the distance. The new hallway had an unfinished look to it, with off-white walls and a course-looking, white stone floor. It was completely empty except for a milky-white, three-meter diameter tube running down its center. It looked almost like a translucent plastic pipeline that led into the distance. He studied the strange scene and twice thought he saw flashes of color in the tube.

Beta spoke up, "This is our internal transportation system. You simply step through the tube and it will take you where you need to go…in our case the engineering center. There will be no discomfort, or any real sense of motion."

"You just step through the plastic?" Kurt asked.

"It's not plastic," Beta replied.

"I should've guessed that," Kurt said softly.

Another flash of color swept by, prompting Don to exclaim, "What the..." but his voice trailed off. Kurt took advantage of Don's pause and asked politely, "How does it work? And, how fast will we be going?"

"I can explain everything when we get to engineering," Beta replied.

"No, I think I'd like to know before I get in," Don pressed.

"You'll be moving at about five hundred k-p-h."

"What?" Don said as he stepped back.

"It uses gravitational field manipulation and inertial control devices. You will simply feel like you're floating," Beta said reassuringly. I will go first, then you two – one at a time. Gamma will follow afterwards."

Without any hesitation, Beta glided into the tube and instantly disappeared from view. Noting their reluctance, Gamma said, "What Beta was trying to say is that we can manipulate gravitational fields so that you will be simply falling along the tubes. It's closest analogy to your technology would be electrical wiring. The copper wire, your conductor, creates a low resistance path that guides electric field lines. This is the means by which your electrons, the components of your electric current, flow along the wire. In this case, we've created a way to guide gravitational field lines along a desired path. Thus when you step through, you will simply be following those guided gravitational field lines, and as a result, feel like you're in free-fall. You won't have any sensation of motion. In fact, it's even the basis of the technology we use to propel our ship."

"Amazing," was all that Kurt could manage. He couldn't begin to imagine even the basics of how it might work. His curiosity pulled him toward the tube and he reached out to touch it. It felt like nothing was there; his hand just passed through its surface. "Simply amazing," he repeated as he stepped in.

His weight instantly disappeared and he felt as if he were floating. He looked back, but everything was gone. All that was visible was a grey blur, disrupted by occasional flashes of bright light. Without warning, his surroundings suddenly became clear and defined. Before he could figure out what was happening, an unseen force gently pushed him onto a platform where Beta was patiently waiting. "Incredible," Kurt whispered. "You have to tell me how all of this works."

"Of course," Beta answered. "We have much that we can share. Though, it will take time."

The platform had the feel of a subway stop, and Kurt took to his old habit of looking down the corridor for the lights of an oncoming train. He smiled upon realizing that he probably wouldn't see any sign of Don until he arrived.

"Where is he," Kurt asked impatiently.

"Dr. Martinez is in transit right now."

A second later there was a blur of motion in the tube in front of him and Don appeared. It took a moment for the scientist to exit and regain his footing, at which point he quickly backed away from the device. Don looked straight at him, but said nothing; his face was a mix of shock and amazement.

Before Kurt could say anything, Gamma glided onto the platform beside them. Beta then said, "Shall we proceed?"

"Yes please," Kurt answered.

They entered a brightly lit oval room that might have been twenty meters across. The floor and ceiling were perfectly white, being separated by a nearly featureless, beige wall. Evenly spaced every few meters around the room's perimeter were small rectangular alcoves, just large enough to fit an alien on one of their carts. Aside from that, the room was empty. There were no tables, chairs or equipment of any kind.

"This is our engineering control center," Beta said. "Before you ask, I'll explain a little. As you likely guessed, we make use of technology implanted in us to interface with the ship. It's similar in nature, but more complex and integrated than the implants we gave you. We can control all engineering and system functions directly with our minds."

Kurt figured Gamma must have seen their confused expressions since he added, "Basically, when we want, we can focus our attention on a sophisticated virtual reality that provides us with all of the...I guess you would call them instruments, controls and data we need to make decisions and take action. It is vastly faster than using physical interfaces like keyboards, switches and screens."

Beta then continued, "The purpose of this room is to allow us to work together in the same control session. By using these alcoves, we can share the same reality."

"Impressive," Kurt said. "And you just switch into this reality or virtual world just like that?"

"Yes," Gamma said, "that is correct. In fact, your implants are capable of receiving and processing some visual data as well as our thoughts. With your permission we would like to use these to help you view and understand some of the information we'd like to share."

"So, we'd be in one these sessions with you?" Don asked.

"In a limited sense, yes," Beta answered. "You wouldn't be able to interact with what you see, but you would be able to see it."

Kurt looked to Don and said, "Well, we've come this far already."

Don shrugged his shoulders and said, "OK."

"Good," Beta replied. The aliens backed into adjacent alcoves leaving them standing alone in the center of the room. Feeling a twinge of self-consciousness, Kurt wondered whether he should walk into an alcove as well.

His attention, though, was quickly drawn back to their hosts as Beta said, "Since there is so much material to see, I think it would be best to start with what interests you most. Please, just ask a question or suggest a topic."

Kurt opened his mouth to start speaking, but Don jumped in ahead of him, "I'd like to know more about how we got here. I don't mean your tram system in the ship or whatever it is. I mean how we managed to jump from star system to star system."

There was a brief moment of silence before Gamma spoke. "Please give us a moment so that we can answer appropriately."

Kurt looked in vain at the two aliens, searching for a hint of what they were thinking; but to his eye, their faces remained expressionless.

Gamma continued, "To some degree you are correct in your thoughts that the devices through which you passed are wormholes. When properly configured, they allow you to travel between two points almost instantaneously."

The room went completely black and an iridescent, flat green table top appeared, floating about chest-high. Centered on it was a small, but perfect representation of their IPV. "Take this flat surface to be a two-dimensional universe," Beta said. "Within it an object may travel forwards, backwards, or side to side." The image of the IPV traced out a circular path on the green surface. "It may go anywhere it desires, as long as it stays on this flat surface. Being a Two-D universe, its inhabitants have no perception of the third dimension: up and down. They don't see anything in this extra dimension, nor can they move in it."

Don interrupted, saying, "We're quite familiar with these concepts."

"I will move ahead then. As you are aware, the Two-D surface itself doesn't have to be flat. It can be curved in the third dimension." The image of the table top changed to a large green sphere, while the miniature IPV continued tracing out its circular path on the newly-formed globe's surface. "The inhabitants can travel along the surface again, and still never be aware that their seemingly flat path is curved around this unseen dimension.

"Of course, as you know from your Albert Einstein, the curvature of this space-time is caused by matter. Each massive object bends or distorts space-time itself." The green globe with its circling IPV vanished. In its place the green table-top returned, but this time with several widely spaced, white spheres; Kurt assumed the spheres represented stars. Each star caused the flat green plane to distort, as if it were a rubber sheet giving way under their weight. "As you know, the more massive the object, the greater the distortion in space-time."

"So you're able to distort space-time enough to move from one point on the surface to another?" Kurt offered.

"In a sense, yes. Keep in mind that this flat Two-D space is just a crude analogy."

"Yes, we understand," Don said. "In the case of a closed universe, the Two-D surface is curved around a three dimensional sphere – a globe like before. In the case of an open universe, its form could be similar to an open, saddle shape, and may be infinite."

"Not really," Gamma said politely. "There are other aspects to the fundamental force at work that complicate things. Some of your theorists were on the right track with the idea of cosmic strings that were massive remnants of the original big bang. In reality, there are sub-dimensional, ultra-dense objects that cause space-time to have a very complicated, undulating shape that's superimposed on its larger structure." The green table top vanished, and Kurt found himself looking at what could only be described as crumpled, ball of paper. However, instead of sharp corners, all of the edges were rounded off. It almost reminded him of a piece of brain coral he'd once seen while snorkeling in the tropics. The surface in front of him meandered randomly, in and out of a myriad of folds, all while maintaining an overall, ball like structure.

"This complex pattern of waves and folds," Gamma said, "is partly a by-product of high-level asymmetries in the original big bang. There are, of course, many other processes at work, but we can discuss those later. Also keep in mind that the magnitude of these folds is exaggerated in this simulation so that we can see them more clearly.

"In the regions where the surface bends away and then back in towards itself, we can use the equivalent of extremely dense objects to distort space-time further, and make the two sides touch. The point of contact simply allows us to move from one fold to the next, and thus cover large distances almost instantaneously. It's not truly tunneling or using wormholes, but it is something along those lines.

"Taking this analogy back to the real-world, we're dealing with three macroscopic dimensions warped in an unseen fourth dimension. The results are, however, exactly as I described in our Two-D example."

Kurt just stared at the undulating green form floating in front of him. The image zoomed in on one of the folds. There were two simplified icons representing the three-ringed form of the AGCs – one on either side of the folded surface. The image showed the AGCs pulling the surfaces toward each other until they overlapped and the folds touched. Gamma spoke again. "As you can see, we use the AGCs to create a stable point of intersection; this is what allows us to travel from fold to fold."

"What about the time travel we experienced?" Don asked.

There was a pause before Gamma said, "I don't understand. There was no time travel."

"What do you mean?" Don pressed. "Of course there was. I mean at Epsilon Eri D we started out in Earth year 2129. After our first transit we used stellar drift to calculate the year to be around 1790."

The lights came back on, and Kurt watched as Beta and Gamma appeared to look at each other from their alcoves. A moment later Beta said, "I think I understand what you mean. Your understanding of time is...is different from how we see it. The first thing that you need to do is take a step back and ask yourself, what is time?"

"Time defines the sequence of events," Kurt quickly volunteered. "You know," he said as he took a pen out of his pocket, "if I drop this pen, it will of course fall to the floor." Kurt let the pen go and it hit ground with a soft thud. "Gravity governed its motion. The effect of my releasing the pen is its falling to the floor. Time defines that sequence."

"Excellent," Gamma said with what Kurt could only describe as excitement. "The most general, qualitative definition of time is that it is the dimension that governs cause and effect. An effect can never come before a cause. Just as the physical dimension of length defines the distance between two points are along a line, so does time define the separation between two events.

"My next question is then, what makes your pen fall? That is, why is *falling* an effect of your releasing it?"

Kurt just stared at their alien hosts, not understanding why they were talking about elementary school science.

"I'm sorry," Gamma said. "Please just bear with us, it will all make sense in a moment."

Their continued silence coupled with Don's impatient gaze, prompted Gamma to continue. "Your textbooks of course state that when you released the pen, the gravitational force accelerated the pen, causing it to fall. The pen followed the gravitational field lines down to the floor. A more precise explanation though would be that it required energy to lift the pen to the raised state. When you release it, it released this energy when it fell to the floor. All motion, whether it be mechanical movement or chemical reactions, in fact all events represent a change in energy states. Time can be defined by this transfer of energy from one state to another. Not by the simple ticking of a hand on one of your antique clocks."

Kurt just stared at his alien hosts and managed a simple, "I see."

"So now I'll define the present differently than you. We define the present as the time period in which an object interacts with its surroundings. More specifically, it is the time period during which the object interacts with force-carrying particles that were emanated from somewhere else. In other words, the moment that one object receives energy from another object. This could be your interaction with a heating element by absorbing infrared photons, or your interaction with a planet's surface via gravity by absorbing its gravitons. Nothing else matters."

"I don't think I understand," Kurt said softly. "You're just talking about very basic physics. This is nothing more than the conservation of energy."

"It goes deeper than that," Gamma answered. "What this definition means is that there is no universal moment that is the present. Let me give you an example. Your Earth is a hundred-fifty-million kilometers from its sun. Because of this distance, it takes light a little over eight minutes to travel from the Sun to the Earth."

"Yes, of course," Don finally said.

"If I were standing on the Earth right now, I could ask you to tell me what was happening on the sun at that exact moment. Would you be able to answer me?"

"I don't see your point," Don said.

"Could you tell me exactly what is happening on your sun before its light rays, its photons, reach you?"

"We know how the sun works. We can predict flares and other phenomena, so yes I could," Don said.

"No you can't," Gamma responded. "You can estimate what may be going on based on your knowledge of nature, but you can't tell me exactly what's happening on the sun. If the sun suddenly brightened, or for some mysterious reason became more massive, you wouldn't know for eight more minutes until those extra photons or gravitons reached you. Physical objects, planets, asteroids, gas clouds, rocks, and so on, can't try to predict what's happening. They don't think or understand nature. They can only react to the flow of energy. The present is defined as that interaction between the energy released from one object reaching another. Following this reasoning, I would define the present on Earth as that moment in time connecting the Earth and the sun. In other words, the moment in time when those photons or gravitons from the sun reached the Earth. In your current definition, you would say that those light rays, those photons, give you an image of how the sun looked eight minutes earlier. We say that they tell you how the sun looks right now. Whatever the sun is doing before the next set of photons reach you is unknown to you. It is the future. It is a cause that hasn't occurred yet, and therefore cannot have an effect."

They sat in silence. Kurt could see where Gamma was going with this, but the connection to the change in year was just out of reach.

"But that still doesn't explain what we saw," Don said. "We saw a change in stellar position. It was three hundred thirty-five years earlier."

"I understand the confusion," Gamma said calmly. "Think more about the eight minutes between the earth and sun. Now think about G3-Alpha.

How far is it from Earth?"

"Three hundred thirty-five light-years," Don said.

"Now picture yourself on Earth, this very second, looking through a very powerful telescope at G3-Alpha. Based on your current understanding of time, what year was the light you're seeing, the photons that are hitting your eye, emitted from the G3-Alpha?"

Don just stared at the alien. The math was simple, but the answer was becoming unsettling. "About 1790," Kurt finally said.

"Correct," Gamma said. "That date which you call 1790 is really the present, not three hundred thirty-five years ago as you label it. That light, those photons, are the interaction between that planetary system and your own."

Kurt saw that there was logic in Gamma's argument, but wasn't convinced. "I think I understand, but I'm still having trouble with your concept of linking different areas of space at different times into a definition of the present. Think of it, if I look through a telescope at the Andromeda Galaxy, it's two and a half million light-years away. Or if I look in another direction, I can see the Large Magellanic Cloud, which is fifty thousand light-years away. The light that I'm looking at took thousands or millions of years to get to me. How can those images that are vastly different ages be the present?"

Gamma answered patiently, "Like I said, you are a thinking being. Your thoughts and perceived understanding of nature allow you to arbitrarily assign a universal 'present' across the universe. However, natural objects can't think or define things. They can only interact via their transfer of energy. It is that energy that can cause something to happen: in other words, create an effect. We use this natural interaction to define the present – nothing else. This law allows us to more precisely define causality. Your definition, on the other hand, led you to believe that you had moved backwards in time and could even try to send a message to your earlier selves to prevent any of this from happening. That of course, was not possible."

As they sat in silence, Gamma continued, "Your scientific literature even shows that humanity is already on the path to understanding this. It refers to solutions of Einstein's General Relativity equations that some people say allow for time travel. The equations, of course, don't allow for that. What those equations did do, was provide you with the details of how the time-dimension of space-time is distorted under some very special conditions: the conditions that we use in the AGCs to move between the stars. In fact, taken a bit further, the results of those equations actually lead to the maximum level of distortion that can be made to the basic fabric of space-time; this maximum level of distortion in turn explains how causality cannot be violated."

"So you're saying that when you bend space-time with your AGCs to connect those different folds, that it actually distorts time too," Don said.

"Yes, of course," Gamma said. "But you shouldn't be surprised. Even your relativity theory shows this connection between space and time."

"And that preserves causality?" Don asked.

"Yes," Gamma said. "If we achieve a maximum level of distortion, then the change you thought you saw in your year, actually corresponds to the light travel time between the two points. In other words, if you were to travel through the AGC from G3-Alpha back to Epsilon Eri-D, using your understanding of time, you would have left in 1792 and arrived there in the year 2129. However, if at the same time, I sent message via radio from G3-Alpha to Epsilon Eri D, it would arrive there at the same time you did through the AGC. It just took the message travelling through regular space exactly three hundred thirty-seven years to get there."

"But now you're saying the AGC would take us forward in time," Don said.

"The direction in which time flows through the AGC, what you would refer to as forwards and backwards, depends on the orientation of the folds we brought together. That embedded directionality is what preserves cause and effect.

"Now going back to your original question, using humanity's current point of view you might say that we exist many worlds spread across thousands of light years and exist across several millennia simultaneously. But reality contradicts this since by following an appropriate route through the AGCs, I can travel from one end of our civilization to the other in only days. Thus I say that all of these worlds exist in one common 'present,' linked by the common events that they experience."

Gamma paused for a moment and picked up Kurt's confusion. "I know that this is a bit much to try and describe in a short amount of time. We will work with you to understand it."

Desperate to steer the conversation to something less abstract, Kurt quickly asked, "Well, can you at least tell us how you build them – the AGCs. I mean it looks like your compressing planetary masses into…"

As Kurt's voice trailed off, Gamma replied, "It is tough to describe our technology in terms that you can currently understand. So, please forgive me if my analogies don't completely answer your question. In a sense, we deploy an automated array of nanotechnology that, for lack of a better word, digests asteroids and other planetary objects into a processed form of matter. Basically you saw the remnants of one of these sites when you were near our colony at Epsilon Eri-D. I believe you referred to the body as asteroid A832. The microscopic robots we use…though they're not really robots…deploy a superconductive sheath across large sections of the terrain. We then use a fluidic suspension containing other nano-devices that precisely control the flow of electrical current across the superconductor. This delivers large quantities of energy used to decompose the surface compounds on the target asteroid. The technology acts at a fast enough speed that it immediately reorganizes the component elements into a crystalline structure that in turn can be used to construct the AGC."

"So you're saying that you can deliver and control electrical currents with atomic-level accuracy across an entire asteroid?" Kurt asked in amazement.

"Yes," Gamma replied. "It's a completely automated process. We deploy the nanotechnology onto the asteroid. It then uses the asteroid as raw materials to synthesize both the superconductive sheath and the controlling fluid. In addition, these robots build more of themselves to accelerate the process until they cover the entire asteroid. Once the asteroid's base material is completely transformed, our technology then decomposes as much of itself as possible into the processed crystalline material that is the raw material for the AGC.

"At this point, I cannot explain the way in which we process this raw material into the AGC in anything close to a satisfactory manner. However, given time, we will be able to describe this to you as well."

Before Kurt could question him further, Don jumped back in, asking, "How do the AGCs work? I mean how do they fold space time?"

"We can show you that too, but it will of course take too much time to explain right now."

"I know, but bear with me. I think I have an idea about this," Don continued. "It's almost as if you use the AGCs to create the effects of a black hole. But the problem I have is that they don't have enough mass; plus, even if they did, the tidal forces should have ripped us or any ship going through it apart."

"You are on the right track. But, keep in mind that it is based on some physics of which you aren't yet aware. Suffice it to say that there is a fundamental universal force, and that gravity is just one manifestation of it. We can manipulate the fundamental fields to create what you perceive as a gravitational effect with only a fraction of the mass you think is necessary. As for the tidal forces, we just create a resonant cavity in which we generate standing gravitational waves. It dramatically amplifies the fields, not unlike the way in which you use an optical resonant cavity to create a laser. This allows us to get around the tidal force issue. There is, of course, much more to it. And, we will help your species learn this, but it will take time."

"How much time?" Don asked.

They sat for a moment before Beta answered solemnly, "Possibly generations. There is much to learn."

Before Don could react, Gamma added apologetically, "Please understand that we do not mean to...to underestimate your capabilities. It's simply that we have over a million more years more experience in science and engineering. So to cover the accumulated knowledge necessary to understand this will take quite a bit of time. To put this in perspective, even with our advanced technology, our own schooling takes over a century of your time."

"I'm sorry, I didn't mean to..." Don started, but was cut off as a shudder ran through the ship.

Kurt stumbled as he tried to regain his footing. The floor shook again and he fell into Don, knocking him to the floor. There was a low roar of distant thunder and he looked up at the aliens for help. They just stared at each other and appeared expressionless.

Beta spoke up, "I apologize. We have a problem."

Chapter 31 – July 29, 2124; 16:27:00

The jolt knocked Jack back into his command chair. He looked to Palmer who was holding on to his terminal to keep his balance. The second shudder sent his first officer to the floor.

"Devon, was that us?" Jack called out.

After a quick glance at his console, Devon answered, "No, sir. Our engines and maneuvering thrusters are off-line; we didn't do anything."

Jack glanced back up at the main screen and saw a wave of ripples flowing up the silver tube connecting them to the alien structure. "What the hell's going on?" he asked rhetorically. "Palmer, get me a damage report."

Palmer answered with a simple, "Yes, sir," as he got back to his feet.

A third shudder travelled through the IPV and sent Palmer back to the floor. Jack held on to his chair firmly as he barked, "Devon, give me a wide field view."

The view screen quickly shifted to a slightly distorted view of the 'city' in which they were docked. The tall silvery structures stood serenely against the pitch black walls of the alien ship. There was no hint as to what was happening.

"Damn it," Jack muttered. "See if you can raise Alpha on the comm. channel."

"Transmitting," Devon replied.

"Captain," Palmer said calmly.

"Yes,"

"I'm reading no structural damage."

"Good."

Palmer continued, "Shall I ready engines?"

"What?"

"Just as a precaution. We don't know what's going on, but we should be prepared just in case we need to..."

"Need to what? We've got two men on that ship out there. We're not going anywhere."

"Yes, sir," Palmer said without trying to hide his disapproval.

"Devon," Jack said without skipping a beat, "have we completed the transmission?"

"Yes, but there's been no reply."

Another strong tremor shot through ship. The tallest of the alien towers showed signs of swaying. Jack ran through their options. Despite their technology, he didn't trust their alien hosts to protect them from an enemy attack. However, the IPV was no match for anything on its own either. They were trapped again, awaiting their fate. He still had to do something, and they couldn't just cut and run.

"Alpha," he called out, with the faint hope of getting some sort of answer. When there was no reply, he said, "Devon, come with me. Janet, take Devon's station."

"Yes, sir," she replied quickly.

Before Palmer could say a word, Jack continued, "I don't like this one bit. We're going after Kurt and Don. Palmer you have the bridge. Your orders are to hold position until you receive further instructions. Do you understand?"

"Captain, I should be the one that..."

"I'm going...period. Hold position here until I let you know otherwise. That's an order."

"Yes, sir," was the reluctant reply. "However, I do want to prep engines for immediate departure on your return."

"Yes, go ahead with that," Jack answered as he left the bridge. He quickly led his pilot to the small armory. As he opened the door, Devon asked, "Won't they just disable any weapons we bring?"

"It's not our hosts I'm worried about. I think their hiding spot's been found."

Jack handed Devon a pistol, along with a thin, protective vest containing extra clips of ammunition. Taking a pistol and vest for himself, Jack then reached for a small palm-sized metal case. Inside it were a half-dozen micro-grenades; though each was no bigger than a marble, they could do significant damage. He tucked the case into a vest pocket and said, "Let's go."

They quickly made their way to the airlock, and continued down the white, alien hallway without a word. On reaching the chamber where he first met their hosts, Jack didn't break stride and headed straight to the glass meeting table at the far side of the room. Looking over his shoulder, he saw Devon had slowed to a walk and was gazing at the walls and ceiling. "Devon, stay focused."

Devon answered with a simple, "Yes," and quickly caught up with Jack. "Where to now?"

"I only see one exit," Jack said, pointing to an open door on the other side of the table.

Proceeding more cautiously this time, Jack walked down the new corridor with his gun drawn; Devon followed closely by his side.

"Captain!"

Jack was startled by the voice, but quickly recovered and said, "Alpha?"

"Yes. I apologize, but our ships are under attack."

"That's what I figured. Where're my crewmen?"

"In our engineering center near the surface of the outer hull."

"I need to get them back to our ship."

"I'm afraid that may not be possible. It appears that we have been boarded in that section. They are cut off from the internal transport system."

"How do I get there?"

"I'm sorry, but it's too dangerous."

"I don't care," Jack said with a deliberate edge. "How do I get there?!"

There was no immediate response from the alien, and Jack shouted, "There's no damned time to waste. Tell me how to get there!"

"Continue down the hall about thirty meters. Go through the entrance on your left. That will take you to the transport system. Simply step through the tube; I have just programmed it to take you to that section of our ship."

Jack didn't bother with a 'thank you,' and ran down the corridor and through the entrance as Alpha had instructed. The plain white room with its plastic tube stretched into the distance. Taken aback by the strangeness of the scene, he proceeded cautiously and walked to within a pace of the transport tube. Lingering doubts about Alpha's instructions were forced from his mind by the urgency of the situation. He continued a few more paces along the tube, looking for a door or hatch, but its smooth surface seemed unbroken. He tried to touch its surface, but pulled his hand back quickly when it simply passed through it as if nothing was there. Turning quickly to Devon, he said, "OK, let's go."

Jack stepped through the tube's wall and instantly found himself floating and struggling to keep upright. It was as if he were adrift in some strange, grey fog. There was nothing to hold on to, or even a way to tell if he was moving. He looked back, but Devon was nowhere in sight. "Devon!" he called out; there was no answer, just perfect silence. His thoughts didn't have a chance to even coalesce before a scene of chaos came into view. Without any warning, a force pushed him out onto a platform filled with dozens of Alpha's people. The room was oddly silent – there was only a frantic, pressing crowd. The aliens were completely oblivious to his presence and just disappeared, one-by-one into the transport tube. Shrieks of pain and panic in the distance broke the stillness of the air. Brief rumbles of small explosives caused the crowd to surge forward, forcing Jack to fight past them.

"Captain!"

It was Devon. Jack turned and shouted, "Over here!" A moment later they met near the rear of the transport platform. There was an exit a few meters to their right, but a blinding flash accompanied by a deafening crack made them freeze in place. Bone-chilling cries from several aliens near him filled the air. Jack looked up in time to see a white bolt of plasma leap across the room and strike the two aliens closest to him. Their glide carts crashed to the floor; their normally expressionless faces twisted in agony before going limp. He reached toward the nearest one, in a vain attempt to help, only to see that he was coated in a warm, dark fluid. As he realized it was their blood, several more bolts mowed down more from the fleeing crowd.

Jack scanned the room and found the source of the weapons fire: two lanky, bipedal creatures, completely covered in a dull, metallic grey armor, were firing indiscriminately at the panicking mass. They stood just over two meters tall, and their limbs seemed impossibly thin. Tinted visors covering the fronts of their heads, prevented him from making out even a hint of their faces or true form. They glanced away from Jack's direction and fired at a small group of Alpha's people who were backed up against a wall. They never had a chance, and fell lifelessly to the floor.

As the soldiers advanced with an intimidating calmness, a wave of aliens flooded toward Jack, forcing him to move out of the way. His reflexive act of keeping his eyes on the enemy, however, didn't go unnoticed. The lead one turned to face him, its posture, however, belied its surprise. Before it could bring its weapon to bear, Jack raised his pistol and fired two rounds at its head. The effect of the electromagnetically propelled projectiles was devastating as the creature's helmet shattered. The second round took its head completely off. Its companion turned with unnatural speed and returned fire. The plasma bolt swept past him, striking Devon in the shoulder. Jack didn't let it get off another shot, though, shooting it in the head and chest. As it fell to the floor, the pandemonium that had filled the room ceased. The attackers lay dead, Alpha's people stopped their panicked exodus and just silently surveyed the scene.

Turning to Devon, who was clutching his left arm, Jack said, "Let me see." The alien's shot had only grazed him, but still managed to tear away a large section of skin and singe the exposed muscle.

"It hurts like a bastard," Devon groaned.

"You'll be OK," Jack said as he opened his first aid kit. He handed Devon a sterile pad and said, "Hold this on it for now. There's not much bleeding – just burns. Keep it covered."

"Yes, sir."

Jack surveyed the room and then pulled Devon a couple of meters to his right, behind a collection of crashed alien glide carts with their now deceased occupants. "You'll be out of sight over here. Can you hold on while I go for Kurt and Don?"

"No problem, sir," was Devon's obedient response.

Jack smiled, but was surprised as Devon's eyes widened. Instinctively, Jack froze in place and surveyed the area around him with his peripheral vision: to his right lay the shadow of an enemy soldier standing directly behind him. Its weapon was aimed at the back of his head. He remained motionless until the creature barked a harsh, but unintelligible command at him. Jack carefully laid down his weapon and stood up. It uttered another command and Jack carefully turned to face the creature. He slowly raised his hands, as much as a sign of surrender as to buy himself time to size up his adversary. The creature stood a few centimeters taller than him, but otherwise was shockingly humanoid in form – it was just thinner than a man. What he originally took to be armor were hard plastic-like pads in its uniform, not too different from what he might find on riot control police. More importantly, Jack noted, its padding left its joints and extremities exposed. It held a pistol-like weapon in its right hand that was currently pointed at his chest. He looked at the creature's face but saw nothing other than his own reflection in its helmet.

No more than a second passed before the soldier raised its weapon again, pointing it directly at his face. Jack pivoted fast to his left and brought his right arm across, knocking the alien's gun off target as it fired. The sound of the shot cut through his ear as he stepped into the creature and grabbed its gun-hand and wrist with both hands. With a single motion Jack twisted its wrist and pulled back. Sensing the move, however, the soldier let go of the gun and yanked back hard, freeing its hand from Jack. They faced each other, barely two meters apart.

Jack wanted to glance back at Devon, but kept his eyes fixed on his enemy. The creature didn't pause and swung at him with a right hook. Jack quickly brought his arms up to deflect the blow, but it was a fake; a lightning-fast kick caught him in the gut before he could recover and block the strike. The force knocked him backward, hard into a pile of wreckage. The soldier didn't hesitate and came at him fast with another punch. Jack dove at its knees, surprising the creature and upending it in the process. They hit the floor simultaneously. As they rolled away from each other, Jack got to his hands and knees first and spotted his gun only a few meters away. He scrambled for it, and was almost within reach when he heard the alien coming up fast behind him. He looked back in time to see it was only a step away, its leg pulled back as it threw a hard kick at him. Jack twisted desperately to avoid the blow, but wasn't fast enough. Its foot struck him in the chest. A sharp pain spread across his ribs, forcing the air from him. His lungs burned as he gasped for air; it took all of his strength to keep his eyes on his adversary as he rolled to his side to avoid another blow. Instead of attacking, the soldier tried to jump over him to get to the gun; but Jack threw a short, quick kick to its knee that sent it sprawling.

Jack gasped again, and managed to get a half lungful of air before lunging toward the weapon. The alien, however, recovered quickly from its fall and got its hands on the gun first. Jack made a last ditch stretch and grabbed the creature's wrist with both hands. There was a deafening crack followed by a searing pain in his arm as the gun fired. Jack fought to push everything from his mind and tighten his hold on the alien's arm. The pistol was firmly in its hands, but Jack's grip was strong enough to keep the it pointed away. They struggled, pushing each other up onto their knees; the alien desperately tried to push the barrel of the gun back towards him. Jack stood up hard, using the quick motion as leverage to keep the weapon pointed away. The gun barrel waved back and forth as neither could gain an advantage. The wound in Jack's arm burned, but he didn't relent. The creature threw its entire weight into pushing the weapon downward, trying to overwhelm him. Jack, however, saw an opening. He suddenly stopped pushing, turned sharply and pressed his back into its chest. The alien stumbled forward, allowing Jack to slide his right arm over its elbow. Its flinch told him it knew what was coming, but Jack was too quick this time. He clamped its elbow against his chest, and pivoted hard to his left as he dropped to his knees. The sickening crack of the bones in its forearm was followed by a loud growl of pain from the alien. As the creature let itself fall to relieve the pressure, Jack maintained his hold on its arm and twisted back in the opposite direction. It shrieked in agony as the break was compounded; the gun slid harmlessly to the side.

Jack kept his eye on the injured soldier as he retrieved his own gun. The alien simply cradled its arm and tried to push itself back from him. As Jack stood up an explosion hurled him back to the floor. A searing pain cut deeper into his already injured left arm. He glanced at his blackened uniform and the singed, exposed flesh of his forearm before looking up – his former adversary had taken the brunt of the explosion and now lay dead in a pool of its own blood. Two attackers ran toward him and Jack instinctively rolled to his left ignoring the pain while raising his pistol to fire. The heat of a plasma bolt just missing him made him cringe as he fired a half-dozen rounds. Both creatures fell to the floor. Jumping to a crouched position, Jack looked for more of the enemy, but only saw the panicked mass of Alpha's surviving shipmates push away from him.

"Devon?" he called out as he turned back. His pilot however, lay motionless on the floor; a small wisp of smoke rose from a tear in the side of his shirt. "Devon!" Jack shouted as he crawled to him. The plasma bolt had left a gaping, blackened hole in Devon's side, exposing cracked ribs and torn, singed muscle.

Jack gently rolled him over only to see another wound in the side of his pilot's skull. Devon's face was frozen in pain, his eyes wide open, staring straight ahead.

"No! God damn it, no!" Jack shouted with pure anguish coursing through him. A wave of rage washed away any memory that he himself was wounded. He used what little self-control that remained to gently lay his pilot back down, and close the man's eyes. The desire for revenge filled his mind as he got up, loaded a new clip of ammunition into his pistol, and walked to the edge of the room's door.

A quick glance around the corner showed three enemy soldiers standing in the adjacent room's center, only a few meters from the bodies of two more of Alpha's people. What caught his attention though was a pair of human legs pulled in behind the alien corpses. Jack eased himself onto his belly and quietly slid himself into the doorway. As soon as he had a clear shot, he fired three short bursts at the unaware targets. They fell without even turning to return fire. Jack took a second to be sure they were dead before calling out, "Kurt? Don?"

The legs moved and Kurt crawled into view. "Jack, is that you?"

Jack kept his eyes on the room's rear entrance and said, "Yes. Now, get over here quick; I've got you covered."

Kurt stumbled toward Jack before leaping behind him. Jack pulled him out of the room before asking, "Where's Don?"

"I don't know," Kurt replied out of breath.

"Tell me what happened."

"We were in another room – their engineering center – when the attack started. Beta and Gamma seemed confused. There were explosions all around, and then dozens of them plowed through the room, trying to escape. I was pulled along with them. Before I could get back to Don, those other ones came in shooting."

Jack put his hand on Kurt's shoulder to calm him. "OK, where's the engineering center?"

"It's...it's the doorway to your left when you go back in there."

"OK, listen to me. They killed Devon; he's over there," Jack said as he pointed behind him. "Take his gun and arm yourself, then get back to the IPV."

"But, what about Don? I can help."

"No. I'm not losing anyone else. Get back to the..." Jack stopped as he heard voices. It was a deep, harsh guttural language. Though he had no idea of the exact words, the voice's tone told him it was a commander giving his troops orders. He looked back to Kurt and said, "Go now. That's an order."

Jack watched Kurt back away before he crouched down by the doorway. After surveying the scene, he pulled a pair of goggles from his vest pocket and detached a mini-drone from its brim. Though smaller than a pea, it was capable of giving him visible and infra-red images of any scene. A quick double tap on the brim of the goggles activated a voice-controlled program for the drone. "Tactical surveillance. Adjoining room," Jack whispered. The drone gently lifted from his hand and shot through the doorway. He put the goggles on and instantly saw the drone's view: an alien soldier stood over the bodies of Alpha's people and pointed at the soldiers Jack had shot. Two others stood by the far door, obediently listening to the first one's instructions. Jack slowly withdrew the grenade case from his vest and took out a single explosive. "Return," he whispered as he tapped the grenade and tossed it into the room. The drone flew out of the room and took up a position beside him. A second later a ball of fire raced out of the room. The accompanying concussion sent the remaining aliens by the transport platform into a new panicked wave away from him.

Jack jumped to his feet and ran through the doorway into the acrid smoke that filled the room. A quick tap on the side of his goggles gave him a clear image of the scene; the enemy commander and his soldiers lay sprawled against the side walls. A moment later, two more of his troops ran in blindly, but Jack didn't give them a chance to react. He dispatched them with two quick shots. Following Kurt's instructions, he made his way to the doorway on the left. "Enter left, surveillance," he whispered. The drone shot ahead as before and gave him an image of what was lying in wait: a group of soldiers were hesitatingly starting to back out of the engineering center. Without exposing himself, he reached around the doorframe with his pistol. He whispered again; "Activate, remote targeting." His drone-eye view now included a read circle, indicating the location at which his weapon was pointing. He quickly turned his wrist until the target landed on the first of the enemy. With three short bursts of fire, he took out the remaining soldiers.

"Don!" he called out in a hushed yell. "Are you in here?"

"Over here!" was the hesitant reply. Like Kurt, Don had taken refuge behind the bodies of Alpha's people. Don jumped up and ran to him. Before he could say anything, Jack shouted, "Get back to the ship now!"

Don took two steps but stopped when he saw Jack wasn't following. "Come on! Let's go," Don shouted back.

Jack didn't look back at the man as he said, "Go now."

"What about you?"

"I'll follow in a minute," he said without any conviction. "Now go." Jack was only barely aware of Don's compliance as anger enveloped him again. He could only think of the fear frozen on Devon's face; there was no turning back. The anger gave way to an intense awareness of his surroundings – an almost calm feeling of complete confidence. As he walked through the room, an injured enemy soldier rolled onto its back. Without hesitation, Jack fired a single round into its head. He stepped around the body as he reloaded his weapon, never taking his eyes off the far side of the room. Two bolts of plasma flew wildly through the door, one barely missing him. Jack dove to his right and pulled out another grenade. Another shot struck the rear wall, but came nowhere near him: they were firing blindly.

Jack moved along the room's perimeter with his back against the wall, approaching the rear door. Two more bolts flew randomly into the room; their trajectory told him they were standing near his side of the entrance. He took a running start, dove past the doorway, and lightly tossed the grenade through before rolling to the other side. He was numb to the sound of the explosion, but felt the sting of heat and small debris strike his back.

"Go through the door. Wide angle surveillance," he whispered. The drone shot through the opening. His goggles gave him a view of long, broad, straight corridor. It was littered with the bodies of dozens of Alpha's people. Their dark maroon blood formed large pools on the metallic grey floor. Not a one had any sort of weapon. The enemy soldier that had fired on him lay motionless against the wall. The drone slowly panned across the scene, when Jack suddenly said, "Freeze position." Four enemy soldiers were retreating down the long corridor. Without hesitation, Jack jumped through the door and gave chase. He squeezed off two quick shots, sending one flailing to the side. As he took aim at another, a familiar voice spoke to him.

"Captain. They are attempting to leave."

It was Alpha, but a quick glance around the hallway showed that he was nowhere to be seen. Jack didn't break stride as shouted back, "You don't allow an enemy like this to retreat." Jack fired again as one of the soldiers spun around to return fire. Jack's shot went wide of its target, and he felt heat of the creature's plasma bolt buzz past his head. He paused for a split second to take aim before squeezing the trigger; this time his shot struck the soldier in the chest. Without saying a word, he sprinted forward again in pursuit.

Alpha spoke again. "You must let them go. If you keep attacking, then they'll have no reason to negotiate."

"The only reason they're retreating is because they don't realize it's only me chasing them. I've got the element of surprise."

"But we need to negotiate," Alpha pressed.

The soldiers picked up their pace, forcing Jack to follow at a full run. Between breaths he answered, "They need a reason to negotiate. We need to show them force — scare them into understanding that they can't just take what they want."

The soldiers leapt through a jagged hole at the end of the corridor.

"That is where their ship is docked," Alpha said.

"Thank you," Jack answered as he chose his course of action. He pulled his last two grenades from the case and threw them as hard as he could at the opening. The explosives bounced into the docking tube as the soldiers turned to face him. Though he couldn't see their faces through their helmets, their posture told all he needed to know. One backed off in shock, while the other leaned forward in anger and raised its weapon to take a shot.

Jack dove to the side as the grenades detonated. A jet of fire and debris shot from the hole, followed by the sharp shriek of fatiguing metal and the sudden whine of a high wind. Looking back, he saw a large crack open in the alien docking tube. It widened, allowing the rush of escaping air to strengthen and pull the debris and enemy corpses out into the void. The tube shook violently before finally giving way, leaving a gaping hole in the wall. Jack watched with both satisfaction and fear as the damaged enemy ship spun away, out of control.

The roar of the wind became deafening, and the sharp pain of decompression cut through his head and lungs. The escaping air dragged him across the floor. He clawed frantically at the smooth surface, but couldn't keep from sliding toward the void. The pain became overwhelming, forcing him to shut his eyes tight in a vain attempt to stifle it. Fear, however made him open them again. Through the blur of pain and fading consciousness, he made out several large objects tumbling toward him. The nearest one suddenly unfolded several long spindly legs and leapt past him toward the opening. Despite the chaos surrounding him, Jack noticed its similarity to the spiders he'd seen at Alpha's table. Three more followed with blinding speed. They linked their appendages in mid-flight and grabbed hold of the jagged edges, creating a make-shift web over the gap. The escaping wind strengthened further, lifting Jack from the floor, and accelerating him toward the creatures and the void beyond. They seemed to be expecting him, though, and caught him in an agonizingly tight tangle of legs and tentacles. Instinct made him fight against their grip, but he soon gave up. When his struggling ceased, the creatures shifted their grasp so that only the nearest one held him. It rose against the force of the wind and climbed along the bodies of the others, dragging him away from the opening. As soon as they were clear, the others tried to follow. But after only a brief struggle, they lost their battle and were carried out into space. The wall suddenly became fluid and flowed toward the opening. The wind died down faster than he imagined possible; a second later, the gap was sealed.

The spider released its grip and carefully placed him on the floor. Without a sound or gesture, it calmly exited through a door in the hallway. The corridor was silent.

Jack took several deep breaths and then heard Alpha ask, "Are you OK?"

"I think so," Jack answered, his voice still trembling. "Thank you. What were those things?"

"They are independent units; part of our ship's systems."

"Robots?"

"No, they're alive, at least in the sense that they are biological. But they were engineered and grown for the tasks that they perform."

"For rescues?"

"No, but we were able to quickly instruct them to do that."

"Including sacrificing themselves?"

"They aren't sentient. The closest analogy that I can give you is that they are biologically based machines." Alpha paused before continuing, "The alien ship that was docked across from you has completely decompressed. We believe all aboard were lost."

"Good," Jack said reflexively. "That should give us some time. Where are their other ships?"

"The ones near us are withdrawing for the moment. However, others from their fleet are still attacking our sister ship. We are trying to take advantage of their withdrawal and contact them to negotiate."

There was an uneasy silence; Jack didn't know what to say. There was no doubt they would regroup and attack more forcefully than before. The question was, how long before the next attack?

Alpha spoke again, this time with what seemed like surprise, "A weapon has been fired at us. Our initial estimation is that it may be an antimatter missile. Impact will be in fifteen seconds."

"Can we try to outrun it or take evasive maneuvers?"

"No. Since we're still in the planet's upper atmosphere, we won't be able to use our main propulsion system and reach a high enough speed. There are only five seconds left, please brace yourself."

Jack looked for a handhold, but there was nothing within sight. All he could do was back up against a wall. There was a distant roll of thunder, followed by a sudden, violent shudder that knocked him to the floor. Before the vibrations subsided, Alpha said, "We're going to try to escape through the AGC."

"What about your other ship?"

"Their drive system has been disabled and they are being boarded in multiple locations. There is nothing we can do."

"You can't just leave them," Jack protested.

"Captain," Alpha said calmly, "The weapon that just struck us had a yield of three hundred megatons. We took significant damage and casualties in the lower portion of the ship, and cannot withstand another attack." Alpha paused for a split second before continuing, "Their tactics suggest that they originally wanted to recover our technology. That's why they attempted to board us. However, since they have succeeded with our sister ship, ours is no longer of value to them. We expect that they will fire more missiles at us in an attempt to destroy us. If we are to survive, then we must escape." Alpha paused again before continuing, "Please walk back toward the engineering control room."

Jack did as he was asked. Alpha was wrong – they had other options. However, the next move a human officer might make could be considered worse. If the enemy was really trying to salvage advanced technology and the other ship was as good as lost, then one should consider destroying the ship to prevent it from falling into enemy hands. Based on what he'd seen, the crew were essentially dead either way. "Is there anything you can do to keep them from getting your technology?" Jack asked quietly.

"No," was the terse response. Jack wasn't sure if Alpha knew what he was thinking, but let the matter drop. He walked into the engineering room, at which point Alpha said, "Please stand still."

Though confused, Jack obeyed. The room disappeared and he found himself hovering above the dark, icy Jovian world in whose atmosphere they were currently hiding. He reached back and to his relief confirmed that the room's wall was still there. The interface was astounding – he truly felt as if he were floating in space. The planet's atmosphere became translucent, and two small silver spheres appeared in the upper cloud layer. "Ours is the nearer of the two ships," Alpha said.

Their vessel dove deeper into the planet's atmosphere, while dozens of bright yellow specks swarmed around the other ship, like bees circling a hive. One by one, they closed in on its surface – the yellow glow of their engines disappearing upon landing. As their own sphere dove deeper, a group of yellow specks broke away from the disabled vessel, and moved away from the planet. Jack assumed it was because they couldn't follow them into the depths of the Jovian atmosphere. Even though the enemy ships seemed little more than bright pinpoints moving through the void, their strategy immediately became apparent; they were forming a blockade in front of the AGC.

"Where are we going?" Jack asked.

"For the moment deeper into the planet. It will provide a measure of safety until we make our next move."

A series of white bolts leapt from the blockade. Their trajectories slowly diverged, creating a fan-like pattern.

"We are quite certain they can't target us," Alpha said. "However, their missiles when detonated in the atmosphere will send potentially damaging shockwaves toward us."

Jack didn't need Alpha's explanation; he knew what they were doing. It harkened back to the anti-submarine tactics used on Earth in the twentieth century. They were effectively deploying depth charges.

"Can you move to the far-side of the planet? You know, put most of its mass between you and them?"

"That is what we're doing right now."

Jack's satisfaction with Alpha's answer quickly dissipated: several of the enemy ships suddenly left the blockade to take up equally spaced positions around the planet. Moments later, they too launched a spread of missiles.

"Thirty seconds until impact," Alpha said.

"Is there anything we can do?"

"We will try to out run them."

Jack studied the scene in front of him. Their sphere changed course sharply, and headed toward the planet's north pole – the only gap in the enemy's coverage. The missiles detonated a second later. Bright white pulses of energy radiated outward, gaining on them as if they were barely moving. Jack stared helplessly as the shockwaves propagated through the clouds. It would take less than a minute for the pulses to catch them. A glimmer of hope crept into his mind: the waves were dimming as they progressed, they would be weaker by the time they reached the ship. The question that remained was, would they be weak enough?

The sphere suddenly accelerated, and pulled away from the approaching wave of energy. Its leading edge, however, began glowing crimson red.

"I thought you said we couldn't out run the shockwave?" Jack asked.

"Not without taking damage to the ship. We've calculated that the damage incurred by increasing speed would be less than that from their weapons."

Their sphere erupted from the planet's upper cloud layer into space. It banked hard to the right, adjusting course to head directly for the nearest AGC. The enemy fighters surrounding the planet turned just as quickly in pursuit, while the ships in the blockade moved to close ranks. The sphere, however, accelerated directly for the blockade with unreal speed, catching them off guard. There was no time for them to react – they burst into orange fireballs as their large vessel tore through them. The floor shuddered from the impacts, but Jack was able to maintain his footing and keep his eyes on the unfolding scene. It was only a matter of seconds though, before the pursuing fighters launched a barrage of weapons in their direction. Every muscle in Jack's body tensed as the missiles closed on them. The silver rings of the AGC lay ahead, but the missiles were closing much too quickly.

"We will reach the AGC in one minute," Alpha said.

The sphere continued to accelerate, giving them a little more time. "Are we going to make it?" Jack asked.

"It will be, as you say, close."

"Don't you have any countermeasures you could launch?"

"As I've mentioned, we are just a scientific expedition. We don't have weapons. We've never needed weapons before."

"You don't need weapons," Jack said with obvious irritation. "Hell, you could just toss debris out the back of your ship. At least some of the missiles would be destroyed by colliding with it."

"An interesting idea," Alpha said. After the briefest of pauses, he continued, "Unfortunately, we cannot open any exterior hatches with the gravitational drive system engaged."

Jack stared again at the unfolding scene. The enemy ships lagged far behind, but a cluster of their missiles was still slowly gaining on them.

"Twenty seconds until transit," Alpha said without emotion.

One by one, though, the leading missiles expended their fuel and fell behind as the sphere continued its relentless acceleration. They reached the AGC with only three of the weapons keeping pace. In an instant, the planet and pursuing ships were gone. The room was pitch black. A second later, a deep blue, earth-like globe dominated his view. Jack's eye quickly found their ship, a relatively small silver ball pulling away from the AGC. Two missiles emerged from it, and maintained their pursuit. The sphere quickly changed course, moving rapidly away from the planet toward a small, grey moon. The missiles matched their course and continued to close on them.

They dove toward the pock-marked moon's surface with the missiles still closing; they were now only a few ship-lengths behind. Jack estimated there were only a few seconds left before impact. A wave of relief hit him before he was fully cognizant of what had happened: the enemy weapons' engines finally died out. They had run out of fuel. The sphere banked left, barely avoiding the planetoid's surface; the powerless missiles, however, continued, detonating on impact. As the blinding explosions faded, Jack saw nothing more than a slowly spreading field of rocky debris.

The image faded and Jack found himself standing in the empty room; he was alone save for the macabre collection of scattered alien corpses. Disorientation took over. He had no idea where to go or what to do.

Alpha's voice gave him a measure of comfort. "We should be safe for now."

The idea of safety focused his thoughts and doubts. "But what about their ships? I don't think they're going to give up that quickly."

"I agree. However, they won't use the AGC to follow us."

"Why? They've got us running."

"They don't seem to trust the conduits. Would you follow us through them?"

Jack was surprised that Alpha's strategic analysis was ahead of him this time. He wondered if their naivety was already dissipating. "No, I wouldn't either," he answered.

"They will still follow, but in normal space," Alpha said.

"How far did we jump?"

"Fifty light-years. But unfortunately that doesn't give us much time."

"What do you mean?"

"Remember how time is distorted when we go through the AGCs – it depends on the specific folds that we connect. Using your view of time, we just moved fifty years ahead. In other words, they left that star system in pursuit of us fifty years ago. Their engine technology is capable of accelerating to hyper-relativistic travel very quickly. We expect that they'll be here in a couple of days at most."

"Then what can we do now?"

"Send you and your crew home before they get here. At least that way, they'll have no knowledge of Earth."

PART 5: RETREAT

Chapter 32 – July 29, 2124; 23:30:00

The small conference room was crowded and buzzed with the sound of a half-dozen hushed conversations. A general feeling of foreboding hung in the air, which Kurt blamed on the meeting being called so hastily; that, and the fact that Jack had insisted the whole crew be present. Nadya leaned close to his ear and asked, "Any idea what this is about?"

"No. He's only been back for an hour, so I haven't had a chance to speak with him. From what I heard, it took them several hours to heal his injuries – especially the wounds in his arm."

"Any word on Devon?"

"None yet. I assume they're still working on him. But..." Kurt stopped as the room went silent. Jack made his way to the center and started speaking in a subdued tone. "Alpha has informed me they could not try to revive Devon. His body was...was too severely damaged."

Nausea and numbness shot through Kurt; Devon was too young for this. Nadya squeezed his hand, but he didn't respond. His wanted to leave, to be anywhere but in this room listening to this news.

Jack continued, "There's not much that I can say at this point that you don't already know. I've listed in our official log that Lieutenant Devon Roberts was killed in action eight hours ago. We will have a memorial service in his honor." There was a noticeable pause before Jack completed his thought, "I'll post the time once we can arrange it."

An uneasy silence followed as all eyes watched the captain. Jack just stood there, his hands on the table, staring down. "There is another reason why I wanted everyone here. Alpha has informed me that they can send us home..."

The room erupted into pandemonium, but Kurt barely noticed. Devon's death dominated his thoughts; still, he thought Jack said 'home.' Hope crept into his mind, displacing some of the fatigue and pessimism that weighed on him. He looked to Nadya who was transfixed by the multitude of conversations. Doubt, though, reasserted itself. He wondered if he misunderstood, and had to shout so that Nadya could hear him. "Is he talking about Earth?"

"Yes. Thank God," she answered as she moved closer to him.

"Quiet down!" Jack's voice boomed. "There's more to this." It took a full minute for the silence to return, at which point Jack continued, "Alpha has offered to give us four small ships that'll be able to take us the hundred fourteen light-years from here to Earth. These will travel through normal space, not an AGC. However, it will be at hyper-relativistic speeds, so the trip will take only a little over a week from our reference frame."

"What does that mean in terms of when we get there?" Don asked.

"In terms of the date, it will be early October, 2129: a little less than two months Earth-time after we arrived at Epsilon Eri."

"So no more AGCs then, right?" Don asked.

"Yes. The conduit we just came through is the last completed one in this particular chain. The other one in this system was never finished. Ironically, Alpha told me that they started constructing it about six thousand years ago to connect this system to Earth. However, one of their scouting teams stumbled on the Sumerians. Once they discovered that there was a written language and the beginnings of mathematics, they were convinced that we might develop into a technological race. At that point they chose to leave Earth alone."

Nadya spoke up this time, "So they're just giving us four ships then to go home?"

"Yes."

"Then, when do we go?" she asked.

"It's not a simple decision. We need to consider what we can accomplish here first. What I'm talking about is helping Alpha defeat this fleet..."

Kurt strained to hear what Jack was saying, but the cross-conversations grew too loud again. He pushed his way to the front in time to hear Don saying, "...are going right? We can't just stay here."

"What's to stop them from sweeping in and taking Earth?" Jack said with obvious frustration in his voice. "There's nothing back home to stop them."

"What are you talking about?" Don shouted. The room grew quiet to as he continued, "You want to stay?"

"It may be the only way that we can protect Earth."

"Why would they even be interested in Earth?" Don asked. "We certainly don't have any technology that they could want."

"Plus, it's doubtful that they even know where Earth is," Palmer added.

"I think it would be trivial for them to track us if we went home. If they were able to access the data from the sphere they captured, they would already know about us. Remember, Alpha downloaded our ship's entire library – I'm sure they shared the data."

"You haven't answered my question," Don said. "What do we have to offer? What would make us a target?" He didn't give Jack a chance to respond, before providing his own answer, "Absolutely nothing! We're too primitive. We've got nothing to offer any of these races, so we've got to leave while we can."

"It's more than that," Jack shouted. "I'm worried that what we're seeing here is much worse than we thought!"

"What do you mean?" Palmer asked in a level tone.

"Look at what this enemy's been doing – they've been systematically wiping out Alpha's colonies. What we're seeing may be analogous to the ethnic cleansing that happened in the twentieth century on Earth, but on an interstellar scale." The room quieted, allowing Jack to continue without raising his voice, "It's brutal but simple logic. If this enemy calculated that the risk of their own annihilation from another technical species was too great, then an obvious solution would be to eliminate any possible risk – that is, any technological race as soon as it was discovered. Acting first would ensure they have the ultimate advantage of surprise. Their tactics show they've got no interest in conquering or negotiating. This is about extermination."

The room went silent as Jack continued, "If this is the case, then Earth would definitely pose a threat as well. We're nothing to them right now, but in a few centuries we could certainly be a potential adversary. As a result, the logical move for them is to strike now, while we're still weak. That's why we need to do something here and now. Not taking any action is too big a gamble."

"You're right that we shouldn't gamble – but staying here is the gamble," Don shouted back.

"Captain," Palmer said, "Our duty is first and foremost to Earth. Before anything else, we need to go back home and warn them. Helping these aliens in some impossible battle against an enemy that probably doesn't even know about us is too big a risk."

"We can stay here and send a message," Jack said.

There was no immediate response to Jack's challenge; the room was quiet, waiting to see what would happen. Despite his complete faith in Jack, Kurt didn't like idea of staying. He couldn't imagine what they could actually do to help. He caught a glimpse of Don saying something to Palmer, but they were too far away to hear.

Don finally spoke up, "I think that Alpha's people can take care of themselves. Our staying here isn't going to make a damned bit of difference."

"Leaving things to them isn't going to help us," Jack shot back, "Right now it looks like they're going to send us home, and then run as well."

"Doesn't that tell you something?" Don said as he slammed his hands down on the conference table.

"It tells me that there'll be nothing standing between that enemy fleet and Earth."

"Then what are you suggesting?" Palmer asked in a calmer tone.

"We convince them to make a stand. Here with us."

"You saw what just happened to them," Don said, his voice hoarse with exasperation. "And, they're over a million years ahead of us! Don't you realize how little we know compared to them or their enemy? There's a reason they're running. I mean, why the hell would they even listen to us? What could we even come up with that they haven't thought of already?"

Kurt couldn't tell if Don stopped because he was out of breath or if he thought he'd made his point. The problem was, the man made sense. He turned to face Nadya and said, "I don't see what Jack thinks we can do here."

She shot an accusing look back at him, but said nothing.

"I've given that a lot of thought," Jack said loudly but calmly. "The key isn't what they know or how much more advanced they are. It's what they're not capable of seeing. They're just a scientific expedition..."

"So are we!" Don interjected.

The murmuring grew throughout the small room until Jack held up his hand. He waited patiently until he could be heard at a normal voice. "Neither they, nor their entire race has fought or even thought about fighting a battle in over a million years. By their own admission, they engineered aggression out of their race. We haven't."

"Do you really think being primitive is going to help?" Don said with sarcasm cutting through his voice.

"Not primitive," Jack answered with continued calmness. "It's a matter of understanding conflict and strategy. Think of it. They have and get whatever they want without any effort. It's just handed to them via their technology. They have an endless supply of everything they need. They don't need to plan, or create strategies. They don't need to compete. This type of thought is completely alien to them. In fact, they're so damned complacent that I've wondered if they're truly alive."

"Do you really think we could make any sort of difference here?" Palmer asked.

Jack turned to face him and answered with a hint of frustration, "Come on. You of all people should see it. The basic tenants of warfare haven't changed for millennia on Earth. The weapons have, but the basic strategies haven't. It goes back to the strategies and foresight taught to us in Sun Tzu's 'The Art of War,' and the game of chess. Arguably all military tactics stem from these."

Don pushed toward Jack, and shouted, "So now you're saying that the writings of a man whose armies used arrows and swords will save us?"

"No, Damn it! What I'm saying is that the understanding and analysis of conflict transcends time and technology. It's a branch of thought and philosophy that we understand and have applied throughout history. We use it in business and economics; we use it in politics. And, yes, we've used it in armed conflict. They haven't and have no experience with it.

"Sun Tzu said, know your enemy, respect his strengths and understand his weaknesses. Use deception. Take advantage of their hubris. These are all things that we can do that Alpha's people haven't thought of. More importantly, it's something that the enemy won't be expecting. I'd be willing to bet that Alpha can provide us with whatever tools we need to do this. Plus, from what we've seen, it looks like their technology is even more advanced than this enemy's."

The room was silent. Don was fuming, waiting for someone to speak up in support of him. Jack stood quietly too, letting everyone digest what was just said. Though Kurt didn't know if he agreed with Jack, he couldn't let his friend just hang out there like this. In the back of his mind, though, he was worried that Jack might be letting a desire to avenge Devon's death cloud his judgement. It only took a second to purge that thought. He looked around once more before speaking up, "This enemy...they're arrogant. Couldn't we lay a trap of some sort?" He instantly regretted his action as all eyes shifted to him. No one said anything, though, which made him feel obligated to explain himself. "When I was on Alpha's ship, I watched their soldiers act like they were hunting...like Alpha's people were nothing more than prey and unable to fight back. I watched them simply walk into rooms without taking any cover, without any hint of defense, and just open fire."

"Kurt, we're not soldiers," a voice from behind said softly.

Another voice called out, "What're you talking about?"

Kurt spun around and answered hesitantly, "They aren't expecting a fight."

"That was my conclusion too," Jack said. "When I was on their ship,

Alpha showed me an orbital view of the battle. What I saw matched what Kurt saw. The enemy ships didn't expect a fight. They approached the whole thing as if they were flushing out their prey and going in for the kill."

"Sir," Palmer said, "I think we need to take a step back from this."

Jack answered him with a simple challenge, "Then what do you suggest?"

"Alpha's ship just escaped one of their attacks. Don't you think they'll take that into account next time?" Palmer asked.

"Running for your life and setting up an ambush are two very different things. They may take an extra step or two to prevent an escape. But, they won't be expecting an offensive move."

"Are you talking about laying traps and then heading home?" Nadya asked.

"For the most part, yes," Jack answered. "There's no way we could even try to engage them in battle. We don't have the ships or weaponry. If all goes well, most of you will head home once the traps are set. A few of us will stay behind with one of their ships to see this thing through. We'll follow after that."

Kurt had to admit that Jack's statement gave him some sense of relief. Though he was pretty sure he'd be one of the ones staying behind with Jack, he was equally sure that he could get Nadya on one of the ships heading home first.

"It's still too risky," Don said. "Our best chance for survival is to go now — not wait to the last minute."

Before there was a chance for the debate to continue, Kurt jumped back in, "They don't use the AGCs, right?"

"Correct," Jack answered.

"Then they'll come in at high speed like we did at Epsilon Eri with the Magellan. Their engines will be pointing towards us as they decelerate. That's when they'll be vulnerable. It'll be tough for them to see anything happening in front of them. The question is, what can we do?"

"Wait a minute," Don interjected. "You're assuming that we're staying. I don't see us having made that decision."

"It's better than running away right now," Kurt shot back.

"You're talking about this as if we were even close to being on an equal footing with these aliens," Don replied. "You're just fooling yourselves; this is nothing more than suicide."

"Don," Jack said in a measured tone, "I need you to give me something to work with. The way I see it, this is our best bet to protect ourselves and Earth. Show me something I missed."

"Something you missed? You've built your whole damned argument on the assumption that they're going to go to Earth. I don't see any realistic basis for that."

"Don, if we stay and I'm wrong, then maybe we've unnecessarily put ourselves in harm's way. If we run and you're wrong, then we will have squandered our best chance at defending Earth. How sure are you that you're right?"

"Captain," Palmer said, "I think you underestimate what can be accomplished by acting as reconnaissance and bringing the knowledge we've gathered about this enemy back home. We could accomplish even more if we can bring some of Alpha's technology with us."

"And how much of a defense do you think we could muster in the few days we'd have before their fleet arrived at Earth? Even with some of their tech, I don't think much. We need Alpha with us to do this. The time and place to defeat them is here and now, with Alpha's ship at our side."

With a deceptively calm tone, Palmer replied, "Captain may I remind you that our mission orders are very clear about how we were to proceed if we encountered superior, hostile forces at Eri-D. We were tasked with gathering tactical data and immediately returning to Earth with that data: no exceptions. We have that tactical data."

"You don't need to remind me – I was involved in writing those directives!" Jack said sharply. "What we've encountered is far beyond the scope of anything we could imagine when we wrote those orders."

"Captain," Palmer pressed, "The orders are explicit – no exceptions."

"The purpose of those orders was for us to do whatever was necessary to protect Earth should the situation arise," Jack countered. "I don't take this lightly."

Kurt was transfixed by the debate as Jack turned to face them. Jack's eyes leapt from him to Nadya, then to the other faces nearest him. "You are more than my crew. You are my friends. The last thing I want to do is put any of you at risk. However," he said as he turned back to Palmer, "I believe the course of action I've begun laying out is the only one that complies with those orders. The only one that protects our home."

"You're still working on assumptions that you can't back up," Don challenged. He spoke fast as if he were grasping at the first thoughts that came to mind, "What if this isn't their only fleet? If there's another one lying in wait, then we'll be destroyed and you'll have accomplished nothing."

"The data Alpha's shown me from the other attacks says that they move their entire fleet each time. They're almost nomadic. They don't leave any ships behind, at least not right now. Alpha did suggest there is the possibility that a more thorough, 'mop-up' force might follow in the future, but only after this one's cleared the way. If that's the case, that force will be back at their home world or some other colony hundreds of light years away waiting for word to proceed. It'll take centuries for them to receive word from this fleet and then return to these targets. That would at least give Earth some time to prepare.

The room was silent again. Kurt looked at Nadya and wanted to say something, but there was too much to absorb. It was best not to think of their chances in battle. He knew he'd already cheated death too many times and was sure this time his luck would run out.

"Don," Jack said calmly. "Palmer's a hundred percent right about the value of the information we have. We have to send it back to Earth. They need to get every bit of data we've collected on both the enemy and Alpha's people. I want you to head this up. It is our top priority. Use whomever you need to get this done."

"Jack," Don protested in a more civil tone, "it's just sending a damned transmission."

"There's more to it than that. Should they somehow intercept our transmission, we can't let them know how much or how little we know of their capabilities."

"I know, I know. I'll use standard quantum encryption," Don said dismissively. "It will be unbreakable; the laws of quantum mechanics will take care of that."

"If we learned anything over the past few weeks, it's that our knowledge of the laws of nature is incomplete. Work with Alpha to find something that is good enough. Just be sure the people back home will be able to read it."

Don took a deep breath before answering, "I can do that."

Jack continued speaking, but Kurt's attention was fixed on Don and Palmer. They were having an animated discussion, though in hushed tones he couldn't hear. His best guess was that Don was being as stubborn as always. It was Palmer's public challenges of Jack followed by his sudden silence, though, that unnerved him. That and the fact that he knew Don was still convinced Jack was wrong. It felt like they gave in too easily at the end. A tap on his shoulder made him turn to face Nadya.

"You think something's up with Don too?" she asked.

He knew it was more of a statement than a question, but answered anyway, "I guess."

Nadya nodded and said, "We need to tell Jack as soon as we can get him alone."

"I agree, but..." Kurt stopped as he realized the meeting was breaking up. Jack was making his way toward them through the exiting crowd. Without breaking stride, he said, "I need the two of you to work on something," and led the way down the hallway to his office.

Kurt glanced over his shoulder and saw that Palmer was following, though the man was far enough behind to be out of earshot. Turning back to Jack, he asked, "So, do you think the crew's agreed to go along with this?"

Jack answered bluntly, "I wasn't asking them. The meeting was to explain the reasoning behind our course of action. I need everyone to understand why we have to do this. I can't have anyone thinking this is reckless...or worse yet, personal."

Kurt was embarrassed that the thought had crossed his mind. He glanced at Palmer, who had just caught up with him, but his stoic expression told him nothing.

"You made a good point in there," Jack continued, "about their vulnerability when they enter a star system. The problem is that we need to somehow figure out how long that window of opportunity will last."

"I can only guess that..." Kurt started, but Jack quickly cut him off. "We can't have any guessing. Besides, we have some data that might help us."

"Sir?" Palmer said.

"During our escape, Alpha's orbital view showed several of the enemy fighters accelerate hard to give chase. They did everything they could to try to keep up with us, but failed. This should give us an idea of their engines' capabilities, and let us calculate the duration of their deceleration phase."

"How can we get this data?" Nadya asked.

"I've already asked Alpha to download it to our systems, as well as detailed charts of this star system."

"Not bad," was Nadya's response.

Turning to face Kurt, Jack said, "I need you and Nadya to review this data and analyze their engine capabilities. We need to know exactly what they can and can't do. We need to keep the element of surprise."

They entered Jack's office as he said, "Computer, display a map of this star system." He reached around Kurt to close the door while the display panel on the far wall came to life. A small, yellow star was set in the middle of seven, white, nearly circular planetary orbits. The last of the planets appeared to be embedded in a myriad of tiny yellow specks: probably a field of icy planetoids comprising the system's Kuiper belt.

"Computer, display the direction to the last system."

A simple green line appeared, stretching from the central star to the upper right edge of the screen.

"I guess we could set up some sort of mine field," Nadya offered. "Maybe put some bait in place, to draw them in, and then set off the explosives."

"Or maybe a debris field," Kurt added. "I mean, yeah, use your idea of baiting them into the area. If they've got dozens or hundreds of ships coming in, it'd be tough to set up enough explosives to get even a large fraction of them. If we set up an area of rocky debris far enough out, I mean far enough from this star, then they shouldn't be able to stop in time. The collisions would destroy them."

They waited quietly for Jack's response, but Palmer spoke up instead. "What if their ships are more maneuverable than we expect? It could be impossible to keep them from steering around a trap."

Kurt answered quickly, "I'm not talking about a few rocks. Assuming Alpha can create some powerful explosives, we could shatter a few of the hundred-kilometer size Kuiper belt objects, there'd be dense clouds with hundreds of thousands of fragments...too many to simply steer around."

"They'd need to be near the outer edge of the belt," Nadya said. "At least two or three hundred AU out in order to be sure they'd still be going too fast."

Kurt smiled. He was beginning to think they had a chance.

"Computer," Jack said, "highlight any objects greater than fifty kilometers across along the inbound enemy trajectory."

The screen's view instantly changed. Gone were the ellipses of planetary orbits and the sprinkling of objects at the outer edge of the star system. They were now looking at a small array of randomly spaced red circles, each with a number beneath it indicating the object's size. The green line along which the enemy would be travelling now had distance indicators starting at three hundred AU at the upper right and counting backwards by twenties as it progressed to the other corner of the screen.

Kurt smiled again: it looked possible. There were several adequately sized objects right along the inbound trajectory.

"We need to be completely sure they can't avoid whatever we put in their way," Jack said. "Especially if they're not as blind as we think on the way in."

The solution flashed into Kurt's head. "What if we use the debris as a sort of reverse bait?"

Nadya elbowed him as she said, "Reverse bait?"

"You know what I mean. Let's use the debris fields to guide them into a trap. We'd create a couple of clouds of debris – not enough to look impossible. If they don't see it and hit it, great. But if they are able to detect and avoid it, the clouds would channel them into a bottleneck close to a few of the larger objects. If we detonate those objects just as they're passing, the fragments would be like buckshot from a shotgun blast. Think of it, in a tight space like that, their ships would be clustered together so we'd have a better chance of getting them all."

Jack nodded as he studied the map. "It's a start."

"I see a problem, here to the right," Palmer said while pointing to two noticeable voids in the map. "You've got a couple of areas where there are no suitable objects. They won't be covered."

Kurt was annoyed that Palmer was poking holes in their idea, but he saw it too. There were no sizeable objects within a hundred thousand kilometers. "I see...there is a chance that some of the ships avoiding the debris field might divert to through those regions instead."

"We could fall back on my original suggestion and lay mines in those regions," Nadya added. "I mean there're only two real voids."

"But what could we place there?" Palmer challenged. "There won't be any objects to break up, and you can be sure that they'd try to steer clear of any smaller ones."

The room was silent. Kurt stared at the screen hoping a solution would just become apparent, but nothing happened. Their plan was starting to look promising, but they couldn't leave any obvious gaps. He studied the shape of the voids more closely, but it didn't help.

"The only thing I can see is a brute force approach," Jack said. "We'd need Alpha to create some high-yield antimatter explosives. If we detonated a large enough explosive near the center of each void, that should cut off any possible escape."

"We'd need a lot of antimatter," Palmer said. "Too much."

"Not as much as you'd think," Nadya answered. "I mean it'd be a heck of a lot for us, but hopefully not too much for Alpha."

"How much are we talking?" Kurt asked.

"A few hundred kilos of antimatter coming into contact with the same amount of matter would produce a blast in the thousands of megatons."

"The question is: can they make it quickly," Kurt said.

"There is also the problem of setting this all up," Palmer said. "Our shuttles aren't nearly fast enough to do it."

"That's where Alpha's people come in," Jack answered.

Chapter 33 – July 30, 2124; 07:47:00

Jack stopped in mid-stride, only a few steps from the bridge, when he heard the word, "Captain," called out. He turned reflexively even though he knew it was Alpha's voice and that he was alone in the hallway. "Yes?" he answered.

"We need to talk. Do you have somewhere private where you can go so that we can discuss the situation?"

"Yes, give me a moment to get to my office. I'll have Palmer meet me there."

"Our preference is to talk only with you."

Knowing that the last thing he should do was start keeping secrets from the crew, he answered, "No. I want my first officer present."

"As you wish."

Jack activated his comm. unit and said, "Palmer, report to my office."

Barely a second passed before Palmer replied, "On my way."

As he walked back down the corridor, his mind raced ahead. He still needed to present the plan to Alpha. How do you convince a species who's only understanding of conflict was to run and hide, to instead take a stand and fight – especially when the odds of your own individual survival were better if you ran? It seemed crystal clear to him: this enemy was trying to exterminate them. There was only one way to deal with such a threat: fight back. There was another equally obvious question though. How do you convince someone with infinitely more experience and knowledge that they should follow you?' Without exception, Alpha had treated him respectfully, but Jack was sure that they viewed their human guests as little more than impetuous children. He needed a way to convince them to place some value on human experience. They needed to see things from a point of view that was truly alien to them.

Jack entered his office, left the door open for Palmer and took a seat at his desk. His blank screen stared at him, as if it were pressuring him to do something; he just didn't know where to begin. Before he could finally formulate his thoughts, Palmer entered. Jack quickly said, "Close the door behind you please."

Palmer did as asked, at which point Jack continued, "Alpha just contacted me. They want to speak with us about our situation."

"Interesting," Palmer replied. "I assume it's a response to your proposal. I would have thought you'd at least let me know exactly what it was you were presenting to them."

Jack allowed his annoyance at Palmer's challenge show as he said, "I haven't sent them anything yet, there're still some details that need to be worked out. You'll see the plan and have a chance to comment before I send it."

Palmer straightened in his chair and replied, "I apologize for my assumption, sir."

Jack nodded in acknowledgment before he activated his comm. and said, "Janet, respond please."

"Here, sir."

"Send a radio signal to Alpha. Let him know I'm ready to speak with him."

"OK," was the quick answer.

A moment later, Alpha spoke. "Thank you for speaking with us."

Jack was still amazed at their continual politeness and answered, "Not a problem. What did you want to discuss?"

"It relates to our current situation. Several members of our vessel are concerned about your idea of setting traps for and attacking the inbound fleet. We still don't know who they are, and at this point, they have not yet done anything to us here, yet..."

Palmer started speaking over the alien, "Jack, you said you..."

Jack cut both of them off, saying, "Stop!" There was an abrupt silence. Rather than wasting time asking Alpha what traps he was talking about, he held up a finger to Palmer and said, "Alpha, can you please tell me how you got your information?"

"There is a separate research group aboard our vessel that has been studying you; they are very interested in your civilization. While doing this, it appears that they have been monitoring your ship in great detail, including all conversations. A member of that team alerted me to the issue."

Palmer responded first, "You assured us that you wouldn't spy on us — that we would still have our privacy."

"Yes I did, and I can still assure you that I have only heard what you have spoken directly to me. This will continue to be the case."

Palmer looked at Jack in disbelief. Jack replied, "But that's obviously not the case if others on your crew are listening in on us. They must abide by your agreement."

"As I said, I am not in charge of them. All aboard our vessel have the freedom to do as they wish. I became your liaison, so to speak, simply because I was first to volunteer for the task."

"But don't you understand how this violates our trust in you?' Jack pressed. "Surely individuals on your vessel can't simply listen in on anyone else whenever they want."

"Any individual can do whatever they want," Alpha replied. "They can listen to, watch or monitor whatever they choose. There are no rules that limit one's actions with us."

"That doesn't make any sense," Palmer said.

"How can everyone just accept such blatant invasions of privacy?" Jack added.

"Captain, as I have tried to explain, ours is a civilization where there are no limitations on any individual, and where no one lacks for anything. As a result, there is no need for your concepts of ownership or privacy. If someone were to watch everything that I do, and listen to every thought that I have, that is fine. It has no effect on me or what I'm free to do; they're not taking anything from me. I know it's complicated for you to understand, but keep in mind that your ideas of privacy are necessitated only by the fact that you still compete with each other. You keep things to yourselves in order to hold an advantage over others. When every individual can have whatever they want, there is no advantage to be had; there is no need to compete. As your civilization and technology advance, you will understand. Please just accept that this is the way things are."

For the first time, Jack was sure he heard a note of condescension in Alpha's voice; if not in his tone, then certainly in his words. How do you respond to someone who just told you that your feelings of betrayal were because you're just a child? He looked to Palmer who sat there speechless, then took a deep breath and said, "Alpha, you've just asked me to accept you for who you are. To accept the basis of your society on faith. This goes both ways. In order to work together, you need to accept us for who we are. And, as a result, respect our own values, whether or not they seem primitive to you."

"I didn't mean to imply that you are primitive," Alpha said apologetically.

"Alpha, it doesn't matter. What is important is that you, and your crew accept our need for privacy. It will aid us in working together with you and trusting you."

"I can understand your need for this. Though, I am confused by your statement. There is no need for us to work together. We will protect you to the best of our ability; there is nothing you need to do."

"There's much more to it than that."

"I don't think so."

"Please, let me explain and then you can judge for yourself." When there was no response, Jack continued, "When the alien fleet found you and began boarding your ship, would your ship have survived had we not taken action against the enemy?"

"I don't see the relevance," Alpha answered. "The only reason they found us was because I exposed our position when we rescued you. To a large degree that conflict was your fault."

"Alpha, that's not the point," Jack said, desperately trying to keep any hint of impatience from his voice. "Look at what happened to your colony on Epsilon Eri D and your cities on G3-Alpha. They were wiped out in quick, brutal attacks. This enemy is trying to exterminate you. Your race had no meaningful response to these attacks. The enemy just came in and killed everyone. The only time anyone survived was when we fought back."

"One example doesn't tell us anything," Alpha countered.

"That's not true," Jack shot back. "You have several examples of attacks where they completely wiped out their targets. They don't want to talk or negotiate with you; they want to remove any possible competition from this region of space."

"Captain, you don't have enough evidence to conclusively prove that."

"No I don't," Jack answered solemnly. "But how sure are you that I'm wrong? What evidence do you even have that your next encounter will be any different than the others? This is about making the prudent move."

An uneasy silence followed. Jack felt the urge to press his case further, but thought it more effective to give Alpha all the time he needed to evaluate the situation. Palmer looked to him and mouthed the words, "I don't trust them." Jack's response was a simple nod.

"We have observed that your crew is not in full agreement with you," Alpha finally said. "That in itself is enough for many here to resist your suggestion."

"Alpha, that has no bearing on this discussion. Many of our people have their own doubts and fears. Hell, even I have my doubts. However, we also know how to choose between a set of unpalatable choices. We work for the greater good even when it means that we as individuals may suffer." Jack paused to make his point, and then said, "I'm not going to hide my true motivation here. If this enemy is interested in exterminating advanced civilizations in this region of the galaxy, then that means Earth is at risk as well as your own worlds. We humans need to do whatever we can to protect Earth. In this case, I see us both benefitting from working together. We can do something to protect your people as well as ours."

Again there was silence. He knew they were overanalyzing the situation, and felt it best to press the issue. They needed to understand how desperate the situation truly was, and said, "Alpha?"

"I understand your point," Alpha said. "But I can't make a decision for everyone on my vessel. This is something each individual needs to decide for themselves. What will complicate things is the fact that I can't see how we can guarantee success."

"There are no guarantees in life," Jack shot back. "Sometimes you need to take a risk. Sometimes you need to sacrifice now for greater good. Let me at least lay out the exact plan I have in mind."

"I will confer with the others, and contact you when we reach a decision. If at that time we require more information, you can present your plan."

"I have one question," Palmer said.

"Yes?" Alpha replied politely.

"What happens if you agree to work with us, and then some aboard your ship change their minds in the middle of the battle?"

Alpha ignored him and simply replied, "Captain, I will contact you shortly."

Palmer looked at Jack, allowed several seconds to pass and said, "I think it's safe to assume they're listening to us right now."

"Agreed," Jack said reluctantly.

"Then how do we discuss this?" Palmer asked with frustration.

"Just be direct. It's best if you speak your mind."

"Understood," Palmer replied. "Then consider this. You know me well, and know that I've got no problem with taking a stand and fighting."

"That goes without saying."

"But, I see two problems. First is their reliability. Alpha just ignored my question as if it weren't a valid point. What if things start going bad and they decide to cut and run? We need to be able to count on them, and I can't see that happening. I mean, he asked for guarantees of success, why can't we ask for a much more realistic guarantee that they'll stick to any agreement that they make?"

Jack just nodded at him.

"Second," Palmer said, "and maybe more importantly, we still don't even know if this enemy is interested in Earth. This really isn't our battle, why are we trying to risk everything to get involved? You've made a lot of assumptions here. How do you know that you're right?"

"I understand your concerns," Jack said.

"More importantly," Palmer continued, "we need to be one hundred percent sure that we get all of our tactical information back to Earth. Relying on Don's transmission is too risky."

"As I said earlier, the risks of inaction are too great. Even if there was only a one-in-four chance that I'm right, could you in good conscience give up this chance to protect Earth?"

"You're speaking as if you had a hint of what the odds really are."

"Palmer, it's pointless to go over this again right now. Our need to stay and fight has already been decided."

"By you," Palmer shot back.

"Yes!" Jack answered harshly. "Unless you can give me anything close to a guarantee that we won't be putting Earth at risk by retreating, then that's exactly how we'll be proceeding."

Palmer just stared back at him.

Jack gave him a second and calmly said, "Let's wait to see what they say. I'll call you back down here as soon as I hear something."

"Understood, sir," Palmer replied as he got up and left.

Chapter 34 – July 30, 2124; 10:30:00

Jack stepped back to let Palmer and Masako review a schematic of the star system. The Kuiper belt objects to be mined were clearly marked with green circles; the expected approach vector of the enemy fleet was depicted as a yellow line diving in from the upper right corner of the screen. Despite Palmer's initial resistance, his tactical input was proving exceptionally valuable. In addition, Masako's expertise in geology was a more than adequate substitute for Don's background; she had succeeded in identifying several features in the small icy bodies where explosive charges would yield a maximum number of fragments. True, Don should have been there too; but as he put it, he "wasn't going to have his hand in any goddamned suicide mission." At least the plan was starting to come together. What remained, however, was perhaps his biggest hurdle: convincing a superior alien civilization to trust their 'primitive' guests and fight this enemy.

"Sir," Palmer said, "we still need to decide when it would be best to detonate the charges."

"I'm still leaning strongly towards Kurt's idea of blowing them at the last second, when their fleet is nearly on top of them. It would be like a shotgun blast."

"There's sense in that. However, even with the improvements we've come up with, I think it relies too much on them being close enough to the targets. We can't guarantee that. Even a few hundred kilometer variation in their position could give them enough time to avoid being hit. I know you're counting on the debris fields we're going to set up ahead of time to limit their room for maneuvering, but I'm worried it'll still give them a chance."

Jack took a breath before replying, "I don't see that we have much of a choice. The only alternative I see would be to detonate them now to create a large field of debris directly in their path – like a natural mine field. But I think we both agreed there's too great a chance that they have the technology to see that debris ahead of time. In that case it'd be simple for them to steer around it."

"There aren't any good choices," Palmer said shaking his head. "We really don't know enough about their capabilities. Sir, I think you should reconsider the idea of abandoning this altogether and simply returning to Earth with the intelligence we've gathered. Especially since we still don't even know if Alpha will agree to any of this, or if we can even rely on him."

Jack knew Palmer's concerns were too valid to be summarily dismissed, but he had to prevent them from sliding back into earlier debates. "Palmer, the real issue is the fact that the risk of inaction is just too great – we have to take a stand," he said with a slight edge. Then continuing in a more conciliatory tone, "You're right that there are no sure bets here, but keep in mind that as with any other battle plan, it really boils down to maximizing our odds – there are no certainties."

Palmer stared back emotionlessly.

"Captain," Alpha's voice said, "please do not say anything. The others on your ship cannot hear me. I need you to excuse yourself so that we can talk in private."

Jack wanted to repeat his earlier admonition to Alpha that anything he had to say needed to be said to his entire crew. However, the simple act of saying that aloud would alert Palmer to the fact that Alpha was trying to hide something. Angry at being backed into a corner, Jack simply held his tongue and turned to stare at the screen.

"I apologize for placing you in this situation, however, what I need to discuss with you must be done alone, and unfortunately, must be done immediately. I will wait a moment for you to find a suitable place."

"Captain?" Palmer said politely.

"Retreat is not an option," Jack said reflexively as his mind searched for an excuse to leave the room. The problem was, most everything could be done by comm. unit or computer. "Let me go talk to Don in person again and see if I can coax him down here. In the meantime, call Kurt. A few more sets of eyes on this problem wouldn't hurt."

"Yes, sir," Palmer said with a hint of uncertainty in his voice.

Jack headed quickly into the hallway and then ducked into his office which was only a few meters away.

"Captain," Alpha said as Jack closed the door, "there have been some disturbing developments here."

"Explain," Jack replied tersely.

"Too many aboard my vessel refuse to participate with any plan you propose. They will not try to fight them."

"Don't you understand what I've been talking about?" Jack shot back. "This is a fleet whose sole purpose is to destroy you, and probably us. You can't seriously…"

"I understand the situation completely," Alpha cut in impatiently.

"Then what are you going to do about it?"

"What do you mean?" Alpha asked with genuine confusion. "I can't do anything."

"Yes, you can. We are facing a clear and unambiguous threat. Doing nothing is the same as committing suicide. So, I'm asking you, what will *you* do about this?"

"You're putting me in an impossible position…"

"I don't care!" Jack nearly screamed. "Hell, I'm not even putting you in any position: they are! If we weren't here, you'd probably be dead by now."

"I can't make a decision that affects everyone."

"Of course you can. You're doing that right now by not taking action. You know the consequence of just sitting still."

There was no answer.

Jack seethed at the indecision and said, "Let me put it to you this way. If you do something without telling the others – and I think you already are by having this conversation with me – will they do anything to stop you?"

"What do you mean?"

"It's clear to me they can't make any decisions on their own – at least anything where they can't be one hundred percent certain of the outcome. That means you can use their indecision against them. So, I'll ask you again, if you go against them and help us, will they stop you?"

"Against them? We don't have 'for' or 'against' in our civilization. We don't have conflict. Do you even hear what you're saying?" Alpha asked indignantly.

"Of course I do!" Jack shot back. "Are you really going to play ignorant with me – an inferior, primitive being? You *do* have conflict. Whether you want to admit it is completely irrelevant. Now I'll ask again: if you go against them, will they do anything?"

"No one's ever done anything like that before."

"You're not answering my goddamned question!"

"I don't know," Alpha answered, his voice trailing of indecisively.

"Yes," Jack replied sternly. "Yes, you do know. It's a simple calculation. Will they unanimously decide to use force to stop you? Keep in mind the fact you're facing a clear danger to your lives and they won't choose to fight. All you would be doing is breaking some unwritten rule or custom."

Before Alpha could respond, there was a knock at Jack's office door.

Knowing it was likely Palmer, Jack said, "Enter."

As Palmer came in, Jack said, "Close the door behind you."

"Yes, sir," was the man's flat response.

"Alpha just contacted me asking for details on our plan."

"Captain?" was the alien's confused response.

Palmer's fixed expression told Jack he didn't hear Alpha's statement. Palmer simply said, "Do you think we're ready to present it? I mean we still have…" Palmer paused noticeably as he searched for a polite way of expressing his doubts, "...have uncertainties."

"At this point we have enough to go on." Taking a deep breath, Jack continued, "Alpha, Commander Palmer is here with me now. We are ready to discuss the situation with you."

Jack was relieved when Alpha chose to play along as he said, "I am here, Captain."

Jack ignored Palmer's glare as he said, "Alpha, you still have access to our computer systems, correct?"

"Yes, that is correct."

"The plan is on the terminal in the conference room down the hall – I assume you can access the file directly."

"I see it," was the terse response.

"In short, we plan on setting up debris fields to funnel the incoming ships into a bottleneck near several larger Kuiper belt objects. At that point we'll..."

"There's no need to elaborate, Captain. The notes you recorded and the schematics in your files explain the idea clearly enough."

Slightly taken aback by the Alpha's abruptness, Jack paused for a second before saying, "Please review this and let us know your answer. I don't need to remind you that we need to act as soon as possible."

"Captain, I don't appreciate you're putting me in this position," Alpha said.

Palmer obviously didn't hear the statement as he said, "Captain, what about the uncertainties?"

Jack answered both of them simultaneously, "I don't care about that right now. The time for debating this is over. We'll take care of the details before we act." Jack took a breath before he said, "Alpha, we'll need to know what you can provide in the next few hours. Palmer, get Don and Kurt. We're going to detonate the mines when they're on top of them. Work out the details of the timing with them."

"Yes, sir," Palmer said as he stood up and left the room.

Jack sat alone, unsure of whether Alpha had ended communications. As the silence persisted, his impatience got the better of him and he called out, "Alpha."

There was no answer.

He got up from his desk, walked to the door, but stopped short of exiting. He needed an answer, but knew he was at their mercy. The seconds ticked by and the frustration boiled within him as he mulled over their options again. The problem was, there were no other options. It was painfully obvious that fear and inaction weren't choices. Alpha should see this; he should know better. Jack stared at the door but didn't want to leave. A smile crept across his face as he realized that it was his own fear of facing Palmer without definitive commitment from Alpha that was keeping him there. They didn't have time for these games. He sat back down and simply waited quietly. Barely a minute more passed before he called out again, "Alpha."

As expected, there was no answer.

"Damn it," he whispered to himself.

Before he could formulate his next thought, he heard the alien's voice again, "They will not assist you."

"That I know," Jack replied without surprise. "Will you?"

"I don't think I have a choice," Alpha said softly.

"Neither of us do. How much assistance can you provide?"

"Our ships are not capable of waging battle. We don't have weapons, defenses…"

"I know," Jack said softly. "The plan is designed for us to do most of the work. We just need your technology to pull this off."

"It will require that I…I lie to them."

"Is telling the truth and dying a better choice?" Jack said calmly.

There was no response. Jack allowed only a few second to pass before he said, "Alpha, do you…"

"I can create the explosives you need: antimatter charges of various sizes," Alpha said. "Plus I can get you a couple small ships to plant them on the targets. Any more than that will be a problem."

"We may need a little more help than that," Jack answered.

"That is all I can do for now."

Chapter 35 – July 31, 2124

The small alien pod took them quickly to their target. Though it was the third of four Kuiper belt objects on which he'd be laying explosives, Alpha's technology still unnerved Jack. Its controls relied on a fully immersive virtual reality and used a direct link to his visual cortex. He saw nothing of their ship, nor of Nadya who was seated behind him. Instead, his eyes told him he was floating alone, unprotected, in open space.

The rapidly growing, dark gray disk of their target loomed in front of him. Designated KB26, it was an uneven spheroid almost two hundred kilometers across. The ship's external lamps revealed dozens of jagged ice mountains rising from the small world, their mottled grey surfaces contrasting sharply against their long inky black shadows. A smooth expanse lay ahead; it had the look of an ancient sea of slush that froze in place while pressing up against the mountains. Their craft swooped in low over the range with unreal speed. Looking to the horizon, Jack could easily see the curvature of the planetoid's surface despite their low altitude. The surreal scene was mesmerizing, however knowledge of their impending battle kept drawing his eyes back to the stars. There he studied a cluster of lights that rivaled the brightest stars in the Earth's sky; belying their almost tranquil appearance, they were the engines of the incoming enemy fleet. It wasn't their presence that bothered him. He'd already accepted the coming battle as inevitable. Their number was the problem; there should have been hundreds ships, not a mere couple dozen.

"Jack, is that ridge to the left the one Masako flagged for us?" Nadya asked.

He scanned the landscape and saw a sheer wall rising from the ground. At some point in its distant past, the planetoid had undergone a cataclysmic collision. A large section of its surface had been cleaved and pushed upward, creating a cliff over a kilometer high.

"I see it," Jack answered. "Yes, that's our target. The fracture runs deep."

"If we set the charges at its base, the fissure should transmit the shockwave to its core. It should shatter nicely."

"I agree." Jack pointed with his right index finger to the base of the wall and said, "Proceed here." The ship instantly adjusted its course. Instinctively he wanted to pilot the craft around a field of jagged ice towers looming in front of them, but its automated functions took care everything. All he could do was watch as they dropped to within a few meters of the surface and danced gracefully around the obstacles.

The craft decelerated quickly, parking itself barely twenty meters from the cliff. "Deploy package here," he said, pointing to a small hole at the wall's base. Two silver spiders, identical to the ones that had rescued him, dropped into view. They carefully carried a suitcase-sized black box between them. Suspended magnetically within it was thirty kilograms of antimatter – liquid antihydrogen to be precise. It was easily enough to shatter the small planetoid. The creatures, or robots – he still wasn't sure what to call them – bounded gingerly in the low gravity across the rough terrain. They carefully secured the box inside the crevice and darted back to the ship with remarkable speed.

"Package three deployed," Jack said. "Kurt, what's your status?"

"We've identified a good location on our third target and should be there in a minute. Janet's taking us in now."

"Good. We're proceeding to number four."

Jack took a moment to ponder the landscape. When the Magellan left Earth, there had only been two manned missions to the Kuiper belt. Here, he was visiting several in a single day. The scientist buried deep within him wanted to stay, but that was not an option.

"Map," he said softly.

The icy landscape was replaced by a sea of blackness. Floating around him were countless small, mottled gray balls: the planetesimals populating this region of space. The nearest globe glowed red, indicating it was their current position.

He admired the view for a moment and then said, "Show target number four."

A short distance to his left, a different small world turned blue. A thin green line indicating the planned course, connected the two objects.

"Proceed to target."

Without a sound, or any sensation of motion, a bright green bead, indicating his ship, climbed along the thin green string, slowly working its way toward the blue target.

"Estimated time of arrival?" He asked.

A voice designed to sound identical to the IPV's computer answered, "Five minutes, twelve seconds."

"External view."

The map disappeared and he was again floating in space. The icy world he just left was little more than a rapidly shrinking grey ball behind him. Their destination was still too far off to make out.

Palmer's voice broke the silence, "Captain?"

"Yes," he answered.

"We've got a problem."

"Explain."

"Alpha reported detecting more enemy ships."

"That could be good. I was worried that they were holding part of the fleet back."

"No, sir; it's not good. There are two distinct formations in addition to the one we knew about. The problem is that they just started decelerating."

"What do you mean?"

"The group we knew about has been running their engines for over a day now and is still a couple of hours away. Like we calculated, they were going so fast they needed to use their engines that long to slow down enough to engage us. These new formations, however, are coming in much, much faster."

Jack turned to look behind him and spotted a small swarm of painfully bright lights. His gut told him it was bad before Palmer came back on the comm.

"Captain, you need to get back here now! Kurt you too!"

"What the hell's going on?" Jack demanded. "We've got to finish."

"Alpha just finished analyzing the new formations. They'll be on top of you in only a few minutes."

"Jack," Kurt called. "Janet and I are already on the surface of target three. Let me just place the charge."

"Make if fast," Jack answered. "Palmer, explain what's going on."

This time Don's voice came in over the comm. "Jack, you don't understand. Alpha says those new ships have engines nearly a hundred times more powerful than the others. While we were watching the first group approach at a distance, these were still closing on us at nearly the speed of light. It means they're already in this star system, and with engines that can decelerate at thousands of g's, they'll be able to engage you immediately. We just couldn't see them until they turned their engines toward us."

"That's impossible."

"It doesn't matter what you think's possible, Jack. They're going to intercept your position in maybe five minutes. You've got to get back now."

Jack didn't answer. He still wanted to plant the last explosive package, but as he stared at the fleet, he knew it was a moot point.

"Captain, do you copy?" Palmer added.

"Understood," he finally answered. "Prepare to detonate the other explosives when they get closer. Maybe we can still do some damage. We'll just wait until the last second."

"Understood."

"Map!" Jack barked at his ship. His view jumped back to the surreal black sea with its array of floating planetoids. The green bead of his ship was nearly half way to target four. "Abort current course," he said loudly. "Identify the IPV and sphere."

Two yellow circles appeared in the distance to his left. He reached out to the one labeled 'IPV,' and said, "Proceed at maximum speed."

Again, there was no sensation that anything had changed. A new thin line simply appeared, leading to the IPV. It traced out a serpentine route, avoiding a myriad of small icy bodies. The course only straightened out when it reached one of the large Kuiper belt voids they had identified earlier. Jack's eye followed the planned course back and forth, but kept coming back to the void.

"Computer, identify the antimatter bomb in void A." A bright orange circle instantly appeared. Located near the void's center, its explosion would destroy anything that entered or even came near the region.

"Alpha," he called out.

"Yes, Captain?" the alien answered.

"Is there any way to eject some of the antimatter in that explosive?"

"What do you mean?"

"I think we can set a trap. What's the density of the interplanetary medium in the void?"

"About a hundred grams per cubic kilometer."

"Ok, back to my first question: can we release in a controlled way about half of the antimatter in that bomb? Is there anything that could act like a valve?"

"Yes, that could be done."

"If we spray that antimatter across this part of the void, it'll immediately annihilate any particles present in the interplanetary medium." Jack said. "Between that annihilation and the resulting shock wave, it should clear a small region of space of every bit of matter, correct?"

"Yes," Alpha replied. "But it won't last very long. Between the local star's solar wind and the thermal pressure of the surrounding gas and dust, it would only take a few minutes for it to fill back in with matter."

"Yes, but that would be long enough."

"Jack, what are you talking about?" Don interjected.

"The way I see it, those ships are moving so fast, and are so maneuverable that I don't think it would be possible to detonate the weapons and get them with the ensuing shockwave and shrapnel. I'm sure we'd get a few, but a large fraction, maybe even the majority would dodge the danger."

"Maybe," Don said reluctantly.

"If we clear this region and then release the rest of the antimatter into the resulting, completely empty void, they won't be able to see it. There'd be nothing for it to interact with. It would be a completely undetectable cloud of antihydrogen. If we time it right, and use my ship as bait, I think I can get them to fly right into it. It'll rip through them before they even have time to react. At very least, we'll get a lot more of them this way."

"Captain, this is too risky. You should…" Palmer started but Jack cut him off. "I don't see any other way."

The comm. unit stayed silent as Jack surveyed the map again; he was only three minutes from the void. "Alpha," he called out.

"Yes, Captain?"

"I'm going to trace out a region near the explosive on my map. You'll be able to see it right?"

"Yes."

"Ok, as soon as I define the area, spray half of the antimatter into that region. I figure it'll take about a minute to expand completely clear the area."

"Yes, that sounds correct," the alien responded.

"Palmer, I want you to detonate one of the Kuiper belt objects I just mined, try KB24. Do it the instant Alpha releases the antimatter. We'll need that explosion to mask the initial effects of the antimatter and its shockwave."

"Understood," Palmer replied.

"Good. At the speed we're going, my ship should pass right through void as soon as the region's been cleared. Once I'm half-way through, Alpha, release the rest of the antimatter."

"That will be risky. There may be some residue that could damage your ship."

"I know, but I need to draw them into it. Do it anyway."

Jack used his two index fingers to trace out an oblong region centered on the explosive. "Alpha, Now," he said.

Almost instantly, an expanding red haze appeared on the schematic. "External view," Jack called out. A blinding white pinpoint, like an intense sun appeared and made him shield his eyes. An instant later there was a flash from behind him; he looked back to see a fireball envelope KB24. Reflex took over, and Jack buried his face in his arm to avoid the intense glare. Squinting, he lowered his arm slightly and looked forward again. The explosion evolved into an oblong orange cloud that was spreading toward him. Years of training told him to pull his ship back, but he resisted: he needed to maintain a direct course toward the cloud. The trap depended on making the enemy think there was no risk ahead. The glow dissipated quickly, and Jack called out, "Nadya, you OK?"

"Yes, I'm fine back here. Let's just hope this works."

"Computer," Jack called, "how long until we pass the explosive?"

"One minute," was the emotionless response.

"Alpha?"

"Yes, Captain,"

"How close is the fleet from..." Jack's question was answered as his ship jumped sharply to the left. A bolt of enemy weapons fire narrowly missed them. He looked behind, but was thrown back into his unseen seat as the ship dodged several more incoming shots. Turning his head again, he spotted at least a dozen ships – their blinding engines still firing at what he guessed was full thrust.

"Alpha, they're still decelerating, right?"

"Yes."

"Is there any way we can see the antimatter once we release it?"

"Yes," Alpha answered. "For all intents and purposes, the antihydrogen behaves exactly like normal hydrogen. I could have our ship fire its maneuvering engines in your direction. It'll emit broad spectrum light. I can configure your pod to view the scene at the wavelength of a regular hydrogen transition. It'll see the absorption and display the cloud perimeter from that."

"Excellent, release the antimatter now."

"But you're not clear of the area."

"Just release it now. We should be able to dodge it. They key is, they won't be able to see what we're doing."

"Be careful captain, I'm starting the procedure now."

Jack ignored Alpha and instead said, "Computer, superimpose the map over the external view."

The artificial colors of the schematic overlaid his view of the stars. An expanding, computer-generated blue haze identified the new antimatter cloud. Jack pointed to an area barely a finger's width away from the edge of the cloud and said, "Computer, continue evasive maneuvers, but take us here."

"The cloud will fill that region before we reach it. The ship will not survive a transit through the cloud," the machine replied.

The ship lurched to the left again, as Jack said, "I know. We'll adjust course in real-time as it expands. I just want to be as close as possible. More importantly, I want to be behind the cloud before they get here. That way they'll fly right into it while trying to catch us."

Without warning, the ship dove down as two more shots flew by, missing by only meters. Faster than he could react, the ship inverted, rolled back over and returned to their original course. The cloud grew unevenly. That unevenness, however, presented them with an opportunity. He studied the undulating curves as if they were billows of harmless smoke, and gained a feel for its expansion. Near the left edge, the cloud bent sharply inward before expanding symmetrically near its underside, creating a small tunnel. Jack pointed to the gap and said, "Adjust course to here."

"Captain," the automated voice protested, "that is a chaotic structure. It is uncertain that a clear path will remain before we reach it."

"Adjust course anyway," he responded.

"Adjustment made. We will reach the structure in twenty seconds."

Jack looked behind him, but the bright lights of the approaching ships were gone.

Though he knew the answer, he asked, "Palmer, what's going on? I don't see them anymore."

"Alpha just alerted us too. They've matched your velocity and have turned to engage you full-force. I count six ships closing in on you at a distance of fifty thousand kilometers. There're another ten right behind them."

His ship's sharp jump to the right followed by three enemy shots confirmed Palmer's response.

"Kurt!" Jack shouted, "are you out of there yet?"

"Just about."

"Move it now, we're taking on fire here. They'll be on top of you any moment."

"Just another second," Kurt answered. "OK, the package is in place."

"Good, get back to the IPV now," Jack said. The ship swerved again as a barrage of missiles whipped past. Jack watched in horror though, as the new set of weapons suddenly turned sharply and came back at him. Responding faster than Jack could follow, his ship dove down at the last second to avoid a head-on impact. The alien weapons missed them by only a meter or two, then turned hard again to come in for another pass. "Warning," the computerized voice announced, "we are within the boundaries of the antimatter cloud. There is no room to maneuver.

As the missiles closed in, Jack called out, "Computer, release the explosive package for target number four, and detonate on my mark."

"Package released."

He watched the small box tumble in space as his ship accelerated away. It took barely a second for the missiles to catch up to it, at which point Jack said, "Detonate now!"

The explosion was as blinding as it was short-lived. The initial glare faded into an expanding blue-white fireball that swallowed the alien weapons. Within seconds, they burst into a series of secondary explosions.

Nadya shouted, "Yes!" from behind him, but he didn't think it was time to celebrate. Instead, he called out, "Computer, how long until the enemy ships reach the antimatter?"

The machine's response was cut off by Kurt's voice, "Jack, we're having problems here. We're taking heavy fire. The ship's dodged everything they've thrown at us, but..."

Barely a moment of silenced passed before Nadya called out, "Kurt?"

After another agonizingly long second, Kurt's voice came through, "Shit, that was close. I don't know how much longer we can keep this up."

"Use the explosive for your fourth target," Jack said. "We bought ourselves a bit of time with ours."

"Can't do that."

"What do you mean?" Nadya demanded.

"We placed both packages on target three since we knew we weren't going to get to number four. We thought we'd give it an extra kick.

"Kurt..." Jack started, but was cut off as his ship swerved hard again.

"Wait...wait," Kurt shouted. "We can still use it. We'll detonate all of them now."

"What do you mean? You're too close," Jack said.

"Think of it Jack. We're way more maneuverable than them. Janet said she'll take us in close to KB53 and draw them in. Have Palmer detonate all of the mines just after we pass, the shrapnel should get a lot of them. Janet says she's sure we'll be able to dodge the debris. Just make sure he blows them no more than a few seconds after we pass or this won't work. Then let's just hope your trap gets the rest. I know that..." Kurt's voice was cut off by a burst of static.

"Kurt?" Nadya called out.

Jack ignored her as sky grew red around them, partially obscuring their view.

"The antimatter cloud is collapsing around the ship," the computer announced. "The outer hull is beginning to sustain damage."

A brilliant purple flash overwhelmed him as he was knocked backwards. When the glow faded enough, Jack looked up. The stars spun wildly and the view directly behind him was gone, replaced by a large, pitch black square. The spinning quickly ceased, and the stars started shifting back and forth in an unreal rocking motion. Before the ship could finish stabilizing itself, it dove again, avoiding incoming fire. "I think we've been hit," Jack said. "Computer, damage report."

"Aft sensors were destroyed," the computer answered.

"Kurt?" he called out.

There was no reply. A moment later, Palmer's voice broke the silence, "Jack, the main part of the fleet pursing Kurt is nearly at KB53."

"Understood." He strained his eyes, looking toward the region where Kurt's ship should be. It was of course, much too far to see, but he had to try. "Kurt, respond please," he said.

Again, there was only silence.

"Captain," Palmer said, "he should be passing KB53 now. If you want to do this, we need to blow the mines now."

"I know," he answered softly.

"Kurt!" Nadya shouted. When there was no answer, she pleaded, "Jack, you can't. If they've taken damage, he'll be destroyed too. You need to give him more time."

He didn't need Nadya telling him what he already knew. But there was more than Kurt's life at risk here. Besides the overall plan, the rest of the crew in the IPV would be sitting ducks if these ships got through; there was no choice.

"Jack did you hear me?" Nadya said.

The simple cold math of the situation helped him force her pleas and his own feelings from his mind. "Palmer, detonate them now," he said with a calmness that surprised himself. He cringed in response even before Nadya shrieked, "No!"

Jack barely heard her. The red haze intensified as he stared at the stars, looking for his pursuers as well as the result of his order. The sudden calm was unsettling.

The computer's voice cut through the silence: "Warning..."

He cut the machine off, saying, "We need to maintain course. Can anything be done to minimize damage?"

There was a barely perceptible pause before the machine responded, "I can ionize the antimatter in front of us and generate a strong magnetic field to shield the ship. The protection will be incomplete."

"Proceed," Jack replied.

A distant, bright violet pinpoint cut through the haze, signifying the demise of KB53. The shockwave swept outward and was accompanied by two more distant explosions as Kurt's other mines detonated. An expanding, shimmering band of glowing debris grew from the destroyed planetoids. Jack ignored its surreally beauty, though, as he continued staring at the evolving scene. Though only a few seconds passed, it felt like hours. His patience was finally rewarded: several small bursts of orange light flashed into and out of existence. The pursuing fleet was being ripped apart by the spreading debris field. Over a dozen white pinpoints appeared as the surviving ships ran their engines hard to avoid the fast-moving rubble. There were only a couple more flashes of orange from the stragglers that couldn't escape. A moment later it became clear that the surviving ships were heading straight for him. Jack felt no fear though; it meant they saw him and with any luck, would soon join his pursuers and fly straight into the antimatter cloud.

His ship lurched again, to avoid incoming fire. As soon as it steadied itself, the computer said, "Warning, you must..."

Jack cut the machine off again and said, "Maintain course." He needed to draw them in; any deviation in trajectory would alert them to the danger. He hoped Kurt's idea had paid off and given him some time to escape. He wanted to call to his friend, but was afraid of what any lack of response would likely mean. His impatience won out, though, and he called, "Kurt?"

Seconds passed with only an occasional burst of static.

"I'm sure he's OK," he finally said, as much to Nadya as to himself.

Her lack of response ate at him as much as Kurt's. "Computer," he called, "Display aft view."

"Unable to comply. Aft sensors are down."

"Rotate ship one hundred eighty degrees, but maintain course." The ship spun around as ordered, giving him a clear view behind him. It was deceptively peaceful; the computer generated image of the surrounding antimatter reminded him of the distant, growing cumulous clouds one might find on a hot summer day. The only interruptions to the tranquil scene were occasional flashes of red haze as the ship clipped the edges of the cloud. "Where are you?" he said as he strained his eyes looking for the pursuing fighters. It seemed logical that they might hang back, waiting for reinforcements.

"Palmer, do you read me?"

Two sharp bursts of static were his only response. He quickly called out, "Computer, check communications status."

"Communications are down. There is too much interference."

"Damn," was all that he could manage. They plowed deeper into the eddy within the cloud, making it feel as if he were gazing up at the stars from deep within some cavern. His attention, though, remained fixed on the distant white pinpoints of the approaching ships: they were closing formation now and coming straight at him.

Without warning, he was slammed into the back of his seat, as the computer announced, "Collision with antimatter imminent...reversing course."

"Computer, explain," he demanded.

"The eddy is collapsing."

He saw it more clearly as the ship accelerated back toward the approaching enemy. Wisps from the surrounding cloud began falling toward them, like a curtain closing off their route of escape. The ship nimbly danced around the collapsing walls of their gaseous cavern, each time identifying a new path before he could see it. The problem was, they were closing in on the enemy ships fast, and dodging back and forth wouldn't save them from incoming fire.

"I need weapons," he said aloud.

"Jack," Nadya said calmly. "Tell the ship to vent any spare atmosphere we have in a jet in front of us. It'll annihilate on contact with the antimatter, and create a pretty serious blast."

"Got it!" he answered without hiding his excitement. "But it won't be very accurate."

"That won't matter," she quickly replied. "Just position us so that part of the cloud is between us and them."

"Understood," Jack replied. "Computer, how much atmospheric reserve do we have on board?"

"Five kilograms."

"It won't be a compressed, efficient explosion," Nadya said. "But, it should yield about five megatons. We'll just use its blast to spray part of the antimatter cloud into them – that's what'll take them out."

"Perfect, Nadya," Jack replied. He scanned the rapidly evolving clouds and saw what he needed: another large eddy lay ahead. If they jettisoned the atmosphere into the center of that gap, it would penetrate deep into the cloud above, collapsing it on top of the enemy fighters. The problem was, they only had a few seconds left to pull it off.

Two plasma bolts flew at them. At this distance, though, their ship still easily dodged the incoming shots. "Computer," he said as he pointed toward the eddy, "adjust trajectory to here. Release three kilograms of reserve atmosphere in front of us on my mark."

"Understood," the machine replied.

"We'll keep two kilos in reserve in case we need to clear an escape path for ourselves."

"Understood," the machine repeated.

They climbed quickly and skimmed along the cloud's upper edge. The rapidly changing swirls and vortices flew by as he forced himself to have patience; they needed to be close for this to work. Barely a second in front of him, the cloud billowed downward. That was their target. The enemy ships saw his quick move up and adjusted course to intercept, unknowingly heading straight for the trap. "Jettison atmosphere now! Pull back now!"

A blinding white flare spread out before them, following the path of their jet of air. It penetrated deep into the cloud, spawning a glowing shockwave that swept ahead of them. The fighters immediately saw the danger and adjusted course, but they weren't fast enough. The nearest three were enveloped by the wave and instantly destroyed. The others scattered, but unaware of the hazard, dove into the surrounding antimatter cloud, lighting up the sky with a dozen brilliant orange explosions. Jack marveled at the morbid beauty unfolding in front of him. A web of glowing streaks surrounded them. Each fiery trail split into smaller and smaller, jagged rays, giving it the feel of iridescent broken glass. They still had to escape the collapsing cloud themselves, though, and his ship dove into the seething chaos. Orange and yellow sparks leapt past as they dodged the burning fragments with unreal speed. Disturbed by the explosions, the vortices of the antimatter cloud changed rapidly, spinning out their tendrils in all directions. The ship danced around them faster than he could register. It all became a blur. Their tunnel widened – they were almost out. A split second later, a flash to his left made him cringe, and he was slammed back into his seat.

There was blackness all around him, save for a small square of visibility directly ahead. The outside world spun wildly. He tried to focus on the blur of stars and explosions, but a biting pain shot through the side of his head.

"Nadya!" he called out.

There was no answer. Jack turned to look for her, but saw nothing. The ship's virtual interface still controlled everything he saw. Frustrated, he wanted to get up from his unseen seat, but it seemed impossible.

"Computer!" he shouted.

"Stand by," it answered abruptly.

The stars ceased their spinning as the ship stabilized its orientation.

"Computer!" he shouted again.

The machine repeated, "Stand by," in an unnervingly calm voice.

Jack stared out of his lone virtual window, trying to decipher their situation. However, his field of view was too narrow – like what one might see from the window on a passenger jet. A simple field of stars lay in front of him. Gone were the explosions, enemy fighters, and even the synthetic blue view of the antimatter cloud. All he could imagine was that they had managed to escape the cloud, but nothing more beyond that.

"Palmer, do you read me?"

As expected, there was no response.

"Nadya," he called again. Her continued silence tore at him more.

"Computer, respond!" he demanded.

The machine answered, "Stand by."

"Goddammit!" Jack shouted. He tried to pound his fists into the wall, but his arms struck nothing. There was no sign of anything that was actually around him – only the virtual reality to which he was connected. As far as he could tell, he was floating in a sea of blackness with a single square 'window' drifting in front of him. There were no instruments, gauges or anything he could analyze.

"Computer answer me now!" he shouted.

"Stand by."

Jack took a deep breath and said in a calmer tone, "You must have some functionality since you can understand and answer me. At least tell me if Nadya's OK."

"Stand by," was its reply.

"Damn you!" He swung is fists wildly again, but they hit nothing. He wondered if he was actually swinging his arms, or if his perceived movements were nothing more than part of the ship's interface. It was probably the latter which meant he was trapped in the machine's synthetic world and couldn't even move his actual body. His only connection to it was the pain from his unseen injuries.

A prisoner in a piece of alien technology, all Jack could do was gaze out the window at the unmoving field of stars. They told him nothing, but he continued staring as there was little else he could do. Time passed, but there was no way to tell how much. Periodic calls to Nadya went unanswered. He finally rationalized that her lack of response didn't mean she was in bad shape, or even injured. It seemed logical that they were each locked into their own separate interface with the ship, but without a means to communicate with each other.

Demands for information from the computer now went unanswered. Only silence and darkness surrounded him. Jack took to replaying the battle in his mind, trying to understand what had happened; maybe even glean some hint of whether they'd succeeded. It was easiest to assume they had achieved some measure of victory as he was still alive. Of course, that didn't answer the question of why he was drifting helplessly in a disabled ship. His mind ran through different scenarios, but he just didn't have enough information to determine what was real.

Time dragged on and his analyses began drawing from his own hopes. He imagined Kurt escaping after luring the enemy fighters into his trap. With any luck, he'd met up with the IPV and the alien sphere. It was better than any alternative.

Fatigue pulled at him, making it tougher to focus. At least he hoped it was fatigue, and not the result of his injuries. A quick mental inventory told him the pain had subsided to a dull ache. But was he simply blocking out something serious? As with everything else, there was no way to tell. Frustration crept back into his consciousness. He forced it out though, by allowing his mind to dabble again in the fantasies of his rescue.

Jack jumped in his seat – the type of startled movement that usually happens when one is about to doze off. He wondered if he'd actually been unconscious or fallen asleep. Again, there was no way to know. The smothering quiet and blackness still surrounded him; the stars outside his window remained unchanged and told him nothing. It felt as if he were simply adrift in this surreal sea.

"Nadya," he called again. When there was no answer, he called for the computer. Again there was only silence. He knew it was futile but decided a while ago he should try calling every five minutes. Without any sort of clock, however, it was becoming difficult to even gauge when five minutes had elapsed.

His mind waded back into a sea of morbid thoughts. He first tried to take inventory of his condition. Aside from the fatigue, and a now very distant headache, there were no other feelings of discomfort: no thirst, or hunger or anything else. He wondered if the ship would be capable of taking care of his bodily needs. There seemed to be enough air, but dehydration might become a real problem. Then again, he had jettisoned most of the ship's atmospheric reserves; how much actually remained? Was his growing drowsiness a sign of oxygen deprivation?

The stars became blurry. He was definitely starting to drift off again. The fear of 'why,' though, jolted him back to awareness. Sleep would be acceptable; but if this was due to an injury, he definitely needed to stay awake. He tried the age-old techniques of stretching, trying to move himself, and taking deep breaths. However, nothing made a difference. He was sure now that none of his actions were real in the physical sense. They were just part of his mind's interface with the ship; his body probably lay unmoving in its reclining chair. The blurriness returned. The fear of the unknown was becoming too routine and failed to push him back to consciousness. The stars faded.

Jack jumped awake again. He was sure he heard a bang: the deep resonating kind one hears when metal strikes metal. "Computer," he called. But there was no answer. "Nadya?" he said. Still there was only silence. Something seemed different – had the stars changed? He gazed more intently at the scene, but the star field remained fixed in place. His mind worked at memorizing their patterns – something he realized he should have done before. After what felt like several minutes, the stars began to grow fuzzy again. The urge to sleep became more tempting each time.

A second metallic bang confirmed that the first was real. The rush of adrenaline made him want to get up, but he knew he couldn't actually move. "Hello!" he shouted. There was no answer. But that didn't bother him this time since the stars outside his window were steadily moving. Something was turning his ship. The IPV came into view – its shuttle bay doors wide open. Excitement drove him to reach toward the window, but the ship's malfunctioning interface kept him locked in place. He simply watched as the IPV appeared to move closer. A moment later the shuttle bay filled his field of view and he heard a deep mechanical noise – the bay doors closing.

The window disappeared from view, but the blackness surrounding him now was different. He could feel the chair beneath him. Jack quickly reached up and banged his hand against the interior of his small pod; the machine had finally released him from its grip. There was a short hiss followed by bright light as the top of the pod slid aside. He squinted, but his eyes adjusted surprisingly quickly as he found himself staring at Don.

"Thank God, Jack," Don said with a shocking amount of relief. "We weren't sure what we'd find when we opened this thing up."

"What about Nadya?" he asked in a hoarse voice.

Palmer answered from behind him, "She's right here and seems OK too."

"Jack?" Nadya called.

"I'm here," he answered. Looking back at Palmer, he continued, "What in the world happened? How long were we gone?"

"Your ship was damaged in the battle. It took us nearly fifteen hours to find you."

"What about Kurt and Janet?"

"We're still searching for them," Palmer replied.

"What do you mean?" he nearly shouted as he struggled to climb out of the pod. A sharp pain in his hip slowed but didn't stop him. He stepped away from the ship, and subconsciously felt around the side of his head. There was dried blood caked on his cheek and temple, but no pain. "Explain what's going on," he said tersely.

Don spoke this time. "Your plan started out Ok. The mines and antimatter destroyed almost all of the incoming ships, but they held two full waves back in reserve. We didn't even know they were there at first. Alpha's ship had joined us in our search for you and Kurt when we spotted them. Our best guess is that they just watched the whole battle and then swept in. There was nothing to stop them…"

As Don's voice trailed off, Palmer continued, "Fortunately, the enemy ships didn't see us right away. As a result, I ordered a complete system shutdown. All power, including life support and communications – everything. I was betting that the mix of warm rubble from the battle and our lack of power signature would keep us hidden. It seems that we were successful, at least for now."

"What about Alpha?" Jack asked.

"We're not sure," Palmer answered.

"It's possible they ran." Don said. "But, just before we shut down, it seemed like they might have been acting like a decoy to draw the enemy ships away from us. I mean, Alpha's ship moved away from us, and then just sat there. When the fighters got close, the sphere took off with one wave in pursuit. If it was a decoy, then it looks like it worked. The problem is, with everything off we couldn't track anything. Palmer said that we needed to lay dormant as long as we could. So we did just that: drifted without power for about six hours."

Jack looked at Palmer and had to admit, going dark was a good idea. He then calmly asked, "What about the other wave?"

"That may be the real problem," Palmer answered. "They didn't go after Alpha."

"What do you mean?"

"Just before we shut down, it looked like they were continuing through this system without decelerating."

Jack continued with frustration lacing his voice, "And where did it look like they were heading?"

There was a noticeable pause before Palmer answered, "Possibly Earth. We don't know for sure because we couldn't track them."

"Damn it!" Jack shouted. "What's our status?"

Don answered this time, "The IPV's in good shape. Better than that even."

"What do you mean?" Jack asked.

"When we told Alpha you were missing, they gave us two of those...those things they used to capture us. I guess I'd call them engines. They just attached to the outside of the IPV like before, but this time Alpha interfaced them with our navigation system. Basically we can use them in place of our engines. They're way more maneuverable than our tech. And they'll even get us close to light speed...like maybe point-nine-c in a day or so. They also gave us another one of those pods you and Nadya were in. Palmer was considering taking it himself to expand our search just before we found you."

"Fine," Jack said. There were more important things to worry about. "Can we track those ships?"

"We can't find them," Palmer said dryly. "The formation that went through the system was coasting at better than point-nine-nine-c. Without their engines on, there's no way for us to see them. As for the ones that chased after Alpha, we've got no idea. I'm sure they're running their engines so we should be able to see them. My best guess is that they're in our only blind spot: the far side of this system's star."

Again, Palmer's analysis made sense. The problem was, they knew too little and had no time to waste.

"Jack?" Don said.

"Yes."

"Right now I think it'd be best if you and Nadya got checked out by Helena. We can take care of things in the meantime."

Jack just stared at them. The last thing he wanted to do was waste time in sickbay. Before he could protest though, Don continued, "Jack, your face is covered in blood. And Nadya, you're limping. Just go see Helena first. I'm sure it won't take long."

Jack didn't move. There was too much to do right now.

"Captain, I have to agree with Dr. Martinez," Palmer pressed. "You need to get checked out."

Looking at the two of them, he finally said, "Work together. Find Kurt's ship and get me some data on where those enemy ships are. I'll meet you on the bridge as soon as I'm done in sickbay."

Palmer gave him a quick, "Yes, sir," and turned to return to the bridge.

Chapter 36 – August 1, 2124; 12:20:00

Jack leaned forward in his command chair. Time was creeping forward just as slowly on the bridge as it did when he was trapped in the alien pod. Barely an hour had passed since his return, yet it felt like nearly a day. There were still no signs of Kurt, Alpha's sphere or the enemy ships. All that lay in front of them was a star system cluttered with the debris from shattered planetoids and wrecked enemy fighters. At five meters in length, Kurt's pod was about the same size as the larger ship fragments, rendering remote radar scans useless. He had Nadya and Palmer searching the region with the IPV's telescopes. Don was looking for power signatures using broad spectrum E-M scans. This left him to plan their next move. But without any data, there was nothing to plan.

"Computer, display schematic of local region," he said softly.

The main screen showed a collection of yellow specks representing the myriad of planetesimals and fragments that populated the vicinity. The map told him nothing though, and he said, "Highlight metallic objects." A small fraction of the specks turned blue: they were the remnants of the attacking fleet. Kurt's ship might be among them, but there was no way to know.

He needed more information, and said, "Computer, display velocity vectors of each target."

A pencil thin arrow emerged from each speck; their rough alignment made the yellow targets resemble a school of fish. They swam to his right, with small, random variations in their orientation. It made sense, though, as this was the general direction of orbital motion in this system. The blue objects, on the other hand, were a chaotic collection of arrows pointing in every direction. This was no surprise either, as violent explosions had sent these fragments careening in all directions. His eyes jumped from place to place, searching for something that stuck out. But nothing caught his attention. His mind slowly grew accustomed to the patterns and they lost their significance. They didn't give him a hint of what was going on.

"Computer...," he started, but stopped as something caught his eye. "Computer, replay – starting five seconds back."

Everything seemed the same, except for a single blue dot whose velocity arrow suddenly changed direction. He stared at the map more intensely, and moments later another blue vector changed.

"Computer, zoom in on and replay the region around the first velocity change."

The blue dot quickly grew into a jagged metallic ship fragment drifting smoothly to his left. His eye followed its trajectory until it impacted a small icy body, sending the remnant spinning away to his upper right. "Of course," he said to himself; the region was littered with debris so collisions were inevitable.

"Computer, highlight all objects whose velocity changed in the last fifteen minutes."

The sea of yellow and blue targets with their pencil thin arrows returned. Scattered among them were a dozen objects highlighted in a bright green, indicating their recent trajectory changes. Jack stared at the map, again looking for patterns to guide him. He only saw the obvious one: all velocity changes occurred in pairs. They were the result of collisions. Aside from that, their distribution was random.

"Computer, display a wide-field view of the star system."

The view zoomed out and the sea of yellow specks was reduced to a hazy, arcing yellow belt surrounding the system's distant sun. "Highlight velocity vector changes again." The computer obliged and two clusters of green points were immediately apparent in the belt. Each was centered around a region where the enemy ships had fallen into their trap. Far off to his left, however, was a third small group. It was much deeper in the system, near the central star. The answer suddenly leapt to the front of his mind. "Computer," he said, "Show me only objects with unpaired velocity changes."

Nearly everything disappeared, only the group close to the central star remained.

"Zoom in on the inner cluster," he said.

His view shifted to show a small earth-like globe with a large, ring-shaped array of green points a small distance away. "There you are," Jack whispered. It was the one of the missing waves of enemy ships in a defensive position around one of the system's AGCs.

"Computer, display all objects with large velocity vectors that are significantly different from the expected orbital motion."

A single object, highlighted in red, was emerging from behind the main star. It moved fast enough that he could easily see its motion across his screen. "Zoom in," he called out.

The view changed, and he instantly saw that it was Alpha's sphere. The ship was moving with enough speed that the surrounding planetoids appeared as little more than thin streaks. Its trajectory said it was likely heading back towards them. More importantly, there were no ships in pursuit. Jack immediately wanted to contact them, but it was too dangerous. Any transmission would give away his position. Hopefully Alpha would find him on his own.

"Computer, display wide field view again."

The hazy, yellow belt surrounding the central star returned. A small red dot, indicating Alpha's sphere, was clearly visible working its way outward. There were, however, no other anomalous objects highlighted – no sign of Kurt's ship.

Palmer quietly walked up to him and said, "Sir, I have a request."

Jack looked up at the man and said, "I thought you were working with Nadya in the observatory."

"Sir, she's quite capable of doing the search without me. Besides, I think I have a better way to help."

He simply replied, "Explain."

"I'd like to take the undamaged alien pod and look for Lieutenant Commander Hoffman. Specifically, I want to search the area near KB53."

"Absolutely not," Jack shot back. "The situation's in too much of a state of flux. I can't have you out there on your own."

"Sir," Palmer said more forcefully.

Jack simply answered again with a firm, "No."

Palmer, however, continued politely, "I understand, but look at the situation. We're shorthanded, and too far from that region to see the difference between debris and a small ship. You're wasting too much time letting me sit here like this."

Jack knew what the right move was, but didn't want to admit it. He already had one missing ship and potential traps all around. He didn't want to risk losing anyone else. However, they were desperate. Every minute longer put Kurt's and Janet's lives in further danger, and he definitely couldn't leave the ship himself.

"Sir," Palmer pressed respectfully, "you need to let me try."

Jack looked around the bridge: Kate was the only other person present and was completely focused on her terminal. Looking back at Palmer, he pushed his fears from his mind – one should never make a decision based on emotion. And fear was the worst of them. Taking a deep breath, he finally said, "Go, find them."

"Yes, sir," Palmer replied and quickly headed off the bridge.

His decision felt wrong, but it was painfully obvious that they weren't making any progress: this was the only logical move. He needed to move on and focused his attention again on the map. However, it told him nothing new: Alpha's ship was inching outward, a contingent of enemy ships was lying in wait near the inner earth-like planet, and the IPV was still sitting helpless in a sea of debris. He studied their positions but realized it was just a waste of time. Activating his comm., he called out, "Don, respond please."

"Here Jack," was the quick reply.

"I was able to identify Alpha's ship. We need to track it."

"Yes, I spotted it a moment ago too," Don replied. "I've already extrapolated its course. It looks like they're heading our direction. My best guess is that they'll reach us in about twenty minutes. But there's a problem."

"What's that?" Jack asked.

"There are enemy ships in pursuit. They're pretty far back, but are definitely following."

"How many?"

"It's tough to tell, but I'd guess it's the bulk of the wave that Palmer and I saw chasing them before."

"Send me your data," Jack said.

There was brief pause before Don replied, "OK, you've got it."

"Thank you."

He looked up at the main screen, and said, "Computer, overlay Don's course calculations on the schematic."

The screen's wide angle view of the system changed slightly. A thin, red arc emerged from behind the central star, swinging out into hazy yellow belt of the star's Kuiper belt before adjusting course and looping toward a white triangle identifying the IPV. Along the arc was a slowly moving red circle identifying the current position of Alpha's ship. A significant distance behind it was a small cluster of blue points: the pursuing wave of enemy fighters.

"Computer, highlight the debris field near Kurt's last position"

A green ellipse buried deep within the Kuiper belt appeared; it lay about a quarter of the way between the IPV and Alpha's ship. "Show Palmer's course," Jack ordered.

The machine obediently added a white line leading from the IPV to the debris field. It was immediately apparent that Palmer would reach the region only a few minutes ahead of Alpha. The enemy ships would follow not long after that. There wasn't going to be enough time for him to do a meaningful search alone. Jack's frustration eased as he recognized that Palmer's idea could still prove useful. True, the IPV was too far away to have a good chance of locating Kurt. But instead of sending just Palmer, Jack needed to take the IPV in as well. If they worked their search from opposites sides, they might have a chance. However, this meant assuming Kurt's ship was near the alien wreckage and giving up on the rest of the system.

"Computer," Jack said, "plot a course to the debris field. Calculate a search pattern to complement Palmer's."

A blue line appeared. It overlaid Palmer's course before diverging when they approached the target region. "Course calculated," the machine announced.

"Good," Jack said. He stared at the map of the debris field for a second longer before continuing, "Take us in."

The computer didn't give a verbal reply. Instead, a bright bead slowly climbed along the IPV's projected course; the alien technology however suppressed any feeling of acceleration. While admiring their progress, the surrounding silence caught his attention. The bridge should have been humming with activity. This, however, was a reminder that half of his bridge staff was dead or missing. Nadya was still running the search from the observatory and lower deck. The rest of the science contingent was pitching in as best they could.

He refocused his attention on the map. Palmer was closing in on the debris field. With the aid of their alien engines, the IPV was close enough now that their radar scans revealed details in the cloud of metal ship fragments. So far, however, no smooth, oval objects indicative of the alien pods could be seen. He tried to take solace with the thought that at least they were making some progress.

"Don," he called into the comm.

"Here, Jack."

"Do you have any updated course calculations for Alpha's sphere and the enemy ships?"

"Yes. Alpha's definitely heading towards us. I expect he'll intercept our position in a little over ten minutes. That's barely five minutes after we reach the debris field. The other ships, however, are a problem."

"What do you mean?"

"It looks like they're fanning out."

"Feed your projections to the main screen up here."

"Give me a sec," Don replied.

The map changed, displaying a close-up view of the region near the broken up Kuiper belt object KB 53. The scene was dominated by yellow-highlighted rock fragments littering the area, along with what must have been several dozen blue-encircled, jagged metal fragments. A tightly clustered set of lines, identifying the paths of the enemy fighters penetrated deep into the region before starting to diverge. It seemed as if they might try to surround the search area.

"It looks almost like they know where we're going. How far back are they?"

"Only a minute or two behind Alpha at most. It's seems they've picked up some speed."

"Captain."

Jack sat up straight in his chair; it was Palmer's voice over the comm. "Yes, go ahead," Jack replied.

"I think I may have found them. There's a smooth five-meter long metal object about fifteen thousand kilometers ahead of me. It looks intact."

"Thank God!" Jack said loudly.

"My ETA to them is about two minutes."

"Good. We'll rendezvous with you there," Jack answered as he studied the map. They would have barely five minutes to get both pods aboard before Alpha's ship and the enemy fighters arrived.

"Kate," he called out.

"Yes, sir?" she replied.

"Send a signal to Alpha. We're going to need their help."

"The signal's been sent," she replied a moment later.

Only a couple seconds more passed before Beta's voice came through, "Captain, we will be in your vicinity in about seven minutes. Our plan is to take your ship aboard ours and outrun the pursuing ships."

"That sounds good," Jack answered with some relief. "We're going to need your help rescuing our other crew members first,"

"That is not possible. Rescuing just your vessel is going to be risky enough. We'll need to come to a stop, deactivate our drive to get your ship inside, and then accelerate again before they catch up with us. Even with pushing our technology to its limits, I'm not one hundred percent sure we can do it. There will be no extra time to retrieve your other crew members."

"I'm not leaving them out there to die," Jack shot back.

"You should be more concerned about the thirteen lives aboard your IPV than the three out there," Beta answered indifferently.

"Where's Alpha?" Jack asked.

"Alpha is no longer available to communicate with you," Beta answered tersely.

The response sent a chill down Jack's spine – he'd underestimated them. For a split second Jack wondered if they'd actually done something to Alpha? Or, were they simply preventing him from talking with them? Before Jack could finish his thoughts, Beta continued, "For us to complete this maneuver, you will need to shut your engines down when we approach. At that point our systems will take control and pull you in. I will contact you when we are in position."

"Beta, you don't understand. We need to get them."

There was no response. He was tempted to call the alien again but knew it wouldn't be of any use. Instead activated his comm. and said, "Palmer, what's your status."

"I'm closing in on the other pod. The outside is undamaged; let's just hope it's like your situation and they're safe inside."

"I was in contact with Beta," Jack said. "Their ship's heading toward us, but…"

"Captain," Palmer interrupted. "Beta had me linked in with your communication. I'm aware of the situation."

"Then you know we won't have time to use our equipment to pull them in. I'll position the IPV alongside both of you, but I'm going to need you to somehow nudge his ship into the shuttle bay."

"Sir, it's too tight in there. We'll end up damaging the IPV and maybe Kurt's pod as well."

Palmer was right but Jack answered quickly, "Then, I'll jettison one of the shuttles."

"Are you sure about…"

Jack cut him off and said, "I don't see any other way. Do you?"

When there was no response, Jack said, "Stand by." He then called across the bridge, "Kate."

"Yes?"

"I need to get to the shuttle bay to do this. Direct all of the command feeds to the terminal down there."

"Understood," she replied.

"Palmer," he said as he left the bridge.

"Yes, sir."

"What's your status?"

"I'm alongside them now."

"Good. Now listen. I just realized it may not be as hard as I thought to get you both in the bay. When we deployed the explosives, we used some sort of robots carried on board the pod. Ask your computer interface if you have any on yours."

Jack dove down the corridor and was nearly at the shuttle bay when Palmer finally responded, "Yes. The system has two of them."

"Tell the machine to use them like a grapple so that you can push the other ship more precisely. It'll figure out how."

"Got it, sir."

"Ok, I'm at the shuttle bay now. I'll jettison shuttle one and then we'll position ourselves by you. Get into position."

Jack looked at his watch: there were barely three minutes left until the rendezvous with Alpha's ship: not enough time to do this by the book. "Computer, connect the shuttle remote pilot to this terminal," he said.

"Connection complete," the machine answered.

"Bypass depressurization and open main shuttle bay door."

"That action is not recommended," the machine said politely.

"We don't have the time to pump the atmosphere out. Just open the damned door."

"Commencing," was the prompt answer.

There was a rush of escaping air accompanied by the clatter of loose equipment being swept out into the void. Jack's error, though, quickly became apparent. The wind started dragging the damaged alien pod he'd piloted toward the opening. The silver ship picked up speed, spun around and clipped the door's frame with a deep bang. A second later it spun away from them into space. "Shit," was all he managed to say as he immediately activated the shuttle's systems from the terminal.

"Release shuttle-one landing clamps," he called out. Once the computer confirmed his order, he brought up a cockpit view of the craft and activated its thrusters. Piloting the shuttle now was little more than moving his finger along the screen to direct the small craft out of the bay. He gave it just enough thrust to get clear and said, "Disconnect shuttle link and display view from external camera three."

The screen showed shuttle-one slowly moving away; the two sleek alien pods were drifting a couple hundred meters directly ahead. Palmer's was positioned behind Kurt's and looked ready to push toward them.

"Palmer," Jack called.

"Yes, sir."

"We'll have the best chance of controlling this if you stay put and I bring the IPV to you. If you push them in, you won't be able to stop them; they'll just crash into the back of the bay. I'll at least be able to use the thrusters stop the IPV's forward motion, and maybe minimize any damage as you and Kurt's pod enter the bay. Use your pod to make small adjustments to their position as we approach."

"Understood."

"Computer," Jack said. "Transfer IPV guidance to this terminal."

"Guidance transferred."

He glanced at his watch: one minute was left. "Feed me the shuttle bay, main-door camera view," he demanded.

The computer complied and Jack found himself staring at the two distant pods, framed by the edges of the shuttle bay door. They were slightly off center. His hands danced across the terminal's engine controls, quickly centering the alien craft. Without taking his eyes off of his target, he used the port thrusters to accelerate toward them. They were moving faster than he preferred, but there was no time.

"I'm going to come in fast and then pulse the starboard thrusters to stop us once you're in. You're going to have to take care of all of the maneuvering. Call out any adjustments you need me to make."

"Understood," was the calm response.

The oblong silver vessels grew quickly— fast enough that Jack wanted to pull back on the thrust, but they only had forty seconds left.

"Captain," Palmer called out, "adjust your elevation up by five degrees."

Jack quickly pulsed his maneuvering jets.

"Now translate forward…twenty meters."

A brief shot from the rear thrusters followed by a push from the front moved them into position.

"That looks good…"

"I show your distance at thirty meters," Jack called.

"Understood, sir."

He brought his hand to the starboard thruster control, ready to quickly stop them when Palmer shouted, "Captain elevate five more degrees, translate three or four more meters forward."

Jack moved quickly, his hands nimbly triggering the controls like a musician, but he wasn't fast enough. Kurt's pod clipped the left edge of the bay door, repeating the same deep bang he heard earlier. He ignored it though, and activated the starboard thrusters. He needed to stop their motion before the pod impacted the back of the bay or the other shuttle.

"Captain."

It was Beta's voice. "Standby," Jack answered urgently as he slowed the IPV. Kurt's pod was still going to hit, but maybe not too hard.

"Captain, there is no time. Disengage your engines now. We will be at your position in ten seconds."

"I need…" Jack started, but Beta cut him off, saying, "Cut them now or we will abort this maneuver and leave you."

He quickly hit the disengage trigger. A second later, Kurt's and Palmer's pods skipped off the shuttle bay floor and slammed into the rear wall. The rebound send Palmer's pod skidding into shuttle-two. Outside, a sudden flash of silver was followed by complete blackness: Alpha's ship had arrived. Jack immediately realized he needed to keep pods contained in the bay, and hit the emergency close trigger for the bay doors. They slammed shut just as Kurt's pod bounced into them.

"Pressurize bay," Jack ordered. The rush of inflowing air was comforting, but taking too long. Looking to his left, he caught a glimpse of Nadya quickly making her way down the hall toward him.

"Are they in?" she asked urgently.

"Yes," Jack answered. They waited an agonizingly long ten seconds in silence before the green "all-clear" light shown on the door. Without hesitating, he hit the "open" control, but the door remained sealed. Its status indicator changed to yellow, and read "pressure warning."

"Computer, status!" Jack shouted.

"There is a leak in the shuttle bay outer door. The room is venting atmosphere."

"Shit, override the warning and open this bulkhead now."

"Unable to comply. Risk to the IPV is too great."

Jack slammed his fist into the hard steel door and barked, "Close the internal bulkheads on this level, now." Heavy steel doors to their left and right immediately slid shut. "That should minimize the risk. Pump additional atmosphere into the bay to maintain pressure and open this door now."

The door slid aside and their ears were assaulted by the loud hiss of escaping air. Ignoring it, Jack and Nadya rushed into the room as the tops of both pods slid back revealing their occupants. A rush of relief swept over him as he saw Kurt starting to climb out of the alien ship. Janet's arms were clearly visible as she tried to pull herself up. Palmer, however, was having a tougher time at it. Jack headed to Janet, while Nadya tended to Kurt. As Jack reached to pull her out, the joy of their rescue was cut short: a loud, metallic snap cut through the room. They spun around to see a small crack forming in the left side of the shuttle bay door. The hiss of escaping air grew to a howling wind as Jack yanked a dazed Janet from her pod. Pushing her to Nadya, he shouted, "Get them both into the hall!"

"What about you?" she yelled back.

"Palmer's still in there. I'm not leaving him!"

Another ear-splitting crack made him cringe. The wind picked up strength as he shouted, "Get into the hall now and close the hatch if the bay door gives out!"

Nadya shouted something back at him, but her words were drowned out by the growing din. He turned back to Palmer without another word. Palmer was sitting upright in his pod, cradling his right arm. Jack guessed that he must have injured it during the crash landing in the IPV's shuttle bay. By the time Jack reached him, a sharp pain was cutting through his head and ears from the loss of pressure. He grabbed Palmer firmly by the waist, and with one swift move pulled with all his strength. Palmer slid out of the pod, but the force knocked him backwards. The crack in the bay door widened, and the rush of escaping air strengthened enough to start dragging them across the floor. Jack had to force the thinning air from his lungs to cough out the words, "Get up…we've got to get out of here now!"

Palmer's eyes rolled back: he was passing out. The tell-tale dizziness of Oxygen deprivation took hold of Jack. He knew he didn't have much time left and pulled hard on Palmer.

"Get on your feet now!" Jack ordered.

All his first officer managed was a disoriented stare back at him.

Jack grabbed him by the belt and tried dragging him toward the hallway door. The smooth, shuttle bay floor, however, didn't provide him with any traction or handholds with which to fight the wind. He started sliding back. Glancing back at the jagged opening, he thought that there must be some way to plug it. Something suddenly struck the side of his head. It stung and he looked up to see that Kurt and Nadya had thrown a long cable to him. Grasping it with one hand, and holding Palmer with the other, he pulled himself toward them. The fatigue and Palmer's dead weight became overwhelming. His lungs struggled in the thinning air, and his vision blurred as exhaustion engulfed him. Simply staying conscious was a battle. A deep resonating groan from behind gave him the jolt of adrenalin he needed to push on.

"Jack, the bay door's buckling!"

It was Kurt's voice rising over the chaos. Looking up, he saw Kurt, Nadya and Janet pulling the cable, dragging him toward them. There were only a few more meters to go. He fought to maintain his grip on Palmer, but his hands and fingers screamed in protest. The roar of the wind grew. A biting cold rose above the pain in his lungs; frost now covered his skin and uniform. His fingers felt like they were breaking. Jack used the pain to stay conscious and maintain a death grip on Palmer and the cable. Reflex took over and he closed his eyes tight: it eased the viselike pain in his head. He searched his other senses for progress. There was a sharp tug of the cable followed by the sensation of being dragged. Two hands firmly grabbed his arms. Another person yanked hard and he was suddenly flung against the hallway wall. A second later the scream of the escaping air was cut off by the hard metal bang of the closing bulkhead. The world around him became distant as he released his grip on Palmer and the cable. Fatigue washed over him. There was the sound of atmosphere being pumped into the hallway. The fresh air rushing into his lungs quenched a thirst more powerful than any he'd ever experienced.

Jack tried opening his eyes, but had to first wipe away the frost from his eyelids. Kurt and Nadya were standing over him. Sitting up, he saw Janet's blurry form hunched over Palmer's motionless body. Jack tried to speak but coughed instead.

Janet looked to him and said, "He's alive, sir. Just unconscious."

Jack allowed a grin to spread across his face as he let Kurt help him up. It felt good to have his friend back. He took a deep breath before gently pushing Kurt and Nadya aside, and moving closer to Janet and Palmer. His first officer coughed and opened his eyes.

"Thank God," Jack finally managed to say in hoarse voice. Exhaustion and relief convinced him to sit down and take a few more deep breaths of the warm satisfying air. He took a second to look behind and saw Kurt and Nadya in each other's arms. Somehow they'd succeeded; nothing else mattered.

"Captain."

It was Beta's voice, but Jack didn't want to answer. He just wanted a second to rest. Duty, however, pushed everything else aside and forced him to say, "Yes, Beta?"

"That was very risky. You are fortunate that you didn't destroy your ship."

Jack ignored the alien and stood up.

"We currently have your vessel aboard ours, and are pulling away from the enemy fighters. When you are ready, we will explain to you what we will be doing next."

"Understood," Jack replied.

"I think it would be advisable if you allow us to repair the damage to your ship."

Jack barely heard the alien as the emergency bulkheads in the hallway finally opened and Don and Helena rushed toward them. He just answered Beta with a reflexive, "Yes, thank you."

Helena got to him first asked, "Are you OK?"

He said, "Yes," while waving her off. Following her over to Palmer, he finally had time to realize that the man was a mess. Small trickles of blood were flowing away from his nostrils and ears. For a split second, Jack was cognizant of the fact that he probably didn't look much better, but it didn't matter. Palmer's eyes were fully open now and he was trying to speak.

They moved closer to hear his hoarse voice say, "What happened?"

"You and Jack nearly got yourselves killed," Helena answered.

Palmer laid back down as Kurt walked over to Jack.

"You OK, Kurt?" he asked calmly.

"Yes. But, what's going on?"

"A lot. I'll fill you in later. Right now, I'm just glad you're safe. I want you to get yourself cleaned up and then we'll talk."

Kurt just stared back.

"Nadya, you can fill him in for now. Just get him ready; I need him back on the bridge as soon as possible. We don't have much time." He watched as she nodded and led Kurt by the arm down the hall.

Jack turned back toward Palmer, but Don quickly leaned toward him and said in a low voice, "Jack, we need to talk."

"I know," he answered without turning to face the man. "Give me a couple minutes."

"This really can't wait. Alpha fed me data just before Beta contacted you."

"Alpha?" Jack asked hopefully. "Give me a second."

Helena was leaning over Palmer, checking his pulse and breathing. "How is he," Jack asked.

"I'm going to need to get him to sickbay to be sure. Plus, I need to check you out too. You don't look much better."

Jack grimaced as he answered, "I'm fine." Before Helena could protest, he leaned close to Palmer and whispered, "Good work today. Now do what Helena tells you."

Palmer nodded.

Jack started to get up, but Palmer reached up and grabbed him by the shirt collar. Jack paused for split second before letting himself be pulled back down.

It took another second for Palmer to get out the words, "Thank you."

Jack nodded in response. Looking back at Don, he said, "Let's get back to the bridge."

Helena turned to glare at Jack, but he ignored the meaning of her gaze and said, "Update me on his condition once you've finished with him."

Reluctantly, she answered, "Understood."

Chapter 37 – August 1, 2124; 14:45:00

Despite his injuries, Jack moved at a quick pace, leaving Don struggling to keep up. He used the lingering pain to purge his mind of any distractions. The entire crew was safe for the moment, giving him the chance to focus on getting control of their situation. He entered the bridge and quickly took his seat before turning to Don and asking, "Did you hear anything else from Alpha?"

Don's face tensed as he tried to speak. The man was obviously trying to hold it together and only managed a simple, "No."

"Let's see the data they sent you."

"I don't think there's anything we can do. It's just…"

Jack cut in calmly and said, "Don, just give me the facts. We'll decide what can be done after."

"It's not good. The portion of the fleet that bypassed this system is large. We're talking a couple hundred ships. They didn't decelerate at all, they just altered course and are definitely heading to Earth."

A wave of dizziness swept over him – a combination of fatigue and shock. Everything seemed distant, as if he was watching the conversation from another room. Don said something else, but Jack's growing anger blocked everything out. The fact that Earth would be helpless dominated his mind.

The words, "Jack are you listening to me?" pulled him back. He looked at Don for a second before saying without conviction, "I'm sure they can get us to Earth first."

"But what will we be able to do?"

That question was already in his mind too, but dwelling on it wasn't going to solve anything. "Did Alpha tell you anything about their plans?" he asked.

"No, he only had time to feed me the data," Don answered.

"What about the other formation?"

"There're two of them. One's taken up a position around the incomplete AGC…"

"Yes, that we knew. But you said there's another?" Jack asked impatiently.

"The other," Don continued, "is bombarding Alpha's colony in this system. It's on the Earth-like planet near the AGC and has been completely wiped out; there are no survivors."

"Shit!" Jack said as he looked straight ahead, staring at nothing in particular.

"Captain." It was Beta's voice.

With forced calmness, Jack answered, "Yes, go ahead."

"We've come to a decision," Beta said.

"Good, we need to discuss what can be done."

"Captain, there will be no discussion. There are no choices."

"I don't understand," Don blurted out.

"You need to understand the situation," Beta said with a hint of condescension. "Our colony has been destroyed and there is a small but deadly contingent of ships in this system waiting to attack us. Our only option is to try to escape. But, please do not worry, we will take you with us."

"What the hell are you talking about?" Don nearly screamed.

"We have a major population center in a system one hundred seventy light years from here. It's listed as star HD 10180 in your catalogue; you will be welcome there."

"We have to get to Earth first!" Don pressed. "After that you can go wherever the hell you want."

"Beta, we need you to explain," Jack added.

"We can't take you there," Beta replied tersely.

"I'm sure your ship can travel faster than theirs," Jack shot back. "It should be possible for you to take us home."

"As you are well aware," Beta said, "they will be traveling along the same trajectory that we would follow. There's nothing to stop them from simply attacking us when we try to pass them. Plus, in the unlikely event that we did get you safely to Earth, it's a certainty that they would then follow us to our final destination. We'd arrive only a matter of days ahead of them. However, if we go directly to our planet, we'll be travelling a hundred seventy light years. By going to Earth first, however, their fleet will end up travelling a total of two hundred forty-one light years. In terms of arrival time, we'll get to our planet seventy-one years ahead of them. That will give us enough time to prepare."

"Prepare for what — an evacuation?" Don said, his voice dripping with sarcasm.

"If that is what's required, then yes," Beta replied firmly.

"Wait," Jack said firmly. "What about those ships you originally offered us? We could still use them to get home on our own."

"That is correct," the alien replied. "However, even with those engines, you would be travelling somewhat slower than them. In other words, you would arrive at Earth after their attack."

"How long?" Jack asked.

"One to two weeks."

The bridge was silent. Kate had long since given up working at her terminal and joined Don in staring at Jack. He knew they needed him to come up something. But his mind was empty. The silence lasted long enough for Beta to speak again, "Captain, we will of course, help you however we can. If that means you want the equipment to go back to Earth, we will give it to you. However, please understand that your crew's chances of survival are vastly better if you come with us. It would be a shame if your species went extinct."

Jack just sat there speechless. It wasn't anger so much as disbelief that filled his mind. The alien was speaking about the end of humanity as if it had already happened — something he simply couldn't accept. He took a deep breath and replied, "I don't see much of a choice, Beta. We have to go back. At very least, we'll be able to help them rebuild."

"I understand your loyalty. But remember what you observed on G3-Alpha. There will be nothing to rebuild."

Desperate to change the subject, Jack quickly asked "What is your ship doing right now?"

"For the time being we are still accelerating toward the outer reaches of this star system. It appears their ships have stopped pursuing us and are joining the others near the AGCs and our destroyed colony. They likely believe that we need to use the device."

"Won't they just follow you when you run for your other colony?" Don asked. He took a breath before adding with an edge, "You won't have your seventy-one-year advantage."

"There are only about twenty ships left here. Their past attacks tell us that they won't go after as big a target as our planet without their full fleet. As a result, we believe this contingent will reunite with the main group near Earth before coming after us."

"Damn you!" Don shouted.

"Captain, please consider your options," Beta said, completely ignoring Don. "We will need your decision within an hour. I will contact you then."

The bridge was silent. Don and Kate just stood there in shock. Jack turned away to try to think, but instead found Kurt and Nadya standing at the bridge's entrance.

"How much did you hear?" he asked.

"All of it," Nadya replied.

"What do we do?" Kurt asked.

"We need to go back to Earth," Jack said softly, "but…" His voice trailed off as he thought about the possibility of finding their home incinerated. Anger grew within him as if the Earth had already been destroyed, then ebbed as years of training took over and pushed the thought aside. There had to be an answer; there always was.

"But what?" Don finally asked.

Jack looked at him. The enemy's strategy was obvious; it was something he would do if he were laying a trap. "It's likely they'll leave a small contingent behind, near Earth waiting for us. If we go back, we'll be killed before we ever see them," he finally said.

"What are you saying?" Nadya asked.

"I don't know," Jack answered as he ran his fingers through his hair. "I need time to think this through."

"Time? Are you actually thinking about running with them?" She said loudly.

"No Goddammit!" Jack shouted. "There's no way in hell I want to live like some sort of specimen or pet of theirs. I'd rather die back home! But…" Jack let his words drift away again. There was no 'but.' There were no other options. He took a deep breath and continued in a calmer tone, "But I can't consign this entire crew to certain death. If nothing else, someone has to survive."

"We'd be the last bit of humanity," Don said softly.

"Shut the hell up!" Nadya shouted at him. "Just shut up. Nothing's happened yet!"

"Jack," Kurt said softly, "there's got to be something we can do."

Jack just looked at each of them. They were his friends – even Don. He didn't want to see them die. But would they really be alive if they went with Beta? Their lives would have no meaning. Either way they didn't have a future. He simply said, "Just give me a few minutes." He walked to the exit and was thankful that Kurt and Nadya let him pass without saying anything. The frustration building within him transformed to physical pain as he made his way down the hall. His stomach felt like it was splitting open. He got to his office and closed the door quickly before finally releasing his anger by pounding the wall. It didn't do anything but move the pain from his gut to his hands. Somehow, though, it helped and he punched it again. He couldn't believe there was nothing they could do.

Jack sat on the edge of his desk and stared at the wall. He'd managed to dent the sheet metal in several places. His mind, though automatically fell back on an old habit: looking for patterns. His fist marks made a tight semi-circle, but the dents weren't evenly spaced. It wasn't the shape that caught his attention though. It was an act of simple analysis. He realized what he always knew: anger and frustration served no purpose. Despite their desperation, they needed to step back and approach this as any other puzzle. It was the only way they'd find the solution.

He got up and rushed back to the bridge. The four of them were still there, and looked quietly at him as he entered. They could have been talking and stopped because of his arrival, but it didn't matter. "Don," he said.

Don looked to him without saying anything.

"You said Alpha sent you all of his data on the enemy ships."

"Uh, yes."

"Good. Is it in our computer system?"

"Yeah, I finished loading it earlier."

"Computer," Jack said, "give me a tactical display of the enemy formations. I want a wide field view showing their course starting from when they first entered the system."

The screen displayed a diagram with several white concentric circles surrounding the system's primary star. Each was marked with increasing distance from the star in increments of twenty Astronomical Units. Three closely spaced, green lines dove in from the right. Near the two hundred AU mark, one gently pulled away and followed a path directly into their earlier ambush: it was the wave of ships they'd successfully engaged. The other two continued together for another forty AU until the they diverged. One swung past the central star before heading off to his left. The other, however, swept in to attack Alpha's colony.

Jack just pointed to the screen and said, "There. They stayed close together until they were well into the system. It wasn't until a hundred fifty to two hundred AU that they spread out. It's the same thing they did before. That's where we'll have to attack."

"When they're a couple hundred AU out..." Don said thoughtfully.

"But how?" Kurt asked.

"It's outside the main part of our sun's Kuiper belt. We won't have anything to use for shrapnel," Nadya said.

"We'd need something way more powerful than last time," a voice said.

Jack spun around to see Palmer standing just behind him. His first officer didn't look near a hundred percent, but that didn't matter right now: the man had a good mind for tactical situations. "Yes, but what?" Jack asked in response.

"Wait, I might have..." Don started, but was cut off by Alpha's voice saying, "Captain."

"Alpha!" Jack said with obvious relief. "What happened to..."

"Simply put, the others did not approve of my actions and do not want me making decisions that affect others again. They don't know I'm speaking with you right now, so we don't have much time to talk before our communications will be terminated. It has been decided that we should leave now."

"Wait," Don said.

"There is no time," Alpha said tersely. "The enemy fleet near the AGC appears to be changing position. They're coming after us."

"No, Alpha. You need to listen!" Don shouted. "What would happen if you activated the incomplete AGC?"

"I'm sorry but there isn't any time for questions like this right now. We can discuss the nature of our devices some other time."

"Alpha, please," Don begged. "This isn't what you think."

There must have been something in Don's voice that caught the alien's attention because he suddenly said, "Without another AGC on the other side, we won't be able to anchor the space-time folds in place. The connection will be unstable. Simply put, the two folds will touch and then immediately snap back to their original positions."

"And that 'snap' you're talking about," Don continued, "will release an immense amount of energy, right?"

"That is correct," Alpha replied with what Jack swore was a hint of curiosity.

"What're you talking about?" Palmer asked.

"An explosion," Don answered. "But, if I'm right, it'll be unlike anything we've ever imagined." He paused for a second, and then said, "Alpha, will that energy release be on both sides? I mean here and wherever the AGC managed to connect us to?"

This time there was a noticeable pause before Alpha answered, "Yes, that is correct."

"How powerful are we talking here?" Jack asked quickly.

"Anything within five AU will be destroyed," Alpha answered solemnly.

"That's over seven hundred million kilometers," Don said in awe.

"To be clear, there will be an explosion," Alpha continued, "but the greater devastation will come from a short, high amplitude gravitational wave pulse. Its high frequency components will disrupt the physical structure of anything in its path. In the case of ships, it will cause their hulls to break apart."

They quietly stared at the map. Kurt broke the short silence, saying, "Alpha, what would that do to the planet with your colony here?"

"It's not very relevant. All of our people in this system have been killed."

"But what about..." Kurt started, but Jack cut him saying, "Alpha, can you trigger the AGC?"

"The only way would be to try to go through it."

"Is that possible?" Don asked. "I mean...would it be stable enough to actually go through and get somewhere?"

Again there was another pause before Alpha replied, "Yes. But in order to survive, you would need to be moving very fast. The connection will only last for a matter of milliseconds. And even then, one would have to be moving fast enough to avoid the energy pulse on the other side."

Jack just smiled at Don: they had their answer. "Alpha," Jack said calmly, "I think we have an idea that will help both of us. First, am I correct in assuming that this AGC will move us forward in time...from our perspective?"

"Yes," Alpha said.

"Then, the question is, can we make sure we come out near the enemy fleet's future location?"

"I can already see what you're proposing. I will do what I can from my side to program the device. When Beta contacts you, tell him you've decided to return to Earth anyway. Ask him specifically for two more of the engines that we attached to your IPV. Their extra power will give you a chance. Go straight for the AGC and do not try to contact me – that will tip the others off to what I'm doing. I will contact you when I can."

"Thank you," Jack said.

There was no response from Alpha.

"What exactly are you proposing?" Kurt asked.

Jack smiled as he answered, "If they can control the point in space where this AGC connects, then it's possible we can defeat them."

"How?" Nadya asked.

"Remember that in this direction, the AGC's are moving us forward in time. Earth is one hundred fourteen light years from here. It should be able to connect us to a location near the fleet, at a point in time a hundred fourteen years from now – just before they enter our solar system. There'll be no way for them to expect this; plus, they'll still be close together…"

"And the explosion from the unstable connection will destroy them," Don said, finishing Jack's thought.

"Exactly," Jack replied. Turning around, he said, "Palmer, I need you to…" but stopped as he realized the man was gone.

Don continued, "We'll have to be careful where we come out."

"What do you mean?" Jack asked.

"If the explosion is as big as Alpha says, then it'll disturb the orbits of any nearby Kuiper belt objects. We can't have them randomly tumbling into the inner solar system."

"You're talking about potential comet impacts with Earth, aren't you," Jack said.

"Yes. Earth, Mars or any of the mining colonies."

"But we have defenses for that," Nadya said.

"For one or two, yes. But here we could be talking about hundreds of fragments," Don answered.

"OK, then I need you to review our solar system's charts," Jack said. "Find me a spot along their inbound path that minimizes risk. Take whoever you need and get this done immediately. You probably don't have much time."

"Got it. I'll get back to you in a few minutes," Don replied as he left the bridge.

Jack looked back at the map, but the ship shuddered before he could put his thoughts together.

"Captain," Alpha said.

"Yes?"

"Nearly all of the enemy fighters have positioned themselves directly between us and the AGC. I don't see how you can get through anymore."

"That could complicate things," Jack answered.

"Jack," Nadya called out.

"Just a second," he replied curtly.

"You should consider Beta's offer to join us," Alpha said.

"There still may be a chance," Jack said. "Alpha, you said they've taken up that position expecting your sphere to go for the AGC, correct?"

"That seems likely."

"Then most of them will break formation when you leave. They'll try to pursue you. That'll improve our chances."

"Jack!" Don called over the comm.

"Go ahead."

"I've found a region that might work. There's a gap just beyond the outer edge of the Kuiper belt, but before a cluster of sub-Pluto sized scattered disk objects. It's relatively clean and about two hundred AU out from the sun."

"Good work. Send the data to the screen here."

"It's on its way," Don answered.

The ship shuddered as Alpha said, "Something's come up here. I've recorded Don's data. I will try to contact you again later."

"Jack, listen!" Nadya shouted.

"What?" he answered with exasperation.

"The shuttle bay door is open."

"What are you talking about?"

"Here look," she said, pointing at a terminal near her. "The IPV's shuttle bay door is showing as open."

"Is it an error? It was damaged earlier."

"Beta said they'd fix it."

"Kurt," Jack called out. "Get down there and confirm this."

Kurt gave him a quick nod and headed off the bridge. Jack looked back at Nadya and said, "Do a quick systems check. Find out what's really going on."

"OK," she answered.

The bridge was silent again as he stared blankly at the map and took inventory of the myriad of potential problems that faced them. Their plan hinged on the alien fleet following Alpha, on Alpha being able to direct the

AGC to the right location, and most importantly, on Beta not stopping Alpha from helping.

Jack barely had time to actually focus on the map before Kurt's voice came in over the comm., "Jack, the door's closed."

"Say again?" Jack replied.

"The shuttle bay door's closed; I'm looking right at it. There must have been some sort of a glitch. The systems have taken a hell of a beating."

"Fine, get back up here asap," Jack said. Turning to Nadya, he continued, "What's your status with the systems check? Was it a bad door sensor?"

"I don't know," she answered. "Right now I'm getting all sorts of electronic interference. I'm not a hundred percent sure, but if I had to guess, it's from Alpha's ship. I think they're about to activate their engines."

"Damn it," he said softly. Then more loudly, he called out, "Beta?"

There was no answer.

"Kate, send a radio signal to Beta. Let him know we need to talk immediately."

A second later, she said, "Signal sent."

Jack fixed his gaze on the map. The seconds ticked by slowly as they waited; it didn't take long for the silence to become suffocating. "Captain," the alien's voice finally said. "Our ship will be heading for HD 10180. As I said before, I believe the most prudent course of action would be for you to come with us."

"That's not possible," Jack said without thinking. The bridge was dead silent. Despite the consequences, the words just flowed from his mouth. "We can't abandon Earth."

"That is unfortunate," was Beta's terse answer.

Suppressing his anger, Jack asked, "Can you please outfit us with two more of those external engines…the same type you've already attached to the IPV?"

Without any hesitation, Beta replied, "That can be done."

"Thank you," Jack replied.

"You do understand that you will, in all probability, perish," Beta said flatly.

Even though he knew it was unnecessary, Jack looked around the room. As he made eye contact with each of his shipmates, they nodded in response. "We have to take our best shot," Jack replied. "I don't see us having any other choice."

"Then please stand by. It will take about two minutes to attach the devices and release your ship."

There was a moment of silence before Don spoke, "Jack, Don't get me wrong, I'm fine with this; but what about the blockade?"

"Let's hope their tech makes us maneuverable enough to get past them," Jack answered.

Silence filled the bridge – there was really nothing else to say.

"Captain," Alpha's voice said, "don't say anything. Your crew as well as the others on my side can't hear me right now. We only have a few seconds left to talk. In a moment we will begin accelerating away from your position toward HD 10180, and a few seconds after that you will begin your run towards the AGC. By that point the distance between us will be too great to have a conversation. So I need you to know one important thing. I've placed a small canister under your desk in your office. Don't bother asking when or how – just suffice to say that it's there. After you make it through the AGC, please listen to its message and decide what you want do with it. I'll leave it in your hands."

The IPV shuddered briefly. A burst of static flashed across the main view screen before a field of stars came into view: they were outside of the sphere. Jack just looked silently at the screen, not sure what to do. Finally, he called out, "Beta?"

The room was quiet until Nadya asked, "Is he going to answer you?"

There was a long pause before Beta replied, "You have noticed a delay in my response. This is because my ship is now accelerating away from yours. This delay will grow rapidly and communications will soon become impractical. I recommend that you begin heading for Earth immediately. If you delay, the enemy ships may try to intercept both your ship and ours…"

"Wait a minute," Don interrupted. "You're not even going to help us? You want us to run interference for you?"

"…only chance is to act simultaneously. It should…"

"Answer him!" Nadya demanded.

"Both of you, shut up!" Jack shouted.

"…best course of action," Beta's voice continued. "If you wish to reply, you should do so now. I will respond as soon as I receive it. I expect this delay to last just under over a minute."

Jack looked at each of them before saying, "Computer, engage engines at full. Take us directly to the AGC."

As before, the alien engines gave them no sense of acceleration. The only indication of their motion was the shifting of the star field on the screen as the IPV adjusted course.

"How're we going to get through the blockade?" Don asked. "There're too many of…"

Jack cut him off as he said, "Computer, how long in ship-time until we reach the AGC?"

"Two minutes."

"Jack, call them. Call Alpha," Nadya said. "We're going to need some sort of distraction to help us get through."

"Asking them isn't going to help," Don said with defeat in his voice.

"What're you talking about?" Nadya shot back.

"Think of it," Don replied. "Their engines are capable of getting both their ship and ours up to relativistic speeds in matter of seconds. Beta said as much at the end of his message. It'll take our message about a minute to get to him. The real problem is by the time they're ready to reply, the distance between us will have grown to the point where it'll take well over a minute before it gets to us. In other words, his response won't make it to us before we go through the AGC. There won't be enough time for them to do anything."

"So we're on our own?" Nadya said softly.

"I wonder if we'll ever even hear from them again. I mean after we pass through the AGC," Kate added.

Jack didn't answer, and instead said, "Computer, display a tactical view of the enemy formations around the AGC."

The screen quickly shifted to show the blue and white globe that once held Alpha's colony, along with an icon identifying the AGC's position. About two dozen red points, identifying the alien fighters, stood their ground near the AGC. Half formed a traditional blockade directly in their path; the remaining ships flanked the device, apparently ready to fire on anything that made it through.

"Jack," Don said. "I'm no tactician, but I don't see any way we can maneuver around them."

The point was painfully obvious. Jack hit the ship-wide intercom and said, "Palmer, report to the bridge."

As he finished his sentence, a cluster of small white points left the blockade, heading directly for them. "They've fired on us," Jack said softly.

"What's our speed?" Nadya asked.

"The IPV's velocity is zero-point-nine-nine c," the computer answered.

Jack quickly looked at them and said, "That can help us."

"What do you mean?" Kurt asked.

"They won't see us until we're nearly on top of them. We'll be right behind our light. But..." Jack's voice trailed off as he saw a flaw.

They stared at him, waiting for the rest of his thought. "But," he continued, "we can't come in straight. They'll expect that. We need to change course and surprise them."

"Do you think this thing's maneuverable enough to come in to the AGC off-axis?" Nadya asked. "Maybe we can slide through behind their formation."

"Maybe," Jack said. "Computer, time to AGC?"

"One minute."

"Computer," Jack called out, "Adjust course as follows." He traced out a sweeping arc on his chair's display. Their course now peeled away from their initial, direct trajectory before looping back toward the AGC from the left.

"What about their missiles?" Don asked.

"They'll only be able to use the light that left us a minute ago for guidance," Jack replied. "We'll be well out of their path by the time they reach this region. And, when they finally do see that we've changed course, I don't think they'll have enough fuel to match our new speed and direction." Seeing the relief on Don's face, forced Jack to add, "But we won't be out of the woods. They'll fire on us again."

Jack took a deep breath and said, "Computer, what's our ETA using our new course?"

"One minute thirty seconds."

"Jack," Don said calmly.

Jack ignored him as he focused on the ships near the AGC. Their approach avoided most of the danger, but they still had to make it through about a half dozen ships on the left flank. Their speed would only give the enemy a few seconds to react. However, with no weapons of their own, that few seconds would be more than enough time for the fighters to stop them. Innumerable thoughts flashed through his mind: Could they jettison the pods and shuttle as counter measures? Could they adjust course fast enough to evade incoming fire? His thoughts were cut off as a new cluster of missiles emerged from the blockade. This time they fanned out covering a broad region of space. It only took a second for him to realize the outer-most ones would intercept them on the way in. "Damn, they're smart," Jack said to himself. "They saw it coming."

"Computer," he called out, "adjust course again." This time, he pulled their sweeping arc much further to the left of the AGC. He then curved it back so they'd come in almost parallel with the plane of the outer ring, diving through at the last second. No Earth-ship should even dream of pulling the g's they'd need to pull this off. Hopefully Alpha's tech could manage it. "Computer, ETA to rings," he called out.

"Sixty seconds."

"They haven't broken formation yet," Nadya said.

"That's because they haven't seen what we've done yet. The light'll get there soon enough. The question is, how fast will they be able to react." His stomach dropped as he finished his sentence. The fighters on the AGC's far-flank suddenly cut across the front of the AGC, reinforcing those on the left side – along the IPV's inbound path. They saw his initial move.

"God no," Jack said as he stared at the new formation. Twelve ships stood directly in their path. "Kurt," he called into the intercom. "Are you still near the shuttle bay?"

"Yes," was the quick answer.

"Stand by, but I'm going to need you to jettison the pods and Shuttle-two. We might need to use them as cover. Maybe even take out a few of their ships with them."

Don called out, "Jack!"

"What?" Jack shot back impatiently.

"What's this?" Don said, pointing to the far right of the main screen's tactical display.

"I don't have time for…" he started, but stopped when his eyes caught sight of what Don was looking at. A small bright blue bead was accelerating away from the IPV toward the newly formed line of fighters. Instinct took over as he shouted, "Palmer!" into the comm. "Respond now."

He was answered by silence.

He allowed only a second of silence to pass before saying, "Computer, locate Commander Palmer."

"Commander Palmer is not onboard the IPV," the machine answered calmly.

"Where the hell is he?" Don demanded.

Jack ignored him and said, "I should have seen this coming. Computer, display video image of the interior of the shuttle bay."

The screen quickly shifted to show the half-empty room. Shuttle-two was docked off to the left; shuttle-one of course had been jettisoned. Jack's eye, however, immediately found what he was looking for: only one alien pod was present.

"Where's the other pod?" Nadya quickly asked.

"Computer, display tactical view again," Jack ordered.

The screen reverted to its earlier view. The blue bead had pulled far ahead of them and was nearly halfway to the AGC and its blockade.

"Goddammit!" Jack shouted. "Kate, open a channel to Palmer's pod."

"Channel's open," she quickly responded.

"Palmer, get the hell back here now," he demanded. "What the hell do you think you're doing?"

"Doing what's necessary," Palmer replied.

"The pods don't have any weapons," Don said in disbelief.

"That's correct, Dr. Martinez," Palmer answered.

"Then what're you going to accomplish?" Don asked. But the answer was obvious.

"I had a conversation with Alpha earlier," Palmer replied. "He told me how to detonate my engines. It should be powerful enough to clear a hole for you to get through. It's the only move left."

Jack answered in a measured tone, "Palmer, this wasn't your decision to make…"

"Captain," Palmer interrupted calmly. "There's no time for pointless arguments. The way I see it, I'm going to die either way. It's either by myself here, or on the IPV with all of you as well. This is the only way that makes any sense."

Jack stared at the screen as Palmer's words tore at him as much as any physical pain.

"Jack, we can't let them just kill him," Don protested.

"Don," Palmer said, "Thanks, but it's over. Let'em come." Another second passed before Palmer continued, "Jack, one last thing."

"Yes?"

"I apologize for doubting your …"

Jack cut in saying, "Palmer, there's no need for apologies. My log will show that you always acted in the best interest of the mission and sacrificed yourself for the crew. And that we…I am in your debt."

There was no answer.

"Palmer?" Jack called out.

They stared at the screen waiting for a reply, but none came. Instead, a barrage of missiles leapt from the enemy blockade. Palmer's ship dove strait toward them, cutting left at the last second to avoid a direct impact. The missiles turned to track their target, but Palmer was too fast and continued his push into the enemy formation. Intent on stopping his apparent run for the AGC, four enemy fighters rose from the blockade to meet him. Seeing the development, Palmer adjusted course and accelerated hard toward them in a desperate attempt to keep the full formation within range of his blast. There was a moment of confusion or maybe fear as the fighters suddenly slowed. In a split second Palmer was on top of them. The screen went black. A moment of a pure silence hung heavily in the air as they waited. Two quick bursts of static flashed across the screen before the tactical view returned. The blue point of Palmer's ship was gone, as was the entire left flank of the enemy blockade. The remaining ships were pulling away from the blast: it looked like they had their opening.

"Don, scan the area for any sign of his ship," Jack said knowing it was hopeless. He then called out, "Computer, ETA to AGC?"

"Twenty seconds."

Before he could fully analyze the new enemy positions, two fighters shot out from the retreating formation. It was instantly clear they were heading for the now vacated left flank. Realizing he might still need to use his last ditch idea, Jack called into the comm., "Kurt, are ready?"

"Yes," was the quick answer.

"Release the docking clamps on my mark and open the bay doors."

"Understood," Kurt replied.

"Computer, exterior view," Jack said. The screen showed the distant, but rapidly growing silver rings of the AGC. The two enemy ships, little more than silver specks at this distance, dove toward their path. Jack knew the chances of hitting them or any of their missiles were nearly zero, but he had to do something. He just needed to know where they would take up their positions to try to pull this off. The fighters grew rapidly, and in a split second cut completely across their path before shooting out of sight. It made no sense. They didn't fire or take up a defensive position.

"Computer, ETA!" he shouted.

"Ten seconds."

"Shit!" Jack shouted as the answer hit him. They were doing what he'd done to them: spraying a cloud of antimatter in their path. He shouted, "Computer, rotate ship one hundred eighty degrees!" and then called out, "Nadya, jettison our all of our ion engine propellant now!"

"All of the xenon?"

"Now, dammit! Now!"

Jack watched her hands dance across a terminal. He clenched his teeth and dug his hands into his armrest, tensing his body for what was to come. In an instant a blinding white light filled the screen: The xenon was annihilating the antimatter cloud. The flash wasn't the problem and he shouted into the intercom, "Brace yourselves for…" But the shockwave hit before he could finish. He closed his eyes tight as he was thrown from his chair. Pain shot through his back and hip as bounced off the floor and struck the far wall. There were shouts of shock or panic from around him. He opened his eyes and twisted toward the main screen in time to see it fill with the ominous blue-green glow from the AGC. A split second later he felt a sharp but brief shudder flow through the ship.

The screen changed dramatically. Gone was the bright white flash of antimatter annihilation. Instead he found himself staring at a seemingly serene field of stars. As he pulled himself up from the floor, he kept his eyes fixed on the screen. Dozens of the stars seemed to be quickly falling behind them. It only took a second to realize the silver-white pinpoints were ships:

they'd landed in the middle of the inbound enemy fleet.

"Computer, rear view," he said loudly.

The screen jumped to show large formations of ships shrinking into the distance. A brilliant violet pinpoint appeared near the center of the fleet – the massive energy release from space-time snapping back into position. It expanded rapidly into a glowing white plume, peppered with sporadic red flashes. Enemy ships in close proximity were exploding. The wave swept outward, engulfing all that lay in its way. The exploding fighters twinkled weakly against the massive surge of energy.

The relief Jack felt with the unfolding destruction was short-lived: the plume was weakening unexpectedly. The outermost fighters took advantage and launched a round of missiles toward them. Though deadly, it wasn't the missiles that frightened Jack, it was the fact that so much of the fleet survived. They couldn't afford to have even one make it through. The bridge was dead silent as everyone recognized the consequences of what was happening.

Something caught his eye. Jack stared more deeply at the screen, trying suppress what he was sure was false hope. Despite the plume's fading energy, enemy ships continued exploding. The wave of destruction continued outward faster than the fleet could react. His eyes drilled into the image until he finally saw the cause. A faint distortion in the background stars swept forward, like a ripple in a calm pond bending the image of the rocks below. It was the gravitational wave pulse Alpha had mentioned – visibly distorting the fabric of space-time before his eyes. There was no defense. It just tore through the enemy formation, shredding them as it flowed forward. His attention was drawn back to the missiles heading toward them. Jack knew the answer, but asked anyway, "Computer, can you increase thrust any further?"

"Engines are at maximum," was the answer.

It was like watching a chase in slow motion. The weapons inched toward them, trying to catch the IPV with its alien engines. The advancing distortion wave crept towards the missiles, slowly but surely gaining ground. In the back of his mind he knew that even if they survived the missiles, they still had to outrun the distortion wave. However, he sat there hoping the wave would somehow move faster, and eliminate the inbound weapons. He knew he was just a spectator; but kept his focus fully on the screen anyway, as if it might give him a hint of something he could do. The seconds passed intolerably slowly, as if they were hours. Still no one spoke a word.

A bright orange flash caught his eye: the wave had caught the first of the missiles. It took only another few seconds before the rest were dispatched in a silent display of orange and red fireworks. The bridge remained still as they watched the progression of the gravitational disturbance. It was weakening, but he couldn't tell if it was fast enough. Soon it was little more than a barely perceptible arc that made the stars twinkle. However, it was nearly on top of them.

"Brace for impact," Jack called into the intercom, though he had no idea of what to expect. The ship lurched sharply forward throwing him against the back of his seat, then backward nearly knocking him to the floor. Pressure alarms, sounded throughout the ship.

"Warning, hull breaches detected," an automated alarm announced.

Jack lunged toward an emergency sealant kit, when the voice announced, "Auto-sealants deployed, stand by."

His patience lasted only a couple seconds before he shouted, "Computer, list compartments with pressure loss."

"Auto-sealants holding in all compartments."

Jack looked around; everyone was standing by their stations, their eyes wide in shock. He glanced at the screen to see the last of the flames from the vanquished enemy fleet flicker out. All that remained was a benign field of stars.

Unexpectedly, in the distance a new star appeared: the AGC in the other system had collapsed. Its explosion destroying the last of the enemy blockade they'd left behind.

"Don do a scan of…" he started; but Don cut him off saying, "Already on it."

"Kurt," he called into the intercom. "Are you OK down there?"

"We're fine. We just got knocked around a bit. What's happening?"

"It looks like we're through…standby."

"Jack," Don said. "Radar scans look clear. Nothing's following us."

"Is that it?" Nadya asked. "Are we home?"

Jack was caught off guard by the question. He'd focused so much on simple survival, that he nearly forgot to check the obvious. "Computer," he said calmly, "Identify this star system."

They waited for only a few seconds before the machine replied, "This is the Earth system…"

"Thank God!" Don exclaimed. Jack blocked out the shouts from the others as he continued his questioning of the computer. "What is the date…Earth-time?"

"September 28, 2129."

"Only six weeks after we arrived at E-Eri D," Don said.

Jack finally allowed himself to smile. It looked like it was finally over. He turned to Nadya who gave him a hug. He was overwhelmed and only managed to say the obvious: "We made it." He took a deep breath and said, "Now go find Kurt and tell the others."

As she bounded off the bridge with a grin, Don surprised him with a quick embrace and said, "Jack, you really pulled it off. I don't know how, but you did it."

He patted Don on the back and corrected him, "We pulled it off." His joy, though, was tempered as he looked at Palmer's and Devon's empty seats. "I just wish the cost wasn't so high," he said softly to himself.

Turning to Don, he continued, "I need to check on the crew."

"Got it," Don replied. "I'll work with Janet to plot a course for Earth."

"Thanks," Jack answered as he headed off the bridge. He had no intention on checking on anyone else at the moment and headed directly for his office. Thankful that he didn't run into anyone in the short length of corridor, he dove into the small room and quickly shut the door behind him. A deep sigh escaped him. "Three dead," was all that ran through his mind: he'd lost too much of his crew. That and the Magellan. It wasn't how he wanted to return to Earth. True, there was good reason to celebrate. A tremendous weight had been lifted from his shoulders. But, the entire crew was his responsibility. They relied on him. Any death meant that to some degree he failed. His thoughts lingered for a while on the three of them – especially Devon.

Fatigue mixed in with his swirl of emotions and his mind drifted back to his last conversation with Alpha. He reached under his desk as Alpha had instructed, his fingers probing until they found a small cylindrical object about the size of a battery. It came loose easily. Before he pulled his hand out he nearly jumped as he heard Alpha's voice.

"Captain, I'll assume that you made it home intact. Let me start by expressing my relief that you made it. I only wish that we had more time. There was so much I wanted to share with you and to learn from you. And, I know there was an immense amount that you and your crew wanted to ask us. First and foremost, though, I apologize for all that has happened. This enemy, whoever they are, was obviously after us. You were simply caught in the middle. I am sorry you lost your crew members and that your world has been put at risk. But as we both know, one cannot change what has happened. This is simply how things are.

"Unfortunately, this will be the last time you will hear my voice. By the time you play this recording we will be large fraction of the way to HD 10180. We will reach our world in your year 2184. After that it will take over a century longer before any ship of ours or any communication we send will reach Earth. So sadly, we will not meet again. That said, it was important to me to let you know that we are also in your debt. Though very few on our vessel will admit it, I do not believe that we would have survived without you. For that I thank you.

"The cylinder that you are holding is my attempt to make up for everything – a gift of sorts. It is a device that contains a significant amount of knowledge. I wanted to share this with Earth. Not just to help you advance, but also for the more practical purpose of helping you prepare should this enemy attack Earth at some point in the future. Our analysis of their attacks suggest that they have a home world or major colony about five hundred light-years from Earth. As a result, the danger is not imminent; you and your descendants will have several centuries to prepare. I do not know if they will come, but it would be prudent for you to use this knowledge to prepare. Keep in mind, it will take your people generations to learn the base concepts of what I have provided so that you can then assimilate and use this information.

"One last thing. And, again I apologize in advance for putting you in this position. As you can imagine, this knowledge will lead to some very powerful and destructive technologies. My understanding of your world is that you do not have a unified government. There are still conflicts between groups of people on Earth, as well as some forms of oppression. In the wrong hands this information could destroy your society or even your world. I was nervous about this, but felt that the danger posed to Earth by our enemy was great enough to warrant taking this risk. I am placing my trust in you to find a way to disseminate this peacefully. As a safeguard against those who might abuse this, I have created the device so that only you can access it. It cannot be hacked in any way. I leave it in your hands to determine how and when its contents should be used. Thank you and I wish you well."

Jack sat in his chair staring at the cylinder. He was at once frightened and relieved to have Alpha's gift. Most important, though, it gave him hope for the future. He was pulled from his thoughts by a knock at the door. "Yes?" he called out.

Kurt entered and said, "Jack, everyone's looking for you. Don said with these engines, we should make it to Earth in only a couple hours, ship-time. It looks like we really made it. We're actually going home."

Jack stood up and grinned at his friend. It was time to celebrate. He patted Kurt on the shoulder and replied, "Yes, we did make it."

EPILOGUE

Jack climbed out of his car into the brisk, late autumn air. Bright sunlight warmed his face – one of several simple feelings he'd never taken the time to appreciate before. Even now, over a year since their return to Earth, it was something he continued to enjoy. Standing at the edge of the small gravel parking lot, he admired the nature trail that lay before him. It wound through a grassy field before heading into a mostly bare forest; its quiet isolation pulled at him. There was near complete silence, save for the rustling of dried leaves in the occasional breeze, and the call of a distant crow. Resisting the urge to follow the footpath, Jack instead checked his watch. It was 1:05 pm: they were late. He didn't mind the delay, however, and instead just continued to enjoy the fresh air. His eyes followed the trees and surrounding hills, searching for that distant bird. Instead he spotted the movement of his ever-present 'protection' detail. Two men, dressed in black, loitered a couple hundred meters away by the tree-line – one to his left, the other to his right. He was sure there were others hidden from view.

The low crackling of gravel under tires pulled his attention back to the parking lot, as a small red car pulled up. Kurt climbed out first while Nadya waved to him through the window. Jack smiled back. It had been over eight months since he'd last seen his friends, or any others from the crew for that matter.

"Jack, it's been too long," Kurt said as he quickly embraced him.

Nadya followed with a quick hug and a kiss on the cheek, before saying, "Have they really been keeping you too busy to even call?"

Jack shook his head and smiled with mock embarrassment as he said, "Let's just say that I haven't had much time of my own." He took a breath before asking, "How was the ride up from D.C.?"

"Not bad," Kurt answered. "At least until we had to show our IDs to your guards at the park entrance."

Jack nodded and asked, "Do you have any phones or other computers on you?"

They responded with puzzled looks.

"Leave them in the car for now, OK?" he said in a hushed voice.

"You know, I'm sure they'll be able to hear everything we say regardless," Kurt replied as he quickly placed their phones in the car's glove compartment.

Jack just nodded in response and led the way down the footpath.

"So, I guess the rumors were true," Nadya said. "Someone did try to kill you."

Jack nodded again. "They felt it was best to cover the whole thing up, but I think most everyone guessed that there was an attempt on me."

"So what actually did happen?" Kurt asked.

"Someone took a couple of shots while I was on the highway," Jack answered. "But luckily the government considered me too valuable, and had insisted that my vehicle be armored. They might have gotten me otherwise."

"Any idea who did it?" Kurt asked.

"The official story was that some lone fundamentalist did it, claiming the knowledge I brought back would destroy the world. But it could just as easily have been an agent from one of the unaffiliated countries that refused to sign the unification treaty. Or maybe even someone from within our own government. Remember, our economic and technological advantage over the rest of the world went out the window as soon as I insisted that Alpha's device be shared with the entire planet."

"Yeah, I bet you didn't make very many friends with that," Nadya quipped with a smirk.

Jack nodded and said, "You don't see my name being tossed about in the press for any awards or anything do you?"

"But you did get a nice title, right?" Kurt said with a chuckle, "Special advisor to the secretary general."

"Like that's what I wanted," Jack shot back sarcastically. They climbed a small hill before stopping at the edge of a pond. Jack stood silently, admiring a pair of ducks paddling toward them.

"So what have they had you doing?" Nadya asked. "I mean we've all been given the pick of nearly any position we wanted: we're still trying to decide. But it was like you practically disappeared."

"After our four months of debriefings together, they brought me back to Washington…for what they called negotiations."

"Negotiations?" Kurt asked.

"Well, it seemed we had to work out the terms of who would have access to Alpha's device, as well as what freedoms I would be given."

"What do you mean?" Nadya asked suspiciously.

"There was a lot of pressure for me to give primary access to the Euro-American union. The way they saw it, they should be the guardians of the knowledge and the planet, and dole out bits and pieces to the Russian block and the Chinese. It's like they forgot the lessons of the past hundred years." Jack kicked some pebbles before continuing with unhidden disgust, "I swear, this place was a lot closer to being unified before we left."

They walked in silence. Jack knew he'd certainly put a damper on their reunion, but it was necessary to talk about it. He took a deep breath before continuing, "It took nearly two months to iron out the details. In their eyes, I was supposed to be little more than a tool used to access this treasure; they didn't want me having a say in anything. First they pressured me to do my duty. Then they pushed hard, saying that I had taken an oath and was expected to live up to it. When I didn't give in, there were threats of charges against me for the deaths of three crewmembers and the loss of a five-trillion-dollar ship. There were investigations – especially into Palmer's death. But none of it mattered: Alpha gave me exclusive access to the device. There was nothing they could do about it. The only question was, how uncomfortable could they make me, and could they wear me down?"

"Who the hell's behind this?" Nadya pressed.

"I'm not really sure. It certainly involves people in the secretary general's and president's offices. But it's not clear who's really running things. The people that questioned me had been fed limited pieces of evidence that made me look like a threat – like I'd somehow been compromised by, as they put it, 'that alien device that was in my head.'"

"Yeah, they did a ton of scans on us looking for them," Kurt said. "But no one ever found even a sign of the implants."

"I'm sure Alpha thought about that in advance and somehow programmed them to disappear or dissolve," Jack answered. "The last thing I'd want is them cutting into me trying to retrieve a piece of alien technology."

"Damn," Kurt said, "I never thought of it quite like that."

"So," Nadya said, "I guess they finally gave in."

"Let's just say it's a stalemate. I'm giving them access to the device, like Alpha wanted. And it's on my terms: everyone who signed the unification treaty gets access. No one gets more or less than anyone else. The flip side is – they don't trust me. At best I'm viewed as someone too naïve for all of this. Most, however, look at me as some disloyal, unthankful ingrate."

"They at least take care of you don't they?" Kurt asked, "I mean you're not in some windowless facility or worse yet, prison. You're free to move about, right?" Kurt then added with a smile, "And it seems they're intent on keeping you safe, considering your contingent of body guards."

"They're there to keep track of everything I do as much as to keep me alive," Jack said matter-of-factly.

They walked a few more paces before Jack stopped beside a towering oak and took a quick look around. His guards were still in sight, one or two hundred meters off in either direction. Without letting anyone see, he pulled a small brown disk from his pocket. "Maybe I'm complaining too much," he said softly. "I can go pretty much wherever I want. And, I've gotten used to my companions back there. Though lately, I have enjoyed my walks in this park. I think that comes from being cooped up in space for over a decade." Jack placed his palm on the tree trunk, pressing the disk into its bark as he said, "Believe it or not, I think it was something as simple as trees that I missed the most."

He paused to look up as if he were in awe at the tree's size. Nadya and Kurt came closer to see what he was admiring. As soon as they were next to him, he pinched the disk on either side.

Nadya caught site of what he was doing and said, "Jack, what are…"

"We only have a minute," he said, cutting her off midsentence. "It's a little device I built using some of Alpha's tech. Right now, all of their surveillance equipment is getting a good burst of static. Keep looking up as if I'm talking about the tree."

They did as asked, while jack pulled a small brown speck from a plastic envelope in his jacket pocket. It was no bigger than the period at the end of a sentence. He quickly stuck it to the back of Kurt's hand where it immediately blended in with his skin. Pointing up, as if he were directing their attention to a bird, he said, "It's something of a failsafe. In case something happens to me, I need you to have it. It'll give you access to Alpha's device – we can't risk losing that knowledge."

Kurt turned to him in shock, and said, "Jack, what's going on?"

"Keep your eyes up there," Jack said as he pointed to an upper limb. "They'll be able to hear us again in a few more seconds. I'm sorry to put you in this position, but after the assassination attempt, I knew I had to do something. You two are about the only people I completely trust. I'm positive if I gave it to anyone in the government, it wouldn't be long before I had some sort of accident."

They stood in silence for a second before Jack said, "You can never speak of this again, OK?"

"Uh, yeah," Kurt said softly.

"Also, if they ask, and I know they will, tell them I was pointing out a blue jay to you. Tell them I'm a bit of an idiot, and have a particular fondness of those birds or something."

Kurt laughed as Jack casually took a quick look around. The two guards were making their way toward them, obviously confused about what was happening. To allay their suspicion, Jack said, "I think there's an interesting nest over here," and led Kurt and Nadya directly toward the man to their left. Confused by their approach he quickly backed off.

"So, now that we've had a breath of fresh air," Jack said, "it's time for the real reason I asked you here."

Nadya looked to him quizzically.

"Despite my own situation, I have had some input in the distribution of Alpha's knowledge. So far, we've set up a scientific and advanced education directorate which filters through the material, chapter-by-chapter, if you will. It decides how best to educate our scientific community. It's almost like perpetual grad school. Now, though, it's time to set up an engineering directorate. Its goal will be to try to apply what we're learning and create usable results. From what we've found so far, it seems most of the initial applications will be related to space travel: propulsion, in particular."

"Are you asking what I think you're asking?" Nadya said with a smile.

Jack returned the grin and said, "Yes. You wouldn't necessarily be leading the team, but the two of you would be senior members. Your experience in seeing Alpha's tech in action, plus the well-known fact that the two of you played a lead role in building the Magellan made the idea an easy sell."

Kurt looked to Nadya and said, "Well, I don't know. I mean it sounds like there'll be too many hours, loads of work. Not to mention the stress of dealing with the government..."

"As opposed to alien fighters and antimatter explosions?" Nadya said as she gave Kurt a light slap in the back of the head.

"Then the answer's yes?" Jack asked unnecessarily.

"Will we be working with you?" Kurt asked.

"Not directly. But we will get to see each other more often," he replied.

"When would we start?" Nadya asked.

"It'll take another month to set the directorate up...so maybe just after the start of the new year."

Kurt looked to Nadya once more, before saying, "I guess we're in."

"Thank you," Jack said with sincerity that went well beyond appreciation for their accepting the job offers. Leading the way back down the path, he continued, "Why don't we get some lunch? I know a nice little seafood spot not far from here."

ABOUT THE AUTHOR

Andreas Karpf is an experimental physicist with a life-long interest in the space program. He enjoys a good space adventure, but lives for the hard sci-fi novel set in a plausible future that doesn't get weighed down by too much technology – a story that takes him for a ride and dream about what may lie ahead for humanity.

As an undergraduate, he earned a degree in Physics and Astronomy, and minored in English. This led him to begin his career as the assistant editor for a physics magazine. He moved into software development, designing business applications. His love of science, though drew him back into Physics where he earned his doctorate and has pursued a research career. Andreas' work focuses on designing new spectroscopic techniques to detect trace gases in the atmosphere. His interests are varied and include art and Taekwondo (where he's a 4th degree black belt). Through his different positions his love of writing has persisted, leading to his debut novel, "Prelude to Extinction." Here he's combined his scientific background with his deep belief in keeping his audience both engaged and entertained. It is his desire to keep his readers thinking and involved in the adventure that drives his writing.

Made in the USA
San Bernardino, CA
19 May 2020

71957129R00212